THE SECRET CARDINAL

Tom Grace was born, raised, and still lives in Michigan. He studied architecture at the University of Michigan, where he developed his strict eye for detail. In just over twenty years of practice, Tom has worked on projects ranging from modest home renovations to major urban designs for Chicago and London. His superior knowledge of technology has found its way into his writing and has earned him tremendous acclaim as a result.

Tom credits his second career as a writer in equal parts to a voracious appetite for books, an over-active imagination, and a compulsive desire to set challenging long-term goals for himself.

Tom Grace lives with his wife, five children and a yellow Labrador. His interests are architecture and current affairs; he also enjoys scuba diving, martial arts and running marathons. To find out more about Tom go to www.tomgrace.net.

TOM GRACE

The Secret Cardinal

AVON

This novel is entirely a work of fiction.
The names, characters and incidents portrayed in it are
the work of the author's imagination. Any resemblance to
actual persons, living or dead, events or localities is
entirely coincidental.

AVON

A division of HarperCollins*Publishers*
77–85 Fulham Palace Road,
London W6 8JB

www.harpercollins.co.uk

This paperback edition 2009

3

First published by Vanguard Press in 2007

A catalogue record for this book is available from the British Library

ISBN-13: 978-1-84756-121-3

Set in Minion by Palimpsest Book Production Limited,
Grangemouth, Stirlingshire

Printed and bound in Great Britain by
Clays Ltd, St Ives plc

To Mary J. Hopps, who believes.

1

CHIFENG, CHINA

August 17

Do this in remembrance of me.

Yin Daoming tilted his head back slightly as he raised the sacramental cup toward heaven. It was only a drinking glass, but he held it as reverently as a golden chalice, and on its glossy surface he glimpsed his reflection – a serious young man with a solid, clean-shaven face. Many of the young women in the village near Shanghai where he was raised thought Yin would make a fine husband, only to be disappointed when he accepted his calling to the Catholic priesthood. A humble man, Yin likened himself to the glass he held high, a simple vessel of God's grace, an instrument for serving God by serving His people.

The glass, with its mixture of water and wine, glinted in the reflected light of candles arranged on a makeshift altar. The sacramental vintage at these clandestine services was typically a few ounces of the locally brewed

1

baijiu – an incendiary 90-proof beverage. No obvious physical change could be detected in the rose-colored liquid, but Yin knew with absolute certainty that the miracle of transubstantiation had occurred – that what he held before him was spiritually the blood of Jesus Christ.

Yin lowered the glass to his lips and took a small sip, the heavily diluted baijiu burning his throat like liquid fire. As a seminarian, Yin had once asked his Bishop if using such a potent alcohol for sacramental purposes wasn't in some way sacrilegious. The Bishop assured him that although Rome might find baijiu a bit unorthodox, it would overlook certain local adaptations, especially given the persecution of the Church in Communist China. The Roman Catholic minority in the world's most populous nation found itself in a Darwinian struggle to survive, and it would either adapt or die.

The shades in the room were drawn against the hostility of the outside world. The earliest Christians had existed in much this way under the pagan rule of imperial Rome. Thirty-three members of the extended family in whose home Yin celebrated this mass knelt around the low wooden table that served as the altar. The youngest, a baby girl, seemed to have forgotten the brief trauma of her baptism and suckled her mother's breast contentedly.

Siblings and cousins waited patiently as Yin distributed communion first to the family elders. The celebration of mass was a rare event, and Yin labored to ensure that each service was memorable enough to be worth the risk of attendance. For a majority of the world's Catholics, the only peril mass presented was to their soul if they failed to attend regularly. But the danger to Yin's persecuted flock was more immediate. The government in Beijing viewed attendance at an illegal mass as an expression of loyalty to a foreign entity over which China's leaders held no control. The penalties for this crime included intimidation, imprisonment, and occasionally death.

Only the oldest of those present at this gathering could recall a time when Chinese Roman Catholics practiced their religion openly. Their children and grandchildren had learned their catechism in whispers and cloaked their faith in a mask of officially sanctioned atheism. In the countryside, people did not abandon the beliefs of their honored ancestors at the whim of rulers in distant Beijing. Nor did they behave in a way that might draw their government's wrath. The underground Catholics of China bent like the willows in the wind, but they did not break.

After distributing the bread of the Eucharist, Yin offered the wine, reenacting a ritual that originated with the Passover Seder Jesus shared with his closest friends on the eve of his crucifixion. The simple act brought Yin and his congregants into communion with a billion other Roman Catholics around the world and with God.

Yin had prayed in beautiful churches, but nowhere did he feel closer to the Creator than with those clinging to their faith against immense hardship. It was in ministering to his endangered flock that Yin truly fulfilled his calling as a priest and became, in the words of Saint Francis of Assisi, a channel of Christ's peace.

'This is the blood of Christ,' Yin said reverently as he offered the glass to a boy just old enough to make his first communion.

The boy bowed his head respectfully and replied, 'Amen,' but barely allowed the scorching liquid to touch his lips. Yin suppressed a smile.

As Yin took the glass from the boy, he heard a metallic sound, the bolts on a heavy door pulling open. It was a sound he knew well, but not from this place.

'Wake up, old man,' a voice barked.

Light flooded in and the sacramental scene faded, erased from his mind's eye by the intrusion. In an instant, the clandestine mass withdrew into his precious trove of memories.

Yin was sitting in the middle of a bare, two-meter-square cell surrounded on all sides by concrete. Legs crossed and hands palm down on his knees, he sat as erect and serene as Buddha. Only hints remained of the lustrous black hair of his youth, scattered threads in a mane whitened by age and hardship. Whiter still was his skin, bleached a ghostly shade by decades denied the warm light of the sun.

A thick steel door and a small air vent were the only suggestion of a world outside the cell. In a tamper-proof fixture recessed into the ceiling, a lone dim bulb provided nearly the only illumination to reach Yin's eyes in thirty years. He had long ago lost all sense of day and night, and of the larger passages of time – temporal disorientation being but one of the techniques employed against prisoners like Yin.

'I said *wake up!*'

The guard punctuated his command by jabbing the end of an electrified baton into Yin's abdomen. Yin exhaled sharply at the explosion of pain and toppled backward, careful not to strike his head against the floor.

'I am awake, my son,' Yin panted softly, regaining his breath.

'I'd rather be the offspring of a pig farmer and his ugliest sow than any son of yours,' the guard spat back. 'Get up!'

Yin rubbed his stomach and squinted at the bright light pouring in from the corridor. His tormentor was a dark silhouette, and beyond the doorway stood several more guards.

The Chinese court had sentenced Yin to death for his many crimes against the state – an order not yet carried out for political reasons. The authorities recognized Yin as a man of great charisma and deep personal faith – a combination that could spread his foreign religion like a plague were he placed with the prison's general population. So unlike most prisoners in the *laogai* – the gulags of China – Yin was not permitted the opportunity to reform himself through the state's generous program of hard labor and reeducation. Instead, he was subjected to lengthy periods of isolation, punctuated by beatings and interrogations.

Yin knew it had been weeks, possibly months, since his last interrogation. The same questions were asked every time, and always he provided the same answers. The brutal sessions came far less frequently now than in the early years of his incarceration, more a task on a bureaucratic checklist than any genuine attempt at reform. After years of systematic effort, the Chinese government seemed to accept the fact that the underground Bishop of Shanghai would die before renouncing the Pope or the Church of Rome.

Yin rose to his feet and awaited the next command.

'Out!' the guard barked.

Yin followed as the guard backed through the door. Compared with the dimness of his cell, the light in the corridor burned his eyes as brightly as the noonday sun. The four guards stared at their charge with disgust.

'Restraints,' the senior guard commanded.

Yin assumed a familiar position with his feet spread shoulder-width apart and his arms extended from his sides. Two guards cinched a wide leather belt tightly around his thin waist. Four chains hung from the belt, each terminating in a steel manacle. Yin showed no outward sign of discomfort as the manacles dug into his wrists and ankles, knowing it would only invite a beating. The arteries in his wrists throbbed, and his hands began to tingle with numbness.

The lead guard inspected the restraints, though he knew they were unnecessary. Yin had never reacted violently toward a guard in all his years of imprisonment. The only danger the Bishop posed was to himself, and that because of his stubbornness. Satisfied that Yin was securely bound, the guard motioned the escort to proceed.

Yin kept his head bowed and his eyes on the floor as he moved down the corridor. The simplest gesture, a nod or glance at anyone, was forbidden and would result in a severe beating, as the badly healed break in his left arm bore testament. Yin's eyes gradually grew accustomed to the light as he shuffled along, taking two short steps for each stride by the guards.

Just up ahead, Yin thought, counting his steps.

The guards stopped. A buzzer sounded the release of the electronic locks securing the door to the solitary-confinement wing. The heavy steel door slid open, and the small procession continued.

Almost there, almost there.

Then he saw it – a glint, a tiny sliver of light on the floor. Yin turned his head a few degrees to the right and gazed upward. A small window, barred and paned with grimy wired glass, but a window nonetheless to the world outside. It was midday, and the sky was clear and blue.

A thin plastic cane lashed across Yin's back, causing him to drop to his knees. The return stroke caught his right shoulder, and Yin toppled to the floor.

'Enough!' the lead guard commanded. 'Get him back on his feet.'

The guard who had struck him grabbed Yin's arm and pulled him up so forcefully that the bony shoulder popped. Despite the blinding pain, Yin found his feet, and when the guard released his arm, the traumatized joint slipped back into place.

The march continued through the concrete corridors of the prison, the light rustle of Yin's sandals lost in the guards' heavy boot steps. Yin knew the route by heart, but only one way – rarely did he emerge from an interrogation conscious.

Yin felt a conflicting mixture of relief and dread when the guards walked him past the doorway that led to the corridor of interrogation rooms. Today's journey from his cell was to be different.

Lord, Yin prayed silently, *whatever is your will, I remain your servant.*

The guards escorted Yin through parts of the prison he could not recall. Then a doorway opened, and Yin felt a breeze kiss his face. It was not the prison's fetid air thick with rotting filth and human sweat, processed and recirculated by dilapidated machinery. This breeze was a whisper from the heavens. Yin detected the faint aroma of prairie in summer and the sweetness in the air that follows a cleansing rain.

So they have finally grown weary of me, Yin thought.

The only reason Yin could fathom for the guards to take him outside was to put a bullet in the back of his head, so he savored each breath of fresh air as if it were his last.

'Stop!' the lead guard barked.

Yin kept his head bowed and focused on his silent prayers. The sound of footsteps crunching on gravel, the measured strides of a long-legged man, intruded on his meditations.

'The prisoner, as ordered,' the lead guard announced respectfully.

Yin heard a rustle of paper and glimpsed a file folder in the hands of a tall man who wore not a uniform but the dark gray suit and polished black leather shoes of a businessman.

'Show me his face,' the man ordered.

One of the guards grabbed a handful of Yin's hair and jerked his head back. Yin's eyes traveled up the elegantly tailored suit past a pair of broad shoulders. The man's face was long and hard, the skin taut over bone and muscle. His jet-black mane swept back from his face, held in place like a glossy veneer so slick that the morning breeze had not dislodged a single hair. The man's mouth was a thin line that betrayed no emotion. Yin guessed his age somewhere between late thirties and mid-forties – only a child when Yin arrived at Chifeng Prison.

When Yin's eyes met those of Liu Shing-Li, the old priest shuddered. Liu was appraising the prisoner with eyes so unnaturally black that it was impossible to discern between iris and pupil. Liu's eyes seemed to absorb everything into their unfathomable darkness while betraying nothing. Yin had always viewed hell not as a sea of unquenchable fire but as a state of being totally removed from God. This was what he saw in Liu's eyes.

'Clean him up,' Liu ordered. 'And put him in a new uniform. The rags he's wearing should be burned.'

The lead guard nodded and gave the orders to his men. They marched Yin a short distance to the motor pool, where they stripped him of his threadbare garments and shackled him to a steel post with his arms above his head. Two jets of icy water pounded the Bishop's frail body, the guards laughing as they directed the high-pressure streams at his face and genitals. Yin choked, coughing up blood and water, his lungs desperate for air.

With the same brushes used to clean the prison's trucks, the guards attacked Yin's flesh until it was raw. Yin shivered uncontrollably, his body confused by the combination of numbness and the burning of industrial cleansers.

'Hold him still,' a guard barked as he pulled out a knife.

A pair of hands roughly clasped Yin's head, and the sharp blade scraped and tore at his facial hair. Years of growth fell away, and blood-tinged water streaked the Bishop's emaciated body. While hacking at Yin's mustache, the guard sliced a narrow strip of skin from Yin's nose, and blood flowed freely from the wound.

After shearing fistfuls of Yin's ragged mane, the guards turned on the hoses once more to finish the job. They then brusquely dried him off and gave him a new prison uniform, its cloth stiff and rough against his skin.

The guards reattached Yin's restraints and again presented him to Liu. At Liu's nod, Yin was handed over to the soldiers accompanying Liu and loaded into the back of an armored military transport. Two benches ran down the sides of the windowless compartment. Yin sat where he was told.

As the soldiers secured Yin's restraints to the steel loop bolted to the floor, Liu signed the paperwork authorizing transfer of the prisoner into his custody and dismissed the prison guards. Liu then donned a pair of sunglasses, slipped into the passenger seat of a dark gray Audi sedan, and signaled his driver to get moving. It would be a long drive to Beijing.

Accompanied by four soldiers, Yin moved across the countryside inside the steel box on wheels. The men did not converse with him, or even among themselves, and they acknowledged his existence only once with a meager meal and a scheduled relief stop. Yin knew this was partly due to his status as a prisoner and an enemy of the state, labels that made him less than human in their eyes. Too, the soldiers' masters feared his faith like a contagion – the Bishop of Shanghai was hazardous cargo. Yin felt no animosity toward the soldiers but rather sympathy for their predicament. To protect them from risk of punishment, Yin kept his silence and prayed for them.

The two vehicles reached the outskirts of central Beijing shortly after sunset. In a modern metropolis teeming with nearly thirteen million people, the rundown district seemed oddly abandoned. Soldiers manning one of the roadblocks that cordoned off the area scanned Liu's papers and waved him past.

The long journey from Chifeng ended a few blocks farther in an alley behind a modest theater. The brick building dated to the waning days of the imperial era, and the intervening years had not been kind. Armed men clad in riot gear stood guard at the theater doors, which appeared both solid and new. An officer approached the Audi and opened the passenger door.

'Is everything ready?' Liu asked as he stepped from the car, ignoring the soldier's salute.

'Per your orders, sir.'

Liu nodded approval. 'Have the prisoner brought inside.'

'Bring the prisoner out,' the officer ordered.

The small pass-through window between the transport's cab and the rear compartment slid open, and the soldiers guarding Yin looked up expectantly. The Bishop took no notice and continued his silent prayers.

'Out!' the driver barked through the opening.

The soldiers unlocked the section of chain connected to the floor bolt and lifted Yin to his feet. Two of them stepped out of the truck and assisted in lowering the manacled Bishop to the ground. Yin glanced heavenward and saw only a handful of stars through the hazy glow of Beijing's night sky.

After the remaining soldiers exited the transport, they escorted Yin into the backstage area of the theater. The air inside the building was stuffy and spiked with the stink of mold. Yin detected something else in the air – the pungent scent of sweat and fear.

Liu approached Yin. He towered over the Bishop.

'Look at me,' Liu demanded.

Yin raised his head to look into Liu's empty eyes.

'Is it true that this man you worship as a god likened himself to a shepherd and his followers to sheep who must be led?'

'Yes.'

'So in this, he was much like Mao Zedong, no?'

'Jesus Christ was a good shepherd, the kind who would lay down his life for his flock. The same cannot be said of Mao.'

'Perhaps, but China has evolved during your time of confinement. Tonight, you have the opportunity to walk out of this building a free man and Bishop of Shanghai.'

'And what price must I pay for the freedom you offer?' Yin asked flatly.

'Spoken like a Jesuit. The price is your cooperation. The government has no quarrel with your religion, only the foreign leadership of your church. Publicly renounce your allegiance to the Vatican and proclaim yourself a Chinese Catholic, and you will be free.'

'I am a Roman Catholic Bishop. If I denounce the Holy Father, I would no longer be a Bishop or a Catholic. You can cut off my head, but you can never take away my duties.'

'But what is a Bishop without a flock?'

'I am the good shepherd,' Yin quoted, 'I know my sheep and my sheep know me.'

'I see. Are you not curious as to why I have brought you here?'

'You have already revealed your purpose. I can only assume that you have assembled an audience for my public declarations.'

'Indeed I have,' Liu said with trace of a smile. 'Over five hundred of your sheep are in this theater, awaiting their shepherd. Their lives are in your hands.'

Yin turned his palms up. 'My hands are empty. All life comes from God.'

Liu had to acknowledge a grudging respect for the strength of Yin's resolve, but recalled the credo that understanding an adversary is one key to defeating him. He turned from Yin and motioned to the officer in charge. A moment later, a small group of soldiers brought a family of five backstage.

The patriarch of the family recognized Yin and immediately dropped to his knees.

'Your Grace,' the man said reverently before kissing Yin's hand.

A soldier pistol-whipped the man before he could receive Yin's blessing, sending him sprawling to the floor.

The granddaughter, a girl no older than ten, pulled away from her parents' arms and rushed to her grandfather's aid. She, too, was brutally struck.

'Enough,' Liu commanded.

The soldier who had beaten the pair stepped back and holstered his pistol. The patriarch cradled his weeping granddaughter as oozing blood matted the girl's long black hair.

'Kneel before your Bishop, sheep,' Liu commanded.

The three adults still standing – a man with his wife and mother – knelt before Yin. As Liu walked behind the family, a soldier handed him a pistol, the barrel lengthened by a silencer. Without hesitation, Liu quickly executed three generations of a family of underground Catholics. Yin forced himself to keep his eyes open – to take in the horror and weep as he silently offered a prayer for the five martyrs.

Liu holstered his weapon and turned to Yin. 'And I say your hands are full.'

'What is your name?' Yin asked softly, his eyes locked on the gory scene.

Liu studied the horrified Bishop and sensed his point had been made. 'Liu Shing-Li.'

'I will pray for you, Liu Shing-Li.'

'Better pray that you choose your words wisely tonight.'

Liu left Yin with the bodies of the slain family. From the stage, an amplified voice exhorted the audience to renounce the foreign Church of Rome and to practice their Christian faith with full government sanction as members of the Chinese Catholic Patriotic Association

(CCPA). Yin ignored the droning propaganda and meditated on the teachings of Christ, wondering what Jesus would do in this situation.

Yin had no idea how much time had passed when Liu returned for him. The soldiers removed the Bishop's restraints, and his extremities tingled with the sudden flow of blood. Unconsciously, Yin rubbed his wrists.

'It is time,' Liu said coldly.

As the soldiers led Yin to the edge of stage right, he heard his name announced to the audience. In the harsh white glow on stage, a smiling priest motioned for Yin to come out.

Yin took a single, tentative step and waited, but the soldiers beside him did not move. He quickly realized he was to enter the stage alone, since a quartet of armed guards would ruin the moment. Yin's first steps out into the light were met with murmuring from the crowd.

The priest moved quickly to the side of the stage, bowed deeply, and kissed the Bishop's hand. All eyes were on Yin, and he felt the burden of the moment. Hundreds of souls were packed into the dilapidated theater – husbands and wives, children and elders – ordinary people who shared with Yin a bond of faith.

Lord, you know I am willing to die for my faith, Yin prayed, *but can I ask the same of these innocent people? Is it a sin for me to act in a way that might result in their deaths?*

The priest led Yin to a microphone at center stage. The murmuring gave way to a silence broken only by the brief wail of an infant. Yin looked out on the frightened, yearning faces. Some people crossed themselves, while others stood with hands folded in prayer, eyes fixed on a man who had disappeared into the laogai decades earlier. They were looking to him for something they could not name, for their spirits to be moved in a way they could not anticipate. Yin inhaled deeply and felt the Holy Spirit give him strength.

'Long live Christ the King!' Yin shouted, his voice erupting from the loudspeakers like thunder. 'Long live the Pope!'

As one, the audience was on its feet.

'Long live Christ the King! Long live Bishop Yin!'

Over and over, the crowd repeated the chant, each cycle growing in strength and confidence. In Yin's desperate moment, his faith and the faith of these people had brought forth the Holy Spirit. The government-sanctioned priests stood uncomfortably, for with two simple sentences, Yin had galvanized the audience in a way they could not hope to understand.

'Cut the power,' Liu ordered, recognizing the danger. 'And get *him* out of here.'

The theater went dark as soldiers rushed Yin off the stage and out the back door, chaining the exit behind them.

'Seal the theater,' Liu ordered as the last of his soldiers exited.

'But, sir,' the officer in charge said, 'what about the people from the CCPA?'

'They won no converts today. Burn it down!'

The order went out, and the soldiers quickly retreated to predetermined safe areas. The transport followed Liu's car, then parked behind the Audi a short distance up the street. Liu sprang from his car and pounded angrily on the side of the transport.

'Bring him to me now!' Liu ordered.

The soldiers rushed Yin out of the transport, half-dragging the manacled Bishop.

'You hypocritical piece of filth!' Liu shouted, looking down on Yin. 'You have led your precious flock to their deaths.'

'I do not wish for them to die any more than I wish for my own death, but to live a life without faith, without hope, is a far more terrible thing.'

'What you did in there condemned those people.'

'What I did was ensure they understood the choice being offered them.'

Bright flashes erupted from several points inside the building as the pyrotechnicians detonated the incendiaries. As the fire grew in strength and began to roar, a second wave of sound rose from the doomed building – the sound of human voices.

'Do you hear them?' Liu shouted. 'With their dying breaths, they curse you and your imaginary god.'

Yin ignored Liu's ranting and listened to the distant voices. What he heard wasn't screams but a familiar melody.

'They're singing,' one soldier said incredulously.

'What?' Liu hissed.

From the raging fire, the song grew as those inside the building added their final breaths. Yin, humbled by the display of faith, added his voice to the chorus.

'*Tu es Petrus et super hane petram aedificabo Ecclesiam mean.*' Yin sang, though his heart heard the words: You are Peter and upon this rock I will build my church.

Liu punched Yin in the stomach to silence him. The Bishop staggered back and fell but continued to sing.

'Return him to his hole in Chifeng,' Liu commanded.

As the transport pulled away, Liu pulled out his cell phone.

'Tian direct,' he said clearly.

The phone matched Liu's voice command to a digital file and dialed the direct number for Tian Yi, the Minister for State Security. Tian answered quickly – he was expecting Liu's call.

'Does Yin Daoming remain unbroken?' Tian asked as calmly as if inquiring about the weather.

'Yes,' Liu replied.

'I see.'

'You don't seem surprised, Minister.'

Tian sighed. 'Not at all.'

'He is a stubborn fool.'

'Yin is neither,' Tian said, 'and it is a mistake to under-estimate him. What about the fire?'

'It's spreading to adjacent structures. I have been assured the entire block will be razed by morning.'

As Liu spoke, the theater roof collapsed, and the song inside was at last silenced.

'Good. Then the clearing of the district will get back on schedule.'

In preparation to host the Olympic Games, Beijing was undergoing a spate of urban renewal that rivaled London's following the Great Fire of 1666. With a hard deadline and the nation's international prestige at risk,

Beijing was removing anything and anyone that detracted from the beauty and harmony of the Chinese capital.

'I should have been permitted to kill him,' Liu said.

'Yin has never feared the loss of his own life. It would have given you no leverage.'

'I wasn't thinking about leverage.'

'Ah, but you forget that a live prisoner is far less trouble than a dead martyr.'

The officer in charge of the theater and the audience wore a concerned look as he briskly approached Liu. He stopped a few feet away and stood at ease, waiting for his presence to be acknowledged.

'A moment, Minister,' Liu said into the phone before covering the tiny microphone. 'Yes, Captain?'

'Sir, our technicians have detected a brief transmission originating from the theater.'

'What kind of transmission?'

'Internet access from a cell phone, specifically a file upload.'

'Were my instructions on searching those people not explicit, Captain?' Liu asked.

'Your orders were clear, sir.'

'Yet someone still managed to smuggle a cell phone past your men. Were your technicians able to intercept this file?'

'No, but they are actively tracing the data packets to determine the intended recipient. The delays we have set on international e-mail traffic will allow us to trap the file before it can cross the border. If the destination is inside China, we will attempt to capture the file while it is still on an e-mail server, before it can be retrieved.

We have since lost contact with the cell phone and it is presumed destroyed, but while the phone was still active, our technicians extracted all the information stored on its SIM card. That information should prove useful in the recovery operation.'

'Do your technicians know what was sent?'

'Based on a few captured packets, we believe it's a video clip of what happened inside the theater.'

'Captain, this lapse in your security is inexcusable, but your failure to quickly contain that file could prove fatal. Keep me apprised of your progress.'

Dismissed, the captain nodded, turned on his heel, and strode away. Liu pressed the phone to his ear as the man moved out of earshot.

'Minister, I apologize for the interruption,' Liu said calmly, 'but I have just been notified of an unfortunate development.'

2

ROME

October 10

This is where it ends, Liu thought as he stared at the front entry of the opulent Residence Barberini in the heart of Rome. Although it had been days since he slept, Liu felt his exhaustion give way to the excitement of the kill.

He sat in the back seat of a dark blue Alfa Romeo 166, watching from behind tinted glass as slivers of early morning sunlight advanced against the shadows in the narrow streets of the Ludovisi District. In the weeks following the theater fire, Beijing's greatest fear was the prospect of having news services worldwide broadcasting Yin Daoming's pro-Vatican outburst and the deadly aftermath. The Tiananmen Square massacre paled in comparison with the wanton immolation of five hundred people, and it was Liu's responsibility to ensure that this political and public relations nightmare never materialized.

After the fire, Liu was certain the damning video clip would swiftly find its way onto the Internet. Of course,

Beijing would denounce the clip as a hoax, but the damage would be done. Still, the underground Catholics he'd interrogated were consistent in their belief that for the deaths of the five hundred martyrs to have any meaning, the world must first learn of the tragedy from the Vatican.

Their strategy of keeping the video clip off the Internet initially served to protect the small group of conspirators, but it also provided Liu with the time he needed to conduct his search and for Beijing to take countermeasures. In addition to establishing a massive data filtering program that all but slowed China's domestic Internet traffic to a halt, the elite hackers working for the Ministry of State Security mounted a denial of service attack against the Vatican that forced the Holy See offline.

Deprived of the instantaneous connectivity of the Internet, the conspirators had only two options. The first was simply to mail a disk to the Vatican, but in an era when packages from unknown senders and data files of unknown provenance were treated with grave suspicion, there was high probability the Vatican would discard the disk upon receipt. The other option was the oldest in the history of espionage: a courier.

A pair of swarthy Italian men filled the front bucket seats of the Alfa – men employed by one of China's main partners in the lucrative trade in arms and heroin. Their associates held strategic positions in and around the hotel and near all the entry points to Vatican City. In the rear seat of the sedan beside Liu sat a stone-faced man named Chin. Chin was a trusted intermediary between the Chinese government and the Italian mafia, and his fluency in both languages provided clear and accurate communication between Liu and the Italians.

Their quarry was Hwong Yi Jie, a successful high-end clothing manufacturer from Zhejiang Province who was in Europe visiting her clients in the European fashion industry. Hwong exemplified the type of citizen Beijing saw as vital to the nation's future, and in her twenty-nine years she had never aroused the interest of the Ministry of State Security. That had all changed a few days ago when a man suspected of handling the video clip broke down after several days of nonstop interrogation and identified Hwong as a member of the underground Catholic Church and his accomplice. Informed that she would present the clip to a representative of the Vatican during her stay in the Eternal City, Liu raced to Rome, arriving last night just a few hours ahead of Hwong. After checking into her hotel, Hwong had ordered a late meal in her room and retired for the night.

'She's in the lobby,' Chin said, translating the report streaming into his earpiece. 'The front desk reports no calls to or from her room.'

Hwong moved purposefully through the front doors of the hotel. Her long black hair was drawn back in a ponytail, and she was dressed in running shorts and a colorful long-sleeve T-shirt emblazoned with the graphics of the Hong Kong Marathon. A fanny pack around her slim waist held a water bottle, and an iPod was strapped to her left arm. After a few minutes of stretching against the wall of the hotel, Hwong started her morning run.

'Search her room,' Liu said, his eyes following the beautiful young woman.

As Chin passed the order on to the men inside the hotel, the driver slipped the Alfa into gear and initiated a loose pursuit of Hwong. Two other cars joined the surveillance, switching every few blocks to avoid detection.

Hwong wound through the narrow streets of the district before heading northwest along Via delle Quattro Fontane. She ran at a modest pace, warming up her legs and finding her stride. A little over a kilometer into her run, she stopped beside Bernini's Fontana della Barcaccia in the Piazza di Spagna for a drink of water and a quick check of her pulse rate. Then with ferocious intensity, she stormed up the Spanish Steps toward the Sallustian Obelisk and the church of Sant' Andrea della Fratte. At the top, she turned and descended the majestic staircase at a comfortable jog, allowing her legs and breathing to recover. She repeated the cycle five times before continuing up Viale della Trinita del Monti toward the Piazza dei Popolo.

The Tylenol caplets rattled like dried beans in a maraca, their hard gelatin shells tapping against the convenient travel-sized container whose compact form Nolan Kilkenny found decidedly inconvenient as he rummaged to locate it within the many zippered and Velcro-flapped compartments of the toiletries kit that hung from the back of the bathroom door. His search was not aided by the hangover-induced headache that made even the memory of pain relievers in his luggage a minor miracle. The black organizer and its thoughtful complement of grooming and health products had been a gift from his bride to replace the tattered wreck that had seen him through sixteen years of adult bachelor life. *Out with the old . . . with love, Kelsey* read the note he found tucked inside when she presented it to him. Ten months later, the note was still there.

Kilkenny located the bottle, its tamper-resistant seal still intact. He peeled off the skin of thick clear plastic in jagged strips, popped off the childproof cap, and quickly downed a pair of pills with a handful of cold water and a prayer for speedy relief.

This wasn't his first hangover, nor was it the worst – those memorable events having occurred when Kilkenny was a newly minted high school graduate and later, while serving as a junior officer in the Navy SEALs, after the successful snatch-and-grab of a terrorist leader residing comfortably in Iran. Those and a few other painful mornings-after followed revelry shared with close friends and comrades in arms. Kilkenny rarely drank, and when he did it was typically in small amounts and on social occasions. But last night he had consumed a lot of red wine with dinner at a nearby *ristorante*, and had done so alone.

What the hell am I doing here?

The image staring back at Kilkenny in the mirror evinced the malaise gnawing inside him, and his futile attempt to marinate that unwanted sensation in Chianti both sickened and angered him. He knew men who had anesthetized their senses with alcohol and drugs for lesser reasons than his, and he vowed that his loss of faith, of hope, would not be his undoing.

After scrubbing the film from his mouth, Kilkenny

splashed some water on his face and head, matting down the disheveled tufts of red hair. His hotel room was small but efficient and, most important, located within walking distance of the Vatican, where he spent most of his time. He had come to Rome at the behest of his father, to work with his father's oldest friend, Malachy Donoher, the Cardinal Librarian of the Holy Roman Church.

Kilkenny's job was to improve the flow of information between the Vatican Library and the Pontifical Academy of Sciences, for it was through these two entities that the Church remained abreast of advances in science and technology while retaining an institutional memory that spanned a millennium. Donoher believed the academy and library, working in concert, could give the Pope a clearer view of advances that might pose moral or ethical problems tempered with a broad historical perspective, the goal of which was to provide the Holy Father with wise counsel when matters of science and faith seemed at odds.

Officially, the invitation to be a consultant to the Vatican drew on Kilkenny's technical expertise at managing information – a fairly simple task to be remunerated with a modest fee. But Kilkenny suspected that Donoher and his father had conspired, creating an assignment that was merely a pretext to force him from an empty home in Ann Arbor, where his surroundings could only remind him of all he had lost. Kilkenny had buried himself in work in the two months since the deaths of his wife and unborn child, but grief remained his constant companion. He existed only in the present, his desired future obliterated by a cruel disease.

He appreciated the thought behind the invitation, even if the job demanded little of his mental energies. Kilkenny's true work – as a venture capitalist with his father's company, MARC (Michigan Applied Research Consortium) – kept him fully engaged with new and interesting challenges. Kilkenny oversaw the transfer of nascent technologies from academic research laboratories into the world of commerce – he was a trafficker in intellectual property. And not just any property. From quantum energy cells to strange organisms hidden for eons in dark waters beneath miles of polar ice, Kilkenny served as guardian and even midwife to innovations that would change the future. His profession was both exhilarating and lucrative, and on more than one occasion deadly.

Travel was part of his job, so living in Rome for a few weeks did not seem at all unusual. And he had to admit, the Vatican did offer a dramatic change of atmosphere, no doubt exactly what his father and Donoher had intended.

Several new garment bags hung in the closet above two boxes of new dress shoes. He had arrived in Rome two weeks earlier wearing jeans, sneakers, and an Ireland rugby jersey, carrying a briefcase and a small overnight bag, but the garment bag containing the rest of his clothing had gone astray. When it became apparent that the bag's MIA status was likely permanent, Kilkenny took advantage of the opportunity to update his wardrobe at several of Rome's finer clothiers.

After drying his face, Kilkenny traded the boxers he'd slept in for running shorts and a T-shirt and began to stretch lightly. His freckled skin gave a boyish look to his six-foot frame – a lean, well-defined body built not for bursts of speed or strength but endurance. He clipped a fanny pack around his waist, retrieved a pair of Saucony running shoes from the closet, and sat on the edge of the double bed to pull them on. A biography of Mark Twain rested on the nightstand along with a black diver's watch and a small triptych frame.

Reaching for his watch, Kilkenny's eyes lingered on the woman pictured in the frame's central panel. The photo was taken in July, when Kilkenny and his wife were vacationing in Harbor Springs, Michigan. Kelsey was wading knee-deep in the placid water of Little Traverse Bay clad in a brightly colored bikini, unaware of the camera trained upon her. She was gazing down at her belly, both hands placed as if cradling the life growing within. It was the middle of her fifth month, and Kelsey was delighted with her maternal shape. Kilkenny remembered the moment and her amazed expression as their child stirred. She had called him over and pressed his hand to the spot where she had felt movement.

The frame to the left of Kelsey's picture contained a slip of light gray paper marked with a pair of black impressions, footprints no larger than the end of Kilkenny's thumb. These were the only marks his son would ever make on the world, aside from the ones Toby left on his father's heart. Framed to the right was a mass card from the funeral of his wife and son this past August.

'I still dream of you and me at the beach, playing with Toby,' Kilkenny said to his wife as he fastened his watch. 'I miss you both so much.'

He grabbed his room key and a water bottle from the minibar refrigerator and left.

As Hwong reached the Piazza del Popolo, a melodic ring tone chimed from her fanny pack. She paused her iPod and answered her cell phone.

'Hwong,' she said cautiously.

'*Ave Maria, gratia plena, Dominus tecum,*' a man said, carefully enunciating each syllable in the first line of an old Latin prayer.

'*Benedicta tu in mulieribus –* ' Hwong's voice wavered as she recited the second line, completing the code phrase for her contact inside the Vatican, '*et benedictus fructus ventris tui, Jesus.*'

'Are you being followed?' The man's English was warmed with an Irish lilt.

'Yes,' she replied.

'I know what you've been asked to do is dangerous,' the man offered sincerely.

'But it must be done,' Hwong said.

'A man will be running across Ponte Cavour shortly. Check your phone for his picture.'

'I don't understand.'

'We never walk alone, my child.'

The call ended and Hwong found on her phone's LCD screen a picture of a man running. He appeared to be about her age, was clean-shaven, and possessed a head of bright red hair. She deleted the photo, stowed her phone, and resumed her run, heading west down Via Ferdinando di Savoia toward the Tiber River. At the foot of the Ponte Margherita, she turned south and ran down the scenic tree-lined *lungotevere* that followed the meandering course of the river.

Hwong saw the runner crossing Ponte Cavour over the Tiber as she moved past the Ara Pacis Augustea and the Mausoleum of Augustus. He turned south on the lungotevere, and she picked up her pace to close the distance. The man stood a full head taller than Hwong and ran with his back straight and head high. He moved purposefully, not a wasted motion in his long-legged stride. She glided up beside him, but he was so lost in thought that he failed to notice. A glint of metal on his left hand caught her eye, a simple gold band around his ring finger.

'Excuse me,' Hwong said politely. 'You speak English?'

Startled, Kilkenny turned his head and was surprised to discover a beautiful young woman running beside him.

'Most of the time,' Kilkenny replied warily. 'Why do you ask?'

'I speak some Italian and French, but my English is better. And you do not look Italian or French.'

Kilkenny nodded with a laugh, and Hwong saw a warm twinkle in his green eyes.

'Command of three languages is impressive, but I'm guessing you know at least one more. Where are you from?'

'China – I live in the city of Hangzhou.'

'That's near Shanghai, isn't it?'

'Yes, south of Shanghai.'

'So, what brings you to Rome?' Kilkenny asked.

'Business. And you?'

30

'The same.'

'Do you run far today?' Hwong asked.

'That depends on what you think is far. Since you're having no trouble keeping up with me, I'm guessing you earned that shirt. How'd you finish?'

'Three hours and eighteen minutes.'

'You beat my personal best,' Kilkenny admitted. 'What I'm running today will probably be easy for you. The route is a little more than ten kilometers, but it has a challenging hill near the end. Care to join me?'

'Yes,' Hwong beamed, relieved. 'This is my first visit to this city, and I do not like to run alone.'

'I'm just getting used to it again. Where are you staying?'

'A hotel near the Spanish Steps.'

The man thought for a moment. 'That'll add another two K. How are you set for time?'

'I have a meeting at noon.'

'You'll be back at your hotel well before then,' Kilkenny promised. 'What's your name?'

'Hwong Yi Jie.'

'A pleasure to meet you, Miss Hwong. I'm Nolan Kilkenny.'

They ran down the Lungotevere, the relatively flat route an easy scenic course for the distance veterans. Hwong stowed her ear-buds so they could talk, and Kilkenny acted as tour guide, pointing out items of interest along the way. Behind them, Liu coordinated the rotating surveillance of the three cars, never letting the runners out of sight.

'We've finished searching the room,' one of the Italians at Hwong's hotel called Liu to report. 'Her laptop and PDA are clean, and we've found no disks or storage devices in the room. The room safe was open and empty, and she's left nothing with the front desk. She must have what you're looking for on her.'

'Are you and your men the only ones who have been in the room since she left?' Liu asked.

'*Si.*'

'Then pull them back and await further orders.'

Liu's driver followed the two runners as they turned at Ponte Aventino, crossing to the west side of the Tiber into the Trastevere District.

'The woman has what I want,' Liu told Chin. 'Tell the men to be prepared to take her on my orders.'

'What about the man running with her?' one of the Italians asked.

'If he gets in the way,' Liu replied, 'kill him.'

'Sir,' the driver offered, 'if you're looking for a secluded place to grab the woman, they're taking the *passaggiata* to the top of Monte Gianicolo. This early in the morning, only a handful of tourists will be watching the sunrise up on the piazzale.'

Liu studied the wooded hill rising up ahead. 'We'll follow the runners to the top, then take the woman there.'

Kilkenny quickened the pace as he led Hwong through the switchback turns in Via Garibaldi.

'That's San Pietro in Montorio,' Kilkenny explained with increasingly labored breaths as they sped past a late-fifteenth-century church and convent. 'It was built because local tradition once held that Nero crucified the Apostle Peter here. That actually happened on Vatican Hill, not far from the other Saint Peter's. Up ahead is the Baroque spectacular Fontana dell'Acqua Paulo. The locals call it *Fontanone*, which means really big fountain.'

Hwong laughed at Kilkenny's joke. 'Why did they build it?'

'According to the plaque inside, it celebrates the restoration of the Trajan Aqueduct in the early sixteen hundreds. The imperial Romans used triumphal arches to commemorate their success in war. Their descendants were happy to get fresh drinking water.'

Kilkenny and Hwong veered right at the fountain, straining on the increasing grade of the road as they climbed the Passeggiata del Gianicolo. City buildings abruptly gave way to lush trees and manicured landscapes. Kilkenny's commentary trailed off in the absence of monuments to point out, which suited him fine. Their rapid ascent of Rome's Mons Aureus – Hill of Gold – left him with little breath to spare.

The road leveled out near the top of the hill and flowed into a broad open space – the Janiculum Terrace. Small groups of tourists clustered alongside the low wall on the eastern border of the piazzale. To the west stood a section of ancient defensive walls built by the third-century emperor Aurelian to protect his capital city. A guardrail of heavy iron chain threaded through a ring of stone bollards defined a circular traffic island in the center of the terrace. Kilkenny and Hwong jogged across the terrace to the island and stopped at the base of a massive equestrian monument. The heroic figure of Giuseppe Garibaldi on horseback towered above them from the very spot where the charismatic adventurer commanded the defense of Rome against the French in 1849.

As their breathing steadied, both runners took deep pulls from their water bottles. Kilkenny extended his arm toward the east.

'Miss Hwong, there is the reward for climbing this hill.'

Rome glistened in the morning sun, the undulating city dazzling from this lofty height. The Tiber sparkled like liquid silver as it snaked between the ancient hills now obscured by roads and buildings. The generations of people who dwelled here had left their mark in the numerous monuments and domes, palaces and bell towers – some instantly recognizable the world over.

Hwong wiped the perspiration from her forehead as she took in the view.

'As beautiful as that is,' Kilkenny added, 'it's even more amazing at sunset.'

He had read about this view while preparing for his assignment to Rome and, though never a romantic about sunsets, knew immediately it was a place Kelsey would have wanted to see with him. Kilkenny ran the hill every morning, pausing at the top to enjoy the view and remember his wife. Before dinner last night, for the first time, he had come here alone to watch the sunset.

Three Alfa sedans raced into the piazzale. Hwong's heart pounded at the sight of the fast-approaching cars, her body instinctively pumping adrenaline in preparation to fight or flee. The water bottle slipped from her trembling fingers.

'Lord, help me,' Hwong stammered.

'What?' Kilkenny asked, lost in his thoughts.

'I have something for the Pope,' Hwong replied, touching the iPod on her arm. 'Evidence of a great tragedy. My government does not want the world to know what they've done.'

Tires squealed against the pavement. The lead car veered left to cover the front of the monument. The second car stopped at the guardrail directly in front of Kilkenny and Hwong, and the third moved to box them in on the right. Two men from the first car, both wearing black balaclavas, leaped over the guardrail as the doors of the second car flew open.

'Run,' Kilkenny said, pushing Hwong away from the four men rushing toward them. 'Head for the woods.'

A bullet ricocheted off granite as they rounded the back of the monument, and several tourists screamed. The third car stopped directly in their path and two more men emerged, charging with pistols drawn. In a quick calculus of their situation, Kilkenny knew they were outnumbered, outgunned, and caught almost completely in the open. Though it had been a few years since his Navy days, Kilkenny's SEAL training kicked in.

Using his only weapon, Kilkenny hurled his water bottle at the nearest assailant. It struck the man squarely in the face as Kilkenny quickly closed the distance. Moving to the outside, he grabbed the man's right wrist and twisted until the elbow locked. A sharp palm strike audibly fractured the joint, and the man's weapon clattered to the pavement. Using the momentum of his attack, Kilkenny spun his opponent around by his broken arm and hammered him into the second assailant.

Both men fell in a heap, the one on the bottom knocked senseless when he toppled back and struck his head against the cobblestones. Hwong ran straight for the walking paths that led into the woods, and as Kilkenny turned to follow her, he scooped up the loose pistol and emptied the weapon at the next pair of pursuers. His shots chiseled the corner of the monument's plinth, buying time by forcing the men to seek cover behind the sculpted mass of stone.

As he emerged from the long shadow cast by Garibaldi's monument, Kilkenny saw the pair of assailants from the first car chasing Hwong. One of them was shouting at her angrily in Chinese and, failing to close the distance on her, took careful aim and fired. A single round caught Hwong between the shoulder blades. Her arms flailed as if to grasp something. As Hwong's legs folded beneath her, she fell to the ground like a wounded bird.

Kilkenny charged angrily toward the shooter, colliding with the man in a vicious broadside and knocking him down. The impact sent the still-smoking pistol clattering across the pavement, and the weapon came to rest near a group of frightened tourists. Kilkenny leaned over and stripped the balaclava from the man's head.

Recovering from the open-field tackle, Liu faced Kilkenny, his eyes a pair of smoldering black coals. He struck quickly, spearing Kilkenny in the chest with the tip of his elbow. The air burst from Kilkenny's lungs, and as he gasped, Liu smashed the back of his fist against

Kilkenny's forehead and raked his knuckles down Kilkenny's face. Liu grabbed a fistful of Kilkenny's hair and rolled. As Kilkenny toppled over, Liu struck the side of his neck with the outer edge of his right hand, stunning Kilkenny to near-unconsciousness.

Liu pushed Kilkenny aside and leaped to his feet. In the distance, he heard the wail of approaching sirens.

'I have them,' one of the Italians teamed with Liu called out, Hwong's iPod and phone clutched in his meaty fists.

Not waiting for the order, the others loaded the two wounded men into the nearest car. Liu considered finishing off Kilkenny, but he had what he came for and the police were on their way.

As the Alfas fled the terrace, Kilkenny struggled to his feet and staggered to where Hwong had fallen supine on the pavement. From the tiny wound, an oozing slick of blood now soaked her T-shirt. She was still alive, though her breathing was quick and shallow. Kilkenny took her hand but dared not move her.

'Hang on,' Kilkenny urged.

'Did they take it?' Hwong asked, pointing weakly at her arm. The armband with her iPod was gone.

'Yes.'

Her look of relief surprised Kilkenny.

'Long live Christ the King,' she said softly. 'Long live the Pope.'

3

VATICAN CITY

Clad in one of his new suits, Kilkenny walked out of the eastern pavilion of the Casina – the sixteenth-century summer residence of Pope Pius IV – and descended a few steps into an oval court paved in a geometric pattern of light and dark marble. A low wall framed the perimeter of the ellipse, a boundary broken at the far ends by a pair of arched gateways and along the short axis by porticos fronting the Casina's two pavilions. The artisans who built the courtyard had envisioned it as an ancient nyphaeum, decorating the idyllic space with a High Renaissance flurry of statues and reliefs, stucco-framed depictions of riders atop water-spewing dolphins.

The Vatican gardens in their autumn splendor surrounded the Casina, and beyond the archway to Kilkenny's left, the white marble dome of Saint Peter's Basilica glistened in the late-day sun. Cardinal Donoher ambled through the southern archway with a warm smile on his ruddy face. He wore the traditional black cassock and mozetta trimmed with scarlet piping and buttons, a broad scarlet sash around his ample waist, and a matching zucchetto atop his thinning head of gray hair. Donoher had received the zucchetto from the current Pope when he was made a cardinal, and the scarlet details in his attire were a sign of his position as a prince of the Church. Suspended from a gold chain around his neck was the pectoral cross that Kilkenny's father gave him at his consecration as a Bishop. The gilded cross bore the embossed image of the risen Christ vested as a priest.

Donoher's face turned solemn when he saw the bruises on Kilkenny's face. 'I see you had yourself quite a morning.'

'I'll live.'

'Sadly, the police tell me the same cannot be said of the young woman.'

Kilkenny nodded grimly.

'The police have nothing as yet on your attackers, but I feel certain the truth of the matter will be revealed in time.' Donoher glanced at his watch. 'We'd best be moving along.'

Kilkenny followed Donoher's lead toward the archway facing the basilica and noticed a slight hitch in the cardinal's stride.

'Are your knees bothering you?'

Donoher nodded. 'My physician thinks I should replace both of these creaky old joints. He tells me there's not much cartilage left between the bones, but I've been putting it off. It's the price for all the fun I had playing football – of course, it's your father's fault.'

'How so?'

'When my family emigrated from Ireland, he was my

first friend when we arrived in Detroit's Corktown – and he's responsible for introducing me to American football. Had he not dared me to try out with him for the team at Catholic Central, I might still be able to dance a jig.'

'But Dad's knees are fine,' Kilkenny offered.

'He wasn't a lineman, and he didn't play in college. Four years I started for Notre Dame, and I feel it every time the weather changes.'

'That's why I run and swim.'

As he walked with Donoher through the gardens, Kilkenny's eyes wandered across brilliant floral displays, teasing out the details of a landscape design that had carefully evolved over the centuries. Deftly orchestrated views opened at precisely the moment that maximized their effect. The organic and the man-made blended harmoniously as a reminder that creation has both a physical and spiritual nature.

'Do you think anyone could ever get jaded working in a place like this?' Kilkenny asked.

Donoher considered the question. 'I can't imagine. You were just a child when I first came to work here, and still not a day passes that I don't discover something new. I believe it was Michelangelo who said "Trifles make perfection – and perfection is no trifle." An inquisitive mind never grows bored. And on the subject of inquisitive minds, how are you coming along on my little project?'

In trying to frame a response to Donoher's question, Kilkenny found he was having some difficulty separating the man from his office.

'Fine,' Kilkenny replied, his answer straddling the line between honest and polite.

'Your enthusiasm is underwhelming.'

'Don't get me wrong—'

'But . . .' Donoher interjected.

'But you have a lot of very bright people working here, and I don't really see why you need my help. To be honest, this job feels like an excuse to get me out of Ann Arbor.'

As he spoke, Kilkenny studied the cardinal's face, expecting to find disappointment. Instead the older man shook his head and smiled.

'Figured it out, did you?'

Kilkenny nodded.

'In a sense, you're right,' Donoher admitted. 'Why I brought you here has nothing to do with shelving my books. And don't tell your father, but it has nothing to do with your grief either. To be honest, I need your help with something that is terribly important, and frankly, any personal benefit you may derive from being here is simply a bonus.'

'I didn't derive much of a bonus today.'

'That much is evident, but you can bear those wounds as proudly as those you carry in your heart. That you would risk your life for a stranger says as much about your character as the relationship you shared with Kelsey.'

'Both women died.'

'But they were not alone in their last moments of life – you were with them. As brief as your marriage was, I thank God for the fourteen months the two of you shared as husband and wife.'

'Eight months,' Kilkenny corrected. 'We were married in January.'

'You and Kelsey renewed your vows in January, but you were married the previous June. I know, because I gave your priest permission to bless your union. I must admit that your sudden elopement came to me as something of a surprise.'

'Kelsey was dead-set against the idea until the *Shenzhou-7* tragedy.'

Donoher nodded. The fiery deaths of three Chinese astronauts had been global news, ultimately involving Kilkenny himself.

'If the worst happened during her mission,' Kilkenny continued, 'she wanted to die as my wife.'

'A brilliant physicist, a daring astronaut, a talented athlete and teacher, a cherished daughter and sibling, a beloved wife, and the bravest of mothers,' Donoher said, recalling his eulogy. 'And a kind and gentle beauty to boot. That woman may have been better than you deserved.'

'I'm sure of it,' Kilkenny agreed.

Barely a month into her long stint in orbit, Kelsey had told him over a secure connection that she was unexpectedly expecting. Their joy was matched only by NASA's perturbation over the logistical nightmare of a pregnant astronaut in orbit, but both were short-lived. Within a week of Kelsey's announcement, her pregnancy ended in miscarriage. She completed her mission as planned and returned home, where she publicly married Kilkenny, and the two resumed their efforts to start a family. Her second pregnancy came as quickly as the first, but on its heels came the illness that would ultimately take both Kelsey and her child. She and Kilkenny had known each other since childhood and been friends long before falling in love. Kilkenny couldn't remember a time when Kelsey hadn't been a part of his life, and every day he found it a struggle to go on without her.

'So,' Kilkenny said, breaking the silence. 'What do you need my help with?'

4

Donoher led Kilkenny through a side entry near the Sistine Chapel. After clearing a plainclothes detail of Swiss Guard security, they ascended to the top floor of the Apostolic Palace. As they reached the papal apartments, a tall, thin man moved to meet them. The attire of the Pope's private secretary was similar to Donoher's except the details were amaranth red.

'Your Eminence,' Archbishop Sikora said respectfully.

'Archbishop, so good to see you again,' Donoher replied. 'Accompanying me today is Mister Kilkenny.'

'Your Excellency,' Kilkenny offered.

'And is His Holiness feeling well today?' Donoher asked.

'A little better. He is waiting for you both in the Redemptoris Mater Chapel. This way, please.'

The Archbishop led them through the second Bramante loggia and into the papal chapel dedicated to the Mother of the Redeemer. Built in the sixteenth century for Pope Gregory XIII as the Matilda Chapel, the room underwent extensive renovation during the late nineteen-nineties.

Kilkenny was stunned as he stepped in from the

formal Renaissance hallway into a space reminiscent of an Eastern Orthodox pilgrim church. Mosaics of startling beauty adorned the chapel walls, scenes from the New Testament rendered in the Byzantine iconographic tradition. A vision of New Jerusalem filled the wall behind the marble altar, and on the ceiling above were a white cross and the Pantocrator. Though only a few years old, the chapel possessed an aura of timelessness.

Amid the splendor of the chapel, Pope Leo XIV sat deep in prayer. The Pope's throne stood against the rear wall of the chapel, a permanent fixture along with a lectern and the altar. Sikora motioned for them to remain by the door as he approached the pontiff. He knelt at the foot of the papal throne, leaned his head close to the Pope's, and spoke softly. Kilkenny saw the Pope nod, and the Archbishop signaled for them to approach.

Elected when Kilkenny was a child, the man seated before him was the only living Pope he could remember. Age and infirmity had eroded the church leader's youthful vigor during his long reign. Shoulders slumped, the supreme pontiff's body seemed to be slowly drawing into itself during his waning years, as if trying to return to the same dimensions it possessed at his birth. The Pope looked up and extended a quivering hand to his visitors.

'Your Holiness,' Donoher said with deep reverence as he knelt and kissed the papal ring.

Kilkenny did the same, and the Pope bade them to sit. As they moved a pair of chairs close to the papal throne, Sikora left the chapel, closing the doors behind him.

'We are sorry to disturb your meditations, Your Holiness,'

45

Donoher began, but the Pope dismissed the apology with a short wave of his hand.

'The matter you have come to discuss has been in my prayers for some time now. So, this is the young man that you spoke to me about?'

'It is,' Donoher replied.

As the Pope studied him, Kilkenny was immediately struck by the intensity and clarity of his gaze. Wrapped within a withering husk of a body was a spirit and intellect that had lost none of its potency.

'Mister Kilkenny, this chapel was a gift to me from the cardinals, one that has brought me great peace. Do you know what it represents?'

'No, Your Holiness, I don't.'

'The inspiration for this chapel was taken from a sermon given by a Jesuit priest named Tomas Spidlik,' the Pope explained. 'The central theme of this sermon was that the Church in the Third Millennium must breathe with two lungs, that of the East and of the West. This space breathes with two lungs and symbolizes unity within the Catholic Church.'

'It certainly is magnificent.'

The Pope nodded. 'I asked to meet with you here because there is something I wish you to see.'

The Pope pointed to the mosaics on the wall behind him. The image spanning the wall immediately re-awakened the dormant memories of Kilkenny's high school theology classes. It depicted the Parousia – the Second Coming of Christ. And on the Earth were those who had been restored to life, the promise of the resurrection fulfilled.

'Do you see the man and the woman near the edges of the wall, leading the processions of the faithful?' the Pope asked.

'Yes,' Kilkenny replied. 'Who are they?'

'Mary, the Mother of Jesus, to whom this chapel is dedicated, and Saint John the Baptist. Please, take a closer look at the people they are leading back to life.'

Kilkenny rose to study the processions, trying to determine who would have earned the privilege of being led into the kingdom of heaven by two of the people closest to Christ. Among those restored to life was a figure in gray stripes, a victim of Hitler's concentration camps. Kilkenny then recalled that during World War II, the Pope and his fellow seminarians hid Polish Jews from the Nazis as the horrors of Auschwitz were occurring just a few miles outside Krakow.

'These are martyrs,' Kilkenny said. 'People who died for their faith.'

'Yes. Martyrs throughout the ages, including the victims of Nazism, Communism, and Islamic fanaticism. I wanted you to see them because martyrs are still being made today. Now please sit, so we can talk.'

Kilkenny returned to his seat beside the cardinal.

'Tell him about the fire,' the Pope said to Donoher.

'I assume you have heard about the theater fire in Beijing back in August?'

Kilkenny nodded. 'The place was a deathtrap; all the exits were blocked. It was a horrific accident.'

'It was *not* an accident,' Donoher declared. 'And nearly every one of those who perished in those flames was a Roman Catholic.'

The Pope bowed his head. 'Over five hundred martyrs.'

'In the minds of those who rule the People's Republic of China, Christianity and democracy represent the most significant threats to their privileged positions,' Donoher explained. 'When the Communists seized control in 1949, they set out to eradicate all religion. Failing at that, they settled for rigid control of the manner of religious practice and the message the faithful would hear. Catholics in China could either worship in a church loyal only to the state or take their faith underground and risk persecution or worse. Efforts have been made over the past twenty years to improve relations between Beijing and the Holy See, but always to no avail. Roman Catholicism remains illegal in China, and not since the earliest days of the Church have we witnessed atrocities like those committed against our Chinese brethren.'

'Beatings, rape, imprisonment, executions.' The Pope's voice trembled as he recited the litany of sins. 'It is a war of faith against godlessness.'

'Religious persecution is a way of life for people of many faiths in China,' Donoher continued, 'and one reason so many Chinese Roman Catholics remain true to their faith is the Bishop of Shanghai, Yin Daoming.'

'I've never heard of him,' Kilkenny admitted.

'I'm not surprised,' Donoher said. 'Bishop Yin is not widely known outside China, and he has been imprisoned almost as long as you've been alive. Yin was born into a Catholic family during the war, but after the Communist takeover, his religious education was conducted in secret. As an underground priest, Yin was instrumental in holding the Catholic community together during the Cultural Revolution. For his efforts, he became both a Bishop and a target for Beijing. When the government was closing in on him, Yin was offered passage out of China. He refused to abandon his people and was eventually arrested and imprisoned. Bishop Yin was in the theater on the night of the fire. The government paraded him on stage and demanded that he renounce His Holiness and the Church of Rome.'

'I take it Yin refused.'

'You might say that his first sermon in nearly thirty years was a succinct expression of where he stood on the matter,' Donoher said with admiration. 'Long live Christ the King. Long live the Pope.'

'Hwong told me the same thing.'

'A profession of a faith that she and many others in China are willing to die for. Of the forty Bishops in China loyal only to Rome, all are either in prison, under house arrest, or in hiding – and some have disappeared completely. Ironically, many of the Bishops in the state church have at the same time quietly asked for and received the Pope's blessing before accepting their ordination. The tangled mess of church and state in China is simply a quagmire.'

The Pope had retreated into prayer as Donoher spoke. When the cardinal finished, he opened his eyes and placed a hand on Kilkenny's shoulder.

'There are two very important secrets that I now need to share with you. Can I trust you to keep them close to your heart?'

'You can, Your Holiness,' Kilkenny replied earnestly.

The hand on Kilkenny's shoulder tightened, the pontiff's

grip surprisingly strong. The Pope's steely blue eyes locked with his, and Kilkenny sensed the true inner fire of this holy man.

'Cardinal Donoher knows what he knows about the Church in China and elsewhere in the world because it is his duty to know. He is the head of the Vatican's intelligence service.' The Pope paused to take a breath and to let Kilkenny absorb the revelation. 'Few people know that first secret, and up to this moment, only I have known the second. Yin Daoming is a cardinal of the Roman Catholic Church. I made him a cardinal *in pectore*,' the Pope placed his other hand over his heart, 'over twenty years ago.'

'Nolan,' Donoher said gravely, 'His Holiness has brought us into his deepest confidence regarding Yin Daoming. You can be certain that if this secret ever reached Beijing, it would be fatal.'

'I will not endanger Cardinal Yin,' Kilkenny swore, his eyes still locked with the Holy Father's.

'I have revealed these things so that you may understand what is about to be asked of you, and to know that this difficult request comes from me.'

'What do you want me to do?' Kilkenny asked without hesitation.

'It is the wish of the Roman Catholic Church that Yin Daoming be free. I want you to help Cardinal Donoher devise a way to make this happen.'

'I will find a way, Your Holiness.'

The Pope smiled as if a burden had been eased. He pulled his hand off Kilkenny's shoulder and turned to face Donoher.

'Cardinal, there is another matter we need to discuss. Our brother in Christ, Cardinal Mizzi, will reach his eightieth birthday in December. He has served the Church well, but I feel it is now time to relieve him of his last official post.'

'A sad day for the Church,' Donoher agreed, 'but he has earned a rest.'

'The office of Camerlengo is now yours.'

Camerlengo. . . . If Kilkenny were not mistaken, as Camerlengo, Donoher would assume control of the Vatican following the Pope's death until the installation of his successor. The position, an ancient and once-powerful title, held little power until that time, but elevated Donoher's political standing in the Vatican considerably.

'Your Holiness –' Donoher protested.

The Pope raised his hand to silence Donoher. 'I understand your desire to maintain the illusion that you are not a powerful man, but the needs of the Church must come first.'

Donoher nodded, acquiescing to the Pope's decision. 'I pray that I will be worthy of this sacred trust.'

Following their meeting with the Pope, Donoher led Kilkenny back to his quarters where they could talk privately. The cardinal ordered a simple meal and offered Kilkenny a bottle of Vernor's from his refrigerator.

'You can get this in Rome?' Kilkenny asked, amazed to see the regional soft drink so far from Michigan.

'The cardinal in Detroit keeps my pantry stocked.' Donoher settled down in an old leather recliner and motioned Kilkenny toward the couch. 'I can only imagine you are filled with questions.'

'Vatican Intelligence?'

Donoher laughed. 'Sounds quite sinister when you say it that way, but it's nothing of the kind. Contrary to what some fiction writers and conspiracy theorists would have you believe, the Pope does not have the world's most formidable spy organization at his beck and call. There was a time, back in the days of the papal states, when the Pope had need of spies and armies, but not for over a century now. When I took over, Vatican Intelligence was an underfunded and understaffed minor office within the Vatican bureaucracy. Pope Leo tasked me with building an organization that could gather and analyze information effectively in this day and age.'

'So you're the Pope's spymaster?'

'Far from it,' Donoher said with another laugh. 'We're more of a think tank than a Catholic CIA, and that's why you're here. I understand that during your time in the Navy, you garnered a reputation as someone who could properly plan something on the order of what His Holiness has asked of us. Which reminds me, I have something for you.'

From a pocket inside his cassock, Donoher produced a small external hard drive.

'What's this?' Kilkenny asked as Donoher handed him the drive.

'That is the fruit of Miss Hwong's sacrifice this morning.'

'But those men took what she had on her.'

'That they did, and they returned to Beijing believing they had prevented the Vatican and the world from learning what truly happened inside that theater. What you hold there is a recording of that tragedy and a great deal more. I pray that it's all you need to plan Yin's liberation.'

Kilkenny tasted the bile rising in the back of his throat. 'You used her. She was nothing more than a decoy.'

Donoher nodded slowly. 'I grieve her death as much as you, more perhaps for the part I played in it. In the end, the decision was hers, and she felt the risk was critical to the deception.'

'Was I part of that deception?'

'You were an afterthought. I knew Hwong was placing herself in mortal danger and felt certain she would be attacked on her morning run. I crossed her path with yours in hope of improving the odds of her survival. I apologize for placing you at risk without your knowledge, but it was absolutely necessary.'

Kilkenny stared at the hard drive, trying to imagine what information could be so valuable that acquiring it cost a human life.

'If we now have the proof of what happened in the theater, why not announce it to the world and use international pressure to demand Yin's release?'

'As damning as the clip is, it provides us no leverage,' Donoher explained. 'The international outrage that followed the Tiananmen Square massacre had no effect on the Chinese government. They won't bow in this matter. Better we act as though we don't know the truth to conceal our intentions. And when Yin is free, he can unveil the truth to the world.'

5

October 12

Kilkenny carefully studied the holographic image of a building that looked like a long, nearly windowless block of concrete. The solitary wing of Chifeng Prison was part of a complex of buildings that housed a large population of inmates. These buildings comprised only a third of the structures on the prison grounds. The brickyard, where inmates were reformed through hellish hard labor, accounted for the remainder.

'Display at two-hundred-meter radius,' Kilkenny said.

The computer controlling the imaging chamber responded to Kilkenny's voice and zoomed out to bring the rest of the penal facility and some of the surrounding countryside into view. The prison stood in the grasslands just north of the city whose name it shared. Also known as the Xinsheng Brickyard, the laogai's kilns produced most of the masonry used by the nearby city of a half million people.

The model, which appeared atop an imaging table six feet in diameter, revealed elements of Chifeng Prison at an extraordinarily fine level of detail. From local topography and roads to door swings and light switches – anything that could be gleaned from architectural drawings, satellite images, and even the recollections of released prisoners had been painstakingly assembled into a computer-generated simulation. Kilkenny could view the prison at day or night, study the patterns of guard patrols and deliveries, even watch stacks of bricks grow in time-lapse fashion, only to disappear into railcars every Thursday.

After combing through the information gathered by Donoher's people in China, Kilkenny found he lacked only two things: the location of Yin's cell and a recent photograph of the man. Of the two images he had of Yin, one was a photograph taken in the early 1950s when Yin was a young man, and the other was a very grainy image culled from the Beijing video clip.

Kilkenny stood braced against the hologram table, the palms of his hands pressed onto the thick black ring of rubber-coated steel that encircled the base of the imaging chamber, puzzling over how to safely breach the laogai's security. At a nearby console of multi-screened Mac Pro computers sat Bill Grinelli, Kilkenny's friend and MARC's resident computer guru. Grin held a frothy cappuccino in one hand while the other danced across a keyboard, working his technological wizardry.

A keen intellect and a mischievous sense of humor had earned Grin his nickname, and he wore the appellation as a badge of honor. A few years Kilkenny's senior, Grin still viewed life with the youthful enthusiasm of a college freshman. What remained of his receding hair dangled from the back of his head in a brown-gray pony-tail. The goatee that encircled his trademark smile grew down from his chin into an often-stroked point. On his forearm, Grin sported a tattoo of an impish elf seated on a crescent moon scattering pixie dust.

Kilkenny had little trouble enlisting his friend's aid in the effort to liberate Yin Daoming. Just one viewing of the Beijing video had put Grin on the next flight to Rome. He admitted a twinge of envy over Kilkenny's private audience with the Pope, despite the fact that his personal religious stance lay somewhere between lapsed Catholic and agnostic. The pair divided the work between them, with Kilkenny tackling operational planning while Grin dealt with technical issues.

Grin's only disappointment with the new project came when he discovered that Vatican Intelligence did not occupy space in any of the historic structures owned by the tiny nation. But what it lacked in dramatic views and Renaissance grandeur was more than balanced by the quality and dedication of its analysts and the tools the Vatican provided for them to do their job. The under-ground facility, located beneath the building that housed the Vatican Mosaic Studio and known as the catacombs by those who labored there, was both stylish and modern, and Kilkenny and Grin had the necessary space and equipment to do their work.

'So, how are you coming?' Kilkenny asked.

'I've tickled the laogai's computer network as well as its link to the mother ship in Beijing, so I'm pretty sure we can keep them out of the loop when your team goes in. And if Donoher can provide me with a few people who speak Chinese like natives, I'm pretty sure I can wreak six kinds of havoc with their emergency responders. You asked for a smoke screen, and I think I can deliver.'

'Well, at least one of us is making some progress.'

'Still banging your head against the wall?' Grin asked.

'With lumps to prove it. There are really only two ways to do this: Hard or soft. Going in hard means guns blazing and a lot of people ending up dead. And to take on a place this size and successfully pull off a snatch-and-grab, I basically need to turn a couple platoons of Chinese volunteers into commandos. On top of that are the twin problems of quietly moving that many armed men into position and then getting them out with Yin after all hell breaks loose.'

'How do you think the Pope would feel about killing in order to get Yin out of jail?'

'His stance on war has been very consistent,' Kilkenny replied, 'so I'm pretty sure he'd veto any plan that includes the words *acceptable enemy losses*.'

'Got any soft ideas?'

'I'm still toying with their regular delivery cycle, but part of the problem is that it *is* regular. Same guy drives up in the same truck at the same time every week. He knows the guards, and they know him.'

'So if anything changes, the guards' Spidey-senses start a-tingling.'

'Soft is clearly the way to tackle this beast, but finding a vulnerability that we can exploit . . .' Kilkenny's voice trailed off as he stared at the long prairie grasses surrounding the laogai. 'If I can just figure out how to get Yin five hundred yards outside the perimeter, the odds of getting him all the way out jump to sixty percent. And they increase with every additional mile the team covers after that.'

'If regular deliveries are a problem, what about *irregular* deliveries?' Grin asked. 'They know the guy who makes the rice and gruel run, and the guy who picks up the bricks, right?'

'Yeah.'

'How about prisoners?'

'Those are scheduled as well,' Kilkenny said.

'Most, but not all. According to the records, Yin's last road trip wasn't scheduled.'

Kilkenny had read the report and realized that Grin was right. Yin's trip to Beijing and back was a unique event and not a normal prisoner transfer. Suddenly Kilkenny found himself pondering how to manufacture an event that would allow movement in and out of the prison without arousing suspicion.

'Did you ever see *Troy*?' Kilkenny asked.

'The movie, or the suburb of Detroit?' Grin asked with a straight face.

'The movie,' Kilkenny replied, ignoring the bait.

'The book was better, but I read it in the original Greek,' Grin remarked without a hint of braggadocio.

'The Trojans accepted the horse from the Achaeans because they believed it was a peace offering. We have to give the folks running that prison something they will accept, no questions asked. That's the only way this can work.'

6

October 13

Three days after his audience with the pontiff, Kilkenny returned to the Redemptoris Mater Chapel, accompanied by Donoher and Grin. Archbishop Sikora announced them and, on the Pope's signal, retired from the chapel. In preparation for this private audience, three chairs had been placed in a semicircle in front of the papal throne.

'Sit here,' the Pope said to Kilkenny, indicating the chair directly in front of the throne.

Kilkenny sat with Grin on his right and Donoher on his left. The Pope studied the three men for a moment, then focused his attention on Kilkenny.

'Cardinal Donoher believes you have found a way to free Bishop Yin. Please, tell me what you have in mind.'

'Your Holiness,' Kilkenny began, 'the plan I'm proposing hinges on a single fact: Beijing will not let Bishop Yin out of prison until after he is dead. And although Beijing appears content to let him live out the rest of his days in a cell, the Bishop was actually sentenced to death for his crimes. The Chinese justice system rarely executes condemned prisoners immediately after sentencing. Instead, it allows these doomed individuals the chance to reform themselves through a few years of hard labor. If, after this probationary period, the court feels progress toward reform has been made, the death sentence is commuted to life imprisonment. If not, then the prisoner is executed. No attempt has ever been made to reform Bishop Yin, so his original sentence still stands. A man in his situation could be executed at *any time* – it's simply a matter of paperwork.'

'You propose a deception,' the Pope said keenly.

'Yes, Your Holiness.'

The Pope smiled conspiratorially. 'Continue.'

'Until recently, Chinese executions were carried out with a bullet to the back of the head. But in an effort to be more efficient and appear more humane, China has begun using lethal injection,' Kilkenny explained. 'Most Chinese prisons are not equipped to perform this type of execution, so the Chinese employ a fleet of mobile execution trucks. I propose to field our own execution truck and to drive right up to Chifeng Prison with all the correct paperwork authorizing the execution of Yin Daoming. The Bishop will be brought out to the truck, apparently executed, and then smuggled out of the country.'

'But what of Beijing?' the Pope asked. 'Won't they know your execution order is false?'

'Eventually, but to paraphrase an old Irish blessing, "May Yin be across the border two hours before the Chinese know he isn't dead." Like any bureaucracy, it'll take a while for the paperwork to move through the system. I'm counting on that lag time. And my associate, Mister Grinelli, has a few tricks to ensure Beijing remains blind to what's happening in Chifeng.'

'This is true?' the Pope asked Grin.

'China has spent a lot of money on communications technology in recent years, but there isn't a bit of it I can't put to sleep.'

'We will do everything possible to protect Yin and the people who go in to rescue him,' Kilkenny promised.

The Pope bowed his head and considered for a moment all that he had heard, then arched an eye toward Donoher.

'Cardinal Donoher, what do you think?' the Pope asked.

'Your Holiness, I believe this plan has a fine chance to succeed. It's simple, and it relies on guile rather than violence to achieve our aim. Bishop Yin could well be in Rome before Beijing realizes what has transpired.'

The Pope took Donoher's advice with a nod, then slipped his right hand into the left sleeve of his simar and withdrew a piece of fine paper folded in thirds.

'In anticipation that you would do as I asked, I have prepared this letter authorizing you to proceed. It is written in my hand and bears the seal of my holy office.'

The Pope handed the document to Donoher, then turned back to Kilkenny. A wry smile curled the corners of the pontiff's mouth, and his blue eyes shone warmly. He shook an admonishing finger at Kilkenny.

'When stealing from dragons, it is wise to be gone long before the beasts awaken.'

61

7

October 14

The Pope sat quietly in the Redemptoris Mater Chapel, his hands slowly working the smooth beads of an old familiar rosary. His prayers were interwoven with meditations on the Immaculate Heart of Mary, for he believed it was only through the Blessed Mother's intervention that his life had been spared from an assassin's bullets early in his pontificate.

He prayed as he had throughout his long life, his daily devotions to a faith that had sustained him through years of suffering and the burden of more than a quarter century as the successor of Saint Peter, whose bones rested nearby beneath the altar of the basilica. One day, the Pope knew, his body would be placed in the crypt with those of the other men who had preceded him as Bishop of Rome.

As he prayed, the Pope heard a distant sound as if waves were crashing on the shore. Thinking it the rushing traffic outside, he ignored the sound and continued with his devotions. But the waves continued to crash, each building in volume and intensity until the sound of water enveloped him. Then the crashing disappeared.

'Jedrek,' a familiar voice spoke softly.

Hearing the nickname used only by his family and closest friends, the Pope paused in his recitation. He detected a faint floral scent in the air, a garden in springtime.

'Jedrek,' the voice called again, this time more distinct. A lyrical voice, familiar, but from his distant past.

Looking up, the Pope saw a woman with blonde hair and blue eyes wearing a plain dress. She stood near the altar, and the air around her was suffused with an ethereal light. The woman was young and beautiful, as he had always remembered her in his heart.

'*Mamusia*,' Pope Leo said, his voice choked with joy. He last saw her a month before his tenth birthday. 'I have missed you so much.'

The woman smiled. 'I have always been with you, my son. Your long journey is over. Take my hand.'

The Pope felt a new strength flowing through his aged body, a vigor he thought lost in the waning years of his life. He rose and stood tall, his first steps poised and confident. He glanced down at his body. His hands were those of a younger man, and his lean frame was clad in a black cassock. Despite the turns his life had taken, the road that led him from an old wooden church in the Polish countryside to the glory of the Vatican, Andrzej Bojnarowicz had never sought to be anything but a parish priest.

The young priest turned and saw his former self, a chrysalis empty as the tomb after Christ's resurrection.

In the face of the dead Pope, he saw the joy he had felt at the sight of his mother.

'Come, Jedrek,' his mother said lovingly. 'It is time to go.'

Andrzej Bojnarowicz took his mother's hand for the first time since he was a child. He felt her warmth and love and followed her into the light.

8

Archbishop Sikora entered the chapel to prepare the Pope for an early evening appointment with the cardinal in charge of the Pontifical Commission for the Vatican City State. He carried with him a BlackBerry PDA filled with the Pope's appointments scheduled several months out.

'Your Holiness,' Sikora said as he approached the pontiff.

The lack of an immediate response did not surprise him; the Pope prayed and slept deeply. As he came around the Pope's chair, Sikora saw the pontiff's rapt expression and dropped the PDA on the floor.

'Jedrek,' Sikora blurted out reflexively.

He placed two fingers on the Pope's neck; the skin felt cool to the touch and he found no pulse. Sikora scooped the PDA off the floor and said a brief prayer of thanks that the device was still functional as he keyed in a call to the Pope's personal physician.

Donoher entered the papal apartments and went directly to the Pope's bedroom. In his wake followed the cleric prelates, the secretary and the chancellor of the Apostolic

Camera, and the master of papal liturgical celebrations – men in whose presence he was officially to declare the Pope's death. The supine body of the supreme pontiff lay on the bed dressed in a clean white cassock. Donoher immediately noted the look of blessed serenity on the Pope's face. Death had been kind.

Nearby stood Archbishop Sikora, the Pope's physician, and several members of the papal staff.

'Your Eminence,' Sikora said, moving to kiss the cardinal's ring.

'Michal, please,' Donoher said, dismissing the polite formality. 'You found him in his chapel?'

Sikora nodded. He handed Donoher a velvet-lined pouch containing the lead seals of the papal office.

'That we would all be so fortunate to meet God in a place that brings us great peace.' Donoher turned to the physician. 'Have you determined the time and manner of the Holy Father's passing?'

'Only that His Holiness died sometime between six and seven o'clock this evening. An area of discoloration on his head suggests the probable cause was a massive cerebral hemorrhage. His death was almost instantaneous.'

Donoher clasped the physician's hand in both of his own. 'Doctor, you and your staff have my sincerest gratitude for all you have done to ease his suffering over these past few years. I will pray for you, always.'

'*Grazie*, Your Eminence, *grazie*.'

Both the physician and Sikora retreated from the Pope's bed, merging in with those who had arrived with Donoher. In his first duty as Camerlengo, Donoher approached the bedside of the Pope. He said a silent prayer as he stroked the cheek of his friend, then turned to those assembled.

'From medieval times to up well into the last century,' Donoher said solemnly, 'the cardinal Camerlengo would ascertain the death of the Pope by tapping him on the forehead three times with a silver hammer. After each blow, the Camerlengo would call out the Pope's given name and ask if he was dead. *Universi Dominici Gregis* makes no mention of this ancient ritual, and I see no need to further insult the body of this great man. I therefore declare that Pope Leo XIV is truly dead.'

With the greatest respect, Donoher gently lifted the Pope's right hand and removed the gold fisherman's ring. As he did so, he recalled the letter the Pope had given him the previous day – likely the last official document sealed with this signet. Donoher placed the ring in the pouch with the seals. In his first meeting with those cardinals present at the Vatican, he would break both symbols of the holy office.

Donoher turned to the chancellor of the Apostolic Camera. 'Do you have the death certificate?'

'I do, Your Eminence.'

Donoher accepted the leatherbound folio and motioned for the physician to accompany him into the Pope's study. Inside the folio was a sheet of pure white vellum inscribed in fluid Latin script with the official pronouncement of the Pope's death. Donoher and the physician affixed their signatures, completing the ritual.

As he looped the 'r' at the end of his name, Donoher

suddenly felt the immense weight of his new office. At this moment, he was entrusted with a sacred duty to safeguard and administer all the goods and temporal rights of the Holy See. Until the election of the next Pope, the cardinal Camerlengo was the most powerful man in the Roman Catholic Church.

'They are ready to prepare the Pope's body,' Sikora announced.

'Doctor, is there any need for further examination?' Donoher asked.

A minor controversy had erupted following the death of the previous Pope, whose reign had lasted a mere thirty-three days. Those sowing rumors that the Pope might have been murdered cited the quickness with which the late pontiff was embalmed as a sign of a Vatican coverup. Had the truth of the late Pope's poor health been more widely known among the College of Cardinals, he never would have been elected.

'The cause of the Pope's death is clear,' the doctor avowed.

'Then I release the Pope's body for preparation to lie in state.'

After removal of the body from the apartments, Donoher cleared everyone from the papal bedroom and study and sealed the rooms. Those members of the late Pope's personal staff who resided in the papal apartments would be permitted to remain until the burial. After the funeral, the entire apartment would be sealed until the new Pope was elected.

Donoher moved purposefully as he left the papal apartments. The next few weeks would likely be among the busiest of his entire life; the list of his duties and responsibilities as Camerlengo was immense.

He flipped open his cell phone and dialed the number for the cardinal vicar of Rome. Upon receiving Donoher's official notification, it would be that man's unhappy duty to make the special announcement to the people of Rome later this evening. Crews representing news agencies from around the world were already setting up just outside the Vatican walls as rumor of the Pope's death spread.

By the time he reached his office, Donoher completed his second call – this one to the cardinal archpriest of the Vatican Basilica, setting in motion the preparations for a papal funeral. He pulled out a file received from the previous Camerlengo and ran down the list of tasks requiring his immediate attention. Throughout his life, Donoher had never owned real estate of any kind. Within the next few hours, he would formally take possession of the Apostolic Palace and the palaces of the Lateran and Castel Gandolfo.

And then, Donoher thought, there was the matter of Yin Daoming.

9

The news had spread worldwide by the following morning. Kilkenny and Grin learned of the Pope's death the previous evening while dining out late. The matriarch of the family that ran the tiny ristorante had burst loudly into tears when the cardinal vicar appeared on the small television she watched at her corner table. The woman had been inconsolable, and like millions of Catholics, she deeply felt the loss of the charismatic man who had led the Church for so long. The pall cast by the Pope's death blanketed Rome like fog, subduing the normally vibrant Eternal City.

Kilkenny sat hunched forward against the imaging table, his arms folded along the edge as a support for his chin. He stared at a hologram of the corridor of rooms in the solitary wing where Yin was imprisoned. Through the nearly transparent holographic walls, he could follow the layout of pipes and ducts that serviced the cells, but his ability to focus on the details eluded him. Hwong's murder and the deaths of the Chinese

Roman Catholics still angered him, and the untimely deaths of his wife and son never strayed far from his conscious thoughts. And now, a man whom he had prayed for every Sunday as far back as he could remember, someone he'd met only twice but whose strength of spirit had affected him profoundly, was dead.

To reach the Petriano Entrance that morning, Kilkenny and Grin had to wend their way slowly through the throng that had spilled beyond the confines of Saint Peter's Square and into the streets around the Vatican. It didn't matter that there was nothing to see – just being there at this moment seemed important to people.

The somber mood of the crowd reminded Kilkenny of a few bitter losses at Michigan Stadium, when tens of thousands of emotionally drained football fans straggled away from the wreckage of a season derailed. He knew the analogy was weak, but the assassinations of President Kennedy and Martin Luther King Jr. predated him, and he simply had no better frame of reference for grief on such a massive scale. Even in the deep seclusion of the catacombs, the aura of mourning was inescapable.

The magnetic lock buzzed as it released the door. Both Kilkenny and Grin turned, then stood as Donoher entered the room. He looked as if he had been up all night and didn't expect to sleep anytime soon.

'Here,' Kilkenny said, offering his chair. 'I can't imagine what your night must have been like.'

Donoher nodded his thanks and sat down with a sigh. 'I have been the head of the Roman Catholic Church for mere hours, and already I'm planning to announce in my opening remarks at the conclave that I have no desire to be Pope, and to promise the most serious consequences to any cardinal who dares vote for me.'

'That bad?' Kilkenny asked.

'I won't trouble you with the details, but never have I borne such a heavy cross. And despite everything that I am now required to do, the two of you have never been far from my thoughts. How soon do you think you can implement your plan?'

'Training is the biggest issue – the people who do this will have to work very well together,' Kilkenny said as he considered the question. 'Six weeks, maybe a month if we really push it.'

'I'm afraid we don't have that kind of time,' Donoher said flatly. 'The Pope's death has set a clock in motion.'

'What kind of clock?' Grin asked.

'In fifteen days,' Donoher explained, 'the eligible cardinals will gather in conclave to elect the next Pope.'

'How does that affect us?' Grin asked, unclear of the connection.

'Pope Leo directed me to pursue this course of action,' Donoher explained, 'and as long as he was alive, we had his blessing. With his death, responsibility for all of the Church's temporal matters devolved to me as Camerlengo. As I am of the same mind as the late Pope regarding Bishop Yin, we can still proceed.'

Kilkenny immediately grasped Donoher's dilemma. 'But you're only in charge until the new Pope is elected.'

'Which could be as soon as fifteen days from now,' Donoher said. 'And if the new Pope doesn't find this idea brilliant, the project is dead.'

'And Yin with it,' Grin added.

Kilkenny stared at the model of Yin's prison, imagining the dark, lonely cell where decades of the Bishop's life had been stolen in a dry martyrdom. The injustice of that windowless hellhole infuriated Kilkenny and fueled his desire to find a way to free the Bishop. Unlike the cancer that took his wife and child, Kilkenny knew how to attack the walls of Chifeng Prison. With a viable plan in hand, Kilkenny could not accept that the Pope's untimely death might condemn Yin to die inside that concrete box.

'Fifteen days,' Kilkenny fumed through gritted teeth, his mind weighing each step of the plan against an impossible deadline.

'Fifteen days is the minimum,' Donoher clarified. 'It could be a bit longer if the conclave deadlocks.'

'How much longer?' Grin asked.

'Thirty ballots, about two additional weeks. After that, a trigger in the Apostolic Constitution kicks in that permits a change in the rules of the election. Instead of requiring a two-thirds majority, the electors can opt for an absolute majority or a runoff between the top two candidates on the previous ballot. These rule changes make it easier for a compromise candidate to garner enough votes to break the deadlock and win election.'

'But we can't count on a deadlock,' Kilkenny said. 'We *have* to get Yin out of China in fifteen days.'

'But just a moment ago you said you needed at least a month to prepare,' Donoher said. 'How is it you now think you can accomplish this in half that time?'

'By using people already trained for this kind of work.' Kilkenny replied.

'Mercenaries?' The cardinal was incredulous.

'Volunteers,' Kilkenny replied. 'Special Forces and CIA, but we'll need permission to use them. I need the kind of people I can trust with my life.'

Kilkenny's eyes remained on the hologram of Chifeng Prison as he spoke, his face eerily illuminated by the computer-generated mirage. But the look of deep concentration that tightened his features waned, leaving behind determined calm.

'You're not intending to go into China yourself, are you?' Donoher asked.

Kilkenny nodded. 'It's the only way to get the job done in time. Grin can handle the tech side of things without me.'

'This isn't what I brought you here for,' Donoher protested. 'Your father will never forgive me.'

'I couldn't forgive myself if I let Yin continue to rot in that hellhole knowing that I could have gotten him out. I appreciate your concern for my father's feelings, but this isn't any different from my time in the Navy, and he should understand that.'

'There's still a chance the new Pope will approve of your plan,' Donoher said, almost pleading.

'Are you willing to bet Yin's life on that?' Kilkenny asked.

Donoher considered the *papabili*, those cardinals considered favorites for the papacy. All were good, deeply religious men, but none possessed the fiery determination of the late Pope. Most, if not all, would find the plan to free Yin provocative and far too risky.

'No,' Donoher conceded.

Kilkenny stood and turned toward Donoher. 'Our choice really is now or never.'

'Then I can think of no greater honor to the memory of Pope Leo,' Donoher declared, 'than to fulfill his last request.'

10

Donoher sat alone in a well-lit conference room in the catacombs. The table before him held several stacks of files covering all aspects of the Vatican's preparations for the upcoming papal funeral and the subsequent conclave. After Pope Leo XIV named him Camerlengo, Donoher's predecessor, Cardinal Mizzi, forwarded to him a file box of information he had collected over the years in preparation for this day. Included were copies of letters from previous Camerlengos about their experiences during past interregnums. Donoher found comfort in the wisdom of those men who had carried this burden before him.

The triangular speaker in the center of the conference table chimed. Donoher glanced at the caller-ID. It was his executive assistant, Sister Deborah.

'Yes, Sister?'

'Your Eminence, the video link you requested is ready.'

'Thank you.'

As he set aside the file he was reading, the flat monitor covering a large portion of the opposite wall filled with a test screen showing the logo of the Holy See. The still image quickly disappeared, replaced by a view inside another subterranean conference room thousands of miles away. Two men gazed back at him. Both appeared lean and fit for their age. The man on the left had a full head of silver hair; the other displayed only hints of gray around the edges. They were dressed in well-tailored suits, and the left lapel of each held a pin of the American flag. Donoher personally knew the man on the left; it was through the CIA director that he had requested this meeting. He recognized the man seated beside Jackson Barnett, though this was the first time he had ever spoken to him.

'Your Eminence,' the President began in a folksy west Texas drawl, 'I would first like to express my deepest condolences and those of the people of the United States on the passing of Pope Leo. I was privileged to have met with him on several occasions and benefited from his wisdom. The Pope was a man of great faith and compassion, truly one of the most inspiring leaders on the world stage. He will be missed.'

'He will indeed, Mister President, he will indeed. Thank you for your kind words.'

'Kind words come easy when they're the truth. Director Barnett informs me you have a delicate matter you'd like to discuss with us.'

'That is correct, Mister President. Are you familiar with the case of Yin Daoming, the Roman Catholic Bishop of Shanghai?'

'Chinese dissident,' the President recalled. 'Been locked up for decades for being nothing more than a man of the cloth. He's got some family here in the U.S., in

Connecticut. I've worked with one of the senators from up there to quietly prod Beijing into letting him go. Talks on that have never gotten anywhere.'

'That has been our experience as well,' Donoher said. 'In August, the Chinese government murdered approximately five hundred of its citizens in a failed attempt to force Bishop Yin into publicly renouncing the Roman Catholic Church and the Pope. Following this incident, His Holiness directed me to find a way to unilaterally free Bishop Yin.'

'Sounds like you're talking about a prison break,' the President said wryly.

'Yes, Mister President. We have devised a nonviolent way to free Bishop Yin. Just before his death, Pope Leo authorized us to proceed.'

'Is this why Nolan Kilkenny is in Rome?' Barnett asked.

Donoher nodded. 'I needed someone with his particular background to study the problem, to see if our aim was even possible.'

'Kilkenny,' the President mused, then he turned to Barnett. 'That the same fella who nailed the folks behind the attacks of the shuttle *Liberty* and that Chinese rocket?'

'*Shenzhou-7*, Mister President,' Barnett offered. 'And yes, the gentleman working with Cardinal Donoher is the same man you remember from that incident.'

'He sure gets around.' The President chuckled. 'The work Kilkenny did last year put a bit of a thaw in our relations with the Chinese – nothing earth-shattering, mind you, but the tone has improved. Too bad we had to keep the wraps on that story – in my mind, the Chinese owe Kilkenny a medal.'

'What you're proposing will infuriate Beijing,' Barnett said to Donoher.

'The continued existence of the Roman Catholic Church in China infuriates Beijing. From the point of view of the Holy See, we have nothing to lose in freeing Bishop Yin.'

'But the United States stands to lose a great deal if we're implicated in any way,' Barnett countered.

'Cardinal, if you have a plan that you think will work, why come to us?' the President asked. 'You have to know that even minor involvement on our part would be politically difficult for the United States.'

'The Pope's death has made time a serious problem for us. In as little as fifteen days, the Church may have a new Pope, at which time my directive from Pope Leo will, in all likelihood, be rescinded. We cannot possibly train our own people, get them into place, and free Bishop Yin in so short a time.'

'What makes you so sure the new Pope won't finish what Pope Leo started?'

'Mister President, you yourself know how difficult it is to make a decision that will put people in harm's way. Pope Leo agonized for years over what to do about Bishop Yin, but after the August tragedy he found his patience at an end. I fear it will take years for the new Pope, whomever he is, to reach the same conclusion – years that Bishop Yin may no longer have.'

'What do you need?' the President asked.

'Logistical support and manpower. Kilkenny intends to lead the team in himself. He wants to assemble a small force of volunteers who would be provided with new identities to conceal their ties to the United States.'

'Special Forces,' Barnett said. 'Kilkenny was a SEAL and still has contacts in the service, including Admiral Dawson.'

'I thought you said your plan was nonviolent,' the President said.

'It is, Mister President,' Donoher replied, 'and if everything proceeds as we hope, Beijing won't realize what has transpired until long after Kilkenny and his team have Yin out of the country.'

'And if everything doesn't go right, a handful of highly trained U.S. commandos might get themselves killed or captured inside China.' Barnett shook his head. 'Mister President, this is a *very* dangerous thing to do.'

'So this jailbreak was Pope Leo's dying wish?' the President asked.

'It was,' Donoher replied.

The President thought for a moment before he spoke. 'Freeing Bishop Yin would certainly have a lot of symbolic value, but the bottom line is it's the right thing to do. If it pisses off Beijing, well, we'll deal with it. Jackson, you're my point man on this operation. I want you to help Cardinal Donoher pull off this jailbreak, but make sure we have at least a fig leaf of deniability.'

'Yes, Mister President,' Barnett replied.

'And Cardinal, best of luck to you on this worthy endeavor. Perhaps we'll have a chance to talk further in Rome after the funeral. Pope Leo left a great legacy.'

'I look forward to it, Mister President.'

11

Jackson Barnett pressed the button for the seventh floor, an action repeated so many times it no longer required conscious thought – which was good, as he was concerned with a difficult problem. The Director of Central Intelligence (DCI) knew the agency's activities in nations hostile to the United States carried an element of risk to the men and women involved. Nothing saddened Barnett more than the somber convocations held in the cavernous lobby, where he unveiled new additions to the constellation of black stars chiseled into the white marble wall. The stars represented the CIA's honored dead.

The doors slid open, and Barnett headed purposefully toward his office.

'Is the link set up?' Barnett asked as he approached the desk of his assistant, Sally Kirsch.

'They're waiting for you now,' Kirsch replied.

Entering his office, Barnett's eyes immediately darted to the flat rectangular display mounted on his wall.

The conversation between the two people pictured there ceased as soon as he walked into view of the camera mounted atop the screen. On the right half of the split image sat Kilkenny, likely in the same Vatican conference room from which Donoher had spoken to the President a few hours earlier. Kilkenny looked tired and a bit disheveled in a sweatshirt and jeans, though Barnett had seen him in far worse condition on several occasions over the past few years.

Beside Kilkenny – virtually, though in reality in a MARC conference room in Ann Arbor, Michigan – sat a beautiful young woman with long black hair and almond eyes. Roxanne Tao was dressed impeccably in a tailored suit. Barnett knew her to be a professional who went to great lengths to look and act the part. Pinned to Tao's lapel was a gold Chinese character representing the word *Qi* – the name of the CIA-backed venture-capital firm she represented in Ann Arbor.

'Good morning, Roxanne,' Barnett said, his South Carolina baritone rich with warmth. 'I hope this impromptu meeting didn't disrupt your day too much.'

'Nothing that can't be rescheduled,' Tao replied.

'Good evening, Nolan.'

Kilkenny acknowledged the DCI's perfunctory greeting with a nod as he sipped on a Diet Coke. Barnett set his briefcase down beside the desk but remained standing. A prosecutor before embarking on a long and distinguished career with the agency, Barnett found he did some of his best thinking on his feet.

'Has Nolan briefed you on his latest project?' Barnett asked Tao.

'No, we were just catching up. It sounds as if things are a little crazy in Rome right now.'

'I have no doubt an element of madness is at work.'

Kilkenny eyed Barnett curiously as he spoke. Donoher had warned him that the DCI was less than enthusiastic about liberating Yin.

'I am just now returning from the White House,' Barnett continued, speaking directly to Tao, 'where the President and I had a most interesting conversation with Cardinal Donoher. As you may or may not know, the cardinal was responsible for hiring Nolan as a consultant to the Vatican. Following the Pope's death, Cardinal Donoher assumed stewardship of the Vatican City State and the Holy See. The subject of our conversation was a Roman Catholic Bishop and Chinese dissident named Yin Daoming. Do you know of Bishop Yin?'

'To many in China, Bishop Yin is a heroic figure, a man of great courage and honor,' Tao replied. 'That he is imprisoned is a crime.'

'Until a few days ago, I'm sad to say I'd never heard of Bishop Yin,' Kilkenny admitted.

'It's not surprising,' Tao said. 'He is little known outside of China, and in China his name is mentioned only with great discretion.'

'Nolan, would you care to illuminate Roxanne on what you've been working on for the Vatican?' Barnett asked.

'I'm going to get Bishop Yin out of China, and I'd like your help.'

'Of course,' Tao replied. 'What do you need me to do?'

'You spent a lot of time in China – I need your experience. I also need to procure some items over there, so if you still have any contacts that you trust, I need them too. And once our team is in place, I've got the role of a lifetime for you to play.'

'I'm certain Nolan wouldn't ask you to set foot in China if he had any idea of the risk it poses to you and to his mission,' Barnett said to Tao. 'And since I have been ordered to provide covert support for this venture, I feel compelled to make full disclosure about your past work in China.' Barnett turned to Kilkenny. 'You already possess the appropriate security clearance for this information, Nolan, and now you have the need to know. Roxanne, tell him.'

As Tao collected her thoughts, Barnett sat down in a brown leather chair, careful to remain in the camera's field of view.

'In the eight years prior to my arrival in Ann Arbor, I was a deep-cover agent for the CIA in Beijing. I was, in the parlance of my profession, an illegal. I had no papers, no diplomatic immunity, no status as a U.S. citizen. If caught, I would have been tried for espionage and, after a thorough interrogation, executed. Those were the rules governing my existence.

'For eight years, I *was* native Chinese. During that time, I built several cells of agents in various government ministries and businesses. My agents produced volumes of intelligence on the actions and intentions of Beijing, information that even led to the disruption of a network of Chinese agents working in the United States.

'In China, I also built a personal life and formed relationships with many people who played no part in my work. I even fell in love and was engaged to be married. I became the person I pretended to be, lived the role as if I'd been born to it, as if Roxanne Tao of California was a fiction and Chen Mei Yue of Beijing was real. In living with the fear that the government could arrest me at any time, I was no different from most ordinary Chinese. The people of China have lived for thousands of years with a government-induced form of paranoia.

'I spent most of my last year in China on the run, my cover blown, my Chinese life in ruins. Many of my cells were exposed, my agents arrested and killed. Some sacrificed themselves to ensure my escape. A few of my people remain in place, dormant, living in dread that the next knock at the door will either be the police, or perhaps me.'

Kilkenny studied Tao as she spoke and sensed equal amounts of anguish and relief. The rules of secrecy with which she lived meant that eight years of her life had to be kept separate, repressed in her memory as something she didn't truly own and could never admit to possessing.

'The very success of Roxanne's operation in China set the stage for her undoing,' Barnett added. 'The Chinese knew something was afoot but had no way to gauge the extent. So, being well versed in the teachings of Sun Tsu, they found an *inward spy* here at Langley who accepted their generosity in exchange for information. The career of the gentleman in question as a mole didn't last long enough to spend even a fraction of his ill-gotten wealth, but the damage he caused in human terms was immense.

'Chen Mei Yue is a known spy of the United States. The Chinese have photographs of her, fingerprints, probably even DNA because she fled her apartment just moments ahead of the police, leaving everything behind. Chen is a wanted fugitive, and the Chinese are still looking for her. Asking Roxanne to return to China is tantamount to asking her to commit suicide.'

'Nonetheless, I'm going,' Tao declared.

'I can't ask you to do that,' Kilkenny said.

'You can't ask me to remain behind, either,' Tao countered. 'Not now that I know what you're after. It may be a danger for me to go, but how much more of a danger is it for you to go without me?'

'Roxanne,' Barnett said, 'I caution you against returning.'

'I'm going in surrounded by a team of meat eaters,' Kilkenny added, 'all big boys who can handle themselves if the *merde* hits the *ventilateur électrique*. You don't have to go.'

'Yes, I do.'

'Why?' Kilkenny asked softly.

'My fiancé was an underground Roman Catholic. I was the spy, and yet Ming kept his secret from me for years. At first, he hid his faith to protect himself, but as our relationship grew he maintained the secret to protect me. Eventually we shared our secrets and planned to have our marriage blessed by a priest. I was raised a Christian but was never very religious until I fell in love with this man. When my cover was blown, Ming hid me in the community of his underground church. He could have saved himself, in fact I urged him to, but in the end he died to protect me.

'What I learned from Ming and the others who

86

sheltered me when I was on the run was the fierce loyalty the Roman Catholics in China have toward one another. I asked Ming why this was so, and he said it was Bishop Yin. Yin stayed with his people when he could have fled. He lived the words he preached. Ming followed that example, and I am alive because of his sacrifice.' Tao's eyes brimmed with tears as she dredged through her store of memories. 'In any other case, I would agree with you both about the dangers of my returning to China, but for Ming and the others who saved my life, I *must* do this.'

As Tao spoke, Kilkenny recalled her boundless support in the days after his wife and son died. Family and friends offered heartfelt sympathy, of course, but in hindsight only Tao seemed to comprehend the depth of his grief and anger. What he had assumed was tremendous empathy he now realized was a wound they shared in common.

'I see there will be no dissuading you,' Barnett conceded, 'so we must do everything possible to keep you off Beijing's radar.'

12

October 16

Max Gates stood atop the dune surveying the carnage below. A stocky, barrel-chested man with forearms that would make Popeye proud, he was clad in a battle-dress uniform of woodland-pattern camouflage with the pants bloused into a pair of black Bates 924/922 boots. The master chief's sandy-brown hair had receded to nothingness long before it had the opportunity to turn gray, though what he lost on top he made up for in a pair of bushy eyebrows and a thick handlebar mustache.

Explosions and gunfire shattered the night, war in all its fury unleashed on a thin strip of sand along the Pacific Coast. The air was thick with smoke, the harsh smell of cordite strong and familiar to CMC Gates – the command master chief and senior enlisted adviser charged with the training of recruits for the Navy's elite SEAL teams.

The CMC stood next to Captain Hunley, the CO and an officer with as many years in the teams as the master chief. Both men were veterans whose vast wealth of experience in this particular brand of warfare was now employed to shape the next generation of naval Special Forces.

On the beach below, the instructors serving under Hunley and Gates set off grenade and artillery simulators, fired full-auto bursts from M-60 machine guns, and shouted commands at the increasingly confused and disoriented class of recruits. Push-ups, sit-ups, flutter kicks, and dive bombers – the instructors drove the recruits through a punishing regimen of physical training exercises, all while soaking the young men with icy blasts from fire hoses. Sand coated every inch of the sodden recruits' bodies, working through their clothing and grinding in every crevice.

'Looks like Hell Week's off to a roaring start, Chief,' Hunley said.

'The men are making a fine batch of sugar cookies out of those tadpoles, sir,' Gates agreed.

Cold, wet, hungry, and tired – for the next five days, the SEAL recruits would experience these four sensations in extremes they could never before have imagined. And at every turn, their instructors would berate, goad, cajole, and tempt them into giving up.

'Hit it!' Petty Officer Portage shouted.

Portage's command sent a sand-encrusted boat crew of seven men into the cold surf for a plunge. One of the men straggled a bit behind his buddies, and the petty officer pounced on him.

'You ain't moving too fast, banana. You got sand in your panties?'

Gates and Hunley couldn't hear the faltering recruit's response as Portage hounded him into the water.

'Looks like Portage has our first bell ringer of the night,' Gates shouted over the din.

A boat crew in the surf lay in a foot of water, linked elbow to elbow, facing the shore. Portage stood at the water's edge, alternating bursts from an M-60 with tender words of encouragement to the shivering men.

'You embryos aren't getting outta that water until one of you quits!' Portage shouted. 'Who's it gonna be? I only need one! There's a hot shower and a dry bed just waiting for one of you.'

A young lieutenant, the sole officer among the sodden boat crew, tried to shout over Portage's banter and encourage his teammates to hang together. A large wave crashed over the men, and one recruit broke away from the others. He struggled ashore and walked with leaden steps toward a brass ship's bell mounted atop a wooden frame. He rang the bell three times to signal his surrender and was taken away.

'That gets us down to forty-eight,' Gates said, unsurprised.

The class was in its fourth week of BUD/S – Basic Underwater Demolition/SEAL training – and already two-thirds of those who started were gone. Only twenty-five percent of recruits in the initial muster of a typical BUD/S class completes the twenty-six-week course and earns the right to display the Special Warfare Badge – commonly known as the Budweiser – on their uniforms.

Despite appearances, the purpose of Hell Week is not to destroy a man but rather to prove to him that his body can do tenfold the work he ever thought possible. It also drives home the importance of teamwork, because men acting as individuals cannot overcome the challenges faced in BUD/S. The recruits that learn these two important lessons through the catharsis of blood and sweat have the best chance of becoming SEALs.

'When do you leave?' Hunley asked.

'Later today,' Gates replied, 'just as soon as I get a few things squared away. I should be back by the end of the month. The guys know the drill.'

Hunley nodded. Earlier that morning, the captain had received an unusually cryptic order that temporarily removed Gates from the active-duty roster. Though curious about this sudden reassignment, Hunley knew not to pursue a matter when the order was authorized by the commander in chief.

'Good luck, Chief.'

Gates saluted his CO, then climbed behind the wheel of a HumVee and drove back to his office on the main base. It was just past midnight, and the complex of buildings was dark except for those areas manned by the night watch. He parked in his designated spot, kicked the sand from his boots, and made his way through the instructors' building to his office. Gates keyed his password into his computer and logged into the base network. He glanced at the new messages in his inbox and was pleased with the responses he found from fellow warriors in the U.S. Special Forces community. He tapped into a secure A/V communications program and keyed in the address for Kilkenny at the Vatican. The two computers shook hands through the Internet, and a window opened into the catacombs workroom.

'Chief, right on time.' Kilkenny smiled.

'Early bird gets the worm, son. Though around these parts the early birds are trying to keep from getting their tail feathers shot off.'

'Ah, Hell Week,' Kilkenny sighed wistfully. 'I still have vivid memories of dining in the demo pit, chowing on a box lunch, knee-deep in that cold putrid cesspool while the instructors lit off smoke grenades and tossed M-80s into the water. You going any easier on the new recruits?'

'Hell no. If it was good enough for you 'n me, it's good enough for them.'

'Glad to hear it. How are you coming with the team for my op?'

'Every spec warrior I polled has signed on,' Gates replied, referring to members of the elite special forces community, 'so we should have a full roster by midday. Amazing how many guys will volunteer for something with so few details.'

'Must be the thought of your charming company.'

'Or the chance to see a crusty old SEAL strap on his fins one last time before he retires,' Gates said in a slow Oklahoma drawl. 'Remember our last op?'

'Haiti? Like it was yesterday. Bet Admiral Hopwood was smiling down from heaven on us after that little foray into the bush.'

'Anytime you can rescue a bunch of hostages and send a steamin' sack of shit to hell – well, my friend, that *is* a good day.'

'This will be a good one to hang up your fins after, Max. Any thoughts on the plan?' Kilkenny asked.

'A few. About six or seven years back, you and I did a stint with the Night Stalkers. Remember those funky ultralights they were toying around with – the BATs?'

Kilkenny clearly recalled one night flight in which the pilot from the Army's 160th Special Operations Aviation Regiment (SOAR) did all he could to get his Navy passengers to lose their dinners. Gates repaid the pilot with a little unscheduled underwater cross training.

'Bitchin' Airborne Things?' Kilkenny mused, recalling the unofficial acronym. 'Think we can use 'em?'

'They've come a long way since the Mark One Mod Zeros we played with. Take a look at the latest iteration.'

Gates uploaded an animation that quickly appeared in a window on Kilkenny's screen. The new BAT sported an open, lozenge-shaped fuselage made with curved sections of piping and seated four occupants in a two-by-two configuration. Like a helicopter, the fuselage rested on a pair of skids, but any resemblance between the two types of aircraft ended there. Tubular tendrils sprouted organically from a slender, three-foot-long turbine engine mounted atop the spine of the fuselage above the rear seats. The tendrils flowed seamlessly like arteries that could draw energy from the power plant. The most distinctive feature of the craft was its wings – a pair of fabric-clad armatures with visible ribs and scalloped along the trailing edge like its nocturnal namesake.

'Looks like something Tim Burton and H. R. Giger might have dreamed up,' Kilkenny opined.

'It ain't a fighter jet, but it sure flies like a sono-fabitch. Can turn on a dime, hover, and do moves in the air that are almost unnatural. I figure with three of these, we can jump across the Mongolian border and reach the outskirts of Chifeng in just a few hours. That'll save us a couple days of transit heading in and out – time that I'd rather use on the ground eyeballin' that prison.'

'As I recall, BATs were just for short-range hops.'

'For the most part, they still are. This beast is totally electric now, powered by a fuel cell. Given the juice it takes to put one of 'em into the air, round-trip range is a couple hundred miles.'

'We're going a lot farther than that.'

'I know, but some of the prototypes they're testing are for long-range insertion.'

'How long?'

'Don't know yet. On these new BATs, they replaced the fuel cell with a radioisotopic thermoelectric generator,' Gates pronounced each syllable carefully as he read the words off a specification sheet. 'A RITEG for short. I understand they use 'em to power satellites.'

'Max, it's a nuke.'

'No shit. I guess that's why they say that with a RITEG, this thing will keep going like the Energizer Bunny. Anyhow, I figure three BATs will do the job quite nicely, and I got a trio of pilots chomping at the bit to try 'em out for real. Best of all, they're not in Uncle Sam's inventory yet – strictly off-the-books hardware.'

Kilkenny reran the animation on his computer. 'Flying in and out would solve a number of logistical problems.

Off the books or not, we better make damn sure we don't leave one of these behind.'

'Yeah, the folks at Boeing who pimped this ride would be most put out.'

'Did you just use the phrase *pimped this ride* in a sentence?' Kilkenny asked.

'Yeah. *Pimp My Ride* is one of my favorite shows. I TiVo it along with *Monster Garage* and *Myth Busters*. Best TV programming since *This Old House*.'

Kilkenny laughed. 'Just send me a full set of specs on the BATs. If we're going to use them, we have to figure out how to smuggle them in and out of Mongolia.'

13

VATICAN CITY

October 17

'Could I interest either of you gentlemen in a glass of wine?' Donoher asked as he entered the catacombs workroom. 'Our evening meal will arrive shortly.'

Grin glanced up from the bank of monitors, his eyes tired but bright. 'I prefer to imbibe only among friends, and if that's a bottle of Italian red I see in your hand, then you must be a friend.'

Kilkenny cleared a space on the worktable, and the cardinal set out three glasses and poured from a bottle of Castello di Fonterutoli Chianti Classico Riserva. The wine looked nearly black, and as Grin inhaled the bouquet, he detected traces of smoke, various fruits, licorice, and wood.

'You've let this little fellow breath a bit,' Grin said approvingly.

'Admittedly, my years in Italy have had a modestly civilizing effect upon me,' Donoher said.

Kilkenny held his glass for a moment and stared at what would be his first drink in a week, then realized that with one bottle split three ways, there was little chance of a hangover. Each man swirled the first sip around in his mouth, tickling his taste buds with the complex, delightful flavor.

'So, where do we stand?' Donoher asked.

'Other than a few minor details, we're ready to go,' Kilkenny replied. 'In fact, Grin came up with a name for our covert op.'

'Did you now? Let's hear it.'

'Operation Rolling Stone,' Grin announced.

Donoher turned to Kilkenny. 'You mean to tell me you've christened our sacred mission after a hedonistic rock 'n' roll band?'

'Actually, it's an allusion to the stone that covered Christ's tomb until it was rolled away on Easter morning,' Grin explained. 'Like Christ, Yin is entombed in Chifeng Prison, and we're going to roll away the stone and let him out.'

'Ah, a scriptural allusion,' Donoher said skeptically.

'Grin assures me the name has nothing to do with the several megs of Stones tunes packed into his iPod,' Kilkenny offered.

'Perish the thought.' Donoher held his glass up. 'Very well then. To the success of Operation Rolling Stone.'

'Here, here,' Kilkenny and Grin chimed in, tapping their glasses with Donoher's.

Kilkenny savored the taste of the red wine and felt it working its magic. He and Grin had been working down in the catacombs almost nonstop since the Pope's death, and he knew the same must be true for Donoher.

'How's it going up there?' Kilkenny asked.

'I am about where you would expect a man to be when he has to stage a state funeral and an election on a mere two-weeks notice, but I'll muddle through. Despite the chaos, what you two are trying to accomplish is never far from my thoughts and prayers. God willing, you'll finish the job before the white smoke rises.'

'Speaking of the election,' Grin said. 'I've been trolling the Web, and Paddy Power is listing odds on the top cardinals. There are five in single digits.'

'The papabili,' Donoher said with an exaggerated Italian flourish. 'It's dangerous to be named a favorite going into a papal election. There's an old saying that many a man has gone into conclave a Pope and come out a cardinal. You aren't betting on this, I hope.'

'I don't gamble at all,' Grin replied. 'Throwing money away is not my idea of a good time.'

'Is it a sin to bet on a papal election?' Kilkenny asked.

'No, but such a wager would be in extremely poor taste. Though were I a betting man, I believe my money would be safe in the top five. Any one of them would make a fine Pope.'

'Who do you think has the best shot?' Kilkenny asked.

'Each papabili has his assets and liabilities. If you follow the conventional wisdom that the Church will not make two bold moves in a row, then Cardinal Magni is the clear favorite. He's the only Italian among the papabili, so he can count on garnering seventeen percent of the vote straight away. He is also very conservative and well-liked by Opus Dei.'

'Aren't those the guys who got slammed in *The Da Vinci Code*?' Grin asked.

Donoher nodded. 'And at sixty-nine, his reign likely will not last as long as Pope Leo's. Magni is a very safe choice. If the European cardinals don't go for him, then they'll likely support Ryff. He's a well-respected moral theologian, a man cut from the same cloth as Pope Leo, which makes him a strong contender. He's middle-European, which to some may make him seem a bit too much like Pope Leo, but the biggest knock against him is his age.'

'Too old?' Kilkenny asked.

'Too young. He's only fifty-seven and in very good health. A man like that could reign for a very long time indeed.'

'What about the other three?' Kilkenny asked.

'Ah, that's where things get interesting,' Donoher said wryly. 'The demographics of the Church have changed dramatically over the past century, and Leo's selection of cardinals reflects this fundamental change. For the first time, cardinals from Third World countries have a real opportunity to win the papacy. Escalante from Honduras would be an exciting choice. Nice fellow, very media-savvy, and wonderful in front of a crowd. His election would be the most dramatic event in the history of Latin America since Columbus washed ashore. Then there's Cardinal Velu from Bombay.'

'India?' Kilkenny said. 'I didn't know there were any Catholics there.'

'Roughly twenty million, and the Church in India dates to the Apostle Thomas. Velu has also spent time in the Vatican ranks, so he's well connected here. He's a conservative theologian, fluent in more than a dozen languages, and has wonderful rapport in Africa and Southeast Asia. And he's the right age – neither too old nor too young – but he's so conservative that the moderate cardinals might have trouble voting for him.

'Rounding out the papabili is Oromo from Sudan,' Donoher continued, 'a very bright fellow and well connected in the Islamic world. He arranged the first visit by a Pope to a mosque. Oromo's election could do a lot of good in building bridges between the largely Judeo-Christian West and the Islamic nations of Africa, the Middle East, and Asia. Africa is also home to more than one hundred and twenty million Catholics, and one of the few places where priestly vocations are on the rise.'

'What's his downside?' Grin asked.

'That depends on the bloc of cardinals. To some, he's more conservative then Velu. Others might object that the Catholic Church in Africa is too young, especially compared with the Church in Latin America. Sadly, there may even be some cardinals who will object to him because he's black.'

'A very un-Christian stance,' Grin opined.

'Certainly one that no cardinal will admit to publicly, but regrettably it's still there. Given the needs of the Church at this moment in history, I pray the Holy Spirit will guide us past any impediments like prejudice to select the right man.'

14

October 18

At one o'clock in the morning, Cardinal Donoher led Kilkenny and Grin out of the catacombs and through a side entrance into Saint Peter's Basilica. Their footsteps echoed off the marble floors and blended like drops of water into the dull hum of reverberant energy that filled the majestic space. Scores of *sampietrini* – the faithful men of Saint Peter's – labored to clean the basilica and prepare it for the third day of public veneration for the beloved Pope. The sampietrini carefully removed traces left behind by the thousands who paid their respects. When the doors reopened at dawn – already thousands were holding vigil in Saint Peter's Square – the basilica would again be immaculate.

As they approached the center of the basilica, Kilkenny found his eyes drawn to the towering structure that soared almost ninety feet above the papal altar. Four ornate tortile columns spiraled upward from marble bases to carry an intricately detailed canopy embellished with a host of angels. With the blessing of Pope Urban VIII, Bernini recast a host of bronze statues taken from the pagan Roman Pantheon into this triumphant baldacchino.

The volume of space above the baldacchino curved inward, the walls warping into mosaic-clad pendentives that supported Michelangelo's soaring dome. As its creators intended, the volume and embellishment of the basilica evoked both awe and majesty. Kilkenny read the gilt band of Latin that circumscribed the circular base of the dome and recognized the phrase as the opening line of the song the Beijing martyrs had sung.

Donoher guided them around a low, U-shaped balustrade that defined the edge of an opening in the basilica floor immediately in front of the papal altar. A pair of bronze gates at the bottom of the U provided access to a double ramp of stairs that led down into the *confessio* – the true heart of Saint Peter's Basilica.

Kilkenny gazed down into the exedra beneath the papal altar and saw an exquisite room clad in multihued marbles. A pair of sampietrini carefully tended to the bronze lanterns of the ninety-five eternal flames that illuminated the confessio. At the far end of the space, behind a niche decorated with ninth-century mosaics and flanked by the statues of Peter and Paul, lay the tomb of Saint Peter. During an earlier visit to Rome, Kilkenny had learned from Donoher that the confessio derived its name from the confession of faith given by Saint Peter that led to his execution by Nero. What had started as a simple tomb on a hill outside the city of Rome became a shrine, then a church, and finally the Renaissance glory of the present basilica.

Christ had been right, Donoher told him then, *Peter was the rock on which the Church was built.*

In the center of the nave, on a crimson-trimmed bier and surrounded by Swiss Guards in full regalia, lay the body of the deceased pontiff. Donoher greeted the officer in charge of the night watch and was permitted to escort his guests to the bier. The three men bowed their heads as Donoher offered a brief prayer.

The pontiff's body had been carefully prepared for burial, dressed in formal papal robes and the head crowned with a golden miter. The body of Pope Leo XIV was first displayed in the Clementine Room of the Apostolic Palace for a period of private veneration by the cardinals and the papal household before being moved to the patriarchal basilica, where it would lie in state until the funeral.

To Kilkenny, the late pontiff's face held an expression of peaceful repose that transcended any mortician's artifice. The sense of loss he felt as he stood at the bier surprised him. He had met only briefly with the Pope twice, but it had been enough to leave an indelible mark. Kilkenny tried to offer a silent prayer, but the sense of a connectedness with God eluded him. Since the deaths of his wife and child, he could mouth the words of a rote formula but summon nothing more substantial.

'Pope Leo was quite something in person,' Grin said.

'That he was,' Donoher concurred. 'I am certain historians will recognize him as one of the great Popes.'

'I don't need a historian to justify my opinion,' Kilkenny said.

'Nor do I,' Donoher agreed. 'But above all things he was a good friend, and I will miss him.'

'Thank you for arranging this visitation,' Kilkenny said, still unable to take his eyes from the Pope's face.

'It was the least I could do given that you two are trying to fulfill his final wish. A shame you won't be here for the funeral, Nolan – it promises to be a most stirring event.'

'Grin can fill me in on what I miss,' Kilkenny replied, feigning disappointment. In truth, he didn't think he could stomach another funeral, the bitterness of his own loss still too fresh. 'I do plan to be back in time for the installation of the new Pope.'

Donoher looked at Kilkenny wryly and smiled, pleased with the young man's confidence. 'By the grace of God, you'll be here with Bishop Yin, and I'll save you both good seats.'

Just before dawn, amid frescos by Fra Angelico that depicted the lives of Saint Stephen and Saint Lawrence, the first Christian martyrs of Jerusalem and Rome, Donoher said a private mass for Kilkenny and Grin in the restored Chapel of Nicholas V. The cardinal's homily was brief, his prayers not only for the Pope's soul but also for the Holy Spirit's guidance of each man's efforts during the difficult days ahead. The *Amen* he received from his tiny congregation was both earnest and heartfelt.

Following the mass, Donoher and Grin saw Kilkenny off for Berlin, his departure setting in motion the first active steps of Operation Rolling Stone. Grin returned to the catacombs to continue what he called the practice of his dark technological arts, and Donoher left for the Apostolic Palace to convene a meeting of all the cardinals now present in Rome.

15

As a constitutional matter, all cardinals and Archbishops in charge of departments in the Roman Curia officially lost their jobs the moment the Pope died. As with any change in national administration, this purge of top officials allowed the newly elected Pope to install his own team of senior advisers.

The deposed secretaries continued to oversee their domains within the Vatican bureaucracy but acted in caretaker mode during the interregnum. Any serious or controversial matters were to be deferred until the new Pope was installed or, in the event of something requiring immediate attention, brought to the College of Cardinals for a provisional decision.

Donoher considered this as he looked over the gathering of unemployed cardinals mingling with their diocesan brethren in the Pauline Chapel. Like the other curial cardinals, he was a lame duck in his dual roles as head of both the Vatican Library and Vatican Intelligence. There was, of course, the possibility that the new Pope would ask him to stay on, but that depended on which cardinal was elected. Although on good terms with most of the papabili, he knew a few would doubtless broom him out. Such was the nature of politics, even in the Vatican, and Donoher had decided early on to leave his fate in God's hands.

Only three of the curial cardinals retained their jobs during the interregnum. The vicar of the Diocese of Rome, who provided for the pastoral needs of the diocese, still enjoyed all the powers he held under the Pope. Overseeing confessional matters related to the Holy See, the major penitentiary also continued at his post, because the door to forgiveness should never be closed.

Third among the Vatican cardinals still employed was Donoher, in his most recent appointment as Camerlengo. Only with the passing of the Pope did the power of this office become evident as Donoher administered all assets of the Holy See. Initially shocked at being named Camerlengo, Donoher came to believe that the Pope sensed his impending death and the effect it would have on the effort to free Bishop Yin. In naming him Camerlengo, Pope Leo gave Donoher the power to act during the interregnum, should he choose to do so. With Kilkenny and his team heading into China, Donoher appreciated the late pontiff's prescience.

One of the cardinals assisting Donoher, a dark-skinned Venezuelan named Ojeda, who headed the Congregation for the Clergy, moved through the crowd toward him.

'They are all assembled, Your Eminence.'

Donoher smiled. 'Would you do us the honor of an opening prayer?'

Ojeda called the congregation to order with a stirring invocation. At the conclusion of the prayer, Donoher nodded his thanks and moved to the lectern. Around him loomed Michelangelo's last frescos: *The Crucifixion of Saint Peter* and *The Conversion of Saint Paul*. The images perfectly illustrated the Church's ongoing battle with evil in the world – a struggle in which martyrs lost their lives balanced against the hope that even their persecutors could be redeemed.

Donoher looked out on an august assembly of men in scarlet-trimmed cassocks and zucchettos. Nearly all those who qualified as electors were now present, with only a few settling last-minute affairs or struggling with difficult travel arrangements from remote dioceses.

Prior to the election of the new Pope, two kinds of congregations would assist Donoher in his duties as Camerlengo. The particular congregation consisted of Donoher and three cardinals, one drawn from each of the cardinal orders of deacon, priest, and Bishop. The trio of cardinal-assistants were drawn by lot and served for three days, after which three new assistants would be selected. The particular congregation would deal with only minor questions, reporting their actions to the general congregation consisting of the entire College of Cardinals.

'My Eminent Lord Cardinals,' Donoher called out, 'it is time for us to begin this preparatory general congregation. I believe you all have received a packet containing a copy of *Universi Dominici Gregis*, which describes our duties and responsibilities during the interregnum. As required by article twelve of this Apostolic Constitution, I shall now read aloud the portion regarding the vacancy of the Apostolic See.'

As Donoher recited from the constitution penned by the late Pope, he recalled the words of Cardinal Antonelli, a layman who served during the nineteenth-century reign of Pope Pius IX and was the last lay cardinal, regarding a conclave:

Nothing, for that moment, nothing stands between us and the Lord Jesus. All our lives we have someone above us – our parents, the priest, the superior, the cardinal, the Pope. But now, nobody. Until we have a Pope, this is it. And we are it. An appeal from us for help can reach no higher authority. We stand at the brink of the chasm between what is human and what is divine.

Donoher then answered a few questions regarding specific clauses in the constitution and how they would be implemented. The questions were thoughtful and reflected the seriousness with which these men regarded the impending conclave. When all questions were answered, Donoher turned the floor over to Cardinal Scheuermann for the swearing-in.

Scheuermann was a lanky German whose salt-and-pepper hair had naturally receded into a medieval tonsure. In addition to his elected position as Dean of the College of Cardinals, Scheuermann also served as cardinal-Bishop of Ostia and Vellitri-Segni and prefect of the Congregation for the Doctrine of the Faith – an office known in earlier times as the Inquisition.

'We, the cardinals of the Holy Roman Church,' intoned the seventy-six-year-old Scheuermann, 'of the order of Bishops, of priests and of deacons, promise, pledge, and swear, as a body and individually, to observe exactly and faithfully all the norms contained in the Apostolic

Constitution *Universi Dominici Gregis* of the Supreme Pontiff Pope Leo XIV, and to maintain rigorous secrecy with regard to all matters in any way related to the election of the Roman pontiff or those which, by their very nature, during the vacancy of the Apostolic See, call for the same secrecy.'

One by one, the cardinals approached Scheuermann.

'I, Norbert Cardinal Clements, so promise, pledge, and swear,' the Archbishop of Toronto vowed. Placing his hand on the Gospels, he added, 'So help me God and these Holy Gospels which I now touch with my hand.'

After the entire congregation was sworn in, Donoher returned to the lectern and reported on a list of business items as required by the Apostolic Constitution, including the schedule for the funeral rites and the status of preparations for the conclave. He also announced the schedule for the requiem masses to be offered by the cardinals at the titular churches in Rome during the *novemdiales* – the nine days of official mourning that would follow the Pope's funeral.

As he neared the end of his list, Donoher motioned to an aide who brought forward a small wooden box. He placed the box on the lectern and opened it.

'On the night of the Pope's death, I took possession of the fisherman's ring and the leaden bull of the Pope's holy office. These items have been continuously in my possession, and I report to you now that they have been destroyed.'

In his right hand, Donoher held the broken fragments of the golden signet ring. A chisel had cleanly halved the image of Saint Peter as a fisherman. Similarly, the leaden bull used to seal all the Pope's public pronouncements lay in pieces. Donoher returned the remnants of papal authority to the box and locked it.

'Last, as there are no extraordinary circumstances known at this time that may delay the start of the election, the conclave to name the successor of Pope Leo XIV will commence in twelve days' time.'

16

SÜHBAATAR PROVINCE, MONGOLIA

October 19

A breeze rustled through the tall golden stalks of grass that grew in thick clumps across the vast Mongolian steppe. The air was cool and dry, rushing down from the mountains north and west of the plains that covered the eastern province.

Kilkenny sat in a low-slung folding chair supported by carbon-fiber struts reading *The Travels of Marco Polo*. Halfway through the Italian adventurer's travelogue, Kilkenny was convinced the man had been obsessed with prostitution. Fall was in the air and Kilkenny was dressed in jeans, Oakley assault boots, and a sweatshirt bearing the embroidered logo of *bd's mongolian barbeque – Ulaanbaatar* restaurant.

He sat amid four traditional Mongolian yurts – circular dwellings with conical roofs framed with wooden poles and covered with sheets of thick felt. The yurts were arranged in a semicircle with their flapped entries facing south. A wispy trail of smoke curled out of an opening in the roof of the yurt closest to Kilkenny.

Max Gates emerged from the steppe on a Mongolian horse, the animal and rider moving as one through the clumps of long grass. He stopped where several other horses were grazing, dismounted, and gave his mount a friendly rub on the nose.

'Any beer left?' Gates called out as he worked his way toward the encampment.

'See for yourself.'

Gates ambled over and peeked into the cooler beside Kilkenny's chair. All twelve bottles Gates had placed inside remained unopened.

'Wuss,' Gates said with a sneer.

He pulled out two bottles, handed one to Kilkenny, and wiped the other across his brow. His face was flushed and sweaty with exertion.

'How was the ride?' Kilkenny asked.

'I'll tell you what,' Gates replied in his thick drawl, 'they got some fine horses here. You should've come with me.'

'My rear end is still sore from the trek out here.'

'I stand corrected – you are a turbo wuss.'

Gates dropped into the chair beside Kilkenny, popped off the beer cap, and drained two inches from the longneck bottle. The beer was dark and carried a strong, hoppy flavor. Gates smacked his lips and bayed like a wolf at the moon.

'Baadog!' Kilkenny said in what had become a running joke between the two old friends.

When provisioning for the trek in Ulaanbaatar, they

had a choice of three domestically brewed beers: Chinggis, Khan Brau, and Baadog. Neither was sure what the name meant, but for guys who enjoyed beers named Pete's Wicked Ale and Magic Hat #9, Baadog seemed the right choice.

'That solar-powered cooler sure put a nice chill on these longnecks,' Gates opined.

'It definitely beats lugging bags of ice all the way out here.'

'Or drinking lukewarm beer.' Gates took another swig. 'As far as bivouacs go, this is definitely one of our better ones, though a bit of a hike on such short notice.'

'Chief, I know for a fact you and I have gone farther faster than what it took to get here.'

'True, but Uncle Sam wasn't paying us to pussyfoot around on those ops.' Gates held up his beer. 'When someone absolutely, positively – '

' – needs their ass kicked,' Kilkenny continued for him, 'it pays to send the very best.'

They tapped bottles, drained another inch of beer, and let out a howling 'Hoo-yah.'

'We've had some good times, my friend,' Gates said.

'That we have, which is why I thought of you when this came up. I know you're pulling the pin pretty soon.'

'Yeah, I got my twenty-five in and as many stripes as the arms on my dress uniform can hold. Any more, and I'll have to stitch 'em on my pants.'

'Not quite up to Navy regs. Any thoughts on what you might do next?'

'I did a little technical consulting on a movie last year, so I'm kicking around marketing myself as a personal trainer to the stars. I think it might be fun to stomp the snot out of some action hero who doesn't even know how to hold a weapon. Of course, I'd probably have to pay the studios to train Halle Berry or Jennifer Garner.'

'You'd have to control that libido of yours first.'

'Hey, I'm a perfect gentleman around the ladies. They always have to ask, and they usually do.'

Kilkenny laughed at how quickly their repartee degenerated into machismo.

'Of course,' Gates continued, 'I could take a clue from our cover as prospective franchisees and go into the restaurant business. Maybe take a slot in your buddy's fast-spreading empire.'

'Billy's a gustatory Genghis Khan all right. He could definitely hook you up.'

'I'd have to be Stateside, though – the one he's got in Ulaanbaatar is bit off the beaten path for me. Hard to believe I have enough time in to retire, it went by so fast, but I guess all good things come to an end.'

'Some before their time,' Kilkenny added.

It took a second, but Gates quickly realized that Kilkenny was referring to his abbreviated tenure as husband and father. The SEAL had attended the funeral of Kilkenny's wife and child along with Kilkenny's former commanding officer, Rear Admiral Jack Dawson. As the senior officer present, Dawson presented Kilkenny with the flag that draped the coffin, and he extended a grateful nation's thanks for Kelsey's brave service as an astronaut aboard the International Space Station.

'I'm oh-for-three when it comes to marriage,' Gates admitted. 'All my blessed unions tragically lasted longer than yours, but not one had a hope in heaven of going the distance. I can't pretend to understand what kind of knots this must have tied in your craw, but I sure envy you for the time you had with Kelsey. Being from the Bible Belt, I can just hear the preacher saying your tragedy is part of God's unknowable master plan. Sounds like a load to me, but if that's the case, then the Almighty's got some explaining to do.'

'Yeah,' Kilkenny agreed.

As Kilkenny took a long pull on his beer, he heard the dull rumble of approaching hooves. Within a few minutes, eight riders appeared from the north. They split into two groups, rounded the crescent of yurts, and rode into the semicircular area where Gates and Kilkenny sat. In addition to the riders, there were several horses carrying loads or pulling small carts. The eight men glared down at them, and Kilkenny wondered if they had trespassed on the wrong pasturelands.

There was a brief conversation among the riders, none of which Kilkenny or Gates understood. Then the apparent leader of the horsemen dismounted and walked toward them. Kilkenny and Gates rose and stood their ground. The man barked out a question and Kilkenny shrugged his shoulders, the universal sign that he did not understand.

'Speak English?' the man demanded, his words thickly accented.

'Yes,' Kilkenny replied.

'Are you well?' he asked.

Kilkenny shot a glance at Gates who looked just as confused.

'Yes,' Kilkenny replied.

'Is your family well?'

'Yes.'

'Are your sheep fat?'

At this question, Gates could barely contain his laughter. Kilkenny grew suspicious.

'Very fat.'

'Is the grass good?'

'If it were any better,' Gates jumped in, 'it would be illegal. You want a beer?'

'The traditional answer to each of the four questions is *yes*,' the Asian replied, his accent now flawless middle-American, 'after which the guest is offered a cup of tea.'

'All we got is Baadog, but I gotta say it ain't bad for cutting the dust out of your throat.'

'Then Baadog it is.' The Asian turned to Kilkenny. 'Lieutenant Gene Chun, SEAL Team One.'

Kilkenny shook Chun's hand and introduced himself. 'Nice outfits, very authentic.'

'Thanks. We didn't want to stick out like American tourists.'

As the other riders dismounted, Chun introduced the team Gates had recruited from U.S. Special Forces. Chun and a petty officer named Jim Chow represented the Navy SEALs. Paul Sung and David Tsui volunteered out of the elite Marine Recon, and medic Chuck Jing jokingly referred to himself as the lone Army Ranger. Rounding out the team were Bob Shen, Terry Han, and Ed Xaio of the Army's Night Stalkers.

As Kilkenny had requested, each volunteer recruit brought with him both the lethal skills of his chosen profession and the cultural and linguistic training necessary to pass easily for native Han Chinese. Some of the warriors were first-generation Americans; others counted laborers on the Union Pacific Railroad among their ancestors.

'You guys have any problems getting into the country?' Kilkenny asked.

'Naw. Our documents were rock solid. Nice touch with that *National Geographic* cover story. Thanks to that and a little creative packaging, our gear breezed through customs, which is a good thing considering what we're packing.'

'Nine-Eleven definitely has made traveling with nuclear material more challenging,' Kilkenny agreed. He turned to Gates. 'Help these fellas get set up while I make dinner.'

Kilkenny stoked the fire inside his yurt and began cooking a mix of steak and vegetables in a shallow wok as the team unloaded equipment and tended to the horses. By the time he finished cooking his version of Mongolian beef, the operators were stepping inside the yurt, cold beers in hand.

'Grab a bowl and find some floor,' Kilkenny announced as he doled out the evening meal. 'And make sure you have a clear view of that blank patch of wall.'

'Why?' Chun asked. 'We getting a movie with dinner?'

'Something like that.'

When everyone was seated, Kilkenny perched himself on a low wooden stool. Beside him stood a small table atop which lay a device that looked like an iPod mated to a medium-sized Maglite.

117

'Gentlemen, I want to start by thanking you for volunteering for this,' Kilkenny said. 'That you all responded to Max's pitch so quickly illustrates the high moral character that I believe exists in the members of our elite profession – either that or you all lost big at one of the chief's legendary poker weekends.'

'Mission?' Han blurted out. 'I thought this *was* one of those poker weekends.'

The men shared a laugh, especially when Gates tossed a pack of cards to Kilkenny. The chief never traveled without a deck. Kilkenny opened the box and began cutting and shuffling the cards.

'If you'll pardon the expression, here's the deal: mission first, cards later.' Kilkenny boxed the deck and tossed it back to Gates. Then he switched on the small projector to display on the wall a grainy black-and-white image of an Asian man in his early thirties. 'This is Bishop Yin Daoming, or at least this is what he looked like before he was imprisoned in the seventies.' Kilkenny moved to the next image. 'This is what a computer thinks Yin might look like today, but there's no way we can predict what three decades in a Chinese prison have done to the man.'

Kilkenny replaced the computer-generated image of Yin with a terrain map of the region.

'We're up here in Mongolia,' Kilkenny said, indicating a point in the eastern province of the landlocked nation, 'and this zigzagging line is the route we'll follow in and out of China. ChiCom air defenses are relatively thin in this part of the country, thanks largely to the fact that Mongolian military technology these days is just slightly better than it was during the reign of Genghis Khan. Our route is designed to take us through the weakest points in their radar coverage. I know the BATs are hard to spot, but no sense making it any easier for them. I'll upload these waypoints into the nav systems as soon as we're ready to go wheels up.'

The next image was a satellite photo of Chifeng Prison.

'At the LZ,' Kilkenny pointed to their landing zone in an uninhabited area northwest of the prison, 'we'll meet with our local support and split into two teams. Chow, Chun, Han, and Xaio are with Alpha; the rest of you are Bravo. Max will head up the Alpha team, which will dig in around the perimeter of the prison, scout the place for a few days so we can get the lay of the land, and set up our defenses in case we need to beat a fast retreat. I'll be with Bravo handling prison insertion and extraction. We already have someone on the ground in Chifeng working with local contacts to procure uniforms, weapons, and vehicles. We'll be working with her to collect these materials at our staging area. Two important points about our person in Chifeng. What we're about to do won't win us any popularity contests in Beijing, but Roxanne already has state's-enemy status there, and the ChiComs want her, dead or alive. Second, she's a personal friend of mine, and if you hit on her, you do so at your own risk.'

'From you?' Han asked.

'From her. She's good people, so let's make sure she gets out of China in one piece.'

As they ate, Kilkenny ran through the finer details of his plan to liberate Yin Daoming and took questions from the team. The briefing lasted through their meal, and everyone switched to water after the first round of Baadog. No one was getting drunk tonight.

After their meal, the team assembled the BATs and suited up for flight.

'We're gonna look like a Chinese luge team,' Han remarked as the men traded their civilian clothes for sleek, form-fitting SEALskin suits.

'You'll love these suits,' Gates assured him. 'We started using them about a year ago. Full mobility, decent body armor, and combat electronics. Best of all, they're good for fighting off the cold.'

'How good?'

'I did a HALO jump over Antarctica wearing one of these,' Kilkenny replied as he holstered a forty-five-caliber H&K pistol and sheathed a combat knife to his leg. 'Double-digit subzero temps and I didn't get a touch of frostbite.'

'No shit?' Han asked skeptically. As veteran of many high-altitude, low-opening parachute jumps, he had endured bitter cold in weather less extreme than over the pole.

'No shit.'

'Amazing. These are about half the weight of our standard flight suits.'

'Hey, what happens to the horses while we're gone?' Chen asked as he patted the head of the gray mare he'd ridden out into the steppe.

'I asked the family that leased us these yurts to look in on them, as we'll be out in the field for days at a time following the wild herds,' Kilkenny said. 'They'll be okay.'

The team broke into three groups, each with one of the Night Stalkers. Clad head-to-toe in dark gray, the soldiers donned helmets equipped with night vision and heads-up displays and climbed into the BATs. The seats were simple canvas hammocks bolted to the frame and fitted with five-point safety harnesses. Kilkenny appraised the aircraft as he buckled in – it was a significant improvement over the first generation. He followed the pipes that sprouted from the engine nacelle to their termini at tiny thrust-vectoring nozzles at various points on the fuselage. By rerouting engine thrust from the large opening at the rear of the nacelle, where it was used to power forward flight, to the nozzles, a BAT pilot could abruptly change direction during flight. The nozzles also allowed the aircraft to take off and land vertically. To the men of the 160th, the BAT was the special forces version of the Harrier.

Gates sat beside Kilkenny in the rear of BAT-2 and strapped in. Bob Shen was at the controls running through his preflight checklist. Terry Han and Ed Xaio were piloting BAT-1 and BAT-3.

'We've got a full tank of gas, a half pack of cigarettes, it's dark out, and we're wearing sunglasses,' Gates said, deadpanning Elwood Blues's pre-chase checklist.

Eyes focused straight ahead, Kilkenny offered Joliet Jake Blues's infamous response, 'Hit it.'

'RITEG is nominal,' Shen said flatly. 'Switching engine on.'

Starting with a low hum, the nacelle mounted to the spine above them quickly spun up, the sound increasing in both pitch and intensity. The horses grazing nearby trotted farther into the field. Sitting in an open-air fuselage, Kilkenny was quick to appreciate that the electric turbine emitted no exhaust. He was also thankful for the noise-canceling hardware built into his helmet that sampled the engine noise and produced an inverse sound to mask it.

The internally shielded RITEG generated almost no externally detectable heat, reducing the threat posed by missiles designed to home in on the hot glow of fuel-burning engines. The aircraft derived another defensive advantage from its unique shape and use of nonmetallic materials. The BAT was not as stealthy as an F-117A, but its radar cross-section was roughly the size of a golf ball, making the low-flying craft difficult to detect amid the electronic noise known as ground clutter.

When all three BATs had powered up, the Night Stalkers gave each other the thumbs-up sign and, one by one, lifted off. Third in the queue, Shen gripped the fly-by-wire controller mounted between the front seats and gave it a twist. The BAT leaped into the air as thrust-vector nozzles redirected the tiny engine's output through the BAT's space frame and outports under the fuselage.

Shen let the BAT hover for a moment until he was satisfied that everything functioned as it should, then he flew the aircraft forward and into position off the left wing of BAT-1.

'Satellite uplink on,' Kilkenny commanded, and an icon appeared on his heads-up display.

SATELLITE UPLINK ACTIVATED

'Message encrypt, three words: *Isengard or Bust.*'

CONFIRM: ISENGARD OR BUST

'Message confirmed.'

SEND TO?

'Bombadil,' Kilkenny replied.

The three-word message shot into the heavens as a brief pulse of electromagnetic energy. Seconds later, after racing through a constellation of satellites in low-Earth orbit, the message sped back to Earth where it was captured by a cluster of dish antennas inside the Leonine Walls of the Vatican.

'Bombadil? Isengard?' What was that all about?' Gates asked, his voice clear through the speakers in Kilkenny's helmet.

'Just letting my buddy Grin know what we're up to. He's not a regular operator, so we decided to encrypt our messages with references to books, movies, and songs that we both would get. In *The Lord of the Rings*, the wizard Gandalf was held prisoner by Saruman at Isengard.'

'So for Gandalf, read Yin?' Gates asked.

'Yeah,' Kilkenny replied. 'Chifeng Prison is Isengard, and Grin is Bombadil.'

'I saw the movies, but I don't remember anyone named Bombadil.'

'Not everything from the book made it onto the screen,' Kilkenny explained.

It was a cool, clear night with a waning moon hanging a few degrees above the eastern horizon. Thirty feet off the ground, the three BATs flew almost due south on the start of a five-hour journey that would skirt the edge of the Gobi Desert as it headed across the border into China.

17

VATICAN CITY

October 20

The funeral mass for Pope Leo XIV was celebrated six days after his death on a beautiful October day in Saint Peter's Square. Donoher stood on the basilica steps studying the nearly half a million people who filled Bernini's piazza and overflowed down the length of Via della Conciliazione, through the Borgo District, to the banks of the Tiber. The streets surrounding the Vatican were packed with millions more as the Church drew together during this time of grief. And around the world, billions watched or listened to what was the largest funeral in history.

The Pope's body lay inside a simple coffin made of cypress, the sole ornament an inlaid cross and the letter *M* near the bottom of the lid, the design taken from the pontiff's personal coat of arms. During the processional, the pallbearers – twelve tuxedo-clad papal gentlemen – had slowly borne the coffin out of the basilica on a red litter. They carried it past the wooden altar and set it in the center of an ornate rectangular rug laid atop the stones of the square. A tall paschal candle stood beside the coffin, and atop the wooden lid lay a red leather-bound book containing the four Gospel accounts of the life and teachings of Jesus Christ.

Three long rows of prelates clad in red vestments framed the sides of a rectangular space that contained the altar and the coffin, and behind these sat more than two hundred world leaders in a sea of funeral black. A choir dressed in white closed the back of the space, with the front open to the square. With a gathering so large that no building could contain it, the people themselves became the architecture, the true body of the Church.

During a private ceremony before the funeral, the Pope's body was placed inside the coffin. Archbishop Sikora then drew a veil of white silk over Leo's face, and Donoher blessed the body with holy water. At the Pope's side, Donoher placed a red velvet bag containing samples of the coins minted during his long reign.

As Cardinal Scheuermann read a Latin eulogy of the Pope's many accomplishments, Donoher reflected on the last item he placed in the coffin – a brass cylinder containing a vellum scroll of that same eulogy penned by a master calligrapher. The scroll was a work of art in itself but more so for the deeds it represented. The Church in the late twentieth century faced many difficult challenges, but it was Pope Leo's clear vision and steadfast faith that had helped change the world for the better.

If pride was a sin, Donoher would permit himself this

indulgence. He was proud of all the Church had accomplished during the reign of Pope Leo XIV, and of his role in those deeds now committed to history.

He did not feel sorrow as the sun warmed his face while he stood on the basilica steps, overlooked by a procession of statues of the saints. He felt joy. The long suffering of his friend and mentor was over, and the wonderful soul that was the essence of that great man had at last received its blessed release and was now with God. For a man of faith, there could be no greater triumph than this.

As the voices of the pontifical choir filled the piazza with the closing hymn, the cardinals followed the Pope's coffin back into the basilica, the procession passing through the great bronze doors in the center of its facade – masterworks by Il Filarete depicting Christ, the Virgin Mary, and the martyrdoms of Saints Peter and Paul.

The cardinals moved solemnly up through the nave and filled the space beneath the great dome, surrounding the confessio and the baldacchino. The pallbearers paused in front of the great pier where Bernini's statue of the mythical Saint Longinus stood bearing the spear that pierced the side of Christ, then descended the stairway into the grotto beneath the basilica. There, the sampietrini affixed red bands to the coffin lid with both papal and Vatican seals. The coffin was placed in a second made of zinc and a third of walnut that bore Leo's name and his coat of arms.

A humble priest, Pope Leo decided early in his pontificate to forgo the traditional papal interment in an ornate marble sarcophagus, wishing instead to be buried in the earth.

'Lord, grant him eternal rest,' Donoher called out at the conclusion of the rite, his booming voice echoing inside the subterranean chamber, 'and may perpetual light shine upon him.'

As those gathered in the grotto sang '*Salve Regina,*' Donoher stared down into the Pope's grave and thought of another holy man in a dark hole, half a world away.

18

CHIFENG, CHINA

October 28

On the night they crossed the border, Kilkenny and the warriors rendezvoused with Roxanne Tao at the landing zone in the steppe twenty miles north of Chifeng Prison. Tao's local contacts provided yurts to house the men and conceal their weapons and equipment. During their second night in China, Gates and the Alpha team dug into camouflaged positions around the prison and began reconnaissance.

Kilkenny had lain low during the past eight days, sequestered in the yurts while the other members of Bravo team ventured into the city of Chifeng with Roxanne Tao, getting a feel for their surroundings. Inner Mongolia's tourist season was all but over, and a Caucasian face would draw more attention than he desired.

Kilkenny sat on the floor on the west side of the yurt – the men's side – with his back to the fire. He was wearing his helmet, comparing Alpha team's observations with information gathered by Chinese Roman Catholics on the heads-up display. The fresh intelligence confirmed much of what he had gleaned from the older data. It held no surprises.

Chifeng Prison ran on a tight schedule. The guards worked in three eight-hour shifts each day. The prisoners started their day in the middle of the first shift and returned to their cells halfway through the third – sixteen backbreaking hours making bricks, seven days a week. Trucks came and went at scheduled times, processed through the two gates with the same security procedures. Kilkenny had confidence in the information he had, but he really wanted the one piece he was sorely missing – the precise cell housing Bishop Yin.

'Computer off,' Kilkenny said, ending the review session.

He stood and stretched, pulled off the helmet, and absently scratched at the prickly red whiskers populating his jaw line. In addition to the scrubby beard, Kilkenny temporarily had suspended several personal grooming habits in preparing for the mission, and the prison pajamas he wore while sequestered in the yurt exuded that fusty odor he associated with a high school locker room.

Opposite the yurt's door, on the north side of the circular dwelling, stood a traditional Buddhist altar. Kilkenny approached the domestic shrine – no different really from the religious items his grandmother kept atop her bedroom dresser – and offered a brief prayer of thanks for the people helping them.

The couple that provided the yurts owned few possessions, but what they had were well cared for. Through halting English, they let Kilkenny know that he and his companions were honored guests and, as if to emphasize the point, showed him their most prized possession. Hidden behind a false panel on the altar was a worn photograph clipped from a Taiwanese magazine – the Dalai Lama and Pope Leo XIV together in prayer. Kilkenny was humbled by the tremendous risk the couple took each day in possessing that image, a risk they accepted only because of a deeply rooted faith. Only here, in the wilderness along China's northern border, could the descendants of Genghis Khan find spiritual contentment in a belief system that wedded traditional Tibetan Buddhism with Roman Catholicism.

Tao stepped into the yurt and removed her hat and coat. Everything she wore was chosen to emphasize that she was Chinese and not American. Even the way she carried herself had changed. Kilkenny considered how easily she had slipped into this native persona. The most significant change in Tao's appearance, though, was the simplest to execute. Before leaving the United States, Tao cut the waterfall of silky hair that reached her waist, trading her tresses for a functional, military bob.

'Time to do your makeup,' Tao said as she placed a low stool and a tackle box on the floor near the fire. She pointed to where she wanted Kilkenny to sit.

'I never thought I'd hear anyone say that to me,' Kilkenny replied.

Tao started by cleaning and drying Kilkenny's face, neck, and hands – areas of skin that would be visible when he was dressed. She laid out various prosthetics and began applying adhesive to Kilkenny's skin.

'Careful,' Kilkenny said. Some of the fading bruises on his face were still tender.

He remained still as Tao affixed bits of latex to simulate edemas and lacerations. In the first pass, she fattened Kilkenny's lower lip, blackened an eye and a cheek, and raised welts on his hands and forearms. Tao next softened the edges around the prosthetics with flesh-toned liquid latex, erasing seams that would destroy the illusion.

'Are you sure you want to do this?' Tao asked.

'Somebody has to let Yin know what's happening. I'd hate for him to have a heart attack when Bravo shows up for his execution.'

'But why *you*? Why not one of the others?'

'You mean someone of Chinese descent?'

'Yeah.'

'Better they stay outside. If something goes wrong, they have a chance of blending in and getting away. It was either going to be Max or me, and I'd rather have him running Alpha and covering my back.' Kilkenny laughed.

'What?'

'On the flight over, Max asked me the same thing.'

'What did you tell him?'

'That I'm the man on a rope, the guy they lower down into a deep hole to rescue someone trapped in the darkness. My job is to find the lost soul and hold fast to the rope. Yours is to pull us out.'

Tao stared into Kilkenny's eyes for a moment and once

more saw the strength of his conviction. They had saved each other's lives more than once, and an absolute trust cemented their friendship.

'That new haircut is still taking some getting used to,' Kilkenny said, breaking the silence as Tao resumed work on his forehead.

'For me too. I've had long hair since I was a little girl. At least it will all grow back and some deserving kids will benefit from my little sacrifice.'

After signing on for this mission, Tao donated her hair – in two twelve-inch-long chunks – to Locks of Love to make wigs for pediatric cancer patients. Kilkenny first saw her new bob when he landed in China. The change in Tao's appearance was so severe that at first he didn't recognize her – which of course was the idea.

She applied a mix of paints and powders to tint Kilkenny's artificially swollen areas in shades of milky yellow, black, and blue. Around the open wounds, Tao dabbed on a dark viscous fluid that, as it dried, formed a crusty, fractured surface like coagulated blood. She also placed droplets of simulated scab on Kilkenny's face and neck, mimicking blood splatter. On two of his fingers, Tao blackened the nails. Last, she smeared and dribbled simulated blood onto Kilkenny's uniform, transforming him into a thoroughly abused prisoner.

'Now, just sit there for a moment and let everything really set up,' Tao said. 'I have to get changed.'

She stepped behind a modesty curtain, removed her civilian clothing, and donned the dark gray uniform of an officer of the Ministry of Justice. Like U.S. marshals, cadres assigned to the Ministry of Justice were an armed force separate from the police and the People's Liberation Army. This force provided security for the courts, oversaw the handling and transport of prisoners, and, as the insignia on Tao's uniform indicated, executed prisoners.

'How do I look?' Tao stepped into view.

'Like a death-row inmate's worst nightmare,' Kilkenny replied.

'I thought men liked a woman in uniform.'

'It depends on the woman and the uniform,' Kilkenny said, recalling the first time he saw Kelsey in a NASA flight suit.

Tao caught the melancholy tone in his voice and dropped this line of banter. 'Let me take a look at you.'

Tao slowly walked around Kilkenny, studying her handiwork at various angles.

'I may not win an Oscar for best makeup,' Tao said, 'but it should do the trick.'

19

It was almost midnight as Bob Shen downshifted, slowing the truck as he drove up to the main gate of Chifeng Prison. The approach was a paved two-lane track covered with a thin layer of wind-driven dirt. The truck's thickly grooved tires kicked up a dusty haze behind the vehicle. A guard stepped out of the gatehouse and signaled Shen to halt.

Shen brought the truck to a stop at a white line painted across the roadway – the entire vehicle now bathed in harsh, cool light. The guard took notice of the Beijing markings stenciled on the truck's body as he strutted toward the driver's door. Two more guards appeared near the gate, their weapons trained on Shen and Tao, seated in the cab beside him.

'Papers,' the guard demanded.

With cool detachment, Tao handed a dossier to Shen, who passed it to the guard. The man quickly scanned the forged documents.

'Prisoner transfer, eh,' the guard said. 'We received no notification of any transfer scheduled for tonight.'

'If you had actually read those documents,' Tao replied,

her voice a blend of superiority and boredom, 'you would have noticed that this transfer is *un*scheduled for reasons of state security.'

Chastised, the guard made a more thorough review of the paperwork and found that the transfer authorization bore proper signatures from the Ministry of Justice and the Ministry of State Security. The packet included a photograph of the prisoner but listed no name, meaning Beijing wanted no record kept of this person's movements within the prison system. The prisoner was obviously not a common criminal.

The guard motioned for the outer gate to be opened and returned to the gatehouse. The barrier – a five-meter-high wall of electrified chain link fastened to structural steel tubing that curved inward near its full height and was topped with a tightly coiled helix of razor wire – rolled to the left along a narrow-gauge rail. When the way was clear, Shen pulled the truck forward to the next barrier. The outer gate closed behind the truck, and only after it was secure was the inner gate opened.

Though no longer aiming at Tao and Shen, the two guards kept their weapons trained on the truck as it passed through the gate. Tao paid no heed to the guards' aggressive stance – it was standard procedure. A lax display at the main gate would have surprised her more.

A jeep arrived at the gatehouse just as the truck cleared the inner gate. The senior guard approached as the jeep came to a stop and handed Tao's dossier to the lieutenant at the wheel. Unlike the guard, the lieutenant took his time reviewing the documents.

The young officer was a tall man, Tao realized as he

stepped out of the jeep, and carried himself ramrod straight. He walked directly to Tao's window, and they exchanged salutes.

'Good evening, Captain,' the lieutenant said. 'The paperwork authorizing this transfer appears to be in order, though I am a bit surprised that we received no prior notification.'

'This is a highly unusual situation, Lieutenant Kwan,' Tao said, reading the name off the rectangular black badge pinned to the officer's jacket. 'My superiors in Beijing wish their actions to leave as light a trail as possible. It is to be as if this prisoner was never here.'

'I understand,' Kwan said.

'The prisoner is to be held in solitary confinement. He is to have no contact with any other prisoners, and contact with your guards is to be kept to an absolute minimum. Under no circumstances is anyone to speak with this prisoner without authorization from the Ministry of State Security. Are these orders clear?'

'Perfectly. We have other prisoners with similar restrictions. The guards in the solitary wing will handle this prisoner accordingly. A question, if I may?'

Tao nodded her assent.

'I saw no sentencing information in the dossier.'

'*All* information regarding this prisoner is classified,' Tao was curt. 'What is your question?'

'How long is this prisoner to be kept here?'

'For the rest of his life, which I expect will not be long.'

Kwan nodded. 'I will arrange for a detachment to take custody of the prisoner for processing and transfer to the solitary-confinement wing.'

'There is no need to process this prisoner,' Tao said forcefully, her anger thinly veiled. 'He does not exist.'

'Yes, but protocol requires the prisoner be stripped, visually inspected by our medical staff, and deloused before being placed in a cell.'

'Have I not made myself clear, Kwan?' Tao asked, her annoyance rising. 'Contact with this prisoner is to be minimal. Preferably nonexistent. Your hygienic protocol is not required. Your detachment is not required. My soldiers will guard the prisoner as he is moved into a cell. All that is required is one person to escort us – *you*.'

Tao's eyes bore into the man, her position firmly delivered. He accepted her authority with a brief shrug.

'If your driver will follow me, I will take you to the entry with the shortest route into the solitary wing.'

'Thank you, Lieutenant,' Tao replied, her tone a hint softer.

As he walked back to the jeep, Kwan barked a string of orders into a walkie-talkie to clear the route through the cellblock. From the reconnaissance photos, Tao knew which building held Yin, but those images did little to soften the brutal impact of the structure. Human beings languished inside those windowless walls, men interred in a mausoleum for the living, some for the crime of daring to believe in a power greater than the state.

They parked at the motor pool beside the prison's small fleet of vehicles. The area was well lit but deserted at this hour. The lieutenant met Tao and Shen at the rear of the transport.

'Bring the prisoner out!' Tao ordered.

The rear door swung open and Chuck Jing and Paul

Sung stepped out. Behind them, Kilkenny shuffled toward the opening, followed by David Tsui. Kilkenny's wrists and ankles were manacled and tethered to chains riveted to a thick leather belt cinched around his waist. He was dressed in a pair of loose-fitting prison pajamas, his head hung low, for all appearances a broken man. Tao noticed that the lieutenant didn't wince when he caught sight of Kilkenny's battered face, either a sign of formidable control or evidence that the man was inured to brutality.

Jing and Sung lowered Kilkenny to the ground. Kwan compared the face of the prisoner with the photograph included in the file and verified the match.

'I see you survived the long journey here with only a few bumps and bruises,' Tao said. 'The road is unfortunately very rough in some places.'

Jing, Sung, and Tsui laughed for Kwan's benefit. Kilkenny shrugged, not understanding a word of Chinese.

'Hood,' Tao ordered.

Tsui draped a baggy black hood over Kilkenny's head and neck. The four soldiers accompanying Tao took up positions around the prisoner, two at Kilkenny's arms to steer him along the way.

'Lead the way, Lieutenant,' Tao commanded.

Each of the heavy steel doors Kwan led them through was secured by a magnetic lock and monitored by a closed-circuit camera.

I hope Grin is watching this, Tao thought, resisting the urge to glance up at the cameras.

The route Kwan chose avoided areas where the prison's general population was housed for their scant hours of exhausted sleep between work shifts, so they saw few guards and no prisoners during the transit. Tao immediately noticed the difference when Kwan led them through a door into the solitary-confinement wing – the floors looked almost new. Elsewhere in the prison, evidence of the daily wear of thousands of footsteps showed unmistakably on the concrete, but the floors in this wing bore no sign of heavily trafficked use. Only the occasional scuffmark from the black sole of a guard's shoe or the wheels of the meal cart marred the glossy gray finish.

A lone guard stood at attention by a flush steel door near the end of the hall. Like the other guards Tao saw, the man wore an electronic earpiece, the thin wire dropping from behind his ear and down his collar. He saluted as Tao and the lieutenant approached.

'Open it,' Kwan commanded.

The guard thumbed the SEND switch on the radio clipped to his belt. 'Open three-four-two.'

The electronic locks on the door buzzed, and the gears slowly pulled the heavy slab of metal to the side. Tao found her eyes drawn to the dark void, horrified at the perverse justice it represented. The thought of her friend spending even one minute in that cell angered and sickened her, but that Kilkenny would do so voluntarily to free an innocent man quelled those emotions. Somewhere close by, Yin Daoming lost decades of this life locked inside an identical two-meter cube.

'Put him in,' Tao said.

Jing and Sung guided Kilkenny through the doorway into the cell. Inside, they removed his restraints and pushed him into the shadows. There, outside the shaft of light from the corridor, they removed the hood and left Kilkenny in the darkness.

Kilkenny's heart was racing as the cell door closed. The steel dead bolts slid home with a dull metallic thud. He briefly heard voices outside his door, though he doubted he would have understood even if they were speaking English. Soon the voices were gone.

It wasn't the darkness that bothered Kilkenny. He had experienced perfect blackness in the depths of the oceans and once in an elaborate science experiment constructed in a cavern far beneath Lake Erie. His apprehension wasn't claustrophobia either. He had faced that fear many times, most recently while searching the ocean floor off South America inside the metal shell of a Hardsuit with a mile of water weighing him down with a crushing force more than a hundred times that of Earth's atmosphere at sea level.

The primordial surge of adrenaline Kilkenny felt was rooted solely in his loss of control. He had allowed himself to be placed inside a box of concrete and steel. That box was surrounded by armed guards and razor wire and situated inside a nation whose government would kill him if it knew of his presence and his purpose.

From his childhood on, Kilkenny's parents instilled in him the virtue of self-reliance – an attribute that formed the bedrock of his personality. It was the lens through which he viewed himself and those around him. His body reacted against the perceived dangers of his situation, confused by an action it instinctively considered suicidal. But his mind knew better.

Kilkenny slipped off the thin-soled slippers and knelt

down with his feet spread about eighteen inches apart and the tops flat against the floor. His arms hung at his sides, the rest of his body tall and upright. He inhaled deeply, and then slowly sat back, his palms resting on his thighs until his buttocks reached the floor. His knees crackled loudly with the increased tension in the joints.

Seated, Kilkenny raised his torso vertical and with each breath widened his chest. He could feel the energy flowing from the center of his body. He interlocked his fingers, turned his palms out, and raised his outstretched arms high above his head.

Virasana. The word suddenly flashed into Kilkenny's conscious mind – the name the young woman who taught yoga at the community center had called this pose. *The hero posture.*

He moved slowly through a series of asanas, loosening his joints and steadying his breathing and the flow of blood throughout his body. The anxiety ebbed as he stretched, some of the ancient postures proving to be a challenge within the restrictive confines of the cell. A sheen of sweat dampened his prison uniform.

Through the exercises, Kilkenny achieved a state of meditative calm. His conscious mind possessed something that his body could not comprehend – faith. Kilkenny's situation, though dire, was not hopeless. That hope was rooted in the faith he had in his friends and the team they had assembled for this mission.

20

VATICAN CITY

October 29

On the morning of the fifteenth day following the death of Pope Leo XIV, the cardinals gathered inside Saint Peter's Basilica to take part in the votive mass *Pro Eligendo Papa – For the Election of the Pope*. They were as one, a sea of scarlet and white in the transepts and nave surrounding the baldacchino. The archpriest of the patriarchal Vatican basilica led his fellow cardinals and the faithful in attendance through the somber Eucharistic celebration. The theme of the mass could be distilled to a single hope – that God would help the cardinals select the right man to lead the Church. As voices of the pontifical choir rose in song, filling the basilica with the closing hymn, each cardinal felt the enormity of the task at hand.

After the mass, the cardinal electors gathered in the pontifical palace, in the four-room suite known as the *Stanze di Raphaello* – the Raphael Rooms. There, they enjoyed a light lunch while surrounded by frescos painted by the Renaissance master and his finest students. Though widely differing in subject matter, frescos ranging from the *School of Athens* and *Parnassus* to *Battle of Ostia* and *Constantine's Donation*, the suite was unified in themes celebrating the power of faith and the Church. In the Room of the Fire of the Borgo, the frescos make specific reference to Leo III and Leo IV, predecessors of Leo X, under whose pontificate the room was decorated. As Donoher studied the figure of Pope Leo III extinguishing the Borgo fire of 847 by making the sign of the cross, the cardinal wondered how Raphael would have depicted the accomplishments of the most recent Leo.

The cardinals, all robed in scarlet, clustered in small groups admiring the paintings and discussing in low tones the needs of the Church or the merits of various papabili. Cardinal Magni sat with a small group of Italian cardinals, among them Cardinal Gagliardi. Considered a papabile before cardiac problems effectively eliminated him from consideration, the gregarious cardinal from Palermo still carried a strong voice in Italy and throughout Europe.

A handful of Latin American cardinals gathered around Escalante, while Ryff, Oromo, and Velu moved among the other electors renewing acquaintances. Donoher sensed that alliances were forming – some geographic, others strategic, but all with the same purpose.

As he sipped an espresso, Donoher considered the unusual politics involved in electing a Pope. An aspirant for the papacy does not openly run for the position as does a politician seeking a publicly elected office. Also, the fine art of backroom deal-making, of granting concessions and promises in exchange for votes, was a practice prohibited under pain of immediate excommunication. Further reducing such temptation – as if the loss of one's soul to eternal damnation was not enough – the Apostolic Constitution nullified all such agreements, freeing the new Pope from any negotiated commitments made to secure his election. Simony simply did not pay.

Despite the global presence of the Church, the rest of the world played no role in selecting one of the last absolute monarchs, thanks largely to the Austrian emperor Franz Josef. During the 1903 conclave the emperor attempted to exercise the ancient veto right of Catholic monarchs against a cardinal he found politically objectionable. Today, anyone involved with the conclave who attempts to influence the election at the behest of a government would suffer immediate excommunication from the Church.

Donoher milled about, looking from face to face. Some he knew well, others hardly at all. Some were dear friends, and others he tolerated as a form of penance. Yet soon, one would be the next Pope.

Who among us? Donoher mused. *Who among us*?

As the Camerlengo considered the upcoming election, Archbishop Sikora approached him. The man seemed to have aged in the days since the Pope's death.

'Your Eminence, may I have a word with you in private?'

'Of course, Archbishop. We still have a bit of time before the conclave begins.'

In the early afternoon, the cardinal electors gathered in the Pauline Chapel. They stood beneath the frescoed walls and ceilings robed in formal choir dress. There, in the presence of the cardinals, all those performing supporting roles to the conclave – including the master of papal liturgical celebrations, priest confessors, an ecclesiastic, two masters of ceremonies, medical personnel, and the cooks and housekeepers at Domus Sanctae Marthae – were sworn to preserve the secrecy of the conclave.

At the appointed hour, a bell was rung and the cardinals proceeded two by two toward the Sistine Chapel. As they walked through the ornate passageways of the Apostolic Palace, the cardinals solemnly invoked the Holy Spirit to guide their deliberations by chanting an ancient hymn.

> *Veni Creator Spiritus*
> *Veni Creator Spiritus*
> *Mentes tuorum visita*
> *Imple superna gratia*
> *Quae Tu creastif pectora*

The procession entered through the large main doorway in the east wall of the Sistine Chapel. For most of the cardinals, it was their first time inside the chapel since preparations for the conclave began. The vast rectangular space measured one hundred and thirty-four feet in length, forty-four feet in width, and sixty-eight feet in height to the top of the flattened barrel vault that soared over the space – the exact dimensions of Solomon's Temple, as described in the Old Testament. Six tall, arched windows punctured the upper half of the walls running the length of the chapel, drawing the light of heaven down onto the marble floor below. The walls flowed up between the windows to form the triangular webs and pendentives supporting the ceiling.

A chancel wall consisting of a low barrier topped with a gilded screen divided the chapel floor into two unequal spaces. The procession filed into the smaller space set aside for the laity to observe mass, then through the opening in the chancel screen into the sanctuary surrounding the altar.

Architecturally unremarkable, the voluminous space inside the tan brick building became instead a canvas for the greatest artists of the Italian Renaissance. In the tradition of the day, the chapel's ornamentation was thematically divided into three epochs. Above the cardinal electors soared Michelangelo's famous ceiling on which prophets, sibyls, and the forefathers of Christ framed illustrated scenes drawn from Genesis. Frescos depicting the life of Moses decorated the long south wall, balanced by the life of Christ on the north.

Directly before the cardinals, as if they needed further reminder of the importance of their task, the resplendent figure of Christ the Judge soared above the altar. *The Last Judgment,* a monumental fresco that covered the entire western wall of the chapel and consumed five years of Michelangelo's life, depicted Christ surrounded by the saints and the elect, and beneath them the damned. Before the altar stood a long table and a lectern. There, beneath Michelangelo's towering masterpiece, the ballots would be counted and the name of the new Pope revealed.

Two rows of long tables draped in red velvet ran the length of the chapel on both sides, from the chancel screen to the altar. The rows closest to the tapestry-lined walls stood one step up on low risers, permitting those seated there an unobstructed view of the proceedings.

146

The cardinal electors moved to the seats assigned them by lot. Behind the chancel screen, those supporting the conclave stood as witnesses to the swearing-in of the electors. Donoher and Scheuermann, by virtue of their duties in the conclave, were assigned seats close to the altar. When all were in place, Donoher approached the altar and bowed his head in prayer, then moved to the lectern.

'My Most Eminent Lord Cardinals, in accordance with *Universi Dominici Gregis*, we must now take our oath. Cardinal Scheuermann.'

The cardinal dean, too, offered a brief prayer at the altar before approaching the lectern. He opened a leather-bound folio and began to read.

We, the cardinal electors present in this election of the supreme pontiff promise, pledge, and swear, as individuals and as a group, to observe faithfully and scrupulously the prescriptions contained in the Apostolic Constitution of the Supreme Pontiff Pope Leo XIV, *Universi Dominici Gregis*. We likewise promise, pledge, and swear that whichever of us by divine disposition is elected Roman pontiff will commit himself faithfully to carrying out the *munus Petrinum* of pastor of the universal Church and will not fail to affirm and defend strenuously the spiritual and temporal rights and liberty of the Holy See. In a particular way, we promise and swear to observe with the greatest fidelity and with all persons, clerical and lay, secrecy regarding everything that in any way relates to the election of the Roman pontiff and regarding what occurs in the place of the election, directly or indirectly related to the results of voting; we promise and swear not to break this secret in any way, either during or after the election of the new pontiff, unless explicit authorization is granted by the same pontiff; and never to lend support or favor to any interference, opposition, or any other form of intervention, whereby secular authorities of whatever order or degree or any group of people or individuals might wish to intervene in the election of the Roman pontiff.

Donoher walked up to the table and, facing his brother cardinals, declared, 'And I, Malachy Cardinal Donoher, do so promise, pledge, and swear.' Placing his right hand on the Gospels, he continued. 'So help me God and these Holy Gospels which I touch with my hand.'

Each of the cardinals made the same declaration, a promise that bound them together in the secrecy of the conclave. After the last elector swore the oath and returned to his seat, the master of papal liturgical celebrations walked to the center of the chapel.

'*Extra omnes*,' he announced, ordering those not taking part in the conclave to leave the chapel.

The audience for the swearing-in departed, leaving only the cardinals, the master of papal liturgical celebrations, and the ecclesiastic chosen to give the second meditation. Donoher and the assistant cardinals had chosen well, as the man delivered a moving sermon that clearly distilled the duty facing the electors and the need to act with the good of the universal Church foremost in their minds.

After this meditation, the ecclesiastic and the master

of papal liturgical celebrations departed, and the doors to the chapel were sealed. Only the cardinal electors and a few people needed to assist with the balloting remained inside. The conclave had begun.

Scheuermann once again stood before the assembly. 'May the election commence, or do any doubts still remain regarding the norms and procedures as laid down in the Apostolic Constitution?'

Scheuermann's question was offered as an opportunity to clarify the rules for the election as prescribed by Pope Leo XIV. Upon their arrival in Rome, each of the cardinals was provided a copy of the Apostolic Constitution, in both Latin and his native tongue, and encouraged to familiarize himself thoroughly with the document. For most, the election would be a once-in-a-lifetime event, and the intent of Scheuermann's question, itself an element of the Apostolic Constitution, was to ensure that each elector understood how the election was to be conducted.

There was a little murmuring among the cardinals, but only one rose to address an issue. It was Donoher.

'I recognize the Most Reverend Cardinal Donoher,' Scheuermann said with a little surprise. Of all people, the Camerlengo should have been an authority on the election procedures.

'My Most Eminent Lord Cardinals,' Donoher began, 'the matter I wish to bring before you is in regard to an amendment to the Apostolic Constitution.'

A cacophony of voices echoed inside the chapel. Cardinals rustled through their papers searching for an amendment that each thought he must have overlooked.

'My Lord Cardinals,' Scheuermann's stern voice cut through the din.

The noise quieted, but the confusion among the electors remained.

'My Lord Cardinal Donoher,' Scheuermann said, 'article fifty-four of the Apostolic Constitution, which addresses this very point in our proceeding, does not permit modification of the norms and procedures for the election.'

'That is true, but I am not proposing an amendment, merely announcing the existence of one. I apologize that the amendment was not included in the packets provided to you all, but I learned of it only moments before the start of this session.'

Donoher walked down the row of cardinals seated beneath Botticelli's fresco *Scenes from the Life of Moses*, and stopped in front of Cardinal Cain, the President of the Pontifical Commission for Vatican City State. Cain did not seem surprised, even when Donoher handed him a handwritten document.

'My Most Esteemed Cardinal, do you recognize this document?' Donoher asked.

'I do,' Cain replied, his booming voice clearly heard by all of the electors. 'It was drafted and signed in the presence of Archbishop Sikora and myself by His Holiness, Pope Leo XIV, one week before his passing.'

'And are the signature and seal those of Pope Leo XIV?'

'They are, and both were made in my presence.'

'And is this your signature notarizing the document?'

'It is.'

'And it was the expressed wish of the late pontiff that

this document not be made known until after the conclave to elect his successor had begun.'

'As expressed to me by His Holiness.'

'Thank you, my Lord Cardinal.' Donoher returned to the front of the chapel before continuing. 'The amendment drafted by His Holiness, Pope Leo XIV, in his own hand, and dated in the week prior to his death, reads as follows.' Donoher looked down at his papers.

I exclude from the provisions of article sixty-one, the introduction into the place of election such technological equipment as required by the Camerlengo for the sole purpose of presenting an audiovisual message recorded by me for the cardinal electors. Following the presentation of this message, the technological equipment is to be removed from the place of election and the original provisions of article sixty-one are to be enforced.

'Are there any questions regarding the amendment just introduced by Cardinal Donoher?' Scheuermann asked.

There were none.

'If there are no objections,' Scheuermann continued, 'I suggest that we now hear the message.'

Several heads nodded in assent. All participants wanted to hear what the late pontiff had to say to them.

Donoher unlocked the side entry and waved a waiting pair of technicians into the chapel. The men rolled in a cart of equipment and quickly erected a large projection screen near the altar. Those cardinals seated at the far end of the chapel moved forward down the center aisle for a better view. When the technicians completed their work, Donoher escorted them out of the chapel and barred the door.

The screen displayed a blue test image from the portable DVD player. Donoher retrieved the disk Sikora gave him just before the opening session and set it into the player. The screen filled with the image of Pope Leo XIV seated in his chair in the Redemptoris Mater Chapel and dressed in formal papal attire.

Greetings, my brothers in Christ. By now the time of mourning is over and the Church awaits a new dawn. Like the Easter season, this is a time of renewal. I pray for you all, and that the Holy Spirit will guide your deliberations. I created many cardinals during my long reign, nearly all of those present at this conclave. But one cardinal I created is not among you because I have held his name in my heart, and with my death he is no longer a cardinal.

It is for this man that I have taken the unusual step of preparing this message for you. Some of you may already have guessed that I speak of Bishop Yin Daoming of Shanghai, who has endured nearly three decades of incarceration in the People's Republic of China. Yin's crime, for which he has suffered greatly, is his faith in the Lord Jesus Christ and his unwavering loyalty to the Roman Catholic Church. We are all called to lead by example, and Yin's example has inspired many in China into religious life at great peril, and sustained millions of the faithful against brutal repression. There is much we all could learn from such a man.

I named Bishop Yin a cardinal in pectore in the second consistory of my pontificate. Through these long years, the Holy See has pursued every diplomatic avenue available to secure his freedom. Sadly, these efforts have borne no fruit. You are seeing this message today because I am dead and Bishop Yin is not among you. Though my successor is not bound in any way by this request, I pray that he, too, will find Yin Daoming deserving of a place in his heart.

At that moment, it seemed to Donoher the Pope was staring directly at him from the screen, and there was a twinkle in the pontiff's eyes.

Of course, my request assumes Bishop Yin is still in China. If the Camerlengo is the kind of man I believe him to be, an extraordinary effort to secure Yin's freedom is already under way. And if, by the grace of God, Yin Daoming is freed before the election of the new Pope, I pray with all my heart that you will give him the same consideration for the papacy as you would any member of the College of Cardinals, for under different circumstances he would be among you now.

I have chosen to speak to you about Bishop Yin in conclave so that my words will be protected by the oath that you all have just sworn. May you all discharge your duties as cardinal electors faithfully for the good of the universal Church.

21

'Is this true?'

A cardinal fired the first question at Donoher before the image of Pope Leo XIV faded from the screen, and dozens more followed as a tide of confused voices surged within the chapel. The decorum observed in such solemn proceedings evaporated, lost in the bewilderment stirred up by the late pontiff's recorded address. Among the most surprised by what he had heard was the Camerlengo himself.

'What did His Holiness mean by an extraordinary effort?' one voice demanded.

'Is something afoot that we should know about?' another inquired gravely.

Donoher caught only fragments of the barrage, his mind wrestling with questions of his own.

'My Lords, please return to your seats,' a stern voice thundered above the din. It was Scheuermann.

'My Lords, if you will all return to your seats,' Scheuermann continued, now that he had their attention, 'I am certain the Esteemed Cardinal Donoher will enlighten us.'

As the cardinals settled down, Donoher moved to the center of the chapel. All eyes were fixed on him, and it seemed even God himself, swirling in the frescoed heavens above, had stopped His labors to hear the Camerlengo's response.

'My Most Esteemed Lord Cardinals,' Donoher began, 'it has been the greatest privilege of my life to serve His Holiness, Pope Leo XIV. One of the goals of his illustrious reign, an aim sadly unmet, was to restore the freedom that was wrongly taken from our brother in Christ, Yin Daoming.

'Those of us who hail from Western nations know little of grave suffering. Our pastoral lives are spent administering well-established dioceses, and our greatest challenge seems to be in creating a sense of relevance for the Church in an increasingly secular and ambivalent world.

'The cardinals of the Third World have a better sense of true suffering. Their flocks are in pain because of punishing debt brought on by corrupt governments; incessant warfare based on racial, tribal, and religious differences; and the ever-looming specter of disease and famine.

'But despite our troubles, great or small, we are all here in this ornate chapel, and Yin Daoming is not. Like Peter, Yin tends a flock that lives each day under the constant shadow of officially sanctioned persecution. As cardinals, we wear scarlet to symbolize our willingness to shed our blood for the Church, to die for our faith. His Holiness held Yin a cardinal in his heart for more than twenty years because this man's blood has been shed for the faith on numerous occasions. Yin has earned the right to wear this color.

'With the failure of diplomacy and the intuition that his reign was drawing to a close, His Holiness charged me with finding another way to free Bishop Yin. A way was found that met with the late Pope's approval, and his assessment of me was correct. As Camerlengo of the Holy See,' Donoher concluded, 'I authorized the effort currently under way to bring Yin Daoming out of China.'

'Is that wise?' Cardinal Enright of Chicago asked, breaking the silence that followed the Camerlengo's statement.

'I think it is wiser to confront evil than to sit back and hope it simply goes away. China's rulers fear Yin, and they will never release him.'

'Does this action exceed the Camerlengo's authority?' asked Cardinal Miralles of Spain, his question directed at the cardinal dean.

'The Camerlengo is entrusted with all the temporal power of the Holy See during the interregnum,' Scheuermann replied. 'But article seventeen of the Apostolic Constitution does, in fact, require the Camerlengo to act with the help of the three cardinal assistants and to seek the views of the college in serious matters. Clearly, my Esteemed Lord Donoher, breaking a man out of a foreign prison is a serious matter.'

'I acted in a manner consistent with the stated wishes of His Holiness, Pope Leo XIV. This matter was merely unfinished business.'

'Perhaps this unfinished business could have waited until after the election?' Scheuermann asked.

'As evident from the message we all just saw, His Holiness believed otherwise.'

'But why act now?' called out Cardinal Drolet of Paris.

'Because it is a sin not to act when you know it is the right thing to do, and the opportunity we have now may not exist in the future. The Chinese government, which thinks little of the Holy See in normal circumstances, would never expect us to act in such a way when we are leaderless. That said, the final decision to act was mine, and I alone will bear responsibility for the consequences.'

'Do you think you will succeed?' the question came from Cardinal Mucemi of Kenya.

'Yes,' Donoher replied without hesitation.

Cardinal Gagliardi stood to address the assembly. 'I think I speak for my brother cardinals when I say I pray for the success of your efforts. Now that this secret has been revealed, My Lord Donoher will keep the college informed of any significant events, no?'

'I will,' Donoher replied.

'My Most Esteemed Brothers,' Cardinal Velu announced. 'I met Yin Daoming long ago. We were both seminarians; he was studying clandestinely. I was having doubts about my calling when we met, but it was plain to my eyes that the Holy Spirit was truly with him. Yin helped me to see my path, and without him I would not be here now. I have never encountered a man so well suited to the pastoral life. Is it possible, My Lord Donoher, that Bishop Yin could be free before the end of this conclave?'

'That is my hope,' Donoher replied, 'so that this matter may be concluded before the new pontificate begins.'

'My question was not made with regard to deniability of your actions by the next pontiff,' Velu explained, 'but the candidacy of Bishop Yin. If, despite his sufferings, or perhaps because of them, he has realized the spiritual potential I recognized in him so many years ago – my brothers, the rescue of Yin at this time could well be the guidance we all prayed for as we entered this chapel.'

'My Lord Velu raises an interesting possibility,' Gagliardi said, 'but as a candidate for the papacy, Yin is unknown to nearly all of us.'

'I indeed may be the only one here who has ever met Yin Daoming – and that was when we were all much younger – but there is no denying the effect he has had on the Church in China,' Velu countered. 'He has led by example in a most powerful way.'

'My Lord Cardinals,' Donoher interjected, 'until that happy day when Bishop Yin is free, the point you are arguing is moot. In looking at the papabili, I have no doubt that this conclave has within it the capacity to break several long-standing traditions and elect a Pope who is neither Italian, European, nor even a cardinal. But so long as Bishop Yin remains in a Chinese prison, he is unelectable because he cannot accept his election. This situation is not anticipated in the Apostolic Constitution, and it places the Church in grave danger. Would we dare set aside the results of a valid canonical election because the one the Holy Spirit has guided us to is unavailable? The Apostolic Constitution clearly states that the conclave ends only after the man elected assents. In such a situation, we threaten to place the Church in a leaderless limbo no different from when the French took Pius VI prisoner for two years. And if leaders in Beijing ever learned of Bishop Yin's election, they would surely execute him.' Donoher let that final thought resonate within the frescoed walls of the chapel. 'Esteemed cardinals, I say this not to dissuade you from voting as your conscience dictates, but so that you will be fully informed. If there is nothing further, then as Camerlengo, I am required by the Apostolic Constitution to conduct one ballot today. It is now time to vote.'

At Donoher's direction, the two masters of ceremonies prepared and distributed the ballot papers to the cardinal electors. Lots were drawn to choose three trios of cardinals to perform specific tasks for this ballot. Selected first were the scrutineers, who would study each ballot and tally the results. The infirmarii were chosen next, their charge to collect the votes of those cardinals too infirm to attend the proceeding in person who would instead vote from their hotel rooms in Domus Sanctae Marthae. Chosen last were the revisors, who would check the ballots and tallies to verify the election results. With the first phase of the voting process complete, all those not casting ballots departed the chapel, leaving only the cardinal electors inside.

Donoher returned to his seat and, with the other cardinals, studied the blank piece of paper before him. It was rectangular, its length twice its width so that when folded across the middle it would form a perfect square. Donoher did this, then reopened the ballot and printed the words *eligo in summum pontificem* on the upper half.

I elect as supreme pontiff. The Camerlengo mulled over the words he had written, considering whose name he would write beneath them, on the lower half of the ballot. As a citizen of the United States, Donoher continued to vote in national elections, but did so with the knowledge that his vote was but one of millions. In this election, his vote was one of only one hundred and twenty, and never before had he felt the importance of his decision. Whoever won the election would be the spiritual leader of a billion-plus people spread across the globe, and he would reign for the rest of his life.

Donoher prayed for a moment, then printed in bold block letters the name of his choice, folded the ballot, and waited. When each elector had completed his ballot, the three cardinals chosen as scrutineers took their places by the altar.

In the center of the altar stood a broad, shallow urn about a meter in diameter, supported on a trio of short, sturdy legs. Crafted in silver and gilded bronze, the urn consisted of a bowl girded by five flat horizontal rings and a shallow-domed lid. The lid bore a delicate design featuring the traditional Christian symbols of grapes and sprigs of wheat, and was fastened to the bowl by a hinge. Two sculpted emblems adorned the urn – the crossed keys of Saint Peter mounted to the rim of the bowl, and a shepherd holding a lamb on the top of the lid. Beside the urn lay a gilded plate.

The urn was one of three crafted by Cecco Bonanotti in accordance with reforms to the election procedure instituted by the Pope in his Apostolic Constitution. The urn on the altar was for collecting the cast ballots. Atop the long table in front of the altar stood the second urn, which the scrutineers would use during the counting of the ballots. Smaller than its brothers and designed for portability, the third urn featured a locked lid and a slot for ballots collected by the infirmarii.

Derided by some in the media as 'flying saucers' and 'too modern' for the ancient ritual, Bonanotti's urns seemed ideally designed for the purpose at hand, and Donoher found them in keeping with the resplendent surroundings.

Mizzi, the former Camerlengo and most senior cardinal in the conclave, rose from his seat and, with his ballot held high for all to see, walked down the center of the chapel to the altar.

'I call as my witness Christ the Lord who will be my judge, that my vote is given to the one who before God I think should be elected.'

As the scrutineers tilted back the urn's lid, Mizzi placed his ballot on the plate, then lifted the plate and tilted it so the ballot dropped into the bowl. The infirmarii followed Mizzi to the altar, each taking his turn to cast his ballot before departing the chapel with the small urn. Then, in order of seniority, the rest of the cardinal electors cast their votes.

After all ballots, including those collected by the infirmarii, had been placed in the urn, the first scrutineer, Cardinal McKernan of Scotland, lifted the lid and thoroughly mixed the contents. The third scrutineer, Cardinal Ranaletti of Florence, proceeded to count the ballots one by one, transferring each to the second urn. Ranaletti's count exactly matched the number of electors – had it been off, the unopened ballots would have been burned and another vote taken immediately.

The three scrutineers arranged themselves at the long table in front of the altar and began tallying the vote. McKernan pulled out the first ballot, noted the name of the person chosen on a sheet of paper prepared for the election, then passed the ballot to Cardinal Elmer of Los Angeles, who did the same before passing it to Cardinal Ranaletti.

'Oromo,' Ranaletti announced, the name rolling smoothly off his Italian tongue.

As the cardinal electors made note of the name inscribed on the first ballot, Ranaletti pierced a needle through the letter 'o' in *eligo* and drew a length of thread through the tiny hole – the first of what would become a string of counted ballots.

Like most of those present, Donoher wrote down each new name as it was announced and kept a running tally as the counting progressed. As expected, each papabile was making a respectable showing with roughly half the votes counted, yet an election with five viable candidates all but guaranteed that none would garner the necessary two-thirds required to win. Then it happened.

'Yin,' Ranaletti called out.

A ripple of conversation had followed the reading of each previous ballot. This time, there was none. Ranaletti strung the ballot and received the next one.

'Yin.'

The imprisoned Bishop of Shanghai received five consecutive ballots before another name was called. As the counting continued, it became clear there were now six papabili in the running. Donoher tried to fathom what had drawn so many cardinals quixotically to Yin.

The five papabili were all good men, any of whom would make a fine Pope. Why, Donoher had to ask himself, were so many electors looking beyond these five – and for what?

It was in the pendentives framing the upper corners of the *Last Judgment* that Donoher found his answer. There, Michelangelo painted angels carrying the symbols of Christ's passion: the cross, the nails, the crown of thorns, the pillar of the scourging. Jesus Christ suffered and died for what he believed in, and His example had inspired followers for two millennia. To lead, one must inspire.

In the conclave that elected Leo XIV, the cardinals had moved past cardinals who could govern and elected instead a man who could inspire the faithful. Donoher knew that any of the cardinals in this conclave could administer the Holy See, but who among them could inspire? And wasn't that what the Church needed?

After Ranaletti read the last ballot – another vote for Yin – he pierced it with needle and thread, then tied the ends of the thread together. The scrutineers reviewed their totals and officially determined what everyone in the chapel already knew – a new Pope had not been elected. The revisers rechecked both the ballots and the notes, ensuring that the scrutineers had performed their duties exactly and faithfully. Donoher's totals perfectly matched the official tally.

'If everyone will please hand your notes either to me or the cardinal assistants,' Donoher called out.

As most of the cardinals rose to hand over their notes, Gagliardi remained seated, staring at the final count.

Magni garnered twenty-four votes – a decent showing in the initial ballot and roughly where the Sicilian expected his man to be. Totals for the other original papabili ranged from the mid- to high teens. But right behind Magni with twenty-three votes was Yin – a man no elector was even considering a few hours earlier.

Madness. Gagliardi shook his head. *To pluck an Asian out of thin air and name him supreme pontiff? It was madness.*

Gagliardi paid little attention to the tightness spreading across his neck and shoulders or the chill of a cold sweat as his olive skin turned ash-gray.

'Your notes, Eminence,' a cardinal assistant said.

As Gagliardi stretched out his left arm to hand over the papers, a burning pain ran up the limb. His muscles from fingertips to shoulder contracted into quivering knots of pained tissue that throbbed with each increasingly erratic heartbeat.

'Are you all right?' the cardinal assistant asked.

Those were the last words Gagliardi heard before the pain in his chest overwhelmed his senses and he toppled forward. The assistant dropped his sheaf of collected papers and slowed the Sicilian's fall to the marble floor.

'The doctors, quickly!' the cardinal assistant shouted as he cradled Gagliardi's head and shoulders.

Donoher ordered the doors to the chapel unbolted, and the two on-call doctors rushed in with a gurney and an emergency cart. Prior to the conclave, both men had studied the medical histories of the cardinal electors and were familiar with the Sicilian cardinal's ongoing struggle with cardiovascular disease.

The doctors lifted Gagliardi onto the gurney and, after a quick assessment, cut open the top of the cardinal's cassock down to his navel and applied a defibrillator to his chest. It took three jolts to return the Sicilian's heart to a normal rhythm. The doctors rushed their stabilized patient to a waiting ambulance.

'Close the doors,' Donoher ordered as soon as the doctors had departed with the stricken cardinal.

The chapel was once again sealed off from the outside world. The cardinal assistants collected the remaining notes and put them on the long table with the official tallies and the ring of ballots. Donoher placed his ballot tally in a leather folio – later, he would prepare a document declaring the results of the voting. He would do this after each ballot until a Pope was elected. Then the collection of documents would be handed to the new pontiff for placement in the archives in a sealed envelope that could not be opened without the explicit permission of the Pope.

The ballots and the other records were taken to a small stove and burned with a handful of chemicals. In Saint Peter's Square, the waiting crowd saw wisps of black smoke emerge from the chimney of the Sistine Chapel.

22

'—*no word yet as to who was taken by ambulance from the Vatican, but unconfirmed reports indicate it was one of the cardinals.*'

Grin muted the sound on the broadcast. Two of the monitors on his workstation displayed feeds from Fox and CNN, and both networks were covering the breaking news at the Vatican but with little to report. Almost as an aside, the reporters mentioned the black smoke billowing from the chimney of the Sistine Chapel. He left the feeds silently running and cranked up his music again. The remaining monitors on his workstation displayed images from the security cameras at Chifeng Prison.

'Any word at all from China?' Donoher asked as he entered the catacombs workroom.

Grin swiveled in his chair and noticed immediately that Donoher was clad in black clericals trimmed with amaranth-red details. From a distance, the cardinal Camerlengo looked like a Bishop, which was apparently his intent. With reporters and cameras on the ground and in the air around the Vatican, footage of a scarlet-robed cardinal outside the secured areas of the conclave would definitely have drawn unwanted interest.

'Nolan's in the belly of the beast,' Grin replied, his voice somber with concern.

'Now we wait to see if he can get himself and the good Bishop out.' Donoher sighed. 'Heaven help him.'

'Your lips to God's ears.'

Roy Orbison's falsetto soared from the computer's speakers into the final chorus of his famous paean to the fairer sex. The final note hung in the air a moment, and then faded, to be replaced by a thunderous ode from Joey Ramone to CNBC business anchor Maria Bartiromo.

'That's quite a leap from "Pretty Woman",' Donoher opined as he sat down. 'Whatever *is* that you're listening to?'

'A weekly radio show called Little Steven's Underground Garage.' Grin leaned back and tapped the pause button on a psychedelic jukebox floating in the corner of the Mac Pro's thirty-inch video display. 'Little Steven is rock 'n' roll's answer to James Burke, thematically connecting songs, history, and cultural trivia. Just before Roy and Joey, he played cuts from The Charms, Nancy Sinatra, The Pipettes, and a clip of Al Pacino at his best from 'Scent of a Woman'. I needed something cool to clear the cobwebs. A session in the Underground Garage usually does the trick. What happened up there today?'

'Before I can answer that question, would you please stand?'

As Grin rose, Donoher pulled a Bible from his briefcase and held out the book with his left hand.

'Repeat after me,' Donoher began, leading Grin through

the same oath sworn by all those providing service to the cardinal electors.

As Grin recited, he wondered what his devoutly religious parents would think of their highly unorthodox son being made a party to the secrets of a papal election.

'—and these Holy Gospels which I touch with my hand,' Grin said, completing the oath.

Donoher slipped the Bible back into his briefcase. 'I swore you in because there are matters we need to discuss that are bound up in the rules of the conclave.'

'And if I'm not in, I'm out.'

'Precisely,' Donoher said. 'Pope Leo has let the proverbial cat out of the bag.'

'Excuse me?'

'Shortly before the start of the opening session, the late Pope's personal assistant took me aside and gave me a disk containing a message from the late pontiff to the conclave. In it, His Holiness, God rest His soul,' Donoher said the last phrase through clenched teeth, 'revealed that Yin was in fact the cardinal he had named in pectore so many years ago, then as much as said that I was mounting a jailbreak to get him out and that the cardinal electors should consider Yin himself for the papacy.'

'You're kidding.'

Donoher's expression was devoid of humor. 'As we speak, my staff is preparing a dossier on Bishop Yin for the cardinal electors to review before the session tomorrow morning. Most of my esteemed brothers know very little about the man, and now that Yin is in the running, they would like to make a more informed decision.'

'The talking heads of the media have been chattering about a secret cardinal,' Grin offered. 'So Bishop Yin is really a cardinal?'

'No, but only because he could not be named publicly and attend a consistory. Yin was a cardinal only in the heart of Pope Leo, and until today, Nolan and I were the only ones brought into his confidence. It's a dangerous secret,' Donoher explained, 'one I would have preferred stayed secret until after Yin was free.'

'Is there really a chance Yin could be elected Pope?'

'Honestly, I don't know. I wouldn't have thought it possible until Velu spoke up on his behalf – resulting in Yin drawing the second highest number of votes. It's either the most selfless act I've ever seen or the most Machiavellian.'

'How so?' Grin asked.

'Just an odd thought, but going into the conclave, there were five cardinals with a strong possibility of being elected. And since graft, bribery, and sex have little to do with Vatican politics these days, and there is no campaigning per se, a papal election boils down to networking and personality. You'd be right in thinking that five papabili would split the electorate five ways, making it unlikely that anyone would secure the supermajority required to win. I'm wondering, perhaps, if Velu might have backed Yin to muddy the waters.'

'But wouldn't that damage his own candidacy?'

'Perhaps. Perhaps not. The introduction of Bishop Yin makes this a completely different race from what we were all expecting. Yin's story evokes a certain amount of sympathy, which has translated into votes. Not enough to get him elected, mind you, but enough to shake the status quo. As long as Yin remains in China, he is unelectable, and once that reality begins to set in, his backers will begin to look elsewhere. They'll remember Velu and the selfless act he performed in front of them all.'

'You have a very devious mind, Your Eminence.'

'This election will play out as God wills, but now I have to contend with a chapel full of cardinals who know we're up to something in China. I pray for the sake of Nolan and the others that none of this information gets out.'

'That would be bad,' Grin agreed.

'It would indeed.'

'Any way to dissuade the Yin vote?'

'Overtly, no, but I will certainly continue to do what I can without violating both the letter and the spirit of the Apostolic Constitution.'

Both of the news feeds on Grin's monitors cut to a live image of a Vatican official delivering a statement to the press. In a split screen appeared a file photo of Cardinal Gagliardi.

'You mind turning up the volume?' Donoher was staring at the monitors.

'Sure.'

'—the Vatican has confirmed that it was indeed one of the cardinals who was rushed just a short time ago to the Gemelli Polyclinic here in Rome,' a newscaster said off-screen. 'The cardinal has been identified as Cardinal Gagliardi of Sicily, a long-time Vatican insider with a *history of heart trouble. No word yet on the cardinal's status, though clearly this is serious enough for him to be removed from the conclave.'*

'That's enough,' Donoher said.

Grin muted the feed. 'You did have an exciting session.'

'Much more than I would have wished.'

23

Donoher displayed his identification to the security guards at the entrance to the cardiac care unit. Although most press members respected the needs of the patient and satisfied themselves with updates from the hospital's public relations staff, there were some paparazzi who would employ any guise to get a photograph of a cardinal stricken ill during the conclave.

Once stabilized in the emergency room, Gagliardi was admitted to the CICU – the cardiac intensive care unit. The nurse station was an island in the center surrounded by glass-walled patient rooms. Cleared to enter the unit, Donoher was led by the head nurse to where the Sicilian cardinal lay under careful observation.

Through the glass, Donoher saw that Gagliardi was with another visitor – a man in his early forties who bore a strong resemblance to the Sicilian churchman, equally large-framed if much more physically fit. The man was talking on a cell phone.

'If you'll wait here a moment, Your Eminence,' the nurse said, 'I must have a word with the cardinal's other visitor.'

Donoher could not hear the exchange, but the nurse was clearly irritated with the man's use of a cell phone inside the hospital. Unrepentant, the man ended his call and slipped the phone into the pocket of his leather briefcase.

'You may go in now,' the nurse told Donoher as she exited the room, satisfied that order had been restored.

Gagliardi reclined in bed, his body connected by wires and tubes to a dozen different medical devices. He was still ashen and appeared old and frail. The cardinal's other visitor leaned over him as Donoher entered the room.

'Uncle, you have a visitor,' he said in a warm, friendly tone.

Gagliardi opened his eyes and smiled weakly. Donoher wrapped his hands around one of Gagliardi's – it felt cool and clammy.

'It is very kind of you to come,' Gagliardi said, his voice a hoarse whisper filled with emotion, 'especially at such a difficult time.'

'Wasn't it you who once told me that caring for the sick is more important than paperwork? The others would be here as well if they could, but I am the only one permitted to leave the area of the conclave. Know that their prayers are with you, my friend.'

'I know, and mine are with them.' Gagliardi lifted his other hand feebly, pointing in the direction of the young man. 'This is my nephew, Guglielmo Cusumano. He's an antique book dealer here in Rome.'

'An honor to meet you, Your Eminence,' Cusumano said before kissing Donoher's ring. 'My uncle speaks very highly of you.'

'It is good of you to be here. Family is very important at times like this.'

'Go finish that call to your mother,' Gagliardi suggested. 'I believe the Camerlengo and I have some matters to discuss privately.'

Donoher nodded, and Cusumano took the hint. 'I'll be back in the morning, Uncle, in time to meet with your doctors.'

'He is a good boy,' Gagliardi said, after Cusumano departed.

'What have your doctors told you?'

'Nothing I haven't heard before. A lifetime of bad habits has finally caught up with me. The doctors are still running tests, but apparently three more arteries in my heart are blocked. Had the doctors not been standing by outside the chapel, I would now be dead.'

'Then perhaps it's not your time.'

'That remains to be seen. The last time they opened my chest, the surgeon offered me a lifetime guarantee on his work. At this moment, I am not comforted. The message from His Holiness was quite a surprise.'

'To us all,' Donoher agreed.

'Can you get Yin out of China?'

'I believe our chances are very good.'

'When?'

'It could be as early as tomorrow.'

Gagliardi paused, momentarily lost in thought. 'Do you think Yin would make a good Pope?'

'Having never met the man, I honestly don't know. But His Holiness found him worthy of being a cardinal, if only in his heart, so I suppose that means he's as capable as any of us. In truth, I don't think it's an issue.'

'But Yin received the second highest number of votes, almost a tie with Magni.'

'Yet neither was even close to being elected. I don't know how to read the votes for Yin. Were they sympathy or a sign? The real test will come in the next ballots, which, sadly, I have to return to prepare for. Before I go, do you wish to be anointed?'

'I do,' Gagliardi replied.

Donoher draped a stole across his shoulders, then placed a small vial and a golden pyx on the table beside Gagliardi's bed. The vial contained the oil of the infirm from Saint Peter's Basilica and the pyx – a thin, coin-shaped vessel – held Holy Communion.

With hands folded and head bowed, Donoher began, 'In the name of the Father . . .'

24

BEIJING, CHINA

October 29

Xiyuan, the site of the Summer Palace, was once in the countryside northwest of the imperial capital, separated from it by an expanse of farms and wilderness. Urban sprawl over the past sixty years had consumed much of that open land, erasing the separate sense of place Xiyuan once enjoyed. The sphere of the Beijing metropolitan area fully encompassed the garden campus of the Ministry of State Security, rendering Tian Yi's ride into the central city paved and urban.

The Chinese spymaster stared absently at the lights of Beijing as his driver sped down the broad avenues toward the center of the capital. A steady stream of cars flowed along the city's main arteries despite the late hour, and towering cranes populated the rapidly changing skyline like a flock of wading birds hovering over a river teeming with fish. Floodlights illuminated the slender structures, the glow evidence of night workers toiling to complete a century of civic construction in a few short years. In China, live cranes were a sign of good luck. Tian Yi wondered what kind of luck the giant steel cranes would bring.

The driver turned on to Xichangan Jie, heading east toward Tiananmen Square, the symbolic heart of China. Ahead on the left, Tian saw the southern portion of the massive red walls that enclosed a two-square-kilometer compound of Zhongnanhai. The compound took its name from the two small lakes contained within its walls, though most in China thought of it as the Sea Palaces. From its origin as an imperial pleasure park during the Jin dynasty, the region of rolling hills and lakes immediately west of the Forbidden City evolved from a place of leisure for residents of the imperial court, filled with pavilions and gardens, into the seat of power for the Communist ruling elite. In 1949, Zhongnanhai became China's Kremlin.

Near the center of its length, the southern wall angled away from the road, receding to form a forecourt in front of an ornate two-story structure with a columned facade and a traditional red tile roof. The eighteenth-century Emperor Qianlong built the Precious Moon Tower – as the Xinhuamen (New China) Gate was originally known – as a gift for his homesick concubine.

As his driver turned into the guarded forecourt, Tian saw two large red signs emblazoned with white characters on the walls flanking the gate.

LONG LIVE THE GREAT COMMUNIST
PARTY OF CHINA!
LONG LIVE THE INVINCIBLE THOUGHTS
OF MAO ZEDONG!

The guards verified Tian's appointment and permitted his driver to proceed. Inside the gate, Tian saw a third sign—

SERVE THE PEOPLE.

As the driver followed the narrow road around the southern lake, Tian thought of the slogans at the gate and recalled Yin Daoming's exhortation to the audience in the Beijing theater. Mao famously said that all political power grows out of the barrel of a gun, yet the very real threat of death did not cow Yin or his fellow Roman Catholics.

How many communists, Tian mused, *would sing the praises of the illustrious Mao while being immolated for refusing to denounce the party?*

The car entered an area northwest of the southern lake called Fengzeyuan (Garden of Plenty). There, guards on night patrol directed Tian's driver to a parking space near a small pavilion that dated to the Qing dynasty. A large contingent of armed men near the building served to alert Tian that the Premier was already inside waiting for him.

A soldier opened the car door and saluted as Tian stepped out. A man in his late fifties, Tian was of average height with a trim build and a lean face with a smooth pate of lightly freckled skin stretched taut over the uneven topography of his skull.

The pavilion doors opened for Tian as he approached

them and closed once he was inside. Premier Wen Lequan sat in a high-backed chair carefully watching Tian. A thickset man in his mid-sixties, the Premier was an electrical engineer who rose through the party ranks before taking the reins of the world's most populous nation four years earlier.

Seated beside Wen were President Chong Jiyun and Minister Fu Yushan of the Ministry of Justice. Chong, a thin bookish man, was an economist and the architect of the country's two-system approach wedding communist politics with capitalist economics. Fu tackled the equally daunting task of modernizing the nation's legal code and processes for administering justice. Trim and athletic, the fifty-three-year-old Fu was the youngest man in the room. His quick political rise was attributed in equal parts to his brilliant legal mind and fiery personality.

Facing three of China's most powerful figures was an empty chair.

'Minister Tian,' Wen said, pronouncing the name with great formality, 'please sit.'

Tian did as the Premier instructed, his expression betraying no emotion despite the attention now directed at him. He gazed past the three men and focused instead on the exquisite brushwork in a painting of the Qutang Gorge hanging on the far wall.

'Throughout your many years of service to our country,' Wen said, 'you have cultivated a reputation as a man of reason and thoughtful, considered action. What most urgent matter has arisen that requires the immediate attention of me and my esteemed comrades?'

'Premier Wen, President Chong, Minister Fu,' Tian began, nodding respectfully to each man in turn, 'I believe the sovereignty of our nation has been violated by forces of Western aggression.'

'Please explain,' Wen said.

'A few hours ago, we received a message from our chief of station in Rome. The Vatican has set in motion an effort to extract a prisoner from the laogai in Chifeng and remove him from the country.'

'Which prisoner?' Fu demanded.

'Yin Daoming, the Roman Catholic Bishop of Shanghai.'

Tian saw Wen tense slightly at the name.

'The Vatican?' Chong mused softly. 'Are they not now leaderless?'

'Yes, and that I believe is the reason behind this provocative action. In a recorded message, Pope Leo himself revealed the plot to his cardinals – the men who are now meeting in secret to select a new leader. This message also revealed that Pope Leo secretly named Bishop Yin a cardinal and asked that he be considered by the committee as the next Pope.'

'Incredible,' Fu said. 'Would they even consider selecting Yin?'

'My information indicates he is one of the top candidates.'

'History often acts with a keen sense of irony,' Wen offered.

'How so, Premier Wen?' Fu asked.

'I was raised in Shanghai Province, in a small village just outside the city – the same village as Yin Daoming.

We attended the same school, so I knew him. I remember Yin as a good student and difficult competitor. We were not friends, but we respected each other. There was an old man in our village – a recluse who many believed could glimpse the future. One summer day, I was swimming with Yin and a group of boys in a small lake. We were racing, and Yin and I were ahead of the others when we reached the far shore. There, we encountered the old man standing in the shade of a willow by the water's edge. We were young, perhaps twelve, and the old man was a frightening figure. He stared at us for a moment, then said, "*One of you will rule, the other will lead.*"'

'Yin is in prison because he leads a dangerous cult,' Fu said. 'He should have been executed years ago.'

'Perhaps,' Chong said, 'but martyrs are more dangerous than prisoners. And once made, they cannot be unmade. If the agents of the Vatican know where Yin is, can we not simply move him?'

'That may not be sufficient,' Tian answered. 'The information we received was provided by our Italian partners. They view the appearance of Yin as a contender for the leadership of the Vatican as a threat to our mutual interests. They correctly recognize Yin as an internal matter and request that we resolve it quickly and quietly before it can negatively impact our business relationship.'

Tian did not have to elaborate. Everyone in the room knew of Beijing's clandestine involvement in the arms and drug trade through the Ministry of State Security. The Premier considered Tian's report and the opinions of Chong and Fu.

'I do not like the idea of killing Yin Daoming, but

I recognize the danger he poses to China. Our society is undergoing a great transformation, and in questioning their faith in the party, the people are vulnerable to subversive influences. If the agents of the Vatican succeed in taking Yin out of China, he will be far more troublesome than the Dalai Lama. If we move Yin, do you think the Vatican will continue trying to free him?'

Tian nodded. 'They are a patient foe with a long memory. I do not see them easily abandoning the course they have chosen.'

'We cannot permit Yin to be set free, and death seems the only way to ensure this,' Wen decided. 'Minister Fu, please draft the order for the execution of Yin Daoming. Minister Tian, have one of your men deliver the order to Chifeng and serve as witness that it is carried out.'

'What of the Vatican agents?' Tian asked.

'I leave that investigation to you. I expect they will disperse once word of Yin's execution is known. If any are found, they are to be killed.'

25

CHIFENG, CHINA

October 29

Kilkenny and Grin found no evidence of monitoring devices inside the cells at Chifeng Prison during their forays through the facility's computer network. This didn't disprove the existence of surveillance equipment – only that no such devices were tied into the network. Kilkenny's next move would reveal if his cell was equipped with anything that operated offline.

Confident that the prison had resumed normal operations since his unscheduled arrival, Kilkenny sat cross-legged on the floor and went to work on the hems of his uniform. While sequestered in the yurt, Kilkenny had practiced unraveling the seams in the dark. At first, the task was frustratingly difficult, but he eventually got the knack of untying the knotted threads to open the seams. He had considered using strips of Velcro but decided the added thickness made the pair of smuggler pouches too obvious.

He extracted a small headset from the first pouch. Two thin wires branched out from a small foam earpiece – one bendable, the other loose. Kilkenny inserted the earpiece in his left ear, the rhythmic throb of his pulse providing the kinetic energy to power the device. He adjusted the first wire so that it wrapped around his temple to suspend a tiny heads-up display screen an inch in front of his left eye. The screen, a thin wafer of transparent plastic, was the size of a small postage stamp. Kilkenny licked the end of the second wire – the adhesive was bitter – and fixed a tiny microphone against his throat.

From the second pouch, Kilkenny retrieved a small plastic cylinder about the size of a nine-millimeter shell casing. With his thumbnail, he peeled off the top to expose the cylinder's hollow interior. He had first learned about microelectromechanical systems (MEMS) when the consortium he worked for became involved with a start-up firm in Ann Arbor that sprang out of the engineering research labs at the University of Michigan.

Carefully packed inside the cylinder was one of the latest miracles of miniaturized electronics: the Fly. The device bore little resemblance to early prototypes, a testament to the great strides made in the young technology in just a few years. MEMS came in as many shapes and sizes as their large-scale mechanical ancestors, and the Fly was the smallest and most advanced breed of micro air vehicle (MAV).

'Activate,' Kilkenny whispered.

The throat mike captured the vibration of his vocal cords and transmitted the command to an object inside the cylinder. The tiny screen hanging in front of Kilkenny's eye flickered and glowed light green, showing the interior of the cylinder. Its walls tapered forward like a tunnel toward a circular opening.

'Take the field.'

The Fly released its hold on the sides of the cylinder and crawled through the tunnel toward the opening. It stepped onto Kilkenny's hand looking very much like a large deerfly. Its creators even programmed in several flylike maneuvers for the sake of realism.

'Begin search.'

The Fly lifted off from Kilkenny's hand, its wings perfectly mimicking the stroke and tempo of its namesake in flight, buzzing as it orbited the cell. It slipped through the small ventilation grille in the wall into a filthy section of ductwork and out into the corridor. Before leaving for China, Kilkenny and Grin had loaded a crude model of the prison's solitary-confinement wing into the Fly's memory. Using visual clues in the corridor, the device determined where it was and began a cell-by-cell search, starting with the one next to Kilkenny's. The Fly landed on the ceiling and panned the room with its night-vision eyes.

'Hold image.'

The fly stopped panning. Kilkenny's neighbor lay curled up on the floor.

'Grid.'

The image on the eye screen divided into nine squares.

'Enlarge A-3.'

The square in the upper right corner grew to fill the entire screen as the Fly zoomed in on the man's face. The prisoner was young, no older than his mid-twenties.

'Move on.'

The Fly wriggled through the vent and flew through the ductwork to the next cell. Kilkenny continued the process, discovering that the cells were either empty or occupied by men too young to be Yin Daoming.

Two hours into the search, the Fly entered one of the few remaining cells at the far end of the corridor. Inside sat a man older than those Kilkenny had seen thus far but strangely ageless in appearance. Unlike the others who slept or fidgeted nervously, this man sat upright like a cross-legged Buddha. His eyes were closed, but Kilkenny knew he was awake because he was softly reciting something.

'Enhance B-1.'

The Fly's camera focused in on the man's shoulder.

'Target site. Land.'

The Fly orbited the room a few times before alighting on the man's shoulder. His voice was barely above a whisper but detectable. Kilkenny could hear his words.

'—benedictus fructus ventris tui Jesus. Sancta Maria, Mater Dei, ora pro nobis peccatoribus, nunc et in hora mortis nostrae. Amen.'

Definitely not Chinese, Kilkenny realized.

'Ave Maria, gratia plena, Dominus tecum.'

'Hail Mary, full of grace,' Kilkenny translated in a whisper.

Kilkenny realized from the cadence of the voice that the man was saying the rosary. After two more Hail Marys, the man completed the decade and began to recite the Lord's Prayer.

'*Pater noster, qui es in caelis, sanctificetur nomen tuum. Adveniat regnum tuum. Fiat voluntas tua, sicut in caelo et in terra—*'

Kilkenny knew the Latin versions of these prayers because both his parents and grandparents had been raised with the Latin mass in use before the landmark Vatican II changes. The old invocations were both familiar and timeless.

'*—Panem nostrum quotidianum da nobis hodie, et dimitte nobis debita nostra sicut et nos dimittimus debitoribus nostris. Et ne nos inducas in tentationem, sed libera nos a malo. Amen.*'

'Speaker on.' Kilkenny commanded. A microphone-shaped icon appeared in the lower corner of his screen. '—but deliver us from evil. Amen,' he whispered into his throat mike.

The man was silent. Perhaps he didn't hear the Fly's transmission, Kilkenny thought.

Then, 'Who is there?' The man spoke softly in halting English.

Kilkenny's pulse quickened. *There can be only one man in this prison who knows Latin and English.*

'A friend. Are you Yin Daoming?'

'I am,' Yin said softly.

'Peter sent me. Your request for deliverance from evil has been granted.'

26

BEIJING, CHINA

Liu Shing-Li's eyes fluttered open with the first trill of his cell phone. His hand was on the device before it could ring a second time.

'Liu,' he answered clearly without any hint of the dreamless sleep that enveloped him just seconds earlier.

A woman lay on the bed beside him, her body tangled in the sheets, felled by exhaustion. He couldn't remember her name, not that it mattered. He assumed it was a professional alias, no different from the one he'd given her or the ones he employed in his line of work. In that way, their professions were similar. Both Liu and the prostitute treated personas as wardrobe, to be worn and discarded as circumstance required – an occupational form of schizophrenia.

'I'm on my way.' He ended the call.

He showered, dressed, and was out of the hotel room in less than ten minutes, and through it all, the woman did not stir. He did not consider the previous evening's entertainment lovemaking. Rather, it was sexual calisthenics.

Sex was a physical pleasure in its own right and, to Liu's way of thinking, not to be complicated with emotion. This detached approach to commingling required increasingly exotic techniques to invigorate his libido.

At this hour, still well before dawn, the drive to the capital's western periphery went quickly. Of course, no traffic officer would consider stopping Liu's car once he saw the special license-plate tag.

Liu cleared the main security checkpoint and was admitted to the manicured grounds of the Ministry of State Security's campus at Xiyuan. Like Langley and Lubyanka, the intelligence agency's headquarters took its name from the place it was located. Xiyuan meant Western Garden. Situated next to the former imperial Summer Palace, the facility boasted spectacular landscaping. The buildings, though modern in design, were distinctly Chinese and respectful of their ancient and illustrious neighbor.

Liu strode purposefully through the ornate corridors of the wing occupied by the senior members of the ministry. He had no interest in the artifacts on display – to him they were merely cultural trophies, spoils to the victor.

'Go in, please,' the executive assistant said, stifling a yawn as Liu entered the anteroom of the minister's office suite. 'He is expecting you.'

The massive wooden door to Tian Yi's office swung open silently and closed behind Liu with a barely audible click. Tian sat on a black leather sofa reading a file while sipping a cup of tea.

'I am pleased you arrived so quickly,' Tian said without looking up from the file.

'There were no delays on the way, Minister Tian.'

'Good. Please sit.'

Tian indicated a chair that faced him. Liu sat. Between the two men stood a low, black-lacquered table that held a tea service.

'Tea?' Tian asked perfunctorily, his eyes still on the papers in the file.

'Thank you,' Liu replied.

Liu filled a porcelain cup with rich black tea and took in the slightly floral aroma. He sipped the hot brew and discovered a smooth, malty flavor with a hint of citrus. Golden Yunnan.

'We have received a disturbing report from Rome. The dead Pope secretly named Yin Daoming a cardinal of the foreign Catholic Church.'

'We had always suspected as much.'

'Yes, but he remained unnamed because the Vatican knew we would not allow it. Now that the Pope is dead, what he kept secret died with him.'

'Then Yin is no longer a cardinal, secret or otherwise?'

'He never was,' Tian replied, 'at least not in a way that posed a problem for us. But now he is something much more dangerous. According to Rome, Yin has become a papabile.'

'Papabile?'

'An Italian term for someone who might be elected Pope.'

Yin a Pope? Liu questioned the proposition in his mind. He would have laughed had anyone other than the minister suggested it.

'Why would they do such a thing?' Liu asked. 'It's madness.'

'All religion is a form of madness, yet such an act might also be politically brilliant. The Pope is not just the leader of a church but the ruler of a nation. If Yin became Pope, he would cease to be a Chinese citizen in the eyes of most of the world. He would instead be a head of state and the spiritual leader of an international organization with as many followers as there are people in China.'

'But what does that matter?' Liu asked dismissively. 'Yin's church has no military, and its billion followers are scattered all over the world.'

'What you perceive as weakness can also be a strength,' Tian countered. 'During the Second World War, Winston Churchill tried to persuade Josef Stalin on the advisability of an alliance with the Vatican. Stalin reportedly scoffed at the idea, asking rhetorically, *How many divisions does the Pope have?* Stalin is dead and the Soviet Union is no more, yet the Vatican endures. The billion who follow the Pope do so willingly. If Yin is elected Pope, keeping him prisoner would be very dangerous for China.'

'Yet we cannot let Yin Daoming go free.'

'No,' Tian agreed. 'The Vatican is aware of this fact too. The information from Rome also indicates that a clandestine effort is under way to take Yin out of the country.'

'Then we should have him moved.'

'Perhaps, but the transfer itself might also provide the opportunity for Yin to be taken. As you well know, millions of Chinese secretly share Yin's religion. No doubt, many are also spies for the Vatican.'

The conversation seemed like a game of Wei Ch'i to Liu, with the thrust of Tian's moves narrowing the options on the board.

'Yin's situation is little known outside China, and that provides us with an opportunity to resolve this situation quietly.' Tian handed Liu the folder. 'This authorization comes from Premier Wen himself.'

Liu smiled as he read the execution order – a document he wished had come to him in August. 'I will see to it personally.'

'And if you discover anything out of the ordinary, take care of it as well. I don't believe anyone you discover illegally inside our borders will be missed.'

27

CHIFENG, CHINA

The door to Kilkenny's cell rolled open, a pair of guards rushed inside, and the beating began. Kilkenny curled himself into a ball to protect his head and chest, letting his back and legs absorb the brunt of the assault. His attackers alternated between jabbing kicks and lash strokes with flexible plastic canes.

Kilkenny deliberately kept his breathing shallow, exhaling sharply in between blows. He felt blood pulsing from ruptured vessels into the traumatized layers of his skin and bruises knotting deep within his muscles. Stricken nerves fired signals of alarm to Kilkenny's brain until he could no longer identify distinct points of injury. Pain was everywhere. Then, as quickly as it started, the violence ceased.

Someone was shouting angrily at the guards who had beaten him. Kilkenny couldn't understand the Chinese words, but the tone and tenor were unmistakable. He stole a glance at the source of his reprieve, and through watery eyes saw a figure silhouetted in the doorway.

The guards manhandled Kilkenny as they shackled his wrists and ankles, and cursed at him violently when they stood him up and his battered legs threatened to buckle beneath him. Again, the officer barked an order and the guards complied. They held Kilkenny upright as the officer stepped into the dark cell and covered his head with a black bag. Kilkenny was half-walked, half-dragged from his cell and down the corridor.

Despite having familiarized himself with the prison layout, Kilkenny quickly became disoriented during the quick march through the facility. He lost count of the doors they passed through, but knew immediately that the last one had led outside. The sound of trucks and machinery and voices filled the air – the prison far more active than when he had arrived in the middle of the night.

Gravel crunched underfoot as the march continued. Kilkenny heard crows cawing overhead. The march suddenly stopped. A voice grunted an order, and the guards holding Kilkenny's arms pushed him down on his knees.

Kilkenny heard a rustle of paper, and a voice began to speak with the official tones of a pronouncement. Whatever the meaning, Kilkenny did not like the sound of it. When the speaker finished, he gave another order.

Again, footsteps crunched in the gravel, though off to Kilkenny's side. He heard what sounded in tone like a question, though directed at someone else. What startled him was the reply.

'As the Lord has forgiven me,' Yin said clearly in English, 'so I forgive you.'

Yin's words were followed by the sound of a muffled gunshot and a body falling to the ground.

Someone tugged at the hood covering Kilkenny's head, pushing his chin down to his chest. Through the bunched folds of the cloth, he felt the barrel of a pistol press against the base of his skull. Among the flurry of thoughts running through his head, Kilkenny imagined the Chinese government trying to bill his father for the bullet and the response they would receive.

As if in slow motion, the sounds of the pistol mechanism vibrated against his skull. Because of his long experience with firearms, he could visualize the trigger bar drawing forward, pivoting the safety lever to allow the firing pin to move while at the same time releasing the hammer. The hammer then struck the firing pin, ramming it into the primer at the base of the chambered round.

It all took scarcely a second. The shock wave emanating like a thunderclap from the guard's QSZ-92 nine-millimeter pistol reached Kilkenny's eardrums just as he felt the impact against the back of his head. He saw stars in the darkness of the hood, then nothing. Kilkenny's legs buckled and he lifelessly fell to the ground.

28

'I am honored by your visit,' Zhong said, greeting Liu Shing-Li with the deference reserved for an important visitor from Beijing.

The warden of Chifeng Prison was a stocky man whose once thickly muscled body had softened over time. He stood a full head shorter than Liu, his pate smooth and hairless by choice rather than genetics – lice thrived inside the prison, and the warden feared a personal infestation. Liu returned Zhong's bow, though with less formality.

'And I at your receiving me on such short notice. I hope my unannounced arrival is not inconvenient for you. The nature of my visit requires discretion.'

Zhong assumed from Liu's polite words that the Ministry of State Security felt it was either unwise or unnecessary to inform him of this visit. He hoped the latter was the case. He motioned Liu to a small circular conference table and sat opposite him.

'Would you care for some tea?'

'No, thank you,' Liu replied with a hint of boredom at the obligatory pleasantries. In situations like these, he envied the directness of Americans.

'How may I be of service to you?' Zhong asked.

Liu opened his briefcase and extracted from it the thin packet of documents he received from Minister Tian. 'The Supreme People's Court has ordered that the death sentence on one of your prisoners be implemented without further delay.'

Zhong appeared mildly surprised by Liu's statement. Execution orders were normally routed internally by the Ministry of Justice, not hand delivered by representatives of the Ministry of State Security. He accepted the documents and quickly read through them. Most contained familiar legal boilerplate authorizing the execution. The signatures, rendered in crisp clear strokes, came from the court's most senior jurists.

'Is the prisoner to be executed by lethal injection or—'

'He is to be shot,' Liu replied without waiting for the rest of the question.

Zhong deliberately avoided reading the name of the condemned man until the end, in a small way granting a few extra moments of life to someone who would soon be dead. It was a small act, but one that created the personal illusion of compassion for a man who otherwise had none. As he read the name, Zhong's right eyebrow arched up like the back of an angry cat.

'Is there a problem?' Liu asked.

'We execute a number of prisoners each year,' the warden replied, 'but never the same one twice.'

Liu's gaze tightened on the man. 'Explain.'

'This is the second time today that I have received an order to execute Yin Daoming.'

'Show me,' Liu demanded.

Zhong went to his desk and retrieved a file from a gray metal tray. He handed it to Liu. The documents from the People's Supreme Court were virtually identical to the ones Liu brought from Beijing, including the signatures.

'Have your men carried out this order?' Liu asked.

Zhong shook his head. 'The officer who delivered the order, a Captain Jiao, and her men are handling the executions. My men are observing, of course.'

'Executions? Someone in addition to Yin is to be executed?'

'Yes. A foreigner. He was brought in late last night pending a final decision from the court on his sentence. A diplomatic issue, I believe. I received the execution orders this morning – both prisoners were being escorted from their cells when you arrived,' Zhong explained. 'Normally, I would be present in my official capacity to observe the implementation of a death sentence, which I expect has just been carried out.'

'I would like to speak with this captain,' Liu said, his steely tone tinged with suspicion. 'Take me to her – now.'

The raw scent of burned gunpowder lingered in Jiao's nostrils, the pistol still warm in her hand. Kilkenny's body lay near her feet, blood seeping through the porous black fabric of the hood onto the ground. Nearby, flies were already hovering over the equally lifeless form of Yin Daoming. Jiao slipped the pistol back into her hip holster, secured the flap, and motioned for one of the prison guards to come forward. The man held a folder of execution paperwork, and she quickly worked through the forms, affixing her signature as the officer in charge of carrying out the death sentence on the two prisoners.

'Will there be anyone to collect the bodies,' the guard asked, 'or are we to dispose of them?'

'The answer to both questions is no,' Jiao replied without looking up as she completed the last form. 'My orders are to transport the remains to Beijing. What happens to them afterward is not my concern.'

Jiao returned the folder to the guard and dismissed him, then turned to the men who accompanied her into the prison. 'Load them on the truck.'

The soldiers laid a pair of black rectangular body bags on the ground next to the prisoners and unzipped the long oval top flaps. They removed the restraints from Yin's wrists and ankles and rolled the body onto its back. Mindful of the blood still dripping from Yin's hooded head, one soldier carefully gripped the arms. The other stood ready at the ankles. On the count of three, they heaved their load up and into the open body bag with the same reverence one would give a sack of manure. The soldier at Yin's feet laid the flap over the body and zipped the bag closed. They did the same with Kilkenny's body, then loaded the cargo into the rear of the truck.

The warden led Liu on the most direct route from his office to the hardscrabble yard near the motor pool where prisoners were executed. Both men squinted as they stepped outdoors, the sun bathing the space with a harsh light that rendered shadows black in sharp detail. The captain in charge of the executions watched as a pair of her men loaded a second body bag into the back of a truck.

'Captain Jiao,' the warden called out. 'May we have a word with you?'

Liu studied the captain as she strode toward him. The woman moved with the confidence that comes with command, and with each stride Liu detected hints of a lithe body beneath the unflattering uniform. Her peaked cap sat low on her forehead, the visor cloaking her eyes in shadow.

'Captain,' the warden began, 'this is Mister Liu from the Ministry of State Security.'

Liu presented his ID, and Jiao nodded after reading the card.

'I am honored,' Jiao said with a crisp bow.

'When did you get authorization for these executions?' Liu asked.

'I received my orders early this morning. Is there a problem?'

'It appears that we both received orders to execute Yin Daoming.'

Jiao laughed. 'Someone must really want this prisoner dead.'

'Perhaps. I would like to see the body, just the same.'

'Of course.'

Jiao led Liu and the warden to the truck. Liu noted that only three of the captain's cadres were now visible. The fourth he assumed was inside the truck given the eruptions of diesel exhaust belching from the idling engine. Though they appeared relaxed, Liu noted a clear difference between Jiao's men and the prison guards.

The guards stood clustered together, arms folded or hands thrust in coat pockets, taking a cigarette break.

All were armed with pistols, and a few carried Type-79 submachine guns, which dangled from straps against their backs. Jiao's cadres stood apart, each surveying a different area of the yard, and their positioning seemed to Liu more deliberate than random. All three were armed with pistols and Type-85 submachine guns that they cradled in the crook of one arm.

'At ease,' Jiao ordered as her men snapped to attention.

Jiao's men are professional soldiers, Liu noted, wondering if that explained their attitude. Men on duty in the presence of a superior officer are unlikely to relax. Chifeng's warden clearly didn't inspire his guards in quite the same way.

The lift gate on the truck was still down, and the two body bags were clearly visible on the ribbed metal bed. Jiao motioned to the closest soldier, who clambered up into the truck.

'Open the bags,' she ordered.

The soldier hesitated for an instant, and Liu caught the brief glance he shot at Jiao. Her response was a barely perceptible nod. He unzipped the upper half of the lozenge-shaped openings and turned down the flaps. Yin and Kilkenny lay on their backs, their faces still covered with black hoods. A freckled arm covered with red hair crossed the abdomen of the body on the right, a body as tall as his own, and Liu immediately knew which one was the foreigner.

'I executed each of these two criminals with a single shot to the back of the head,' Jiao reported.

'I see,' Liu replied.

Liu leaned into the truck and grabbed the hood

covering Yin's head. The fabric resisted at first, the co-agulating blood sticking to the saturated cloth and cooling flesh. He gave a sharp tug to pull the hood free. Yin's head lurched up with the tug before falling back into the body bag with a hollow thump, the thin layer of plastic offering no cushion atop the truck's metal deck. The Bishop's jaw dropped open exposing a mouthful of long, crooked teeth. Despite the streaks of congealing blood on the face, Liu immediately recognized the man he took to Beijing in August.

The weight of the hood in Liu's hand surprised him. It seemed to be simple cloth, yet the hood felt unusually heavy. He held it up and pressed his palm flat against the fabric where faint contours of Yin's face still wrin-kled the coarse weave. Something flat and stiff lined the interior of the hood.

Liu turned the hood around and found the charred perimeter of the entry hole. A thin trail of blood slowly dripped from the opening, and Liu stuck his finger through it and discovered the smooth interior of a plastic bladder. Liu pulled out his finger, the digit stained with bright fluid that against his skin looked too red to be real.

The dull thump of an explosion interrupted Liu's thoughts. A small plume of smoke and dust rolled up from behind the concrete wall at the far end of the yard.

Roxanne Tao dropped her guise as Captain Jiao and struck as Liu reflexively turned toward the source of the sound. She snapped three kicks in rapid succession – the first to Liu's right knee, the second a punishing shot to his kidney, and the third a sweeping roundhouse that caught the side of his head.

The last blow stunned Liu and sent him sprawling atop the body bags into the bed of the truck. Jostled, Yin's head rolled to the side facing away from Liu. The pain clouding Liu's vision quickly faded and his awareness returned. Inches from his eyes, he saw a smooth curved surface of alabaster covered with thin strands of matted white hair. The back of Yin Daoming's head bore no sign of violence, no hint of injury – the skin taut and perfectly intact.

Staccato bursts of gunfire filled the air, brief and precise. Liu felt a pair of hands run roughly over his body, expertly stripping him of his pistol and the balisong knife strapped just above his ankle. Both weapons clattered to the ground some distance away, the pistol in pieces. Several pairs of hands then hoisted Liu from the truck bed and tossed him to the ground in a heap.

Blurred vision returned as waves of pain pulsed from Liu's bruised kidney. He heard the distant thump of several more explosions and the roar of an engine as the truck fled the yard. The air around the prison filled with sounds of shouting and the high-pitched wail of an alarm.

29

A cloud of gray dust swirled around Liu as he hauled himself up from the ground. He coughed, the gritty particles coating his mouth and nose with a dry, chalky residue. The truck carrying Yin and the foreigner disappeared around a building, heading toward the main gate.

Liu moved as quickly as he could toward a heap of bodies on the ground nearby. The three guards were clearly dead; entry wounds marked their chests and heads – expertly placed kill shots. The warden moaned on the ground a few feet away from the guards and clutched his leg, the shattered limb bent unnaturally at midthigh.

A squad of guards in riot gear rushed into the yard, their assault rifles carried shoulder-high, ready to fire. Liu made no sudden moves and kept his hands in plain sight.

'They are gone!' he called out to the point man. 'The warden is injured and requires medical attention.'

The guard approached warily, his eyes and weapon trained on Liu. The men behind him swept the fields of view to right and left, searching for threats in every direction. A corpsman moved up from the middle of the group to deal with the warden's injuries.

'Report,' the point man growled into a throat mike.

One by one, the members of the assault team sounded the all-clear for the yard and motor pool.

'Check the others,' the point man ordered the men behind him, his Type-85 still drawing a bead on Liu's forehead.

'Your comrades are all dead,' Liu said icily. 'Anyone with a weapon was killed.'

'Your papers, slowly.'

Liu pulled open the left side of his blazer, revealing both the interior pockets and an empty holster. With everything in clear view, he reached into his breast pocket and extracted a thin black leather wallet containing his ministry photo ID card. He held the wallet open, which let the soldier see it without having to take a hand off his weapon. A simple gesture, but one that helped to build trust and establish rank.

'Sir,' the guard said, lowering his weapon.

Liu put away the wallet and buttoned his blazer. Nearby, the corpsman injected Zhong with morphine.

'Who is the warden's second in command?' Liu asked.

'Mister Tang, manager of brickyard operations. He is being escorted to the security command center.'

'Please inform Tang that I am commandeering vehicles from the prison motor pool and that you and your men are accompanying me in pursuit of the fugitives.'

Liu recovered his weapons and moved as quickly as the pain in his back and leg allowed, alternating between a jog and a brisk walk with the prison strike team following his lead. The corpsman remained with the injured warden awaiting an ambulance for transport to Chifeng City Hospital No. 3.

The chief of the motor pool, still shaken by the outbreak of gunfire, offered no argument and quickly provided Liu with a pair of heavy trucks and drivers. Unlike their chief, the two young drivers found the excitement a welcome change from their normally tedious routine.

The officer in charge of the strike team sat up front in the lead truck. Liu positioned himself in the second vehicle. With the soldiers aboard, the drivers wasted no time starting the pursuit. The two trucks raced across the yard, following the same route to the main gate taken by their quarry.

'Posse's heading out,' Gene Chun reported silently, the vibrations of his vocal cords amplified by the throat mike.

Max Gates and his quartet of spec warriors lay camouflaged in the semi-arid scrub surrounding Chifeng Prison. Existing on bottled water and energy bars over the past few days, the soldiers were an insurance policy they hoped Kilkenny's team wouldn't have to cash in. A coded request for *divine intervention* notified Gates and his team that something had gone awry and that their people inside the prison needed to make a fast retreat.

'Two heavies outbound at the main G,' Chun continued.

'Copy that,' Gates replied. 'Fire in the hole.'

Chun retreated into a foxhole he had dug less than a hundred yards from the main gate. He could hear the low growl of diesel engines growing louder as the trucks approached, seeming to gain aural dominance over the high-pitched wail of the sirens.

* * *

The wreckage of the double gates lay stacked like toppled dominos; the coils of razor wire were trapped beneath the chain-link mesh and flattened by the escaping truck. The driver of the lead truck in pursuit accelerated, building speed to climb over the tangle of metal. So intent was he on guiding his rig over the debris that he never saw the rocket-propelled grenade racing toward his truck grille.

The RPG round exploded on contact, stripping the hood and fenders from the front of the truck and tearing the engine from its mounts. The driver and the soldier seated beside him died instantly, their bodies torn by shards of metal and glass. The shock of the blast ripped through the undercarriage, cracking open the fuel tank and triggering a secondary explosion that separated the body of the truck from the frame. Though protected by the cab from the initial detonation, the men in the back of the truck were incinerated by the second blast.

Liu's driver veered from the flaming wreck, piloting the truck through a turn nearly sharp enough to roll the heavy rig on its side. Shrapnel from the double blast rained down like blackened hail, and the air was choked with the acrid smell of burning rubber and plastic. Fuel from the ruptured tank spread out on the ground, flames impatiently transforming every ounce of the liquid into heat, light, and smoke.

The second truck stopped a safe distance from what remained of the first, the driver's hands fused, white-knuckled, to the steering wheel. The man was almost hyperventilating, his heart leaping inside his chest. Any closer to the lead truck and they too would have been engulfed in the conflagration. Liu unbuckled the shoulder harness and stepped out of the cab, leaving the driver to recover alone.

Over the roaring fire and the unrelenting siren, came the sound of another explosion ripping through the air. A thick black cloud rose from the opposite side of the prison, and Liu knew the brickyard had also been struck. There were only two roads out of Chifeng Prison, and Liu envisioned a burning semi and several tons of bricks now blocking the second.

'*Cao*,' Liu cursed, the profanity flowing from his mouth in a slow hiss of breath.

30

'Wake them up!' Roxanne Tao shouted.

She knelt between body bags, her jacket folded into a pillow beneath Kilkenny's head, the aged Yin's head cradled in her lap. Both men looked cadaverous, their lips and fingernails tinged blue with hypoxia. The ride out of the prison was jolting, and she had tried to protect the two unconscious passengers from injury.

'Pull up their shirts,' Chuck Jing said as he ripped open his med kit.

Tao rolled Yin's loose-fitting top up to his armpits, exposing a hairless chest of smooth white skin stretched taut over a rib cage so clearly articulated that the poorly set breaks in Yin's bones were unmistakable.

'Jeez, they really gave him a beating,' Paul Sung said, catching sight of the mottled bruising and lash strokes on Kilkenny's torso.

'I'll take a look at those in a sec,' Jing promised. 'Who first?'

'Yin,' Tao answered. 'At his age, he shouldn't be kept under any longer than necessary.'

Jing swabbed Yin's chest with Betadine, the antiseptic

a bright shock of color against the bleached canvas of skin. He thrust a long syringe into the concave valley between a pair of bony ribs into the man's heart and pushed down on the plunger. The synthetic adrenaline poured into the imperceptibly beating cardiac muscle as the medic worked to initiate a strong, steady heart rhythm. Yin's body suddenly tensed, his back arching. His eyes bulged, and his first panicked breaths came in rapid gasps, as if he were a drowning man clawing to the surface for air. Stimulant delivered, Jing retracted the needle and pressed a sterile dressing over the tiny wound.

Gradually, Yin's breathing and heart rate returned to normal. He blinked several times, squinting, his eyes not accustomed to light.

'These should help, sir,' Jing said, slipping a pair of wraparound sunglasses from his med kit onto Yin's face. Before leaving the States, Jing had consulted with doctors who treated POWs from the Vietnam War about the needs of patients long deprived of light.

Now Jing pressed a stethoscope against Yin's chest, listening for any sign of a dangerously irregular rhythm and found none.

'How do you feel?' Tao asked in Mandarin.

Yin looked toward the comforting voice, then reached up and touched Tao's face.

'Like someone who has been reborn from darkness and pain into the light.'

'Do you know where you are?' Jing asked.

'Outside the walls of Chifeng Prison,' Yin replied.

'Sounds lucid to me. Now for our other escapee.'

Jing plunged a second syringe into Kilkenny's chest.

Kilkenny bolted upright as an energized flow of blood raced through his body. His skin felt prickly, each nerve hammered by the throbbing that pulsed through even the tiniest capillaries.

'Sit – rep' Kilkenny gasped, his breathing ragged, asking for a situation report.

'The execution went fine,' Tao replied, 'but things got a little crazy after that.'

Kilkenny glanced at the frail man whose head lay in Tao's lap. 'He okay?'

'Near as I can tell, he's coming around nicely,' Jing replied. 'Just a little spent by the zapper.'

Kilkenny nodded. 'I haven't felt this hungover since – ' His words trailed off as he recalled his last brutal morning-after.

'You are the one who spoke with me last night, yes?' Yin asked in English.

'I am,' Kilkenny replied.

Yin smiled. 'That is the answer I always expected to hear upon my release from prison, though not to that question.'

'What was the question you thought you'd be asking?'

'The one Moses asked the burning bush on Sinai,' Yin replied. He changed the subject. 'How did you create the illusion of our deaths?'

'Better living through technology.' Kilkenny grinned.

'The hoods we placed over your heads,' Tao explained, 'contained a pouch of fake blood and a squib charge. That was to give the illusion that you'd been shot, because the pistol I used was packed with electronics instead of bullets. You both received a jolt to your nervous systems near the base of your brains that suppressed your breathing and heartbeat, simulating death.'

'I still think a fake lethal injection would have hurt less than zapping the back of my skull,' Kilkenny groused.

'That may be,' Tao replied, 'but it wouldn't have worked without the right kind of truck, and trucks equipped for lethal injection are hard to come by.'

'Ow!' Kilkenny howled as Jing tended to his wounds.

'I'm sorry about that,' Tao said. 'I stopped the guards as quickly as I could.'

'Professional hazard. Just a few new dings for my collection.'

'Judging by what I'm seeing,' Jing offered, 'I think you got the whole set now.'

'It sure feels like it. So what happened after you popped me in the back of the head?'

'A man from the Ministry of State Security arrived with orders to execute Bishop Yin,' Tao replied.

'Then it is fortunate you executed me first,' Yin said.

Tao smiled at the Bishop's show of gallows humor. 'This guy insisted on inspecting the bodies –'

'I see where this is going. How'd we do?' Kilkenny asked.

'Not a scratch on our side,' Jing replied, 'but we had to take out a few of theirs. Gates's squad covered our exit. No sign of pursuit.'

Yin tensed in Tao's lap, his arms folded and drawn tightly against his chest.

'Are you all right?' she asked.

'Have you killed to win my freedom?'

'Yes,' Kilkenny replied. 'We had hoped deception would

be enough, but my team did what was necessary to save their lives and ours.'

'To kill in self-defense is no sin,' Yin said calmly, 'but still I grieve for the lives that were lost.'

Tao said, 'I got quite the opposite feeling from Liu Shing-Li.'

'Who?' Kilkenny asked.

'The man who was sent to end my life,' Yin answered.

'A soulless monster if I ever met one,' Tao added.

'Oh, Liu has a soul,' Yin corrected her, 'but his actions put it at grave risk.'

'Two minutes to swap point,' David Tsui reported from the front seat.

Jing and Sung checked their weapons and reloaded their magazines. Tao traded her stun pistol for a real one and offered another to Kilkenny.

'You up to this?' she asked.

Kilkenny held out his hand and noticed a slight tremor. 'I won't win any medals for marksmanship today, but I shouldn't embarrass myself in a fight either.'

'Are you expecting trouble?' Yin asked.

'No,' Kilkenny replied, 'but I prefer to err on the side of caution.'

Bob Shen guided the truck through the old industrial district on the northern periphery of Chifeng, an urban landscape of narrow rutted roads and squat, window-less buildings clad in tile roofs and soot-stained masonry. He drove into the open end of a long, single-story ware-house, now an idled facility. A rolling steel door dropped to seal the entry.

Kilkenny heard a voice outside the truck, a man

conversing rapid-fire with Shen and Tsui. He glanced at Tao, who was straining to catch both sides of the exchange, for any sign of alarm. Jing and Sung listened too, but both men focused their eyes and weapons on the rear door.

Several questions were asked and answered, then the voices on both sides grew friendly.

'It's our contact,' Tao said, relieved.

'Tsui and I will run a perimeter sweep,' Shen called from the cab. 'The rest of you can offload.'

Sung was first out the back of the truck, his assault rifle held at the ready. Jing filled the doorway with his muscled frame. Both men visually swept the warehouse for targets.

A small group of people cautiously approached the truck, men and women of widely varied ages and a few young children. None were armed. Sung and Jing lowered the muzzles of their weapons.

'*Ni hao*,' a young girl with long black hair said, breaking the nervous quiet.

'*Ni hao*,' Sung replied softly. 'What is your name?'

Now the center of attention, the girl shyly looked to her mother for permission to answer. The mother nodded.

'Ke Li.'

'How old are you?'

'Six,' she replied, holding up both hands with the correct number of digits extended.

'I have a little boy who is just your age.'

The girl's face brightened and she pointed at the truck. 'Is he in there?'

'No, he is far away.'

'Is it true?' asked an old man who stood beside the girl's mother. 'Have you freed Bishop Yin?'

'It is,' Yin answered from within the truck.

A nervous energy swept through the people gathered around the truck, a palpable excitement that comes when a fervent prayer is answered.

Jing jumped down from the truck and stepped aside, revealing Yin in the doorway. Awestruck, the people dropped to their knees, hands clasped and heads bowed reverently – all but the little girl.

Sung offered an arm for support and helped Yin dismount the truck. Ke Li stared at the disheveled prisoner, a confused look on her face.

'Are you really a priest?' she asked skeptically.

The faces of Ke Li's parents and grandparents blanched, but Yin gazed warmly at the child.

'Yes, my child, I am.'

'But you are so dirty,' Ke Li remarked.

'I know, but like sin, dirt can be washed away.'

Ke Li considered this for a moment, then suddenly remembered something and began patting her shirt. Finding what she was looking for, she looped a thumb around a thin cord that ran across the back of her neck and fished out a simple wooden cross, which she proudly held out for Yin to see.

'My grandfather made this for me when I was born.' The girl's voice dropped to a whisper. 'It's a secret. I have to keep it in a special place or someone will take it away. Do you have one?'

'I did once, long ago. I was not very good at keeping it a secret.'

With the impulsiveness of her age, Ke Li removed her cross and offered it to Yin. 'You can use mine until you get a new one.'

Yin beamed at the child's generosity and knelt down to her level. 'Will you put it on me?'

Ke Li nodded enthusiastically and slipped the cord loop over Yin's head, her tiny hands brushing the sides of his face. In return, Yin placed his hands on the child's head and whispered a blessing.

Yin stood and, to Kilkenny's eyes, seemed taller. Ke Li scampered back to her mother's proud embrace. Kilkenny didn't understand a word of the exchange, but the imagery could not have been clearer.

'Blessed are the children,' Kilkenny whispered to Tao.

'I guess so.'

'Please, everyone,' Yin said, motioning for the people to rise. 'I am honored to be among you and humbled by your faith.'

The people stood, and Ke Li's grandfather approached Yin. The two old men bowed. The grandfather knelt down on his left knee, took Yin's hand, and kissed the finger where the ring of the Bishop's episcopal office should be. Yin blessed the man and asked him to stand.

'Is this your work?' Yin asked of Ke Li's cross.

'Yes, Your Excellency.'

'It is the finest I have ever worn.'

'I am honored.'

'That you have passed the meaning of this cross on to your children and grandchildren does you far greater honor than the praise of an old priest.'

Tsui and Shen returned with several young men dressed in coveralls.

'How's it look out there?' Kilkenny asked.

'Good,' Shen replied. 'The perimeter's clear of hostiles, but I can't say for how long. We should put some distance between this truck and ourselves. Everything we need is here.'

Kilkenny nodded. He got to his feet and stepped out of the truck, followed by Tao. The appearance of the tall, freckled Caucasian startled many of those surrounding Yin. Though no longer rare, the sight of a foreigner in Chifeng, especially one with red hair, was still unusual enough to elicit a curious glance. Ke Li tugged at her mother's pant leg and pointed at Kilkenny. Yin looked at Kilkenny and smiled.

'These are all good people, even the one who looks like a foreign devil.'

Tao and the soldiers laughed, leaving Kilkenny, who didn't speak Chinese, out of the joke.

'What did he say?' Kilkenny asked.

'He vouched for you,' Tao replied.

'As if his standing here isn't enough?' Kilkenny turned to Yin. 'Your Excellency, we need to change and get moving.'

'I understand,' Yin replied.

Their contact at the warehouse, a round-faced man named Su, led them to a small office suite where they were provided with new clothes. Both Yin and Kilkenny were stripped and quickly scrubbed raw by a group of matronly women with a greater regard for hygiene than for the men's modesty. As Kilkenny's prosthetic wounds were peeled away, he wished the real ones could be removed as easily.

As soon as Kilkenny had a towel wrapped around his waist, one of the women ushered him to a chair, where she sat him down with his head tilted back. The woman opened a bottle and poured a pungent, viscous liquid on his hair. Kilkenny tried to relax as she massaged the liquid in, quickly dying his red hair black.

'How do I look?' Kilkenny asked when Tao walked over to inspect his transformation.

Tao considered the question carefully before rendering a verdict. 'Less conspicuous.'

'That's it? I'm not dark and mysterious?'

'No, just less conspicuous.'

'I can live with that.'

'But when we get home, go back to red,' Tao advised. 'This is not a good look for you.'

With a fresh change of clothing, Yin, Tao, and the Asian-American soldiers could now easily blend in with the local population. As this was not possible for Kilkenny, Su and his people assembled a wardrobe typical of a tourist from the United States. Complementing the ubiquitous jeans were a pair of hiking boots, a gray sweatshirt with *Michigan College of Engineering* silk-screened across the front, and a navy blue L.L. Bean squall jacket.

'How do I look?' Kilkenny asked Tao.

'Like you're ready for a football Saturday in the Big House.'

As they dressed, Su's people cut the prison garb and soldiers' uniforms into strips and burned them along with the body bags and hoods.

A woman trimmed Yin's hair, then covered his jaw and upper lip with a layer of soapy foam. She went about the task of removing several weeks of growth with gentle skill, but despite her care, the honed edge of her razor nicked open the remnant of a scab on the crease of Yin's nose.

'I am so sorry,' the woman said, blotting the tiny wound. 'Curse my clumsy hands.'

'The last person who shaved my face showed neither your ability nor your concern, as your blade has just discovered,' Yin said. 'I bless you and your hands, and thank you for your kindness.'

Beaming, the woman joyfully completed her work, transforming Yin's haggard appearance into a more civilized look. Su stood Yin against a light gray screen and snapped a photo. Kilkenny was last to be photographed. The images instantly appeared on a nearby laptop computer, and a college-age man quickly fabricated a new set of identity documents.

'Nice job,' Kilkenny said, looking over the young man's shoulder.

The man beamed. 'I am number one-hacker. Next year, I go to University of Michigan.'

'This yours?' Kilkenny asked, pointing at the sweatshirt.

'I ordered on Internet after government say I can go. You know this school?'

Kilkenny nodded. 'You'll love it.'

Su and Tao carefully reviewed Yin's new identity papers and declared the forgeries acceptable.

'These are for you, in case we're stopped,' Tao said, handing Yin the documents.

Yin read the name listed beside his photograph. 'Feng Zhijian.'

'That mean anything?' Kilkenny asked.

'The loose interpretation is a phoenix who remains strong in spirit. I thought it appropriate.' Tao turned to Yin. 'Once you have this information memorized, I'll give you a few more details to flesh out your new identity.'

'Such as?'

'I am your daughter, Feng Xiu Juan.'

'Then your mother must have been quite beautiful, because you thankfully look nothing like me.'

Tao blushed, embarrassed at both Yin's flattery and how easily he disarmed her emotional control.

'If you are wondering,' Yin said to Kilkenny, 'her name means elegant, graceful phoenix. Fitting, no?'

'Quite.'

Su made a brief announcement, and the people began moving back into the warehouse.

'Time to go?' Kilkenny asked.

'That's basically what he said,' Tao replied.

'Would you look at that,' Shen said, amazed.

In just twenty minutes, the young men in coveralls had reduced the truck to its smallest component parts. Rubber tires sat stacked along with belts and hoses; copper wires stripped of their insulation lay bound in coil loops. Steel, still at a premium in China, had been carefully collected. A pair of sweat-soaked men sporting welder's goggles had cut the larger pieces of frame and body panels into manageable chunks. Anything painted was dipped in a fast-acting solvent that stripped the surface to bare metal.

'This gives a whole new meaning to chop shop,' Kilkenny said, knowing that by the end of the day, black-market smelters would recycle the metals, and anything else that could be identified as part of the truck would be as impossible to find as Jimmy Hoffa.

They left the warehouse in a collection of cars, taxis, and vans. Some of the vehicles were privately owned; others belonged to small businesses. The exodus was orderly, with only one or two vehicles leaving at a time in order to carefully blend Kilkenny's team and their Chinese collaborators into the midday flow of traffic in Chifeng.

31

Liu sat in the warden's office and stared at the tiny fragments clinging to the bottom of his teacup, but the abstract composition revealed no hint of the future. Not that he held any stock in tasseomancy or any other form of divination – he did not believe the future was knowable. Even luck he ascribed not to fate or supernatural whim but to one's ability to control unfolding events. And Liu's luck since arriving in Chifeng had been uncharacteristically bad.

The prison was on high alert, the brickyard idled, and the prisoners were locked down in their cells. Fire crews had finally extinguished the blazes at both gates, and mechanics now labored to remove the blackened wreckage and clear a way out.

The prison's technical staff faced similar difficulties recovering from a crippling attack on the computers that controlled the security and communications network. Unable to establish an encrypted line to Beijing, Liu decided the need to report Yin's escape far outweighed any potential security concerns, and he risked using his cell phone. The sleek device's tiny LCD screen displayed two words: *No Signal*. Until the prison's physical and electronic links were restored, the facility was quite effectively cut off from the outside world. And every minute that passed put Yin farther out of reach.

Someone rapped sharply at the door.

'Come,' Liu answered, annoyed.

Tang Hui stepped inside, a thin file clasped tightly under his arm. The manager of the prison's brickyard was a paunchy, middle-aged man with thinning hair matted down by perspiration. Tang's suit matched the man, gray in color and rumpled.

'You have something to report,' Liu said, more a command than a question.

'Yes, sir. Our phone system should be operational in the next few minutes. Once testing is complete, the line you requested to Beijing will be established. Our security system has been partially restored, and I have staff reviewing feeds from our cameras to see if we have any usable images of Captain Jiao and her accomplices. Also, we have located the file on the prisoner who escaped with Yin.'

'Finally. What took so long? The man was just brought in last night.'

'That was the problem. The paperwork had been processed by the receiving officer but hadn't yet reached the records department.'

Tang handed the file to Liu. It contained several pages of information about the prisoner – official-looking documentation so perfect it could pass a forensic examination. Yet everything in the file was worthless except for the color photographs and physical description of the man.

Liu studied the two pictures of the prisoner – one head on, the other in profile. The man's red hair was short, framing an oval face with a slender nose, thin lips, and green eyes. At nearly two meters in height, such a man would stand out in a crowd anywhere in China. The rest of the team that spirited Yin from prison would be far more difficult to spot. As Liu studied the photographs closely, his eyes narrowed with recognition.

The multiline phone on the warden's desk lit up and emitted a soft electronic purr. Liu looked up from the file at Tang and nodded for the man to answer the call.

'Tang,' the man said clearly into the handset.

He listened for several seconds, then complimented the caller on a job well done and cradled the handset.

'The phones are for the most part working again, and our technical staff should have an encrypted line to Minister Tian's office connected to this phone shortly.'

'Good.' Liu laid the file on the desktop with the page oriented toward Tang. 'Given all that has happened, can I trust that these photographs accurately depict the man who was brought here last night?'

Tang scanned the page. 'Yes. Official procedure requires the receiving officer to confirm that the paperwork matches the prisoner. Lieutenant Yu signed the transfer papers, verifying that everything was correct.'

'And Yu would have actually seen this prisoner and made a visual match?'

'Yes.'

Liu scrawled an e-mail address on a Post-It note and affixed it to the page. 'I want these photographs and the physical description of this man sent to this address at the Ministry of State Security. Perhaps they can find out who he really is. And as soon as you have useful images of Captain Jiao and her men, send them along as well.'

The phone rang again, and Liu motioned for Tang to leave. He waited for the office door to close, then picked up the handset and prepared to deliver the most difficult report of his career.

'So, the matter of Yin Daoming is now resolved, eh?' Tian asked with uncharacteristic directness.

'No, sir, it is not,' Liu replied.

'Explain,' Tian commanded.

Liu chronicled the events as they unfolded upon his arrival at the prison, then added what he knew about the foreigner who was brought into the prison during the previous night.

'This foreigner, are you certain he is the same man you encountered in Rome?' Tian asked.

'Yes.'

'Then it is unfortunate you did not kill him there. A fake execution,' Tian mused. 'The Vatican has tasked some very clever people with liberating Yin. The political damage that could be caused by Yin's escape is incalculable, but perhaps there is still time to correct the situation. I will contact the Ministry of Public Security and the People's Liberation Army with regard to securing our borders and airspace.'

'What are my orders?' Liu asked.

'Hunt down and kill Yin and these Vatican terrorists before they flee the country. You will be provided whatever resources you need, but you must not fail.'

32

VATICAN CITY

'Any word from Nolan?' Donoher asked as he entered the subterranean workroom.

Grin sat in front of a large-screen monitor watching a grainy black-and-white video. In the days since Kilkenny's team entered China, he had kept a patient vigil here, maintaining a fragile electronic lifeline halfway across the world.

'Just this.'

Grin reset the clip to the beginning. The camera panned out, revealing its position some thirty feet off the ground. The sun cast harsh shadows on the sandy yard. Several guards were visible on the left side of the screen. Then a group of soldiers marched two hooded men into view. Both were forced to their knees and executed with a shot to the back of the head. Donoher winced as the bodies toppled to the ground.

'Were they captured?' Donoher asked, horrified.

Grin paused the video and zoomed in on the officer

who shot the two prisoners. He enhanced the image enough to show the woman's face clearly.

'Even without the hair, I know that's Roxanne Tao. What you just saw was the riskiest part of Nolan's plan – if you'll pardon the pun – executed flawlessly.'

'But it looked so real.'

'That was the whole idea,' Grin said as he panned back and hit the resume key.

Donoher watched as the two bodies were zipped into bags and loaded into the back of a truck. Two men in suits appeared, beckoning to Tao. After a brief discussion, she led them to the truck. The rear of the vehicle was turned slightly away from the camera, so it was impossible to see what was happening until the soldiers accompanying Tao opened fire. The one-sided exchange ended quickly, and the truck bearing Kilkenny and Yin fled the scene. The bodies of the two men and several guards littered the yard.

'What just happened there?' Donoher asked, stunned.

'I don't know, but if our people opened fire, they had no other choice.'

The image switched to the prison's main entry seconds before an explosion tore the large paired gates apart. The fleeing truck cleared the burning debris, and the screen abruptly turned blue.

'As soon as they got out, I took the prison offline,' Grin explained. 'That's what cut the feed we were watching. With any luck, it also gave our people a head start.'

'When did all this happen?' Donoher asked.

'Just a few hours ago.'

'I wonder where they are now.'

'God only knows,' Grin said, 'but I'm keeping an eye out for clues.'

'Well, I had best return for the morning session.' Donoher rose and smoothed out the folds in his cassock. 'I'll visit with you again during the midday break.'

'While you and the rest of the cardinals have God's attention, try to slip in a good word for our people in China.'

'I'll be driving the good Lord to boredom with the monotony of my prayers on that subject,' Donoher promised.

When the cardinal electors had taken their seats and the doors to the Sistine Chapel were closed, Donoher walked up to the altar. He bowed his head and prayed quietly for a moment before turning to face the other princes of the Church.

'My Venerable Brothers, before we begin the next balloting, I would like to apologize for my absence at the meeting of the general congregation this morning, but under the circumstances it was unavoidable. I can report only that Cardinal Gagliardi's condition remains quite serious. Many of you know of the cardinal's ongoing battle with heart disease, and I ask that you all remember him and his family in your prayers.'

A murmur of approval rippled through the conclave, heads nodding at the suggestion. Several cardinals touched their own chests, their hands unconsciously drawn to the scars that ran like hedgerows down their sternums. Cancer and cardiovascular disease were frequent companions of men past a certain age.

Cardinal Aquaro of Brazil rose and nodded to Donoher, indicating that he wished to speak.

'I recognize my Lord Cardinal Aquaro,' Donoher said, ceding the floor.

'A question only, Eminent Brother. Do you have anything to report regarding Bishop Yin?'

Donoher's brow furrowed as he considered how to answer Aquaro's question, and he felt every eye in the room studying him.

'My Lord?' Aquaro prodded, attempting to rouse the Camerlengo from his thoughts.

'Bishop Yin is no longer a prisoner of the People's Republic of China. Earlier this morning, our effort to liberate him succeeded – but only to a point. The Chinese government is unfortunately aware of Yin's escape, and I can only assume the authorities are making every effort to prevent his departing the country.'

Cardinal French of Philadelphia stood, and Donoher acknowledged his request to speak.

'My Lord, are the Chinese aware of our involvement in this matter?'

'I don't believe so, but I have no information as yet to accurately answer your question. I continue to pray for the success of our effort, but I must also be mindful of the sacred duty of this conclave. Both Cardinal Gagliardi and Bishop Yin are wise and holy men, and either I am sure would serve the Church well as Pope. But at this moment, both are in mortal danger, which in my mind precludes them as candidates for the papacy. It is not my intent to dissuade any of you from casting what I am certain would be a vote made in good conscience, but we must all consider the needs of the Church. If there are no further questions, we should begin.'

After Donoher returned to his seat, the masters of ceremonies distributed the ballot papers to the cardinal electors. Lots were then drawn for those who would assist in the day's balloting. Wheeler of Australia, Unkoku of Japan, and Hielm of the Netherlands were selected as scrutineers. The infirmarii were Freneau of France, Oromo, and Siegfried of the Curia. Veblen of Miami, Garay from Quebec, and Prati of Florence were drawn as revisers. With all in place for the second ballot, those assisting the conclave departed the chapel, leaving the cardinals alone to vote.

No Pope was elected on the first ballot, triggering an immediate second. Though no candidate garnered more than forty votes, Donoher noted certain trends emerging. Cardinals receiving fewer than ten votes in the opening session all but disappeared, their supporters moving on to stronger candidates. Magni held steady through the morning ballots due to the strong backing of the Italian cardinals, but lost the lead. Oromo and Escalante surged into the mid-twenties, with Yin, Velu, and Ryff hovering in the mid-teens.

As the notes and ballots were tossed into the stove, Donoher wondered who would eventually emerge from the crowded field of candidates. Although Yin lost ground, doubtless because of what Donoher had said, the Camerlengo was amazed that the imperiled Bishop continued to find support among the cardinal electors. That a conservative group of men so bound in tradition would even consider so bold a move as to elect Bishop

Yin heartened him. As a student of American history, Donoher believed Jefferson was correct when, in a letter to James Madison, he wrote, *A little rebellion now and then is a good thing.*

33

XIYUAN, CHINA

Peng Shi responded quickly to the summons and presented himself in the anteroom of Minister Tian's office suite. The young officer was dressed in a dark gray suit with black wingtip shoes, a starched white shirt, and a patterned silk tie. He looked very much like a member of the diplomatic corps, though in fact he was an intelligence officer and had in the previous year distinguished himself over the course of an investigation into an attack on a manned Chinese spacecraft. That notoriety had the unfortunate effect of rendering his cover as a junior member of the embassy staff in Washington, D.C., useless, necessitating his recall to Beijing until a new identity could be created for him. As the glow of his hero's welcome in the halls of the Guojia Anquan Bu faded, Peng found himself missing the excitement of working in a foreign capital.

'The minister will see you now,' Tian's assistant announced politely.

The man opened the ornate wooden door, allowing

Peng to pass through into the minister's office. Tian sat in a leather chair behind a large desk of black lacquered wood. In furnishing and objects, the space surrounded its occupant with the visible trappings of his office and reminded all visitors of the power directed from inside this room. Glancing past the minister, through a panoramic span of ribbon windows, Peng saw the famed gardens of the imperial Summer Palace in their autumn splendor.

'How are they treating you in the Tenth Bureau?' Tian asked.

'Quite well, Minister.'

'Good.' Tian pointed a wireless remote at a large flat screen wall monitor. 'Please look carefully at these photographs and tell me if you recognize this man.'

Peng walked up to the screen and studied the images. It had been more than a year, but the man's face was still quite fresh in his memory.

'This man is Nolan Kilkenny,' Peng declared, though his voice betrayed some confusion.

'Are you certain?' Tian asked.

'Absolutely, but these photos – has he committed a crime in China?'

'Several.'

'But Nolan Kilkenny uncovered the murder of our *yuhangyuans* aboard *Shenzhou-7* and brought the criminals responsible to justice. This man is a hero.'

'*Was* a hero,' Tian corrected. 'Today, he is an enemy of the state. But before I elaborate, I have a few more photographs for you to look at.'

The images changed. On the left, Peng saw Kilkenny

233

standing in the lobby of a building next to an Asian woman with long black hair. A black-and-white image of a woman in an officer's uniform filled the right side of the monitor. The date and time index at the bottom of the image indicated that it had been taken that morning.

'I took this first photograph in August of last year,' Peng said, 'in Washington, D.C. The woman was identified as Roxanne Tao, an associate of Kilkenny's.'

'She is also an American spy wanted for espionage in this country. Once the preliminary identification was made on Kilkenny, putting a name to her was not difficult. Can you confirm the woman on the right is Tao?'

'The quality of this photograph is poor.'

'It was taken by a surveillance camera at Chifeng Prison,' Tian offered.

'I cannot confirm a match with absolute certainty, but it appears so, and it makes perfect sense. They have worked together before.'

'That was our analysts' thinking as well.'

Tian moved on to the next pair of images. One was a recent photograph of Yin, the other taken at his arrest in the late 1970s. Peng studied both and felt a faint sense of recollection about the older photograph.

'This is the criminal that Kilkenny extricated from the *laogai* in Chifeng this morning.'

'An American spy?' Peng asked, assuming he had seen the picture during his training as an agent.

'A Roman Catholic Bishop. You have a sense for Kilkenny and Tao, followed them for a few weeks, no?'

'That is correct.'

'Good. I want you to fly to Chifeng and assist the man tasked with hunting them down. You are to be his second.'

Peng nodded.

'You performed well on your last assignment – I expect the same effort now. On your way out, pick up your flight information and a briefing package from my assistant. This is a matter of great political importance, Peng. These people *cannot* be allowed to leave China.'

'I will do my best, Minister.'

34

CHIFENG, CHINA

The Chinese Catholics aiding Kilkenny's team led them on a circuitous route out of Chifeng and into the grasslands of the Inner Mongolian steppe. Northwest of the city, they switched from cars and trucks to horses and rode off into the wilderness. Yin beamed like a child when he mounted a soft brown horse with Kilkenny, thrilled with the experience. Throughout the journey, the smile never faded as he rode tall in the traditional wooden saddle, stretching his body like a sail to capture the sunlight and fresh air that he had been without for so long.

The journey ended near sunset as they approached a large circle of yurts, the original encampment having grown since their departure the previous night. Trails of smoke spiraled from openings in the conical roofs, and the aroma of grilled meat and vegetables filled the air. Several people, all ethnic Mongolians, ran to meet them, while others excitedly announced their arrival to those inside.

'You made it!' Gates roared as Kilkenny and Tao dismounted. 'Everybody in one piece?'

'Pretty much,' Kilkenny replied. 'How'd you guys make out?'

'Still shaking the sand out of our boots, if you know what I mean. Nothing a few bottles of Baadog and some barbecue won't cure. What the hell happened back there?'

'Beijing decided today would be a good day to execute Yin,' Tao replied. 'The man they sent to do the honors showed up just as we were preparing to leave.'

'Sorta sent things right down the shitter. Think it's a coincidence?' Gates asked in a low voice.

'No,' Kilkenny replied. 'So quietly remind the guys to stay sharp because we don't know where the leak is.'

'At least we covered your exit pretty well. There's been a distinct lack of movement from Chifeng toward the prison, so I suspect your buddy Grin cut 'em off real good.'

Kilkenny nodded. 'The brief time we were in the city it was business as usual – no checkpoints or increased police patrols. In that regard, our luck is still holding.'

Gates rapped a couple of knuckles against the side of his head. 'Knock on wood, it'll hold until we're outta Dodge.'

'Seems our hideaway has gotten popular with the locals.'

'Yep. The folks who collected me and the boys from our extraction point planted roots overnight. Gives the place a real lived-in look, and as a bonus, three of those yurts are hangars for the BATS. When you give the word, we can be wheels-up in ten minutes.'

'Good work. Where's my gear?' Kilkenny asked.

'Hangar number three,' Gates replied, pointing at the third yurt from the left.

Inside the yurt, Kilkenny discovered a group of grinning children playing in one of the BATs. He checked the aircraft to verify the controls were locked out and that the children could not accidentally start the engine.

Kilkenny unzipped a small duffel bag and pulled out his helmet. A few children climbed out of the BAT to watch him. He made a great show of struggling to put on the helmet, acting as though it was too small, and the children laughed at his performance. When the helmet was on, the children peered through the dark visor but could not see his face. They waved hands in front of the visor to test if he could see them, and he played along with the game.

As the children roared with laughter, a woman poked her head through the open doorway and, with a flurry of rapid-fire Mongolian, cleared the children from the yurt. Kilkenny was sorry to see the youngsters go.

Alone, he toggled the BAT's electronics and, through the helmet, tapped into the aircraft's powerful burst transmitter.

'Message encrypt, three words: *Gandalf Isengard Eagle.*'
CONFIRM: GANDALF ISENGARD EAGLE
'Message confirmed.'
SEND TO?
'Bombadil.'

The uplink compressed Kilkenny's message into a focused pulse of energy just a few picoseconds in length. A pair of satellites in a constellation circling the earth in a low orbit, and tuned to the frequency of the uplink, captured the pulse and redirected the three-word message toward Rome.

Kilkenny rejoined the others as the evening meal was being served. Several families had gathered inside the largest of the yurts, the men on one side, the women on the other, and Yin seated in the center at a place of honor. Kilkenny started to sit down with his team when the patriarch of the family beckoned him forward.

'Please, sit,' the man said in halting English, indicating a place beside Yin.

Kilkenny hesitated, then caught Tao motioning sharply for him to do as the man asked. He bowed to their host and sat on the floor at Yin's left side. Yin smiled warmly at him, intoxicated with joy during his first hours of freedom. In his youth, Kilkenny had enjoyed his moments of athletic glory and the fleeting glow that followed a hard-fought victory. But here he felt like an interloper in a moment that belonged to Yin and his people.

'The food smells so wonderful,' Yin said, his voice almost choked with tears. 'I had forgotten.'

'Try to go easy,' Kilkenny advised. 'Your stomach might not be up to real food just yet.'

Despite their modest means, their nomadic hosts put on a feast worthy of a visiting Khan. Traditional courses of shaomai dumplings, buckwheat noodles, cheese, and roast lamb, all served with milk tea, sated everyone with delirious warmth.

When the inevitable bottles of baijiu came out, Kilkenny leaned close to Tao. 'Please inform our host that we mean no disrespect, but my men and I won't be drinking tonight. We'll be leaving when it's fully dark and will need our wits about us.'

Tao relayed Kilkenny's message, and though disappointed, the host seemed to understand Yin's safety mattered most. After a brief exchange of questions and answers, he walked up, placed a glass in Kilkenny's hand, and filled it to the brim.

'Roxanne?' Kilkenny asked, unsure of the etiquette of the situation.

'It's a compromise,' Tao explained. 'I told him we would be flying tonight, and he countered that not all of us could be pilots. He point-blank asked if you were a pilot. Nolan, you are responsible for Yin's liberation, and these people know it. You *must* drink.'

'Here, here!' Gates shouted. 'You have the honor of the team to uphold. Drink up!'

Kilkenny glanced up at Yin, who smiled, holding his own glass of liquor. The alcohol in the baijiu was so strong, Kilkenny was thankful the fumes didn't ignite in the confines of the yurt.

'To freedom!' Yin toasted.

'Amen to that,' Kilkenny seconded.

Both men drank heartily, much to the roaring approval of the assembled families. Kilkenny nursed the rest of his drink slowly, but the host made sure his glass was never less than half full. After several rounds, the host called for quiet and approached Yin. As he spoke, Tao quietly translated for Kilkenny.

'Bishop Yin, you have honored my family and me with your presence among us.'

240

The man bowed deeply as he spoke, showing both humility and deeply felt respect.

'And we are truly thankful that God has bestowed such a gift upon us. For many years, we have prayed for the day you would be free.'

'God answers all prayers in time, even those of a stubborn priest.'

'I hope you will forgive my rudeness, but I have a request that I hope you will consider,' the man trembled as he spoke. 'The priest who used to visit us was arrested last year; we do not know his fate. We continue to pray for him, but without him we have had no mass, no sacraments. Will you celebrate mass for us?'

Yin's eyes teared up at the request, his voice too choked with emotion to speak. As he regained his composure, Yin turned to Kilkenny.

'Do we have time?' Yin asked.

'Just enough for a mass, I think. Are you up to it, though? It's been thirty years.'

'I celebrated mass on each day of those thirty years,' Yin said, 'except for today.'

'The day's not over yet,' Kilkenny replied.

35

VATICAN CITY

In the dimly lit workroom in the catacombs, Grin dozed at his workstation, exhausted from ten days with far too little sleep. He was bathed in the glow of multiple screens, a dizzying flow of electrons containing fragments of information gleaned from computers half a world away. Some of the screens contained moving images; others were filled with scrolled panes of arcane symbols – the poetry of the machines.

A window displaying a countdown timer reached zero, and Bing Crosby launched into his rendition of the twenties' chestnut 'The Red Red Robin.' Grin's eyes fluttered as the late crooner and orange juice pitchman roused him from a dreamless sleep with his dulcet baritone and impeccable phrasing.

Wake up, wake up you sleepy head.
Get up, get up, get out of bed.

'All right, all right. I'm awake,' he said with a yawn.

With one hand, he keyed in the command that cut Crosby off in the middle of the second verse. Blinking away the sleep, Grin made contact with a stealthy piece of code he left embedded deep inside the main server at Chifeng Prison. Even after the system administrators at the prison had taken the drastic step of wiping the server's hard drives clean and reloading every bit of software, his program survived.

When he tapped into the security camera feeds, he saw armed guards patrolling empty corridors and the idled brickyard – the facility completely locked down and in a state of heightened alert. Hastily erected barricades protected the two main gates. Nearby lay the scorched and twisted wreckage of the original entries along with the gutted remains of the vehicles destroyed during the breakout.

Now to see what the cops are up to, he thought.

The screens windowing the central computer that served the Ministry of Public Security in Chifeng showed a marked increase in activity. Grin culled several pages from the steady stream of data and fed them into a Chinese-to-English translation program.

'They're setting up roadblocks, covering the airport and train stations,' he mused, skimming through the rough translations. 'Rousting the usual suspects in the community of Catholic subversives.'

'And what might that be, Mister Grinelli?' Donoher asked as he entered the workroom.

'Reports from Chifeng's finest,' Grin replied, his eyes remaining fixed on the screen.

'Have you learned anything?'

'That I should never again complain about the jack-booted meter readers in Ann Arbor. The words *To Serve and Protect* may be stenciled on cop cars in Chifeng, but the question I have to ask is, Who are they serving and protecting? See for yourself.'

Grin quickly keyed in several commands, activating windows linked to surveillance cameras throughout Chifeng. Long queues of vehicles blocked the main roads as uniformed police searched each one and interrogated the occupants.

'The Chinese are casting a wide net,' Donoher said.

'Uh-huh, and check this out.' Grin pointed at a pair of windows listing arrival and departure information. 'They've diverted all incoming flights and grounded everything that's already there. The trains are shut down as well. I hope our guys got out of town before the clamp-down, because they have pictures of Nolan and Roxanne for the wanted posters.'

'At least this tells us they haven't been caught yet.'

'You one of those silver-lining types?' Grin asked.

'An occupational requirement.'

A window popped to the surface of the monitor in the center of the workstation, a white square containing a vibrant-hued version of Andy Warhol's famous Rolling Stones logo.

'Dare I ask?' Donoher inquired.

'Operation Rolling Stone,' Grin answered as he keyed in a new command. The dot in the center of the window spiraled open like an iris diaphragm, revealing a three-word message.

'Gandalf Isengard Eagle?' Donoher read aloud, puzzled.

'A message from Nolan,' Grin said warmly. 'A good one.'

'What does it mean, beyond the literary reference to Tolkien's literary opus?'

'Yin is Gandalf,' Grin explained, 'a pretty straightforward substitution. Early in the story, Gandalf is imprisoned in the tower at Isengard by the wizard Saruman.'

'So Isengard stands for Chifeng Prison.'

'Exactly. The king of the eagles plucked Gandalf from the tower and flew him to freedom. They got Yin out of prison and, as of—' Grin checked the time stamp on the message, 'a few minutes ago when Nolan sent this, they haven't been caught.'

Donoher clasped his hands together and bowed his head to offer a brief prayer of thanks.

'Cardinal?' a young nun called from the doorway.

'Yes, Sister?' Donoher replied, still smiling from Kilkenny's message.

'I was hoping to catch you before you returned to the conclave. We're setting up a video link with the United States. It's Jackson Barnett, and he'd like to speak with you both.'

'Would you please put it through in here?'

Grin cleared the largest of his displays, and a moment later Jackson Barnett appeared on the screen.

'Your Eminence,' Barnett said with respect for both the man and his title, 'Mister Grinelli. I am pleased to have reached you both. I am certain you have been monitoring the situation in China.'

'Like a cable news network on a political sex scandal,' Grin replied.

'We've noted a significant increase in activity within the Autonomous Region of Inner Mongolia,' Barnett said, 'specifically around the city of Chifeng and along a rather large stretch of the nearby Sino-Mongolian border. I take this to mean that our mutual friends were successful in extracting Bishop Yin from the laogai.'

'That is our sense of the situation as well,' Donoher concurred. 'Nolan's subterfuge was apparently discovered by prison officials, but he and his team managed to escape with Bishop Yin despite this setback.'

'I see.' Barnett paused, carefully considering his next words. 'Cardinal, may I be blunt?'

'Please.'

'A source within the Chinese Foreign Ministry reports that around four in the morning of October twenty-ninth, Beijing received a coded message from its embassy in Rome. The message informed Beijing of Yin's status as an unnamed cardinal and papal candidate, and of a Vatican effort to liberate him. Cardinal, you have a leak.'

Donoher felt his body tighten, a sickening wave of nausea washing over him. He slumped into a chair like a boxer staggered by a series of body blows, trying to regain his senses.

'Somebody ratted out Nolan and Roxanne?' Grin asked.

'Yes,' Barnett replied. 'Our source only had access to the sanitized version of the message that provided no clues as to its provenance. As soon as this information came to light, I felt it important to alert you.'

'Thank you, Jackson,' Donoher said solemnly. 'I assure you we will act on this in order to bring all of our people home safely.'

'A goal we both share. Perhaps we should talk again later today?'

'The conclave reconvenes this afternoon, and I expect there will be a meeting afterward to discuss matters of state.' Donoher checked his watch. 'Will two o'clock, your time, be convenient?'

'Fine. Good day, gentlemen.'

Barnett signed off, and the screen went blank.

'Hellfire and damnation!' Donoher growled. 'A Judas Iscariot in our midst. Only those present in the Sistine Chapel heard the Pope's message. So how in bloody blazes did the son of a – How'd he do it? How did the traitor get word to the Chinese?'

Grin scratched his goatee. 'Let's think about this a second. Of the hundred-odd people who now know our little secret, only you and I have access to the outside world. Everyone else is basically incommunicado, right?'

'That is correct.'

'What about Cardinal Gagliardi? He was at the opening session.'

Donoher shook his head. 'The man has just suffered a massive heart attack.'

'I'll check his hospital phone records anyway, just to make sure. Whipping out my Occam's razor,' Grin continued, 'I see that the rest of the cardinals have neither the means, motive, nor opportunity to betray us. And if they didn't do it, and you and I didn't do it, then either there's a bug in the chapel, or someone else saw what was on the Pope's DVD.'

'The chapel has been swept for bugs, and we have devices installed at each of the windows to interfere with any laser microphones that might be trained on the building from outside.'

'You need to sweep the chapel again, just to make sure,' Grin advised.

'There won't be time before this afternoon's session. If we're still without a new Pope, I'll have it done tonight. But now that I think of it, there is someone outside the conclave who may have had prior knowledge of the Pope's message. As much as it pains me, I think we should have a chat with him.'

36

CHIFENG, CHINA

Peng Shi arrived at Chifeng Prison shortly after sunset. The driver brought the sedan to a stop at what was left of the main gate and submitted their papers for inspection. Peng's eyes lingered on the blackened hulk that sat off to the side and wondered about the men who had been trapped inside as the vehicle burned. His thoughts drifted back to August of last year when he was aboard the destroyer *Hangzhou*. There, he had observed the recovery of a charred space capsule containing the remains of three murdered yuhangyuans – remains that Nolan Kilkenny located for China.

With the visitors cleared for entry, the guard directed Peng's driver to the administration building where they would be met. Metal halide lights bathed the prison grounds and buildings with an artificial glow devoid of the warmer visible wavelengths, causing the red sedan to appear a deep maroon. The placement of the lights around the prison all but eliminated shadows, a security measure that reinforced the unnaturalness of the scene.

The driver guided the sedan into a visitor's parking space in front of the administration building. A uniformed guard and a middle-aged man in a gray suit stood waiting for them by the entry. As Peng got out of the car and collected his briefcase, the man approached him.

'Welcome, Mister Peng. I am Tang, manager of the Chifeng Brickyard.'

'Good evening,' Peng replied. 'Where can I find Mister Liu?'

'Mister Liu was unavoidably detained,' Tang replied. 'He is expected back at any time. You may wait for him in the warden's office.'

'I prefer to make better use of my time. Tell me, Mister Tang, is the officer who received the foreign prisoner last night available? I have some questions for him.'

'Lieutenant Kwan is right here,' Tang replied.

'There was also a report of a guard detailed to observe the executions who survived the attack. Is he also available?'

'Neither man may leave the prison grounds without the permission of Mister Liu.'

'Good. I would like Kwan to escort me to the yard where the executions took place. Have the other guard meet us there.'

'I will see to it.'

'Thank you, Mister Tang. Lieutenant Kwan, take me along the path used by the escaping truck.'

'This way, sir,' Kwan replied.

Through the glare of the prison's lights, Peng found it difficult to see the terrain much beyond the perimeter fence. Last night, those who attacked the prison watched from beyond the halo, exploiting the prison's nocturnal blind spot.

'Have you located the firing positions yet?' Peng asked.

'Yes. We found four used PF-89 launch tubes within two hundred meters of both gates.'

'Serial numbers?'

'Unreadable. The tubes have been sent on to an army lab for further analysis.'

'Describe the foreigner who was brought in last night.'

Kwan collected his thoughts for a moment. 'A little taller than me, about two meters in height, eighty kilos. He had red hair and many freckles on his face and hands. There were deep bruises on his face, neck, and hands, but I've seen men arrive looking worse. He was dressed in a standard prison uniform.'

'Did he speak at all?'

'He made no sound the entire time I was with him.'

'How long was that?'

'Less than ten minutes, just the time required to escort him from the transport to a cell.'

'Was he searched?'

'No, we were ordered not to.'

They rounded the corner of a building and entered an open yard with the motor pool at the far end.

'This is where executions are carried out,' Kwan announced. 'Prisoners are brought out of that door and escorted down here. Once dead, they are usually loaded onto a truck and taken to the crematorium in Chifeng.'

A guard stepped through the door Kwan had pointed

to and walked toward them. After closing the distance, he snapped to attention and saluted the lieutenant.

'At ease,' Kwan said after returning the salute. 'Mister Peng, this is Au-Yang, one of the guards.'

Au-Yang was younger than Kwan, in his late teens or early twenties, with a full, round face and thickset body.

'You were present at the execution this morning, yes?' Peng asked.

'I was part of the detail that brought the foreign prisoner down to the yard.'

'Were you armed?'

'Yes, with a pistol.'

'Then why are you still alive?' Peng asked pointedly.

'Excuse me?' Au-Yang replied, puzzled.

'I understand that anyone in the yard with a weapon was killed.'

'I left the yard after the prisoners were executed. I was not feeling well,' Au-Yang explained, placing a hand on his stomach.

'Your first execution?'

Au-Yang nodded sheepishly.

'Where were the prisoners executed?' Peng asked.

Au-Yang looked at the ground and found a pair of black stains on the gravel. 'Here, and here.'

'And where was the truck parked, the one that fled with the two prisoners?'

Au-Yang pointed to a spot several feet away.

'Did anything unusual happen while you were present?'

'Before he was shot, the old one said something I didn't understand,' Au-Yang replied.

'What did he say?'

'I'm not sure, it wasn't Chinese. I think it was English, but I don't really know.'

'Was he speaking to the foreigner?' Peng asked.

'I don't think so. He couldn't have known the man was there.'

'Why is that?'

'The prisoners were brought out separately, and both wore hoods,' Au-Yang explained. 'They never saw each other.'

'And everyone else who was present was Chinese?'

'Yes.'

Peng tried to imagine the scene and empathized with the young guard. Peng had killed before, but he did so only when necessary and took no joy in it. Capital punishment, he felt, should be reserved for only the most heinous murderers, and he found it troubling when it was applied as punishment for political crimes.

'That's all for now. You may return to your duties.' Peng dismissed Au-Yang, then turned to Kwan. 'Please show me where the prisoners were held.'

'This way,' Kwan replied.

The interior of the prison was eerily quiet. The inmates were locked down, the guards extraordinarily vigilant. Kwan led Peng down long gray corridors, their footsteps echoing off the smooth hard surfaces. They stopped in front of a heavy steel door stenciled with the number 342.

'This cell is where the foreign prisoner was held,' Kwan announced.

'Open it,' Peng commanded.

Kwan radioed the request to the monitoring station and released the door. Peng peered into the dark cell, then stepped inside and shuddered. The cell was cold, as if the thick concrete was siphoning the heat from his body. He sat on the floor, trying to understand the mind of the previous occupant. Even with the door fully open, the cell enveloped him like a tomb. Peng wondered how anyone could retain their sanity locked inside this room for any length of time, and yet Kilkenny had volunteered to do so.

'What are you doing in there?' an irritable voice demanded from the corridor.

Peng turned and saw that Kwan had stepped away from the doorway. The silhouette of a different man filled the opening.

'Thinking,' Peng replied.

'Unless you prefer to remain in there with your thoughts for an extended period of time, I suggest you come out now.'

'Of course,' Peng said.

Peng rose and walked out into the corridor where he met Liu and a pair of guards. The three men looked flushed from exertion. Liu stood slightly taller than Peng and glowered at the younger man.

'This cell and the one that housed Yin Daoming should be searched thoroughly,' Peng suggested.

'For what?'

'Anything that would have allowed the two prisoners to communicate – something very small that could have been smuggled in without arousing Lieutenant Kwan's suspicions. I can think of no other reason Kilkenny would place himself in that cell other than to communicate his intent to Yin. And this morning, Yin certainly knew something was going to happen. His last words were in English – I assume a message to Kilkenny.'

'If a device was smuggled in, wouldn't the foreigner have taken it with him?' Liu asked dismissively.

'Perhaps, but that possibility shouldn't deter us from looking for evidence. Are you not seeking the source of the RPGs?'

'We are, but the priority is the manhunt.'

'Of course,' Peng agreed, 'but in our zeal to recapture Yin, we must not sacrifice our investigation of the broader conspiracy.'

'Close that cell,' Liu ordered Kwan. 'No one is to enter this cell or Yin's until after a forensics team has completed a thorough search. Peng, come with me.'

As the junior man, Peng trailed Liu by a half step, and with a pair of guards in tow, they moved down the corridors in silence. Liu was fuming, though Peng suspected it had more to do with the escape than his brief investigation. When they reached the warden's office, Liu dismissed the guards.

'Report,' Liu demanded of Peng.

'The foreign prisoner and the woman known as Captain Jiao have been identified as Nolan Kilkenny and Roxanne Tao – both of the United States.'

'So the Americans are involved with the Vatican in this?'

'A strong possibility,' Peng replied, 'but the level of that involvement is not clear. Nor is their motive. Of course, Beijing is asking what the Americans could hope to gain from this provocative course of action.'

'Has Beijing moved to enhance border security?' Liu asked.

'Yes. All border crossings are temporarily closed until sufficient forces are in place to process each individual and search every vehicle. Units of the army and air force are patrolling our borders with North Korea, Russia, and Mongolia. Army units have also been stationed at all transportation hubs, and all travelers within the country are required to provide identity papers. Coastal defense is on heightened-alert status and has stepped up patrols in our territorial waters.

'Beijing has also requested assistance from Mongolia in preventing Yin's escape. Photographs of Yin, Tao, and Kilkenny have been delivered to the authorities in Ulaanbaatar, along with a list of their crimes. Our formal request for immediate extradition of these criminals was accompanied by a diplomatic note indicating cooperation in this matter would have a strong bearing on the foreign trade and investment package currently under consideration before the central committee.'

'Effectively closing that avenue of escape,' Liu concluded, pleased.

'The local army unit is working with Chifeng police to cordon off the city,' Peng continued, 'assuming that's where they went after fleeing the prison and that they may still be there.'

'Are they also searching the surrounding country-side and rounding up known and suspected members of Yin's cult?'

'A system of beliefs that survives intact for two millennia and boasts over a billion followers is hardly a cult,' Peng offered. 'But yes, those with ties to the underground church are being located for questioning.'

Liu appeared satisfied with Peng's report. 'I was informed you are familiar with Kilkenny and Tao.'

Peng nodded. 'That is why I was sent to assist you.'

'Tell me about them.'

'Until a few years ago, Kilkenny was a junior officer in the American Navy's special forces. He is presently a businessman involved in technology research and investment. He is also connected to the CIA, but tangentially and not in the agency's direct employ. He was married briefly to an astronaut who died this past August. I met him during the previous summer, when he was investigating the incident involving their space shuttle. In my opinion, Nolan Kilkenny is an honorable man.'

'Honorable men do not break criminals out of prison.'

'I suspect he does not view Yin as a criminal – they share the same faith.'

'And Tao?'

'She is a spy,' Peng said matter-of-factly. 'Much of her background is unclear, but she now runs an investment company with ties to both Kilkenny and the CIA. Several years ago, under another identity, she operated a widespread espionage network in China. That network was dismantled, but she eluded capture and the Sixth Bureau lost track of her. I uncovered her during my surveillance of Kilkenny. If possible, Beijing would like Tao taken alive.'

'And the others?' Liu asked.

'Their fates are left to your discretion.'

37

CHIFENG, CHINA

After Yin's mass, the Night Stalkers completed flight prep on the BATs while the team members still clad in civilian clothes changed for the trip across the border. The children, much to Kilkenny's discomfort, huddled around the doorway of the yurt, peeking in with rapt fascination as he changed. He further entertained them by demonstrating the chameleonlike characteristics of his SEALskin suit, changing from a solid dark gray to camouflage stripes.

'Having fun?' Tao asked, drawn into the yurt by the children's laughter.

'They are. At least my striptease was only PG, or I would have had to post a guard.'

'Or charge admission.'

'I can't think of anyone who would pay to see me naked. How's your suit?'

Tao did a slow spin, allowing Kilkenny to view her at all angles. The sleek nanotech fabric wrapped her lithe curves like a second skin.

'It's a good fit,' Tao replied.

'That's an understatement. I bet the tailor who put that outfit together never worked with a set of measurements quite like yours. Slip on a pair of stiletto heels and you'd be set for a late night of after-hours clubbing.'

Tao glowered at Kilkenny. 'You first.'

Bishop Yin appeared in the doorway looking puzzled, his suit bunched up in places around his light frame and Ke Li's cross dangling from his neck.

'Have I put on this uniform correctly?' Yin asked.

'There's really only one way to wear it,' Kilkenny said as he looked over Yin's suit. 'Unfortunately, it's not a one-size-fits-all, and I guessed a little too big for you. I apologize if it's uncomfortable, but it will keep you warm.'

'Then I will be fine.'

'We'll find you a good tailor once we're out of China,' Kilkenny promised. 'Your cross might be a problem when we're airborne. Would you like me to stow it for you?'

Yin placed a protective hand over the symbol of his faith. 'No, I wish to wear it.'

'Then let's get it inside your suit so it won't bat around in the wind.'

Tao loosened Yin's collar and carefully slipped the cross inside. It barely telegraphed through the loose fabric covering Yin's torso. Tao placed a reassuring hand on his chest over the shrouded symbol.

'That should protect it,' Tao said.

The Bishop folded his hands over hers, 'And *it* will protect *us*, my child.'

Outside, they heard the sound of hoofbeats racing toward the encampment.

'Stay with him,' Kilkenny said as he unholstered his pistol and slipped through the doorway.

The hoofbeats stopped abruptly, replaced with orders shouted harshly in Chinese. The horses whinnied and snorted, sounding winded from the ride. In the darkness beyond the halo of campfire light, Kilkenny saw movement in the shadows. The forms of two men with their arms clasped behind their heads grew more distinct. They were Asians and dressed in civilian clothing. Gates and four warriors followed closely behind, weapons trained on the unexpected arrivals.

Recognizing the two men, the patriarch of the clan rushed toward them, his hands waving frantically in the air.

'You catching any of that?' Kilkenny called out.

'The head man just vouched for these guys,' Chow answered. 'That good enough for us?'

Kilkenny holstered his pistol. 'Yeah, cut 'em loose.'

Weapons were lowered, and Chow informed the men of their release. The patriarch escorted them to the fire and ordered others to fetch water for the riders. Both men were caked in dust from a hard ride, their horses frothy around the muzzle. The men brightened when Yin and Tao emerged from the yurt. After they had drunk their fill, the patriarch questioned them. The exchange flowed quickly, with the men talking rapidly.

'What are they saying?' Kilkenny asked Tao softly.

'Apparently we got out of Chifeng just in time. The whole city is locked down – no one going in or out. The local police with army backup are running house-to-house searches. Phones, TV, radio – all shut down.

Curfews. They've imposed martial law as part of their effort to apprehend a group of very dangerous criminals who escaped from the prison.'

'That would be us,' Kilkenny said.

'Before the lines were cut,' Tao continued, 'they received word that all border crossings are closed. Also, you and I and the Bishop are the latest additions to Mongolia's Most Wanted.'

'Would they really arrest us?' Kilkenny asked.

'If the Chinese asked them to, yes,' Tao replied. 'When you're landlocked between two very powerful neighbors, you learn to get along.'

'Is there a problem?' Yin asked.

'Yes,' Tao replied. 'We planned to go north and take you out through Mongolia, but that way is now closed to us.'

'Which means we go to Plan B,' Kilkenny added.

'Plan B?' Yin questioned, unfamiliar with the phrase.

'Our second choice,' Kilkenny explained. 'It's a much longer flight, but it should still work.'

'A *longer* flight,' Yin repeated, a childlike twinkle in his eyes. 'Having never flown before, I think I would like that.'

'Then I hope you find our BATs comfortable, because we'll be spending a few nights in them.'

Tao motioned for Kilkenny to quiet down as she tried to glean more news from the riders. The patriarch nodded his head gravely and looked at Kilkenny and Yin.

'What is it?' Kilkenny asked.

'Helicopter searches. They're looking for camps like this one, any place where we could have found refuge. And they're arresting suspected Roman Catholics.'

'Then we're out of here,' Kilkenny decided. He looked at Gates and the team. 'Time to saddle up. We need to put some distance between these kind folks and ourselves. Roxanne, please express our sincere thanks to our host and to these brave gentlemen for this information. They may have just saved Bishop Yin's life.'

'Permit me,' Yin said.

Starting with the patriarch, Yin bowed deeply to each of the men and offered what Kilkenny could only imagine was a glowing tribute at the end of which he blessed them, then all who dwelled in the house of their host.

'I don't know what he just said,' Kilkenny whispered to Tao, 'but clearly the man can work a room.'

'You have no idea.' She also was moved by Yin's eloquence.

Kilkenny showed Yin how to don the balaclava and adjust his helmet. Tao slipped into the rear seat of the BAT piloted by Han and held her hand out for Yin. As the Bishop carefully climbed aboard, Kilkenny took the co-pilot's seat.

'Team Comms on,' Kilkenny said clearly, activating the short-range receivers in the rest of the teams' helmets. 'Listen up, people. Our Mongolian egress is a no-go, so we are switching to Flight Plan Marco Polo.'

One after another, the three Night Stalkers confirmed Plan Marco Polo and tried to load the coordinates into their navigation computers.

'Uh, Nolan?' Han called out. 'Our NAVCOM is negative on Plan Marco Polo.'

'That's because we're going to make it up as we go along. I have a few tentative waypoints roughed in that

I'll upload to you once we're airborne. For now, just head west.'

'Why do you call your plan Marco Polo?' Yin asked.

'He was the most famous Westerner to travel the Silk Road. Since he successfully returned to Italy from China, I find him inspirational.'

As Kilkenny spoke, the pilots warmed up the engines and completed their preflight checks.

'Those who traveled the Silk Road did so mostly by day,' Yin offered, 'but I recall one group who made the journey west traveling only at night. They were guided by a star.'

Kilkenny laughed. 'Then you will be very pleased to know that we will be guided by a constellation of twenty-four stars. They're not as bright as the one that guided the magi, but ours are accurate to within a few centimeters.'

'Twenty-four is eight threes – a very lucky number.'

'I can take a hint. People, Plan Marco Polo is now Plan Magi.'

One by one, the three BATs lifted off and quickly gained speed.

Yin craned his head back, watching the nomad's camp disappear behind them. Tao noticed that his hand pressed tightly to his chest.

'Are you all right?'

'I am fine,' Yin replied.

'Terry,' Kilkenny said to the pilot, 'once things settle down, I'd like to get a little time behind the stick and brush up my piloting skills. We have a lot of flying ahead of us.'

'When we're over a nice flat stretch of nothing, I'll run you through a refresher course.'

After flying several hours under a clear, moonless sky, Kilkenny watched the grasslands gradually succumb to the Gobi Desert. He was piloting the aircraft, and behind him Tao slept and Yin stared out with rapt fascination at the stars. Han busied himself with checking various systems while keeping an eye on Kilkenny to verify that he was on course to the next waypoint.

'Anybody out there sniffing around for us?' Kilkenny asked.

'No, but when my kids are this quiet, I get nervous,' Han replied. 'You got any?'

'Any what?'

'Children. I have two boys and a girl – all under six. My house is a zoo. Those kids back there really latched onto you, so I figured you must have some of your own.'

Kilkenny thought for a moment before replying. 'My son was to be born on the first of November. He died with my wife in August.'

'I'm sorry,' Han said empathetically, imagining Kilkenny's loss.

Kilkenny shrugged. 'Look, I'm going to let Rome know what we're up to. If you need me, just send a ping or rap on the side of my helmet.'

'Roger that,' Han replied meekly.

'Comms off,' Kilkenny said, disconnecting his link to the rest of his team. 'Satellite uplink on.'

Yin turned his attention from the stars to the man seated in front of him and prayed for his rescuer.

38

VATICAN CITY

SETTING SON SEVEN SAMURAI

What are you trying to tell me? Grin stared at the four cryptic words he had written in neat block letters across the top line of the legal pad.

Kilkenny's latest message departed from the *Lord of the Rings* theme of the first two. This in itself told Grin something had happened – some event that forced his friend to follow a different storyline from the one he envisioned. At this point in Kilkenny's plan, the extraction team would have waited until dark before flying north across the Sino-Mongolian border. Under their guise as tourists, they would then depart from Ulaanbaatar for Rome via Germany.

The magnetic lock securing the workroom door buzzed loudly as it released, emitting a discordant note amid the middle movement of Mozart's 'Violin Concerto No. 3 in G.'

'No rock 'n' roll tonight?' Donoher asked.

'Wolfgang Amadeus is better for solving puzzles.'

'Puzzles? A crossword or that infernal sudoku?' Donoher asked as he sat down by the workstation.

Grin handed over the legal pad. 'A message from Nolan. I know I should get this, but for the moment it's eluding me.'

'That's because you're exhausted.'

'Maybe, but I'm not on the run with half the Chinese military after me. I promise to get a solid eight in the sack right after our team gets the hell out of China.'

'I share your sentiments.' Donoher shrugged and placed the pad on the desktop. 'Sadly, I can't make heads or tails of this message either.'

As the digital clock display on Grin's largest monitor reached 8:00 p.m., the screen cleared and filled with the image of Jackson Barnett seated in his office at the CIA's Langley campus.

'Good evening, gentlemen,' Barnett said. 'I see from the news that black smoke has once again emerged from the chimney of the Sistine Chapel.'

'Yes,' Donoher replied, 'and I apologize in advance, but I am not permitted to discuss the election.'

'No offense taken. Regarding our friends in the Far East, I have a great deal to report.' Barnett flipped open a folder. 'All crossings along China's borders with Russia and Mongolia are closed. The normal complement of border guards has been augmented with PLA troops, and army helicopter units are out patrolling over three thousand miles of border, including the stretch China shares with North Korea.' Barnett glanced up from his notes. 'The last I heard, the Vatican's relations with Pyongyang were as frosty as our own.'

'A move in that direction would be out of the frying pan and into the fire,' Donoher concurred.

'The size of the troop movements we're seeing has more than piqued the interest of the Russians,' Barnett continued. 'They've placed their own forces on an elevated-alert status. The Chinese are being typically closemouthed about what they're doing, and the Russians, being Russians, are suspicious.

'The city of Chifeng is under martial law, and PLA forces are visible in significant numbers at every transportation center in the country. The Chinese Navy is also making its presence known in the Yellow Sea and the Formosa Strait, countering any attempt to fly over water to South Korea or Taiwan. Antisubmarine warfare vessels have also been deployed, presumably against a submarine extraction.'

'I wasn't aware the Vatican possessed a submarine,' Grin offered.

Ignoring the comment, Barnett pulled a page from his file and placed it on a document reader just off camera. The image on the screen immediately split into two windows, with Barnett on the right and a facsimile of a printed flier on the left. Three photographs ran down the side of the flier – prison shots of Yin and Kilkenny and a grainy image of Tao in uniform. Two blocks of text accompanied each image, one in Cyrillic and the other in Mongolian.

'This information has been issued to all law enforcement and border personnel in Mongolia – the Bishop and our associates have been accused of a litany of offenses. As Mongolia is quite interested in fostering good relations with its neighbor to the south, the Chinese have effectively cut off this avenue of escape. It will also be only a matter of time before the authorities in Ulaanbaatar generate a match for Nolan from his tourist visa, albeit under a false identity. The question is whether they will choose to share this information with the Chinese.'

'Why is that?' Grin asked.

'Embarrassment,' Donoher answered.

'By now, the Chinese have combed their database of foreign visitors and come up empty, which means Nolan entered their country illegally,' Barnett continued. 'In confirming that he was in Mongolia just days before appearing at Chifeng Prison, the Mongolians would be conceding he crossed their border into China.'

'So they'll get with the program and try to broom that inconvenient detail under the rug,' Grin said.

'I'm certain the entry paperwork for Nolan and his team has already disappeared,' Barnett agreed.

Grin skimmed the notes on his legal pad. 'So Mongolia is out. Same with Russia and North Korea, and I'm not sure Nolan would risk flying low over large expanses of open water.'

'What are you getting at?' Barnett asked.

'Nolan's last message,' Grin replied. 'He changed the reference he was using, which means his plans have changed. The next step was to fly north into Mongolia. If north is out, he has to go somewhere else.'

'But where?' Donoher asked. 'You've already eliminated north and east, and south would be equally dangerous flying over the densely populated regions of China to where? Vietnam, Laos, or Burma.'

'Oh, that is *so* bad.' Grin groaned. 'They're heading west.'

'Are you certain?' Barnett asked.

'Nolan wrote it down twice, just to make sure I got it. He threw me with the *Seven Samurai* reference because I knew there was no way they would try to fly all the way to Japan. But his reference to the "son" of the *Seven Samurai* is a different story. The original film has been rehashed a dozen different ways, most of which I own, including the animated film *A Bug's Life*. One of the best reworkings of Kurosawa's masterpiece is *The Magnificent Seven* – and the setting for this particular son of the *Seven Samurai* is the Old West. And in case I missed it the first time around, Nolan used the words "setting son", and for "son" read our local star and not a male offspring.'

'The sun sets in the west,' Donoher said, paraphrasing the now obvious.

'Considering their options, a westerly route would take them over the least populated regions of China,' Barnett said. 'The question remains is where they intend to cross.'

'I'm sure Nolan will let us know as soon as he figures it out,' Grin replied.

'Doubtless,' Barnett agreed. 'What about the leak? Have you made any progress?'

'Possibly,' Donoher replied. 'I hope to know more tonight.'

'Well, that's all I have, so don't let me keep you.'

'Thank you for all your help,' Donoher said.

'We both have a vested interest here,' Barnett replied, before terminating the link.

'So, what's happening tonight?' Grin asked.

'Many things,' Donoher replied, 'but first we must speak with an old and trusted friend.'

39

Donoher and Grin found Archbishop Sikora in the Redemptoris Mater Chapel. He was seated near the late Pope's empty chair, deep in thought. A digital video camera mounted on a tripod stood aimed at the papal throne.

'Archbishop, thank you for meeting with us,' Donoher said warmly, announcing their arrival.

Sikora rose and moved to greet them. It seemed to Donoher that the man had aged since Pope Leo's death.

'Your Eminence,' Sikora said respectfully.

'This is my associate, Mister Grinelli.'

Grin extended his hand, 'Your Excellency.'

'A pleasure.' Sikora took Grin's hand in both of his own and greeted him warmly.

'I've asked Mister Grinelli to join us as he is assisting me in the matter I wish to discuss. I see you've brought the camera.'

'Yes, though I was curious why. Is our conversation to be recorded?'

'No,' Donoher replied. 'We simply wished to see the device.'

Grin stepped to the camera and began studying it. Donoher walked slowly past the Pope's empty chair, recalling the last time he was here. He motioned for Sikora to resume his place and moved a chair in front of him.

'How are you, Michal?' Donoher asked.

'All right, I suppose. I am greatly relieved the Pope's suffering is finally over. The past few years were most difficult for His Holiness.'

'For someone who was so physically active, his illness was particularly cruel,' Donoher agreed. 'Thankfully it spared his mind. But what of you? Any thoughts on what you will do?'

'I have no idea. I served His Holiness ever since I was newly ordained and he was the Archbishop of Krakow.'

'More than once he admitted to me he would have been lost without you,' Donoher offered kindly.

'He was a man of vision,' Sikora demurred. 'I just kept track of the details. And now I am just one of those details, something to be attended to once the new Pope is elected. What does one do with an old Archbishop with no diocese?'

'I have always fantasized about finding a small parish somewhere in need of a priest – an old country church where you know the entire congregation by name. A small flock to tend in my waning years.'

'That would be nice,' Sikora agreed.

'All will be revealed in God's time, but now to the matter at hand. The disk you gave me before the opening session – it was made with this camera?'

'Yes.'

'And you were present when His Holiness recorded his message to the cardinals?'

'No, the Pope was alone.'

'Alone? Who operated the camera?'

'His Holiness, with a remote control.'

Donoher glanced at Grin.

'Remotes are standard equipment,' Grin confirmed. 'It lets dad be in the picture with the rest of the family.'

'The Pope's instructions to me were quite clear. His message was for the cardinal electors only. I set up the camera, made certain everything was ready, and handed the Pope the remote control. Then I left. He used this camera many times to send birthday messages and such to close friends and relatives. He knew how to switch it on and off. He called for me when he was finished.'

'And what happened then?'

'I removed the disk from the camera and placed it in a plastic case.'

'There was only one clip on the disk you gave me,' Donoher said. 'Me, I require several attempts to record even a brief message on my answering machine. Did you edit the footage the Pope recorded, trimming it down to show only the best version?'

'No, the disk I gave you was the one from the camera. His Holiness rarely required more than one attempt to deliver a message.'

Donoher nodded, conceding that fact.

'What is the reason for these questions?' Sikora asked. 'Was there a problem with the disk?'

'Someone revealed the contents of the Pope's

message to an audience His Holiness did not intend,' Donoher replied. 'What happened after the disk was recorded?'

'The Pope signed an amendment to the Apostolic Constitution in the presence of Cardinal Cain and me. The document and the disk were placed in a large envelope, which the Pope then sealed.'

'And all this took place here, in the chapel?'

'Yes. Cardinal Cain was with me outside the chapel when the Pope recorded his message. After the Pope sealed the envelope, Cardinal Cain and I placed it in a secure box at the IOR.'

The Istituto per le opere di Religione – the Institute for Religious Works more commonly known as the Vatican Bank – held as many secrets in its vaults as notes and securities. As the head of Vatican Intelligence, Donoher knew both were valuable forms of currency. That the Pope would place this secret in one of the bank's vaults made perfect sense.

'What were the Pope's instructions regarding the envelope?' Donoher asked.

'The IOR could release it only to the Pope himself, or, in the event of his death, to the Cardinal Camerlengo on the morning of the opening session of the conclave. My instructions were to bring you to the IOR to retrieve it. If I was unable to perform this duty, the IOR was to notify the Cardinal Camerlengo directly.'

Sikora spoke easily, without a hint of nervousness. Donoher also noted that he maintained eye contact as he spoke.

'So, from the time you removed the disk from the

camera until you placed it in the vault,' Donoher posited, 'the disk was never out of your sight?'

'That is correct,' Sikora replied.

'And you were never alone with it?'

'Never. Cardinal Cain and I delivered the envelope to the IOR together.'

'Do you have any questions for the Archbishop?' Donoher asked Grin.

'Just one. Did you program the camcorder to put a time and date stamp on the DVD?'

'I always do that, for posterity.'

Grin nodded to Donoher that he was finished.

'Thank you, Michal. That's all the questions we have for now.'

Donoher led Grin out of the Apostolic Palace and along the broad path that ran behind the basilica. Above them, the basilica's dome glowed in an aura of artificial light that obscured the stars above.

'What do you think?' Donoher asked.

'He was being straight with you. You going to double-check his story with Cardinal Cain?'

'Of course, but I'm sure I'll get the same answers.'

'Did you think Sikora was the leak?'

'Not really. I thought perhaps there was a time when the disk was left unattended, or maybe the files were copied onto a hard drive. I hoped we'd find an opportunity when someone could have seen the Pope's message beforehand.'

'In the legal thrillers my lady likes to read, it's called the chain of evidence, and the chain here looks pretty solid. I suppose Sikora and Cain could have sneaked a look at the disk, but that depends on how much time elapsed between the recording of the DVD and when they dropped it off at the bank. The IOR should have a record of the deposit, and the camera burned the file data onto the disk.'

'Even if opportunity and curiosity somehow led a pair of churchmen to conspiracy, you're forgetting the seal. If they opened the envelope, they would have broken the Pope's seal. Closing it again would have required a new seal, and to make one of those you need the Pope's ring.'

'Did he ever take it off?'

'Not to the best of my knowledge,' Donoher said. 'And when I received the envelope at the IOR, the seal was still intact.'

'Barnett told us Beijing received word from their embassy in Rome around four in the morning – eight o'clock last night, our time. If Sikora and Cain are the leak, they sat on what they knew until after the conclave started, which begs the question, Why? If it's not them, we're back to either someone eavesdropping on the Sistine Chapel or a cardinal has broken his oath.'

'I don't find either possibility to my liking,' Donoher admitted, 'but I pray it's not the latter.'

40

CHIFENG, CHINA

October 30

Ke Wen-An could not feel his arms. The thin steel cable from which he was suspended dug deeply into his wrists like a dull saw blade. At first, the pain was excruciating, but numbness brought some relief. Blood streaked down his arms from where the skin had given way, the deep red trails dry and hard in the hours since the wounds were fresh.

The ordeal began late the previous day, when the police arrested Ke, along with his wife, his father, and his young daughter. Initially, they thought they were just one of the many families of Roman Catholics detained by authorities for questioning, but a unique interest in them became quickly apparent. Over the past twelve hours, the gray concrete interrogation room became hell for Ke and his family.

Ke's feet dangled just inches from the floor, and he wondered if the weights strapped to his ankles would eventually lengthen his body enough to gain even a meager foothold. The floor was close enough to tempt him with the possibility of a respite, but the price to end his anguish was still too high.

Blood and saliva trickled down Ke's throat, triggering a spasm of coughing. His body reflexively fought to prevent fluid from collecting in his lungs to avoid drowning, but with each breath his exhalations weakened. Carbon dioxide, the waste product of normal breathing, was slowly building to toxic levels inside Ke's body.

And he was naked. Not that Ke cared at all about his state of undress – agony has a way of rendering the superficial concerns of modesty irrelevant. Bruises mottled his flesh – whorls of blues, blacks, and sickly yellows – a visual record of abuse by clubs, batons, whips, and fists. Burns scarred his flesh where cigarettes had been extinguished and firecrackers detonated. Blackened stubble was all that remained of the tufts of hair that grew in various places on his body. And when the fire beneath his arms failed to elicit the information his interrogators demanded, an accelerant was applied to his genitalia to assure adequate fuel for the flame.

As a physician, Ke understood the trauma his body was enduring. Injury and reaction. Cause and effect. And little by little his body's defenses were failing, unable to keep up with the increasing scope of damage. He was past the tipping point and knew with all certainty that he would never recover. Not that he wanted to.

Ke was not tortured alone. The body of his wife lay atop a large table in front of him. In between his own beatings, he was forced to watch as the woman he loved and the mother of his child was tormented, her body defiled with vicious depravity. A succession of guards raped and sodomized Gan Yueying, splaying her nude body across the table for their warped, deviant pleasure. The last wrapped his meaty hands around her delicate throat and nearly strangled her to death as he climaxed.

The worst torture came from the man who led the interrogation. When his wife's ravaged and beaten body no longer amused even the most cruelly imaginative of the guards, Liu questioned Ke again. With each refusal to answer, Liu severed another piece of Gan's body.

Gan was never allowed to lose consciousness for long, and once she revived, Liu would cut her again. Digits littered the floor amid pools of blood, vomit, and waste. The skill with which he amputated her breasts with a balisong knife bespoke experience unimaginable. Gan screamed in agony as she was dismembered, but between her wails she locked eyes with her beloved husband and urged Ke to remain strong, to keep their faith.

Ke never imagined he would pray for his wife's death, but when it finally came, he wept tears of joy. Her suffering was over. On the journey to heaven, he would not be far behind.

Liu leaned against the wall as the police doctor vainly tried to revive Gan, but finally the doctor shook his head and retreated from the interrogation room. Ke's father and six-year-old daughter wept in the corner of the room, the old man trying to console the horrified child, unwilling witnesses to the barbarity inflicted upon the couple.

'One less whore,' Liu sneered.

The butchered remains of Gan Yueying barely looked human. Liu moved close to the old man and his grand-daughter like a stalking animal approaching prey. He towered over Ke Tai-De, showing nothing but contempt for the old man and his family of cultists.

'It's not too late to save your son,' Liu said.

'He, and my family, are already saved,' Ke Tai-De replied stoically. 'Nothing you do changes that.'

'We'll see, old man,' Liu replied.

Liu slowly walked around the table to where Ke Wen-An hung from a metal pipe in the ceiling. With each feeble breath, the physician swung lightly, and the cable around his wrists dug in a little deeper.

'So, doctor, as a *Catholic*,' Liu hissed the word, 'I'm certain the irony of your situation isn't lost on you. Much of what you are experiencing, medically speaking, is what that criminal you worship felt after the Romans nailed him to a tree. Did you know that it normally took days for a crucified man to die? The Romans often broke the prisoner's legs to hasten death by suffocation or shock-induced heart attack. Do you think, doctor, that such an injury would have a similar effect on you?'

Liu pulled out his pistol and gripped it by the barrel. Crouching down, he grabbed one of Ke's ankles, straightened the leg, and swung the pistol like a hammer onto the kneecap. The triangular bone cracked, and an electric jolt of pain rushed through Ke's nervous system. Pleased with the effect, Liu swung again and shattered the other knee. Ke's head slumped, and Liu sprang to his feet.

'Don't pass out on me now, doctor.'

Ke's eyes fluttered, his mind hovering on the border of consciousness.

'Tell me what you know of Yin, and I will end your pain.'

Ke shook his head, conscious enough to reject the worthless offer.

Liu moved to Ke, his mouth near the dying man's ear. 'If you don't speak, your daughter will be next.'

With every last bit of strength that remained, Ke raised his head and groaned, 'Long live Jesus Christ.'

Infuriated, Liu drove the barrel of his pistol under Ke's chin and squeezed the trigger. The nine-millimeter round ripped through Ke's head, erupting from the top in a violent spray of blood, bone, and gore. Ke's head drooped forward, much of the crown missing.

As the echo of the gunshot died down, someone knocked at the door.

'What?' Liu shouted angrily.

A uniformed police officer opened the door. Peng stood in the corridor behind him with several more officers.

'Is everything all right?' the officer asked.

'Everything is *fine*,' Liu snapped grimly.

Liu holstered his pistol and wiped a speck of gray matter from his cheek, flicking it onto the floor. Peng peered into the interrogation room and saw the bodies.

'How long has he been at it?' Peng asked the officer softly.

'Twelve hours. Since they were first brought in.'

If Liu heard Peng's question, he ignored it. Instead,

he pushed Gan's mutilated remains off the table and onto the floor at the feet of her daughter and father-in-law. Peng leaned into the interrogation room and was immediately struck by both the horror and the witch's brew of stench that lingered inside.

'I have some information,' Peng said, trying to stifle the rising contents of his stomach. 'Perhaps this would be a good time for a break.'

Breathing heavily, Liu nodded. 'Think about what I want to know, old man. When I come back, your granddaughter is next.'

Liu exited, leaving Ke Tai-De and his granddaughter alone with the mauled, desecrated bodies of their loved ones.

One of the officers handed Liu a small towel, which he used to wipe blood, sweat, and bits of tissue from his face and hands.

'Report,' Liu commanded.

'The northern border is secure, and there has been no sign of any attempt to cross it. Troops are in position at critical points, and aerial reconnaissance is ongoing. I've received word from our people in Ulaanbaatar confirming that Kilkenny and another American entered Mongolia on a flight from Germany. Kilkenny was traveling with false papers, and we assume the same of his companion.'

'What about the spy?'

'Twelve days ago, Roxanne Tao flew to Shanghai from the United States and entered the country with a forged tourist visa. From there, she traveled to Beijing. She was not seen again until the twenty-eighth at the prison.'

'Walked right through the front door,' Liu spat angrily.

'Her papers were quite good, and she has altered her appearance.'

'They still *missed* her.'

Liu looked haggard and agitated, the skin around his eyes dark and swollen.

'Have you gotten any rest since I've been gone?' Peng asked.

'I'll rest after Yin and these foreign terrorists are dead.'

'Have you learned anything from your interrogations?' Peng asked.

'Not much,' Liu admitted, 'but everything points to the old man – he's an important figure in the illegal church in Chifeng. We know there was local support for the raid, so he must have been involved. Breaking him is the key to unraveling this conspiracy.'

'And the rest of the family?'

'All are members of the foreign cult, which is crime enough. I'm using them to break the old man down.'

'But they are dead, and he has told you nothing.'

'There's still the granddaughter. Now that he knows how far I will go, I'm certain he will talk to save her.'

'I am not so sure. The history of this religion is filled with revered martyrs, starting with the one they believe was the son of their god.'

'Lunatics!' Liu spat. 'He *will* tell me what I want to know.'

'Assuming that he knows anything himself.'

'He knows.' Liu paused briefly. 'Anything else?'

'Sweeps continue in the outlying areas around Chifeng, and troops are questioning herdsmen. We have found no sign of the raiding party,' Peng said.

'All the more reason for me to continue with the old man.'

'You are exhausted. Would it not be wise to rest and let another interrogator continue? Perhaps a change of tactic to disorient the man.'

Liu waved his hand dismissively. 'Anything else?'

'No,' Peng replied.

'Perhaps you would like to assist me with the child?' Liu said, almost taunting the younger man.

Peng felt his stomach rising once again at the thought of torturing a young child. 'I think it best that I continue following other avenues of our investigation.'

'Very well. Report back in a few hours.'

Peng bowed and departed. As he walked away, he wondered what hold the Catholic religion had on the Ke family. What was it about their faith that allowed them to die for a man they could not have known, to sacrifice themselves as a parent would to protect a child? At his sides, Peng felt his hands trembling.

41

INNER MONGOLIA

Yin awoke from a restless sleep. It was midday, and he lay beneath the wing of the BAT that had carried him more than seven hundred miles west from Chifeng. They had landed before dawn beside an escarpment that promised to cast a deep shadow over their hiding place. Once on the ground, the soldiers had quickly draped camouflage netting over the three aircraft, concealing them from all but the most intense scrutiny. Kilkenny and the pilots slept nearby, exhausted by one long flight and restoring themselves for another. The other soldiers, some unseen yet he knew they were there, protected the hidden camp from discovery. Tao saw Yin sitting up and approached him.

'Good afternoon,' Tao said softly. 'Did you sleep well?'

'My sleep was troubled.'

'That's not surprising. You've been through quite an ordeal.'

'Perhaps that's it,' Yin said.

Tao noticed Yin's right hand was rubbing a spot near the center of his chest.

'Are you feeling all right?' she asked.

'My heart is heavy. I feel something is wrong.'

'Don't move,' Tao said sternly. 'I'll get some help.'

Tao returned a moment later with Jing, the team's medic, and Kilkenny.

'Can you describe how you're feeling?' Jing asked as he opened his med kit.

'A heaviness here,' Yin replied, indicating his chest.

'Do you have pain or numbness anywhere?'

'No.'

'Any dizziness?' Jing asked.

'No.'

'I need to examine you, sir. Roxanne, help me undo the top of his suit.'

Jing and Tao carefully peeled down the upper half of Yin's SEAL-skin suit to reveal a lean torso of skin and bones. Ke Li's cross hung from a cord around Yin's neck, the symbol of his faith close to his heart.

'That will need to come off too,' Jing said, indicating the cross.

Yin nodded and gently lifted the cord over his head. He kissed the hand-carved cross reverently.

'Please, hold this for me,' Yin said, handing the cross to Kilkenny.

Kilkenny took Yin's cross and stepped back, out of the way. Jing checked Yin's heart rate and blood pressure, listened to his lungs, then connected the Bishop to a small electronic monitor.

'You can pull your top back up if you're cold,' Jing told Yin, 'but try not to loosen the contacts on your chest. I want this to run for a while. It should give us some idea of how you're doing.'

'Thank you for your concern,' Yin replied.

As Tao helped Yin with his clothing, Kilkenny motioned Jing over to talk.

'What do you think?' Kilkenny asked.

'Everything seems okay. He's got a strong heart and no problem with his lungs.'

'So he's not having a heart attack?'

'Not that I can tell. Other than the heaviness in his chest, he has none of the classic signs. I'll know more after we've run the monitor a while, but right now, I'm leaning more toward stress. Just look at everything he's been through in the past twenty-four hours.'

'Try the past thirty years. Thanks, Chuck. Let me know when you're done with him.'

As Jing returned to his patient, Gates joined Kilkenny.

'He okay?'

'We'll know more in a bit,' Kilkenny replied, 'but Chuck's thinking at the moment is that it's stress.'

'We all got a touch of that.'

'I just hope in his case it's not enough to kill him. After all that man has been through, I'd hate to think he died because we broke him out of jail.'

After Jing completed his examination, Kilkenny rejoined the Bishop. Yin was fully dressed and eating a meal of light rations.

'I've brought you your cross,' Kilkenny said.

'Thank you.'

In donning his pectoral cross, Yin repeated the simple ritual of reverence.

'How are you feeling, Your Excellency?' Kilkenny inquired.

'Better. And how are you feeling?'

'I'm fine,' Kilkenny replied, surprised by the question. 'Why do you ask?'

'The burden you carry is heavy. Such weight can wear upon a man.'

'I've heard it often said that the Lord doesn't give us burdens greater than what we can carry.'

'An interesting thought. Do you believe it is true?'

'I don't know, but if it is, there are times I think He has greatly overestimated me.'

'Is this one of those times?' Yin asked.

Kilkenny considered the question for a moment and wondered if Yin's symptoms might be the result of fear of being recaptured.

'I'll get you out of China,' Kilkenny vowed.

Han approached Kilkenny and Yin; the two other pilots sat in the front of BAT-2.

'Sorry to interrupt,' Han said, 'but it's time for our pre-flight meeting.'

'If you'll excuse me, Your Excellency.'

Yin bowed and Kilkenny departed with Han. The Bishop carefully watched the man who engineered his rescue, and he contemplated the immense burden on Kilkenny's shoulders.

42

VATICAN CITY

'Don't you make a fine-looking priest,' Donoher declared, finding some amusement in Grin's obvious discomfort.

It was near dawn, and Grin stood in the foyer of the Vatican Mosaic Studio dressed in a black cassock with a traditional Roman collar encircling his neck. The long sleeves covered his whimsical tattoo, and only the tips of his leopard-print Chuck Taylor canvas basketball sneakers peeked out beneath the cassock's hem.

'I'm sure I do, but either the Church's manpower shortage is worse than reported, or you really need to upgrade your background-check procedures.'

'As I recall, Saint Ignatius Loyola lived a very *full* life before changing his ways,' Donoher said as he eyed the fit of Grin's cassock. 'Regardless, you are more believable as a priest than a Swiss Guard.'

'Dressed like this – I'll bet God's going to zap me as soon as he has a clear shot.'

'My personal view of God is that of a just being who combines infinite forgiveness with a wry sense of humor.'

'If this getup helps our cause, I can put up with a few guffaws from the Almighty. So, the chapel is clean?'

'As the proverbial whistle,' Donoher replied, disappointed. 'No sign of any clandestine devices was found inside or out.'

'Which shifts suspicion onto the cardinals. It's still possible we're up against a new technology.'

Donoher nodded. 'Yes, but as your hero Occam would suggest, we must look to the more likely cause first, no matter how unpalatable it may be. While the conclave is in session, I expect you and the sweeper teams to leave no stone unturned.'

'You realize this search will take time. What happens if a new Pope is elected before we have our answers?' Grin asked.

'Then we may never know if a cardinal has indeed betrayed the Church.'

After the cardinal electors vacated their rooms, Grin met in the lobby of Domus Sanctae Marthae with several plainclothes members of the Swiss Guard and the two trustworthy technicians specified in the Apostolic Constitution to assist the Camerlengo in ensuring the secrecy and security of the conclave. The two technicians, Aldo and Tommaso, looked tired from a long night of sweeping the Sistine Chapel and adjacent rooms in the palace for electronic listening devices. The guards detailed to the search snapped to attention as Grin approached.

'That's okay, guys,' he told them. 'Who's in charge?'

A lean young man with chiseled features and hair the

color of straw stepped forward. 'I am. Lieutenant Tag Jordan.'

'Okay, Tag, please tell your men to take it down a notch. I appreciate your professionalism and all, but it's not required.'

'But it is,' Jordan countered. 'You represent the Camerlengo, and he *is* the caretaker of the Church. We will treat you no differently from a personal representative of the Pope. If it will make you more comfortable, I can have the men stand at ease.'

'Please.'

Jordan issued the order in crisp German, and the soldiers spread their feet shoulder-width apart and folded their hands behind their backs. Each stood so ramrod straight that plumb bobs could have been calibrated against them for accuracy.

'Gentlemen,' Grin began, 'we have a lot of ground to cover and not much time to do it. Also keep in mind that the rooms we're searching belong to the cardinal electors, so treat their personal property with the appropriate respect. This respect complements another aspect of our search – we don't want anyone to know we were here, so the rooms are to be left as we found them. Getting down to particulars, we are looking for any device capable of sending or receiving a message. If you find anything, notify the sweepers or me and we'll come check it out. The sweepers and I will be circulating through the building looking for any listening devices that may have been planted. Any questions?'

There were none.

'Good,' Grin said. 'Let's get to work.'

43

Gentle arcs of water streamed from the galleon's sixteen cannons, an endless broadside from the centerpiece of the *Fontana della Galera*. The sails of the ornate and intricately rigged bronze vessel were forever furled about the crossbars, and on the prow the figure of a young boy blew a spray of water through a horn.

Donoher let his thoughts wander as the sight and sound of rippling water eased the tension in his mind. It was nearing one o'clock in the afternoon on a cool, clear day, and the shadow cast by the Hall of Bramante and the Palezzetto del Belvedere now covered the ship and half of the fountain. In another hour, the rest of the long narrow courtyard would slip into shadow. Donoher stood along the side still in sunlight, absorbing the warmth before he returned to the conclave.

Grin, still clad in priestly garb, emerged from the palezzetto and strode purposefully toward the Camerlengo.

'A euro cent for your thoughts,' Grin offered as he approached.

'You'd receive a mighty poor return on that investment.'

'Oh.'

'I was just recalling a conversation I had with Nolan before this all began. He asked if I had yet grown so accustomed to the splendor of my surroundings that I no longer noticed them.' Donoher nodded his head toward the seventeenth-century fountain. 'In the whole of the Vatican, this place is one of my favorites. There's an inscription on the ship: *The papal fleet does not pour out flames, but sweet water that quenches the fires of war.*'

'A worthy sentiment, history notwithstanding.'

'Of the two hundred and sixty-three men who have succeeded Saint Peter as Bishop of Rome, only a handful ever sent men into battle,' Donoher countered calmly. 'What's nice about today is that there are no tourists, making for a most welcome reprieve.'

'I heard about the black smoke.'

'The only good news of the day, unless you have something to report.'

'That depends on how you look at it. We've searched about a quarter of the apartments, and we've found only a few replacement batteries for hearing aids. Either your fellow cardinals are Luddites, or they left all their gadgetry at home.'

'I suspect a combination of the two, though the few of my brethren who comfortably employ such devices turned them over to my office before the start of the conclave. So you'll be back at it this afternoon?'

'Just as soon as they lock the doors to the chapel.'

'Then we both should be heading back. Please walk with me.'

The Camerlengo set the pace, his worn knees creaking

audibly beneath the crimson choir dress. Abrupt changes in the weather, such as the cold front that crossed the Italian peninsula just before dawn, wreaked havoc with his battered joints.

'I take it there's been no word from Nolan,' Donoher said.

'None, but I don't expect to hear from him until he has something important to say.'

'It's night there now. I hope the Lord provides our people with a bright star to guide their journey.'

'Amen to that,' Grin replied.

44

After the ballot papers for the afternoon session were distributed, the junior cardinal deacon ushered the master of papal liturgical ceremonies and the masters of ceremonies out of the Sistine Chapel and closed the doors. The cardinals were once more in conclave.

From his seat near the altar, Donoher studied his fellow cardinals, wondering what kinds of subtle deal-making had transpired during the midday break. Ryff, the German, effectively scuttled his candidacy the previous evening, throwing his support behind Magni. It was a shrewd move, and one that played on the old adage that fat Popes followed skinny ones. At sixty-nine and with proportions matching those of Pope John XXIII, Magni's pontificate would certainly be far shorter than Leo's impressive reign. In supporting Magni, Ryff demonstrated solidarity with the European cardinals, who as a block controlled nearly fifty percent of the votes. The German cardinal could afford to wait, and his sacrifice would not be forgotten the next time around.

Though Magni surged to thirty-three votes in the morning's second ballot, it was clear that Europe wasn't voting as a monolithic bloc. In his conversations between sessions, Donoher detected in some of Europe's non-Italian cardinals a sentiment that the wrong European stepped aside. Donoher also noted that the loss of Gagliardi took some of the wind out of the unified Italians' sails.

Escalante garnered twenty-five votes, drawing support not only from Latin America but portions of the United States, Canada, and the Philippines. Oromo's candidacy was unusual in that it combined the undeniable growing importance of Africa to the Roman Catholic Church with a charismatic man who promised to be a staunch defender of the faith and a powerful voice to the Third World. As a Vatican insider, the Sudanese cardinal was well known by his fellows in the college, and this familiarity, Donoher believed, helped him retain his base of support through the consolidating ballots.

Yin and Velu, too, held onto their core of support, and even gathered a few additional votes, though not enough as yet to threaten the front-runners. Donoher was certain that those two names were the subject of much discussion during the break, with cardinals hoping Velu would follow Ryff's example and others politely lobbying against the quixotic candidacy of the endangered Bishop of Shanghai.

Ryff rose from his seat near the center of the chapel, beneath Michelangelo's *Creation of Eve*.

'My Most Eminent Lord,' the German called out, his voice directed at the Camerlengo, 'a question, if I may, before the next vote.'

Donoher nodded. All eyes were on Ryff.

'Is there any news of Bishop Yin?' Ryff asked.

After scuttling his own candidacy, the German became the perfect choice of the Europeans to address this issue. If asked by any of the remaining papabili, the question might have appeared self-serving, an attempt to free up fifteen votes, but from Ryff it expressed the sincere curiosity of the conclave.

What Donoher found interesting about Yin's support, at least as he perceived it, was that it came from all over the globe. The other papabili found initial backing from ethnic or geographic blocs, then drew in uncommitted electors as they gained momentum. Yin's core defied conventional wisdom, and Donoher believed these electors represented a different dynamic in this conclave – an expression of pure faith that God had given them a sign.

'Bishop Yin and his liberators are at present seeking a way out of China. At the same time, the Chinese government is vigorously attempting to prevent his departure. The situation is dire but not without hope. I am certain the Bishop of Shanghai remains in your prayers as he does in mine during this most difficult time.'

Murmurs of approval rippled through the chapel, the desire for the safe deliverance of those in danger unanimous among the cardinal electors.

'And now,' Donoher continued, 'with the guidance of the Holy Spirit, let us continue with the sacred task of electing the next supreme pontiff.'

'Oromo,' Cain announced, reading off the final ballot.

Donoher didn't need to hear the name called to know

that after three days the conclave remained deadlocked. Though the tallies varied by a few votes, the order of the candidates remained unchanged.

The ballots and notes were again collected and burned, the coils of black smoke symbolic of the dour mood that permeated the chapel. After nine rounds of balloting, the cardinals were no closer to electing a new Pope than on the opening day of the conclave. They felt the eyes of the world's Catholics upon them, a billion souls urging them to choose wisely and challenging them to rise above the status quo.

Yet the man who held the narrowest of leads in the balloting was also the safest, least objectionable of the papabili, the embodiment of time-honored Vatican tradition. Pope Leo XIV would be a tough act to follow, but the waiting Church wanted and needed an encore.

Donoher left his seat, said a brief prayer before the altar, and turned to face the other cardinals.

'My Esteemed Brothers, I believe our present impasse requires a pause in our deliberations. Per article seventy-four of the Apostolic Constitution, I suspend voting for one day to provide us with time for prayer and reflection.'

45

GANSU, CHINA

During the second night, the BATs crossed from Inner Mongolia into the harsh and barren Gansu Province, a region traditionally considered by the Chinese as the outer limit of the Middle Kingdom. A thin sliver of a moon hung high above, casting an eerie light on the mountainous terrain. Early in tonight's flight, they passed over a remote section of the Great Wall, the famous barrier against invasion from the north.

'It is a shame we are not following the ancient route through the Hexi Corridor,' Yin mused as he gazed at the landscape below. 'I recall it was most impressive.'

'Sightseeing is not on the agenda,' Kilkenny said curtly.

Tao scowled at Kilkenny and placed a gloved hand on Yin's. 'I've traveled quite a bit in Gansu, and it was spectacular.'

Tao's instinct told her Yin was feeling homesick for a land he hadn't seen in three decades. And once out of China, he could never return. As he passed into the west, everything Yin had ever known was slipping away. Yin nodded, and Tao glimpsed a hint of his warm smile through his dark visor. The quiet Bishop returned his gaze to the windswept land below.

'If our circumstances were different,' Tao said, 'what would you recommend we see?'

'The land below us has much history and much beauty. The Buddhist caves at Dunhuang and Bingling Si contain magnificent works of art. Maiji Shan near Tianshui is also quite spectacular. If we were on foot – '

'God forbid,' Kilkenny interrupted.

' – then we would have little choice but to follow the Hexi Corridor,' Yin continued. 'It was the only route west. From the south, the corridor follows the edge of the Qilian Shan Mountains – the foothills of Tibet. Only desert and mountains are to the north. Chinese civilization originated in Gansu, and control of the corridor was very important. All trade passed through here, and the Great Wall protected much of the corridor. It was a critical piece of the Silk Road. Many saw the importance of this region, and control over it changed hands many times. The descendants of all those conquests are still here.'

'Sounds like Ireland,' Kilkenny offered.

'Among those who came were Tibetans. Monks settled in a beautiful valley south of Langzhou and founded the monastery of Labrang Si at Xiahe. It is the most important monastery outside of Tibet and one of the centers of the Yellow Hat Sect. I found refuge with the monks at Labrang Si. It was very good for the spirit in difficult times.'

As Yin spoke, he stared into the distance as if his

memories lay there. Absently, he moved his right hand to his chest. Tao noticed immediately.

'Is your heart bothering you again?' Tao asked.

Kilkenny turned in his seat. Despite Jing's initial diagnosis of stress, Kilkenny knew a combat medic was no substitute for a cardiologist.

'My heart is troubled,' Yin replied, his voice a choked whisper.

'Do you want to have the medic look at you again?' Kilkenny asked.

'No. You said we must keep moving.'

'But you are the reason we're here,' Kilkenny countered. 'Do you need a doctor?'

'I am fine,' Yin lied. But behind his helmet, unseen by Kilkenny and Tao, tears streamed down his face.

Second Lieutenant Sun Tonglai of the People's Liberation Army Air Force paced along the side of the unpaved stretch of road south of Dunhuang trying to keep warm, a futile effort against the mass of cold air flowing down like an icy river from the mountains. He lit another cigarette and thrust his gloved hands back into the pockets of his long blue coat. He drew in each breath deeply and held the warm smoke inside his lungs, the cigarette tip a glowing ember. After a pleasant leave home, Sun did not relish the idea of freezing to death on a desolate road in the middle of nowhere.

Sun was stationed at Base 20 outside Jiuquan, and the small bus that was taking him back sat by the side of the road with a flat tire. The driver, with the help of a few passengers, had removed the damaged tire and was mounting the spare. With any luck, they would soon reload all the baggage and once again be on the road.

'What is that sound?' one of Sun's fellow passengers asked.

At first, Sun heard nothing. Then a sharp note rose above the rushing wind, almost a whistle but constant and growing in intensity.

'Is that a plane?' another asked.

'I'm not sure,' Sun replied. 'It sounds too small, and too low to the ground. Perhaps it is just an echo coming through the mountains.'

Because he was an Air Force officer, most passengers accepted Sun's explanation of the phenomenon, but the sound continued to puzzle him. He scanned the heavens, looking for running lights that would reveal a passing aircraft's position, but he saw only stars and a sickle moon.

Something black crossed the bright band of the Milky Way, large enough to blot out handfuls of stars. It was followed by a second shape, then a third – three distinct black forms with scalloped wings.

'Too big for birds,' one passenger said.

'They are making the noise,' another offered.

'You're military,' a fellow passenger demanded. 'What is it?'

'I don't know,' Sun admitted before catching himself. 'Listen, people, do not tell anyone what you have seen. If it is military and they are flying at night, you are not supposed to see it. Just forget about it.'

46

VATICAN CITY

'Where did you find this?' Donoher asked.

The sleek black device was rectangular with rounded edges, about the size of the Camerlengo's palm, and less than a half inch thick. The face consisted of an LCD screen framed in silver and an array of tiny silver oval buttons. Above the LCD screen were three small holes for the speaker and the name *BlackBerry*.

'In Cardinal Velu's apartment,' Grin replied. 'It was packed in among his things.'

Donoher switched on the phone. A screen graphic appeared as the BlackBerry booted up and tried to acquire a signal.

'It won't work down here,' Grin said, reminding Donoher that they were in the catacombs. 'I tried it in the apartment as well – I don't think Velu's carrier in Bombay has a roaming deal with any of the local providers. Then one of the Swiss Guards noticed something interesting about this particular BlackBerry.'

'Did he now?' Donoher asked.

'This model is WiFi-enabled and compatible with the Vatican's wireless network,' Grin continued. 'And it's standard issue for the Swiss Guards. From his apartment, Cardinal Velu can send and receive e-mail and text messages.'

'Has he done so?'

'I haven't checked. I thought I'd better bring it up with you before rifling through his e-mail.'

'Of all the cardinals, Velu makes the least sense for this. He's been involved in our negotiations with the Chinese regarding Yin and our other clergy for years.' Donoher handed the BlackBerry back to Grin. 'I want you to review Velu's messages, but before you do, let's have a chat with him.'

They found Velu deep in prayer, alone and kneeling at the grave of Pope Leo XIV in the Old Grottoes beneath Saint Peter's Basilica. The claustrophobic space was all that remained of the original basilica, its volume so reduced that a man of average height could touch the ceiling with little difficulty. All around them lay the intricately fashioned tombs of Popes dating to antiquity.

As the sound of their echoing footsteps drew closer, Velu lifted his head and turned in their direction.

'So sorry to disturb you, Esteemed Brother,' Donoher apologized.

Velu slowly rose to his feet. 'Just visiting with an old friend. I was unable to pay my respects before the funeral. I do not believe I have met your associate, Father?'

'It's Mister,' Grin corrected him. 'I'm not a priest.'

'I do not understand,' Velu said, eyeing Grin's cassock.

'Mister Grinelli's sole oath is to the conclave,' Donoher explained. 'He is dressed in this manner so that he may move about the Vatican without drawing undo attention to himself. He is involved with liberating Bishop Yin.'

Velu extended his hand and clasped Grin's tightly. 'Then my prayers are with you.'

'Uh, thanks.'

'What has brought you both here?' Velu asked.

'We're looking for answers,' Donoher replied.

Grin reached into his pocket and pulled out the BlackBerry. 'This device was found in your room. Is it yours?'

'Yes,' Velu replied.

'Please think quite carefully about the next question,' Donoher said, 'because we do intend to investigate this device. Have you employed it since swearing the oath to secrecy?'

'Yes.'

Donoher seemed almost pained by the admission. 'Then you admit to breaking your holy oath?'

Velu nodded. 'I had to.'

'But in heaven's name, why?'

'My mother is dying. That's why I did not come to Rome immediately. I stayed with her until the last possible moment. I even offered to claim grave impediment and forgo the conclave, but she would not hear of it. She hopes that I will be Pope.'

'What does your mother have to do with Yin?' Grin asked.

'Nothing at all,' Velu replied. 'I just pray the new Pope will be named soon so I can be with her at the end.'

'Just so we are crystal clear about this,' Donoher said, 'with whom have you been in contact?'

'My brother, Raji. He and his wife are helping to care for my mother.'

'And no one else?' Grin asked.

'No one.'

'Was your communication with Raji strictly about your mother's health,' Donoher continued, 'and you at no time relayed information about the conclave?'

Velu nodded. 'My oath regarding the secrecy of the conclave remains intact.'

'Still, you broke your oath to refrain from contact outside the conclave,' Donoher said, 'and you will be subject to penalties as judged appropriate by the next Pope. Also, your BlackBerry is forfeited for the duration of the conclave, and you will from this moment abide by *all* the norms and procedures of the Apostolic Constitution.'

'I understand,' Velu said.

'You are also forbidden to mention to anyone that your room was searched – this is a matter of life or death.'

'Yin?' Velu asked.

'Yes. You should have come to me with this,' Donoher said in a softer tone. 'The particular congregation could have worked something out. Now that I know your situation, I will certainly urge them to do so on your behalf.'

'Thank you,' Velu said.

Donoher turned to Grin. 'Do what you can with that device, and be ready to continue your search as soon as the conclave reconvenes.'

47

ROME

The Mercedes S500 Guard glided up to the curb at the Piazza di San Giovanni in Laterano. It was late in the afternoon, and the Lateran Obelisk that once stood at the Temple of Ammon in Thebes cast a long, slender shadow east toward the Scala Sancta. Two bodyguards stepped from the car and surveyed the area before permitting their charge to exit the armored sedan. Enzo Bruni appeared small in the company of the men sworn to protect him, though he stood five-eight and added a couple inches more with a thick head of wavy black hair. A stylish man, Bruni wore a perfectly tailored suit and expensive leather shoes. He took pride in his appearance, just as he took pride in his standing in the leadership of the Neopolitan Camorra – one of the four primary criminal organizations operating in Italy.

The bodyguards led the Camorra don to the side entrance of the basilica. A devout man despite his profession, Bruni sought the sacrament of reconciliation each week. He did so at a randomly different church, which pleased his chief of security because it avoided predictability.

The Basilica di San Giovanni in Laterano was the true basilica of Rome and the diocese administered by the Pope as Bishop of Rome. Throughout the Middle Ages, the basilica and its adjacent palace were the seat of papal power, eclipsed only by the Vatican in the late fourteenth century. Bruni entered through the medieval portico, passing a statue of Henry IV of France, the protector of the basilica.

Bruni crossed himself as he passed the tomb of Pope Innocent III and continued toward the narthex. His footsteps echoed on the Cosmatesque floor – a work of art fashioned in swirling patterns of marble. From modest beginnings in the fourth century, the interior of the basilica was continually modified over time. An ornate wooden ceiling floated high above the floor, lit from beneath by clerestory windows and supported by arches and pillars designed by Boromini. The basilica's history matched that of the Church itself, for it had been the scene of both glory and tragedy, all the while growing bit by bit through the ages.

As in Saint Peter's, the narthex of San Giovanni contained a confessio and a papal altar covered by an ornate ciborium. Rendered in the Gothic style, the structure featured twelve frescoed panels by Barna de Siena and a reliquary chamber containing the heads of Saints Peter and Paul. Bruni genuflected before the altar, then continued down through the center of the church to the confessional.

Bruni examined his conscience as he waited his turn,

reviewing any actions through which he spiritually turned his back on God. Only one weighed on his mind today, but Bruni feared it would be the one that damned him to hell for all eternity.

An elderly woman stepped out of the confessional and shared a meek smile with him. Nearly everyone who sought regular confession was Bruni's age or older, people raised in the Church before Vatican II. Ironically, while the woman confessed her angry thoughts at an inconsiderate neighbor or some other minor transgression, many of those in greatest need of reconciliation rarely availed themselves of the sacrament.

Bruni stepped into the confessional and was greeted by a young priest barely a few years out of the seminary. The priest had the kind of face that made a person feel welcome in this most awkward and revealing of church rituals. Gone were the screens and kneelers in the confessionals of the old Church, visual barriers between supplicant and confessor. Bruni sat down and bowed his head.

'In the name of the Father, and of the Son, and of the Holy Spirit,' the priest began, Bruni crossing himself in time.

The priest read a brief passage from scripture that emphasized the love in which God held all people, then invited Bruni to talk. In the modern Church, the sacrament evolved from rote formula into a more substantive conversation.

'Bless me, Father, for I have sinned. It has been one week since my last confession,' Bruni began. 'Father, while I am seeking absolution from my sins, I voluntarily omit some of what I am about to tell you from the seal of confession. What you decide to do with this information I leave to your conscience, but for the sake of my own soul I feel I must give you that opportunity. The matter I wish to discuss is a serious one.'

'I understand,' the priest said calmly, his voice belying the concern he felt.

'I am a leader of the Camorra. I and other men of my profession are seeking to influence the selection of the next Pope. The cardinal we support is a good man and will serve the Church faithfully, but we also believe his selection will serve our interests as well. Two nights ago, we received information that Pope Leo, God rest his soul, sent some men into China to break a Bishop out of jail and get him out of that country.'

The priest's eyes narrowed. What remained of his warm smile melted into a thin straight line.

'Your face says you don't believe me.'

'I'm sorry,' the priest stammered, trying to regain a sense of neutrality.

Bruni smiled. 'Not necessary. I had the same look on my face two nights ago. This Bishop has been in jail a very long time – the Chinese do not approve of the Church – and the Pope wanted him out. The Camerlengo, Cardinal Donoher, is in charge of this mission. My associates and I had no problem with this until we learned that Pope Leo secretly named this Bishop a cardinal and has asked the conclave to consider him for the papacy. After the first vote, this Chinese Bishop has emerged as a viable candidate.'

'How did you acquire this information?' the priest asked, shocked by the detailed revelation.

'We have a source.'

'*Inside* the conclave?'

Bruni shrugged. 'The introduction of this Chinese Bishop to the conclave was viewed by my associates as a potential threat to our plans. We do a great deal of business with the Chinese, so we informed them of our concerns and asked them to take care of the problem.'

'What do you want me to do about this?'

'I do not like the idea of killing a priest. Get word to Cardinal Donoher. Warn him that the Chinese know what he's up to. The rest is up to him.'

48

CHIFENG, CHINA

October 31

Liu leaned against the corridor wall outside the interrogation room, eyes closed, a cigarette dangling from the corner of his mouth, his body exhausted beyond anything he could remember. More than forty-eight hours had passed since Tian ordered him to Chifeng to end Yin Daoming's life. His knee ached, and the bruise on his head compounded the sensation of a spike being driven up into the base of his skull.

Technicians from the coroner's office rolled a gurney down the corridor and parked it next to where Liu stood, narrowing the passage to half its width. They were dressed in white, and each man had smeared a strong aromatic balm across his upper lip as a defense against the stench of death that awaited them inside. Liu masked the smell with his unfiltered cigarettes.

Liu heard a rattling sound moving down the corridor toward him. At once, he knew it was Peng.

'Do you have to make so damn much noise?' Liu asked.

'The officer up front asked me to bring you these.' Peng tossed him the bottle. 'Headache?'

'What do you think? *Cao!* My skull is splitting. These cultists will drive me mad.'

Liu poured out a pair of tablets and swallowed them dry, eager for relief. Peng stepped aside as the technicians emerged from the interrogation room with a white plastic body bag. The underside dripped as they carried it out, though with what Peng didn't want to know. As they laid the bag on the gurney, he could tell it contained a body that was small and light.

'That's the last one,' the technician said, handing Liu a clipboard of paperwork.

Liu signed the release forms allowing the bodies to be cremated and disposed of – there were no next of kin. He returned the clipboard, then leaned his head back against the wall and closed his eyes.

'Did they tell you anything?' Peng asked.

'Just religious nonsense, nothing of use.' Liu snorted a laugh. 'You know what the old man said before he died? He forgave me. Do you believe that? The criminal forgave me. Upside-down world and you wonder why I have a headache.'

'The cure for your headache is rest and good news.'

'You have either?'

'A promising lead. An Air Force officer was returning to Base 20 near Jiuquan last night when the bus he was riding on broke down. As they changed the tire, he and the other passengers saw three objects fly overhead. They had large wings, scalloped like those of a bat.'

312

'Maybe they were bats.'

'Bats do not have engines.'

Liu's eyes opened. 'Continue.'

'The officer could not see the aircraft clearly, but each had an engine that was powering their flight. They were no more than eighty meters off the ground, and he estimates their speed at one hundred kilometers per hour. When the officer returned to his base, he reported what he saw and inquired about any experimental aircraft being tested at night. Fortunately, his superior officer was aware of our investigation and made the connection.'

'Gansu, eh?' Liu pondered.

'The use of light aircraft capable of night flight fits perfectly with the needs of their mission. And we know Kilkenny and at least one accomplice arrived in Mongolia – this answers how they crossed into China. The question is, Why did they not return the way they came?'

'Because they are being aided by these cultists,' Liu replied, the answer painfully obvious to him. 'They were kept in hiding until dark and warned to avoid the border.'

Peng nodded. 'Based on the time of the sighting and the officer's estimate of speed, we believe they are covering between one thousand and twelve hundred kilometers per night. And always over sparsely populated areas.'

'Which is easier to do the farther west they go. That still leaves a large border to protect.'

'Yes,' Peng agreed, 'but now we know what we're looking for.'

49

VATICAN CITY

The sounds of Billie Holiday and Her Orchestra greeted Donoher as he entered the catacombs workroom, the jazz legend's seductive voice dancing with Oscar Peterson's piano through 'These Foolish Things.' Grin sat at his workstation eating a croissant, a steaming cup of espresso nearby. His freshly laundered cassock hung from a coathook near the door.

'All's quiet on the eastern front,' the computer guru said before the Camerlengo could ask the question foremost on his mind.

Donoher pulled up a chair and sat down. 'I heartily approve of your choice of music this morning.'

'I'm weak when it comes to a woman with a great set of pipes, and few can deliver raw emotion like Lady Day.'

'That lovely woman had more than her share of pain to draw upon,' Donoher agreed. 'Have you learned anything from Velu's BlackBerry?'

'He was telling the truth. Since arriving in Rome, he's corresponded only with his brother – all updates on mother Velu's condition. Some very depressing reading.'

'Velu and I spoke with his brother last night – his mother's life is near an end.'

'Then I hope he makes it back home in time. I did check the server handling all the Vatican WiFi traffic, and it came out clean. Just a handful of e-mails that sync perfectly with what's on his PDA.'

'Then Velu's not our leak.'

'Doesn't look like it. While I was in the server, I checked out all the other message traffic. I can identify all the devices used by the guards and other Vatican personnel, and even which hot spots they tapped into to send their messages. Velu's PDA is the only one that connected with the hot spot in Domus Sanctae Marthae.'

'Poor Velu. Among the penalties for what he's done is excommunication *latae senteniae*.'

'I know what excommunication is, but what was that bit of Latin at the end?' Grin asked.

'There are two types of excommunication,' Donoher explained. '*Ferenda senteniae* is a judgment imposed by a Church superior or a Church body. *Latae senteniae* happens automatically, at the moment the sin is committed.'

'Do not pass GO; do not collect two hundred dollars.'

'In a manner of speaking. Historical interference with papal elections made such an extreme penalty a necessity. In a way, it's a direct attack on the papacy.'

'What's on the agenda today?' Grin asked.

'Prayer and reflection coupled with an exhortation by the senior cardinal deacon, which should shake things up as he's an old fire-and-brimstone man. I expect there will also be a bit of discreet politicking going on. With any luck, we'll see some progress when voting resumes tomorrow.'

'With any luck, we'll see Nolan and his team cross the Chinese border with Yin.'

The workroom phone rang, and Grin checked the caller ID.

'It's your assistant,' he said as he offered Donoher the handset.

'Good morning, Sister.'

'Your Eminence, I have Colonel Gergonne, the commandant of the Swiss Guard, holding for you. He says it's a most urgent matter he needs to discuss with you.'

'I'll speak with him.'

The line went silent for a moment as Sister Deborah transferred the call.

'Good morning, Colonel,' Donoher said.

'Your Eminence, I apologize for disturbing you during the conclave, but I have a young priest in my office who is most insistent on speaking with you. In fact, he has been here with us for much of the night. I have verified that he is who he claims to be – a priest assigned to the Basilica di San Giovanni in Laterano – and that he has no history of mental illness and is unarmed.'

'Has he given you any indication about why he needs to talk to me now?' Donoher asked.

'He claims to have information for you about a threat to the conclave and a Chinese Bishop.'

'Colonel, have him brought to my office straight away. I'll meet you there shortly.' Donoher shook his head, amazed, as he rose and cradled the handset. 'The Lord indeed works in mysterious ways.'

'How so?' Grin asked.

'Would you believe that this very morning, a priest has appeared on our doorstep with information regarding the source of our leak? I'll let you know what I learn.'

After Donoher left, Grin looked up at the ceiling and whispered, 'God, don't get me wrong. I like divine intervention as much as the next guy, but right now our people in China need it more than we do.'

50

After interviewing the priest, Donoher attended a brief service in the Pauline Chapel, where Cardinal Cain, the senior cardinal in the order of deacons, lived up to his reputation and delivered an exhortation to princely brethren in a basso profundo that shook the foundations of the Apostolic Palace. As the rest of the cardinals returned to their rooms to reflect and pray, Donoher changed into less conspicuous priestly attire and was taken by a Swiss Guard in an unmarked car to the Gemelli Polyclinic.

Cardinal Gagliardi was asleep when Donoher arrived, and the Sicilian looked no better than during the Camerlengo's previous visit. Donoher closed the door behind him to dampen the noise from the corridor. Outside, it was cool for this time of year, but the sky shone clear blue and the midday sun created a warm pool of light by the window. Donoher found an old rosary on the table beside Gagliardi's bed, its ebony beads polished smooth by thousands of recitations. He moved a chair into the patch of sunlight and began to pray.

Donoher lost track of the time as he prayed, his

thoughts gliding in and out with the rosary's familiar cadences. He had completed two circuits of the rosary – contemplating the joyful and luminous mysteries of Christ's life – and was about to start the sorrowful mysteries when Gagliardi stirred.

'Water,' the Sicilian rasped, his voice thin and hoarse.

A pitcher of ice water and a plastic drinking glass with a straw sat on a bedside tray table. Donoher filled the cup and placed the straw close to Gagliardi's lips, which were cracked and dry. The cardinal sipped gingerly, the parched interior of his mouth absorbing the liquid like a dry sponge. When he had drunk enough, Gagliardi turned his head away. Donoher removed the cup and wiped a droplet that escaped from the corner of the patient's mouth.

'You're looking better,' Donoher lied.

'If I looked any worse,' Gagliardi's words came in barely audible gasps, 'I'd be dead.'

'What do your doctors say?'

'That I will die soon.'

'Does your family know?'

'Just my nephew. I don't want a death vigil. Do we have a new Pope?'

Donoher shook his head. 'Deadlocked. Voting is suspended until tomorrow.'

'Papabili?'

Donoher pulled his chair close to the bed so that his face was just a few inches from the Sicilian's.

'In the last balloting, Magni was the only one with more than thirty votes. Escalante and Oromo are both mired in the mid-twenties, followed by Velu.'

Gagliardi tallied the votes in his head and recognized the shortfall. 'Who else?'

'Bishop Yin. He fell back a bit after the first ballot and has languished in the teens. I expect his candidacy will falter in the next round.'

'For the best. Ryff?'

'He threw in with Magni's supporters rather than split the European vote. That's been the only real change. There was some interesting movement between those backing Velu and Oromo this morning, so we might yet see a Third World consolidation to challenge Magni.'

'He needs the North Americans,' rasped Gagliardi.

'Don't they all, but the United States is divided. The older urban areas favor Oromo, but the regions with a growing Hispanic presence are backing Escalante. The Canadians, I suspect, are more inclined toward Europe.'

'All good men, but two bold moves are not good for the Church.'

'You may be right,' Donoher offered. 'Perhaps the Church needs a caretaker after a Pope like Leo.'

'Magni would be best,' Gagliardi agreed.

'If that is God's will. Is it yours?' Donoher asked pointedly.

'Eh?'

'Is it your will that Magni become the next Pope? Is it your hand I see in the shadows deftly orchestrating his ascension?'

'What are you talking about?' Gagliardi asked.

'Motivation. You missed a wonderful sermon this morning. Cain really outdid himself – I wouldn't be surprised if he won a few votes in the next round, despite his age. He asked each of us to question our motivation, to question what was truly behind our previous votes. He got me thinking. The Italian cardinals have always been a very loyal group, true both to the Church and one another. As a bloc, they've enjoyed the historical position as king makers in the Church. Then I thought about the papabili, how these five good men all found their way to this point in history, and it struck me that from the moment they became cardinals, you played a part in each man's career. You guided their appointments on committees; you made sure they traveled and became known among the college. From your position in the Curia, you nurtured them, but your actions, when viewed through Cain's lens, now seem calculated. Did you get your thirty pieces of silver?'

'What are you accusing me of?' Gagliardi gasped.

'Betrayal. You conspired to interfere with the election. You broke your solemn oath to the conclave. And you betrayed Bishop Yin, endangering his life and the lives of those sent to save him. For what, money?'

'I don't know what you're talking about.'

'The mafia's sole purpose is making money, and only Italians can be mafia. The Chinese learned about Pope Leo's message to the conclave from the mafia here in Rome, and you are the only Italian cardinal to leave the conclave. Is making Magni Pope so important that you would allow blood to be shed to see it happen? Bishop Yin and the people I sent to rescue him are at this very moment being hunted. Among those whose lives you've endangered is the son of my oldest and dearest friend. I baptized this young man, and in just this past year presided over both his wedding and the funeral of his young wife and unborn son. This brave young man is *family* to me.

'And today, there are whole families of martyrs in China because of your betrayal,' Donoher continued. 'People with faith far greater than yours and mine, people who gave their lives to protect the man you betrayed. Their blood is on your hands, and you will have to answer to the Almighty for their deaths.'

Gagliardi closed his eyes tightly against the irate Camerlengo's condemnation. In his mind, he envisioned his impending day of reckoning with the Creator. He stood naked and alone before an unimaginably bright light, his hands soaked in blood.

Donoher leaned back in his chair, flushed with anger and revulsion. His eyes followed the tubes and wires that connected Gagliardi to a phalanx of medical devices, and he wondered if pulling the plug on any of them would hasten the traitorous cardinal's demise. For the first time, Donoher entertained a desire to kill.

'Forgive me,' Gagliardi croaked in a whisper.

'What?' Donoher asked, struggling to dispel the temptations of his homicidal fantasy.

'Forgive me.'

'I don't know if I can,' Donoher replied, unprepared for Gagliardi's request.

'I admit it,' Gagliardi pleaded. 'All you've said is true. Money, all for money. The IOR, money laundering.'

Donoher recalled the Banco Ambrosiano affair that rocked the Vatican Bank in the early eighties. The IOR had become entangled in the spectacular collapse of an

Italian bank involved in money laundering for criminal syndicates.

'Is Magni a party to your betrayal?'

Gagliardi shook his head. 'He knows nothing of this. He is a good man but with no head for numbers. It would be easy to hide the details from him.'

Donoher knew Magni to be a pious man who couldn't balance his own checkbook, and even the best accountants would find it difficult to ferret out a well-conceived scheme of financial chicanery in the Vatican's complex account books.

'How were your criminal associates informed about Bishop Yin?' Donoher asked.

'My nephew. He is trusted. I know I don't deserve it, but please, I beg you. Forgive me.'

Gagliardi held out a trembling hand to Donoher. Tears streamed from the stricken man's eyes and trickled along the oxygen cannula tubing from his face down onto the bed sheets. The depth of Gagliardi's remorse turned Donoher's anger to pity. He wrapped Gagliardi's hand in both his own and stilled the tremors.

'Forgive me,' Gagliardi pleaded again.

'I forgive you,' Donoher said softly, 'but I cannot absolve you of your sins.'

'You would deny me the sacraments?'

'I am powerless in this matter. From the moment you betrayed the conclave, you were excommunicated latae sententiae. Only the new Pope can absolve you of these grave sins.'

Having engineered the conclave's deadlock, Gagliardi knew it might be weeks before a new Pope was elected

– time he did not have. The monitor at his bedside began beeping frantically, and the display of lines monitoring the cardinal's heart function lost their rhythm and became erratic. Gagliardi gasped, his breathing shallow and strangled as if his chest were in a vice.

Three nurses and the physician on call rushed into the room with a crash cart. Donoher released Gagliardi's hand and stepped back by the window, out of the way but still in the stricken cardinal's line of sight. They checked his airway and vital signs, performed CPR, and applied increasing levels of electric shock to arrest the erratic fibrillation of Gagliardi's heart, but the organ was past recovery.

With each fluttering heartbeat, the blood circulating in the Sicilian's body slowed until it finally stopped. When death came, Gagliardi did not sense the presence of loved ones who preceded him, nor did he feel drawn out of his body into a radiant light. Instead, his consciousness closed in around him, contracting tightly like a black hole. The darkness that enveloped Gagliardi felt infinite and in its vastness empty.

The on-call physician noted the time of death, and the nurses began switching off the monitors.

'There was nothing more we could do for him,' the physician told Donoher.

'Thank you for making his last days comfortable. I'll notify the Vatican of his passing, and if it is permitted, I wish to inform his next of kin.'

'That is very gracious of you,' the doctor said. 'This kind of news is best delivered in person.'

51

TIBET

MESSAGE UPLOAD COMPLETE

'Satellite uplink off,' Kilkenny said.

The heads-up display disappeared and Kilkenny removed his helmet. Gates reclined beside him in the co-pilot's seat, resting up for the final leg of their flight.

'Think your buddy Grin will get that?' Gates asked without opening his eyes.

'He'll figure it out.'

'I hope so 'cause it'd be mighty nice if there was someone friendly there to meet us on the other side.'

'I'm more concerned about the unfriendly ones who are trying to keep us from getting there.'

Kilkenny pulled himself out of the BAT and stretched, his joints stiff from two long flights. The temperature had dropped considerably as they ascended to the Tibetan plateau, and Kilkenny's breath now billowed in steamy wisps as he exhaled. At a little over three thousand meters, the altitude relative to sea level here was ten times higher than where he lived in Michigan. The air was noticeably thinner, too, but Kilkenny found he had little difficulty acclimating.

He left Gates in the BAT and found Tao in conversation with the team's medic. The three pilots were clustered together around one of the BATs, reviewing the night's flight plan over what qualified as their evening meal. Food was a traditional grumbling point among soldiers, and Kilkenny was certain that even a Memphis barbecue served by the Hooters girls would receive complaints by troops in the field. The remaining team members were either on watch, checking equipment, or, like Gates, trying to catch some shuteye.

Yin sat back on his heels, his legs tucked beneath him, knees parted in a wide posture Kilkenny was familiar with from his years of martial arts training. Yin's upper body stood tall, and his palms lay open on his thighs. He was alone on a grassy patch of ground facing the western horizon. The sun had just slipped behind the highest peaks, painting the entire range in a warm golden glow. A gentle breeze ruffled Yin's white hair but did not disturb his meditation.

'How's he doing?' Kilkenny asked out of earshot of Yin.

'Vitals are strong,' Jing reported. 'His heart rate is good for a guy his age, and his rhythm is textbook. If there's a glitch in his ticker, I'm still not seeing it.'

'Is he having any trouble with the altitude?'

'Actually, I think he's handling it better than some of us. I'm keeping everybody hydrated and passing out the Tylenol as needed.'

'Good.'

Jing left to stow his medical supplies in the ebbing twilight. Kilkenny and Tao studied the man they had come to China to save, wondering if their actions might instead shorten the cleric's life.

'What do you think? Is he okay?' Kilkenny asked.

'Something *is* wrong, but maybe it's not physical. The shock of reentering the world like this after what he's been through – I can't imagine.'

'An institutional man.'

'A what?' Tao asked.

'An institutional man. Morgan Freeman's character used the term in *The Shawshank Redemption*. It refers to a man who's been in prison so long that he can't function on the outside – a man who needs the walls of the prison to feel safe. Looking at him now, though, I'd say he's enjoying the great wide open.'

'His sleep is troubled.'

'I was in a box just like his for only one night, and it messed up my dreams. He'll get the best treatment available for whatever's bothering him once we get him out of China.'

'I'm worried about him,' Tao said.

'Yeah. Me too.'

Yin prayed as the sun set, his thoughts moving beyond scripted formula into a personal conversation with the Almighty. His prayers sought protection for those who risked their lives to free him, and forgiveness for their persecutors. He asked nothing for himself, knowing that each day was itself a precious gift.

He felt a surge of warmth in his chest, swelling from

his heart, embracing him, enveloping him. The sensation rushed to his extremities, and his mind seemed to expand beyond his body into the horizon. In that instant, Yin felt a small pair of hands touch his cheek and the cross on his chest, and he knew the child Ke Li was now with God.

52

VATICAN CITY

Grin was deep inside the PLA's Air Force network when the Rolling Stones logo reappeared in the center of the monitor, accompanied by the familiar opening chords of 'Gimme Shelter'. As Jagger sang the opening lyrics, Grin tapped the window to retrieve Kilkenny's latest message.

MISTY MOUNTAIN HOP 111
ZOSO BEST 41

'Nolan, my man, you are really putting me to the test.'

Grin wrote the message in block letters across the top of a legal pad, then allowed his mind to wander. The first thought that came to mind was the Led Zeppelin song 'Misty Mountain Hop' – the wording in the message too exact to ignore. The song derived its name from the long mountain range that ran down the center of Tolkien's Middle Earth, though the mountains figured more prominently in *The Hobbit* than in the epic on which Kilkenny had based his initial messages. Grin pondered Kilkenny's last message that indicated the team was traveling west across China.

'Imaging chamber on. Display Earth, wire frame with longitude and latitude.'

The chamber glowed as it powered out of its sleep mode, and soon a skeletal rendering of Earth floated in midair. Land masses were defined with bright green lines, the navigational divisions in white with numerical markings.

'Enhance region between fifteen and fifty degrees north latitude and sixty and one hundred and twenty degrees east longitude.'

A bright line appeared, defining the boundaries of the region Grin requested. The globe expanded in size and appeared to sink through the bottom of the chamber, and as it did so, the highlighted region spun into view. A domelike portion of the Earth's surface now covered the bottom of the cylindrical chamber.

'Display national boundaries.'

Yellow lines raced across the visible section of Asia, tracing out the familiar puzzle pieces of the political map.

'Display topography and render.'

The computer controlling the holographic display assumed for the purposes of the rendering that the sun was directly over the equator, as it would be on the first day of spring or autumn, and that it was also solar noon above the center of the selected area. Mountain ranges swelled up where tectonic plates collided eons ago. Rivers snaked through valleys and splayed into deltas. Oceans flat and blue contrasted with the wrinkled green texture of the land. The curvature of the earth was still apparent at this scale, and Asia appeared without the cartographic distortion of flat maps.

He studied China's western border and discovered that nearly its entire length ran through mountainous terrain. China's Misty Mountains ran more than two thousand miles and included some of the world's tallest peaks. Somewhere in all that jagged topography, Kilkenny intended to exit China.

'*Mi hermano*, you've got solid brass *cojones* the size of grapefruit.'

Fairly confident of what Kilkenny meant by 'Misty Mountain Hop', Grin set to work on the number that followed.

'Display one hundred eleven longitude east.'

A white line shot through the eastern half of China, north to south, just a few hundred miles from Beijing.

'About three time zones off, if China had more than one. Delete one hundred and eleven longitude east.'

The white line disappeared. Grin sat back with the legal pad and played around with the numbers, trying to ascertain their significance. He recalled that *Lord of the Rings* opened with the celebration of Bilbo Baggins's eleventy-first birthday.

'Eleven-one,' he said, breaking the digits apart. 'One-eleven.'

He drew a backslash between the second and third numeral – 11/1 – and he saw it.

'November the first. They're crossing the border some-time tomorrow.'

Satisfied he had cracked the first line of code, Grin went to work on the second. He took the word ZOSO as another reference to Led Zeppelin and sketched the logo associated with the band's lead guitar player, Jimmy Page.

It took him a while to recall the logo exactly – he'd last drawn it in the margins of his notebooks in high school. As he doodled, the phone purred and he answered it.

'Gagliardi was our Judas,' Donoher said, sounding tired and depressed. 'It was all a scheme to get the mafia's tentacles back into the Vatican Bank. What a mess. Before I return to the Vatican, I plan to pay a visit to Gagliardi's nephew to inform him of his uncle's passing and perhaps send a message of my own.'

'Gagliardi is dead?' Grin asked.

'He passed while I was with him,' Donoher replied. 'I went to the hospital this morning mad enough to kill Gagliardi, but in the end, I could only pity the man.'

'Want some good news?'

'You have to ask?'

'I'm pretty sure Nolan plans to cross out of China sometime tomorrow, which from his point of view starts in just a few hours.'

'Do you know where?'

'I'm still working on that – the second part of his message is trickier than the first. I'll let you know as soon as I have something.'

'God willing, tomorrow will be a bright and glorious day indeed.'

'Speaking of good news, I hear this day off has been a real boon for the environment,' Grin offered. 'All that black smoke billowing out of the Sistine Chapel really jacked up the city's smog index, not to mention global warming.'

Donoher laughed, forgetting for just a moment the burden he carried. 'Now I see why you and Nolan get along so well. You've got a wicked sense of humor.'

'Between Nolan and me, all puns are intended.'

'Keep at that message,' Donoher said. 'Once Nolan and his team are across the border, I want to be ready to move them as far from China as humanly possible.'

53

ROME

Donoher's driver dropped him off in front of a four-story townhouse in the Trastevere District of Rome. Like its neighbors, the building was well maintained for its age. The ground floor was clad in a rusticated base of cut stone blocks; the upper floors were dressed in tan stucco with smooth limestone trim decoratively framing the windows. An arched opening in the center of the symmetrical facade provided entry into the building. At shoulder height next to the opening was a polished bronze sign:

G. CUSUMANO
LIBRAIO ANTIQUARIO

He rang the bell and waited. A small closed-circuit camera mounted off to the side of the door about twelve feet off the ground relayed Donoher's image to a monitor inside the townhouse. A moment later, Guglielmo Cusumano appeared at the door.

'Your Eminence, what can I do for you?' Cusumano asked.

'I am afraid I come bearing sad news.'

'My uncle?'

Donoher nodded. 'He passed just a short time ago. I was with him at the end.'

Cusumano withdrew into his thoughts for a moment, then collected himself once again. 'My manners, please, come in. Can I get you anything?'

'A glass of wine perhaps.'

'I think I can find something suitable to toast uncle's memory,' Cusumano said.

The ground floor of the townhouse was laid out in large reading rooms and served as Cusumano's place of business as a dealer in fine antique books. The air carried the barest scent of old leather and vellum; a state-of-the-art environmental system maintained ideal conditions for book preservation inside the townhouse. If the furnishings in the shop and the number of volumes on display were any indication, Cusumano was very successful at his trade.

They climbed a spiral staircase to the second floor, and Cusumano left his guest in his personal library while he went in search of the vintage he had in mind. He returned a few moments later with a pair of broad-bowled glasses and a well-aged Barolo. Cusumano poured two generous servings and handed one to the Camerlengo.

'To my uncle, a man of faith and family all the years of his life.' The nephew settled into a plush leather sofa.

'To Cardinal Gagliardi,' Donoher added. 'May his soul find the rest that it deserves.'

The Barolo lived up to its reputation as one of Italy's finest red wines, this mature example offering a rich bouquet to the nose and a complex, flavorful palate. In the Corktown of his youth, Donoher recalled the tradition of toasting the deceased with a fine whiskey. The Poles of Detroit's Hamtramck enclave did the same, only with vodka. Spirits for the spirit.

'Death came quickly,' Donoher said. 'His heart could take no more.'

'I'm thankful you were with him at the end. No one should die alone.'

'I agree. In the end, your uncle was able to make a full confession and unburden himself of all the troubles of this world.'

'Then he meets God with a clear conscience.'

'This is a fine wine,' Donoher said, changing the subject, 'and no doubt expensive. Thank you for sharing it with me.'

'My uncle always said that wine, like talent, was meant to be shared. Wasn't Christ's first miracle the wine at the wedding feast in Cana?'

'He also shared wine with his closest friends at the Last Supper, though I doubt it was a Barolo. Your uncle was quite proud of you, and I can see you've done well for yourself,' Donoher said as he surveyed the room. 'I would never have guessed the trade in old books was so financially rewarding.'

'I deal in rare, prized volumes. Just this morning, I completed the sale of an exquisite first edition of Palladio's *I Quattro Libri dell' Architettura* to an American collector. Rare books are works of art as well as sound investments.'

'Such a unique and profitable enterprise no doubt requires specialized accounting and bank services. Your uncle mentioned your interest in our bank at the Vatican.'

'Did he?'

'Yes, and regardless of who becomes the next Pope, I'm sure you will be pleased to know that regulatory oversight of the IOR will be most exacting. Many of the laws governing our bank, though providing a desirable measure of privacy, also make it difficult to monitor accounts for criminal activity. The IOR is not just a bank, it is the Church's bank, and we must hold it to a higher standard. Otherwise, some unscrupulous persons might try to launder money through our accounts or obtain valid letters of credit for fraudulent purposes. We won't allow the Church's bank to be abused by anyone.'

Cusumano leaned back, slowly swirling the deep red wine in his glass, his eyes narrow and fixed on the Camerlengo. A hint of a smile curled the corner of Donoher's mouth, the message delivered.

'Are you a religious man?' Donoher asked.

'In my own fashion.'

'Then you are of course familiar with the concept of excommunication. Are you aware that of the grave sins resulting in this form of censure, there are twelve that only the Pope can absolve? Attacking or murdering a prelate, or *aiding* those who do so, is one. If you, for example, were to commit such a terrible sin, even I, the Camerlengo of the Church, could not restore you.'

'Then it would be best to avoid such a sin, especially now when there is no Pope.'

'It would indeed.'

Donoher finished his wine and set the empty glass on the table beside his chair. Cusumano did not offer to refill it.

'One final matter, before I go,' Donoher said. 'The laws of the Vatican are not the same as the laws of Italy. One major difference is the death penalty. Though not imposed by a Pope for well over a century, capital punishment remains an option. And for murderous crimes against the Church, I don't think Italy would quibble over extradition.'

54

VATICAN CITY

'Have you learned anything?' Donoher asked upon his return to the workroom.

Grin was standing by the imaging chamber studying several hundred miles of mountainous terrain.

'In his latest message, Nolan is playing seven degrees of trivial separation. The first line reads MISTY MOUN-TAIN HOP 111, which I've taken literally as he's crossing the mountains on the first of November. But 'Misty Mountain Hop' is also a song on Led Zeppelin's fourth album. In the second line, ZOSO is the graphic symbol representing Jimmy Page, the lead guitarist for Led Zeppelin. This symbol first appears in the record sleeve of the aforementioned fourth album.'

'So Nolan is pointing you to this particular recording.'

'More like beating me over the head with it. Zeppelin's fourth album is a fan favorite and considered by many to be their best. Personally, I prefer *Physical Graffiti*, but that's just me. In telling me ZOSO BEST 41, I read not only that album number four is number one – the best

– but also that I should look at the fourth song on side one. That's tough to do in the CD age, but I'm old enough to own a copy of the album on vinyl, and the fourth song on side one is "Stairway to Heaven". It's a classic.'

'Okay. What does it mean?'

'The name "Stairway to Heaven" was coined by the fourth-century Indian poet Kalidasa to describe the Himalayas,' Grin explained. 'Display view one.'

The hologram in the imaging chamber dissolved and was instantly replaced with a view of a significantly larger piece of real estate.

'The Himalayas are approximately eighteen hundred miles in length, running from Afghanistan in the west to India's Arunachal Pradesh in the east.'

'That doesn't narrow it down much.'

'No, it doesn't. When most people consider the term *Stairway to Heaven* in relation to the Himalayas, they think of Tibet and Nepal.'

'That's where Nolan intends to cross?' Donoher asked.

'No. The BATs are designed for low-level flying, so I'm not sure if they can handle that kind of altitude. Even if they could, our people would probably need bottled oxygen. And then there's the weather – it's a little late in the season to be crossing the Himalayas on foot or in a motorized kite. I kicked this scenario around a dozen different ways, and what really made me reject it is that this clue is too straightforward. It's not like Nolan. That's why I had to dig deeper, and I finally figured it out. Do you know the film *Fast Times at Ridgemont High*?'

'Should I?'

'Only if you enjoy well-written comedy interspersed with teen angst and adolescent coming-of-age trauma, all set in the early eighties.'

'Not exactly at the top of my list,' Donoher replied. 'Please continue.'

'This movie featured what was, in my humble opinion, one of Sean Penn's best performances, though after my recent stint in a cassock, I have a newfound appreciation for his later work in *We're No Angels*. But I digress.'

'You most certainly do,' Donoher agreed, tempering his impatience. 'How does this film fit in with Nolan's message?'

'In *Fast Times*, the dweeb nicknamed Rat seeks dating advice from the cool guy Damone. Among the pearls of wisdom Damone has to offer is the suggestion that side one of Led Zeppelin's fourth album is the best make-out music ever recorded. This gets us back to ZOSO BEST 41.'

'But that's the album that pointed you to the entire Himalayan range?'

'Yes, but that's not the clue. Rat took Damone's advice but, being a dweeb, got it wrong. During his ill-fated date with the ingenue Stacy – portrayed by the fetching Jennifer Jason Leigh – Rat played the wrong side of the wrong album.'

'This *is* going somewhere?'

'This reference forces me to acknowledge Nolan's genius. The album Rat used wasn't Zeppelin's fourth album but *Physical Graffiti*. And the song heard playing during the date is not the make-out classic 'Stairway to Heaven' but the far superior 'Kashmir'. Nolan is heading for Kashmir.'

'Can you show me where?' Donoher asked.

Grin nodded. 'Display previous view.'

The hologram dissolved and then reformed to display a three-dimensional view of the troubled Indian state of Jammu and Kashmir. Black lines snaked through the mountainous region, defining the internationally recognized borders. Thinner, dashed lines identified militarized lines of control around disputed territory encroached upon by Pakistan and China. Starting high in the glaciers of western Tibet, the Indus flowed northwest through Kashmir and into Pakistan.

'What you're looking at is an area roughly the size of Michigan,' Grin explained, 'and where it abuts China is about as long as the shoreline from Toledo to Mackinaw City. Biggest difference, aside from the lack of fudge, is obviously the terrain. Where China touches Kashmir is a region called Ladakh.'

'Where do you think he'll cross?'

'A couple of large valleys run diagonally from Tibet through Ladakh – the Indus runs down the middle of the larger one. If I had to guess, I think he'd let the geography lead him out of China.'

'Is there any place nearby where we can land an aircraft?'

'At Leh,' Grin answered. 'It's the heart of Ladakh and the only commercial airport.'

'Once they're across the border, they'll be in India, but illegally and without documentation,' Donoher mused, 'and with the exception of Nolan, all looking very much like Chinese soldiers.'

'Or asylum seekers. Do you think India would send Yin back?'

'I doubt it – India and China are not the best of neighbors – but by the same token we don't want the Indians tossing our people in jail either. We need to place somebody in Kashmir to help smooth things over once they arrive. And we probably need a friendly word through the back channel from Washington to tilt the situation in our favor.'

'Barnett?'

Donoher nodded. 'Please ask Sister Deborah to set up a video conference with him in an hour. In the meantime, I need to enlist Cardinal Velu for some help.'

55

TIBET

November 1

The first hint of dawn painted a line of deep blue across the eastern horizon and erased the faintest stars from the heavens. The waxing crescent moon hung just above the jagged mountains to the west as if waiting for sunrise before dropping from view. Kilkenny was at the controls, piloting BAT-1 over some of the world's most breathtaking scenery, regretting that his view was filtered through the greens and blacks of night vision.

'I have the new numbers,' Han announced.

'How bad?' Kilkenny asked.

'We took a big hit from that headwind over the plateau.'

'I know,' Kilkenny said. 'We're supposed to be in India by now. Any good news?'

'We're starting to make up some of the lost time.'

'Enough to get us across the border before dawn?'

'It will be close, but if we get some good wind on our tail in the last valley, we might make it.'

'You ready to take the stick again?' Kilkenny asked.

'Yeah, and thanks for the break,' Han said. 'My shoulders were sore as hell after fighting that wind.'

'Get us across that border, and I'll find a nice Indian masseuse to work you over,' Kilkenny promised.

'I always work better with an incentive.'

'Can I have one too?' Gates squawked from BAT-2, his request parroted by the rest of the warriors.

'Gentlemen, as we are in a very real sense "on a mission from God",' – here Kilkenny did his dead-on imitation of Dan Aykroyd's mantra in *The Blues Brothers* – 'I cannot in good conscience promise you an all-expense-paid trip to the Kama Sutra Spa and Fornicatorium.'

Low groans filled Kilkenny's ears.

'I will, however, gladly authorize a real masseuse to remove the damage inflicted on our joints and muscles by these long flights and an open bar to provide nourishment of a spiritual nature.'

'Hoo-yah!' bellowed Gates, Chun, and Chow above the chorus of other positive if not profane responses.

Kilkenny knew the feeling. The men were getting excited as the mission neared completion.

'Comm, two-way Kilkenny,' Tao said.

The voices in Kilkenny's ears faded.

'Nolan,' Tao said, 'take a look at Yin.'

Kilkenny looked over his shoulder and saw Yin reclined in his seat, arms folded across his chest, still and quiet.

'Is he—'

'Sleeping,' Tao cut him off. 'I checked and he's sound asleep. He hasn't stirred in hours.'

'Good for him.'

'So we're close to the border?' Tao asked.

'Yeah, I just hope we cross it before dawn. Otherwise we'll have to put down.'

'When will you know?'

'Within the hour. If he were awake, I'd ask him to pray for a steady tailwind.'

56

Woo Sun studied the landscape below, a mixture of sharp peaks and undulating forms rendered even more surreal by the night-vision goggles that allowed him to fly so close to the ground in low light. His right hand was on the pickle stick of a Harbin WZ-9 attack helicopter – a Chinese variant of the Eurocopter Dauphin II. It was one of sixty flown by the PLA's Aviation Corps, and nearly all of them had been rushed into service along the western border the previous day.

To Woo's right sat his weapons operator, Gong Yuan. The two men had trained together for three years, logging thousands of hours in a variety of flight conditions. They knew every sound the WZ-9 made and could tell how the twin turboshaft engines were performing by their vibration through the airframe.

Both men scanned the valley, searching for three low-flying aircraft with fixed wings scalloped like those of a bat. Woo had laughed at the description of their quarry, but not at their orders should they locate them. The enemy aircraft were to be shot down and all aboard killed.

The intelligence officer who briefed the crews of Woo's

squadron reported that the enemy aircraft was designed for stealthy insertion and removal of special forces personnel. It was a lightweight, slow-moving craft that featured an open fuselage and a negligible radar cross-section. To Woo's and Gong's satisfaction, their prey was also reportedly unarmed.

Woo and Gong had flown out of Tianshuihai and were patrolling a section of the border where China abutted the Indian state of Jammu and Kashmir, including the disputed region of Askai Chin that was under Chinese control.

'Could you imagine being posted to this place?' Gong asked.

'I'd give a city boy like you a week before you sucked on your pistol.'

'*Qin wode pigu,*' Gong replied, profanely suggesting that Woo kiss his posterior.

Woo followed a valley southwest out of Changmar heading toward Bar – a village on the northern shore of the Tibetan lake of Bangong Co. There, mountain streams collected in the narrow strip of briny water that stretched one hundred and thirty kilometers. The western quarter of the long, thin lake lay on the Indian side of the border, where it was called Pangong Tso. Water flowed from Bangong Co into the Shyok River, then on to the Indus River before turning south through Pakistan toward the sea.

'Crossing eighty degrees east longitude,' Han announced, 'and in a few moments you should see the eastern end of Bangong Co. As we begin our descent into India,

I remind you that smoking on this flight is prohibited and to please put seats and tray tables in the upright position. Again, thank you for flying Night Stalker Air.'

Yin looked around trying to determine how to adjust his seat as Han requested.

'It's a joke,' Tao explained. 'The kind of thing you would hear every time you flew in a commercial jet. Those planes have a few more amenities than our BATs.'

'Maybe, but our view is better,' Han countered.

More stars had faded from the predawn sky, and the moon winked at them from behind passing mountain peaks as they flew low through the valley. Numbers flicked by on Kilkenny's heads-up display – speed, position, distance to waypoint, and time – and the moment for a decision had arrived.

'Team comms on,' Kilkenny said. 'Bad news, people. Looks like we're going to spend another day in China. We've got a clear sky and about an hour of flying time before we reach the border. Sunup's in twenty and we're losing dark fast.'

A chorus of disappointed groans answered Kilkenny's report.

'You heard the man,' Gates barked. 'Same drill as before. Let's find a good place to hole up. No sense getting this far only to have our asses shot off while trying to jump the border in broad daylight.'

'Check it out,' Han said.

The valley ahead narrowed where it formed the basin of the glacial lake. A thick white fog floated above the still surface of the lake, a distinct mass like a cloud that had fallen from the sky.

'Let's cut around it and look for an LZ on the southern shore,' Kilkenny said.

'You got it, boss.'

At Bar, Woo turned the helicopter southeast into the canyon that cradled the narrow lake. He flew above the fog, the wash from the four main rotor blades churning the upper layers of the mist. The canyon widened into a bowl at the eastern end of the lake, and the fog spread out like a blanket over the water below.

'I got something,' Woo said.

'Where?' Gong asked.

'One o'clock. Moving to intercept.'

Gong scanned the horizon and spotted three distinct forms gliding above the mist.

'Too solid to be a flock of birds.' Gong switched on the radio. 'Dragon One Five to Base.'

'Base. Over Dragon One Five.'

'Report probable contact. Zero three three point five north by zero eight zero point two east. Moving to intercept.'

'Roger, Dragon One Five.'

'I think I hear a chopper,' Han said. 'And it's hauling ass toward us.'

'Bogey at three o'clock,' Gates reported from BAT-2.

'That scrubs the landing,' Kilkenny called out. 'Get into the fog and run like hell for the border.'

Han put BAT-1 into a sharp dive toward the white cloud of mist. The other BATs followed his lead as the Harbin rapidly closed the distance.

'Nuts!' Gates cursed, then he opened the Velcro seal on the pouch beneath his seat and fished out a pistol.

'What do you think you're going to do with that?' Shen asked, his hands wrapped tightly on the flight stick.

'Hey, I might get off a lucky shot.'

'Base, we confirm positive ID of target aircraft. Preparing to engage.'

'Roger, Dragon One Five. Good hunting.'

Once in range, Gong activated the weapons system and tried to acquire a target.

'There's nothing to lock onto,' Gong reported. 'I'll have to do it manually.'

'We'll take the one in the middle of the flight, scatter them like birds.'

Woo dropped down, the underside of the Harbin skimming across the fog. Gong selected the Harbin's fixed twenty-three-millimeter cannons and opened fire. Tracer rounds drew bright lines through the air, allowing Woo to adjust his angle of attack.

BAT-2 shuddered when the first rounds punched through its wings. With the pistol gripped tightly in both hands, Gates lined up his shot and squeezed the trigger. His nine-millimeter response ricocheted harmlessly off the Harbin. The dogfight was a lopsided mismatch.

The Harbin slowed to nearly a hover and Gong fired again. One round pierced the nacelle, shattering the lightweight turbine engine. Tiny shards of the ceramic blades exploded in all directions, and the crew compartment was engulfed in a halo of shrapnel.

'Son of a bitch!' Chun swore as razor-sharp debris sliced through a few unprotected areas of his uniform.

Fragments pierced arms and legs, other pieces lodged in the warriors' helmets and body armor. Seated up front, Shen and Gates caught the worst of the damage, their bodies peppered with dozens of tiny wounds. Deprived of power, BAT-2 fell from the sky. Shen fought his pain, struggling to guide the battered aircraft safely to the ground.

'Look sharp, people!' Gates shouted. 'As soon as we touch down, haul ass for some cover.'

BAT-2 struck the ground hard just as the first rays of dawn lit the mountain peaks. They landed on a rocky slope, and the four warriors released their harnesses and raced toward the fog. The Harbin swooped down to block their way, and Gong switched to the twelve-point-seven-millimeter gun pods and opened fire.

Xaio swung BAT-3 around, approaching the helicopter from behind. All three men with him took aim on the Harbin's tail rotor, but turbulence from the helicopter buffeted their craft and their shots flew wide.

'This fucker is picking off our guys down there!' Jing shouted.

'And we're next,' Xaio added bitterly. 'We're dead one way or another. But if we can take down this bastard right now, Yin gets out alive.'

'Do it!' Jing urged.

Agreed to a man, Xaio guided BAT-3 into a steep climb above the Harbin.

'You guys know what sound shit makes when it hits the fan?' Xaio asked.

Proud members of the Corps and familiar with the old joke, Sung and Tsui answered in a yell, '*Mareeeeeene!*'

BAT-3 swooped straight down like an eagle after a river salmon. Xaio aimed for the center of the Harbin's main rotor and called for as much power as the nacelle could deliver. The warriors aboard BAT-3 survived just long enough to know they had saved the lives of some of their company, then their aircraft disintegrated in the blur of the helicopter's rotating blades.

The collision snapped the Harbin's main shaft just below the hub, tilting the rotor assembly forward. One after another, the four long blades pounded into the side of the helicopter. Gong lost his arms and legs as the first blade sliced into the cabin. Slowed as they cut into the fuselage, the composite blades broke into large and lethal projectiles. Gong and Woo died instantly, their bodies torn apart.

Deprived of lift, the two fatally entangled aircraft obeyed gravity and plummeted to the ground. The knot of metal struck the bare, rocky slope and tumbled over. The twin engines, still racing furiously, tore free of their mounts, severing the fuel lines. Fumes and liquid ignited, detonating the half-empty fuel tanks. An expanding fireball tore through the fog, rising into the air like a beacon.

57

'Report!' Liu demanded.

'We've lost contact,' the communications officer replied. 'Everything is operational on this end. Dragon One Five is not responding.'

'*Gou shi!* Peng, where are they?'

Peng stood at a large wall map of the region, estimating the intersection of the Harbin's reported sighting.

'The last reported position was in western Tibet,' Peng replied, 'near Bangong Co. The nearest village is Rutog.'

'Captain, do you have any other aircraft in that area?'

The officer checked the current status of all aircraft assigned to this mission. 'The closest are near the end of their range. They don't have enough fuel to make it to Rutog and back. We do have one being refueled now that can be there in little more than an hour.'

'Peng and I will be on it.'

Han piloted BAT-1 in a wide arc around the wreckage, careful to remain upwind of the plume of oily, black smoke. Kilkenny and Tao surveyed the ground below while Yin prayed for the lives just lost. Two-thirds of their company lay either dead or wounded around the burning hulk of the Chinese helicopter.

'We should have put down earlier,' Kilkenny grumbled.

'It's not your fault,' Tao said reassuringly. 'We're in danger every minute we stay in China.'

'If we were on the ground they wouldn't have spotted us.'

'Perhaps, but if they had we would all be dead.'

'I found a place to land,' Han said, happy to change the subject.

'Do it,' Kilkenny ordered.

Kilkenny had his harness and helmet off as soon as the BAT landed, and he ran down the slope toward the crumpled airframe. The bodies of four men littered the field, the ground around them raked by heavy fire. Shen and Chun were clearly dead, their bodies perforated with bullet holes.

He found Chow by a large boulder and pressed his fingers to the man's neck but failed to find a pulse. He rolled the body over and saw the blood pooled on the ground beneath it. A sliver from the engine's ceramic blades had pierced the young SEAL's neck, and the exertion as he ran for cover proved fatal.

'We found Max,' Tao called out. 'He's alive.'

Kilkenny raced to where Tao and Yin knelt beside his former chief. They had removed his helmet, and Gates was both conscious and in pain.

'I know this is a dumb question,' Kilkenny said, 'but where does it hurt?'

'Be easier to say where it doesn't. Any of my guys make it?'

Kilkenny shook his head. 'And if it weren't for BAT-3, we'd be having this conversation in the next life.'

'I saw. Brave s-o-b's took that fucker out just as he was drawing a bead on me.'

Gates rubbed the Kevlar panel covering his badly bruised chest and dislodged a flattened slug. Several more dotted his body armor.

'Remind me to send a real nice letter to DuPont when we get home.'

'Make sure you enclose one of the slugs.'

'Here's the med kit,' Han said. 'I'll go check the RITEG on BAT-2, make sure it shut down.'

'Good thinking,' Kilkenny said. 'And pull it off the frame – I don't want to leave a nuke behind.'

'How's it look?' Gates asked as Kilkenny and Tao dressed his wounds.

'Some of these cuts will need stitches, but most are superficial. You might have a few cracked ribs as well, but nothing a tough old SEAL like you won't recover from,' Kilkenny replied. 'Of course, you've at least doubled your collection of dings.'

'Just what I needed,' Gates said grimly.

'I don't know,' Tao mused as she set a dressing. 'I think a few scars give a man character.'

As Kilkenny treated Gates, Yin tended to the remains of the three fallen warriors. He carefully ordered their bodies on the ground and removed their helmets, treating each man with great dignity. Yin said a prayer for the repose of their souls, that each would find eternal rest. Although he could not reach them, Yin offered the same prayers for the men whose bodies were being consumed by the fire.

After Gates's wounds were tended, Kilkenny joined Yin by the burning wreckage and offered his own prayer for the men who had sacrificed themselves for the team.

'They were brave men,' Kilkenny said. 'They saw what had to be done and took action.'

'But what of the other men?' Yin asked.

'They got what they deserved.'

'Did they? But for an accident of birth, could they not have been your men? Did they not share many of the same hopes as your men? I find no joy in any of these deaths, and I forgive those who sought to harm us.'

'Of all the lessons my catechists tried to drill into my head, I still have the toughest time with that one.'

'Truth is like water,' Yin explained. 'Both are necessary for life, but both may come in forms that are difficult to grasp. Forgiveness can be hard to give, and is often harder to accept. But the true paradox is that the forgiveness we need most must come from ourselves. It is a lesson I struggle with as well.'

'Why do you need forgiveness?' Kilkenny asked. 'If anything, you're owed a very large apology.'

'We *all* need forgiveness. You and your companions have risked your lives to win my freedom, and some have been killed in the effort.' Yin touched the cross hidden beneath his suit. 'I fear that members of my flock who have helped you have also paid a terrible price. All because of me.'

'None of that is your fault,' Kilkenny said dismissively.

'Had I chosen a different vocation, many people would still be alive, and we would not be having this conversation,' Yin countered calmly. 'And for better or worse, choices you have made have brought you here at this moment.'

'If it's any consolation, I forgive you for being a man worth saving.'

'All of us are worth saving.' Yin paused. 'You were to be a father today, yes?'

'I was.'

'What happened to your wife and child?'

The directness of Yin's questions angered Kilkenny, but he felt an overwhelming urge to answer.

'Kelsey and I wanted to start our family once we were married, and she became pregnant last February. In the spring, we learned she had cancer. The disease was treatable, but it required a horrible sacrifice.'

'The life of your child.'

Kilkenny nodded. 'Because she was pregnant, my wife's cancer was very aggressive and required equally aggressive treatment. The doctors gave us three choices: end the pregnancy and attack the cancer; attack the cancer while she was still pregnant with the knowledge that it would either kill or seriously injure our child; or postpone treatment until after our child could be safely born and hope the cancer hadn't spread too far.'

'A difficult choice,' Yin agreed. 'What did you two decide?'

'We both wanted Toby, and we wouldn't do anything to endanger his life. Kelsey and I chose to postpone treatment to give our baby the time he needed to be born. We knew this choice was the most dangerous one for her, but Kelsey was already thinking like a mother, and she was willing to risk death for our child. It was a race against time, and we lost. Kelsey was dying when the doctors delivered our son. He was so small,' Kilkenny's voice cracked as he recalled the scene, 'he fit in the palm of my hand. Toby died just a few hours after his mother.'

'And now you carry the grief of a devastating loss, and the anger. They are your constant companions, lurking on the fringes of your consciousness. You can hide from them in your work, or numb yourself with alcohol or opium, but the grief and anger will continue to gnaw at you like rats until you confront their source. You loved your wife, yes?'

'Of course.'

'Yet you chose not to treat her illness, knowing that it could cause her death. Why?'

'Because we believed that it was morally wrong to do anything that would have killed our child.'

'But still your child died, along with your wife. Knowing that, would you have decided differently?'

'Kelsey and I talked about that, and we couldn't trade his life for hers. With the choice we made, we still had hope.'

'So you did what you believed was right. You acted in accordance with your faith?'

'Yes.'

'Do you pray?' Yin asked.

'Occasionally.'

'Near the end, did you offer your life to save your wife and son?'

'Yes,' Kilkenny admitted.

'And still they were taken from you. Who took them?'

'Nobody,' Kilkenny shot back. 'They died because my wife had cancer.'

'But when you offered your life for theirs, who did you think would accept the exchange?' Yin demanded. 'And when He didn't, and your family died, who did you blame?'

'God,' Kilkenny replied.

'But the decision that led to their deaths was not God's. It was yours.' As Yin spoke, the tone of his voice remained calm without a hint of accusation. 'I do not believe God causes earthquakes or floods, nor do I believe He afflicts people with disease or allows some to commit acts of evil. All of this is part of His creation, including the gift of free will.

'You and your wife made a decision based on faith and hope, yet still suffered a great tragedy. I believe God is aware of this tragedy, and in His own way seeks to restore harmony. This is akin to the Chinese belief that crisis and opportunity are two sides of the same coin. But in keeping with our free will, God does not force harmony upon us. Instead, He presents opportunities, but it is up to us to recognize them. To overcome your grief and anger and to survive your loss, you must forgive yourself.'

'We got company!' Han shouted.

Drawn by the tall column of black smoke, five men were striding down the slope toward them. They moved as easily over the uneven terrain as the yaks that thrived in this region. All wore long *chubas*, felt boots, and richly embroidered hats. Except for the two youngest – who looked to be in their late teens or early twenties – Kilkenny found it difficult to estimate the men's ages. Their faces glowed with a rich bronze patina acquired from a lifetime of harsh weather and brilliant sunlight.

Kilkenny and Yin joined the others by BAT-1. The men stopped about twenty feet away, carefully assessing the group.

'Think they're here to pick over the bodies?' Gates asked.

'More likely curious,' Tao replied.

The men spoke quietly among themselves, keeping a careful eye on the five strangers in their land.

'The younger ones seem curious about you,' Kilkenny said to Tao. 'I'm sure you're dressed more provocatively than they're used to.'

'It is our clothing that intrigues them,' Yin offered. 'They wonder how we stay warm in something so thin.'

'You understand what they're saying?'

Yin nodded. 'I may be a little out of practice.'

Kilkenny walked up to the men, smiling and keeping his hands where they could see them. He held out his arm and rubbed the fabric, indicating they could touch it if they liked.

At first only one accepted Kilkenny's offer, then the others joined in. A rapid discussion ensued that ended with the apparent spokesman asking a question about the suit.

'Bishop Yin?' Kilkenny asked, looking for help.

'Our suits do not appear to be felt or silk. They wonder if they keep us warm and what kind of animal produced the fabric.'

Kilkenny smiled. 'Tell them we are very comfortable, and the fabric was made by a very small insect called a nanotech.'

Yin relayed Kilkenny's answer and the five men nodded, pleased with a new piece of knowledge.

'Na-no-tek,' one of the men said to Kilkenny, enunciating the syllables carefully.

Kilkenny nodded. The leader asked Yin another question, his tone more serious.

'Three of us are Chinese and two are not,' Yin translated. 'He wonders where we are from.'

Kilkenny pondered the question. Although all but Yin were from the United States, their presence in China was not officially sanctioned and something Washington would deny. In telling the Tibetans the truth, Kilkenny feared exposing them to reprisal from the Chinese government.

'I'm having a little trouble with that truth thing again,' Kilkenny said to Yin. 'If Beijing thinks these people knew where we were from and suspects they helped us in any way, it could be bad for them.'

'I think I may have an answer,' Yin replied.

Yin walked up beside Kilkenny and offered a response. The Tibetans all nodded and talked excitedly.

'What did you tell them?' Kilkenny asked.

'I said that I was a priest and that you and your associates came to China to accompany me to the West.'

The spokesman offered another question, and Kilkenny noted that he said one word with a particular reverence: *Kundun*. Yin clasped his hands together and bowed before answering – the word clearly had special significance.

'They ask if I am a lama, a holy man, and if I am going to the West for my own protection, like the beloved Kundun.'

'Kundun?'

'A Tibetan name,' Tao explained. 'It means *the presence*. They're talking about Tenzin Gyaltso. In the West, he is known as the Dalai Lama.'

'A fair analogy,' Kilkenny said.

The Tibetans greeted Yin's response warmly and drew close around, questioning him further. All but ignored, Kilkenny stepped back and left Yin with his enthralled audience.

'Seems the natives have taken a liking to our holy man,' Gates opined.

'He definitely has a way with people,' Kilkenny observed.

'What are we going to do about them? You know the Chinese are going to come for that,' Tao said, nodding her head toward the burning helicopter.

'You can bet they reported sighting us before starting their attack,' Han added.

'And what about the bodies of our people?' Gates asked. 'We can't let the ChiComs get 'em.'

'I was thinking the same thing,' Kilkenny replied, 'and I have no intention of leaving our buddies behind.'

'How can we take them with us?' Han asked. 'We have more passengers than seats.'

'One problem at a time. First, I think we need to offer a hecatomb to our fallen warriors.'

'A heck of what?' Han asked.

'He's going Greek on us.' Gates rolled his eyes. 'I've seen this before. It's what happens when you read too much.'

'Would our Tibetan friends be offended if we cremated the remains of our dead?' Kilkenny asked Yin. 'We don't want their bodies desecrated by the Chinese military.'

Yin posed Kilkenny's question to the group. After a brief discussion, he had an answer.

'Tibetan Buddhists bury their dead in earth or water, or in the sky.'

'The sky?' Kilkenny asked. 'You mean cremation?'

'No. Sky burial is an old and honored tradition in Tibet. After the spirit has departed, the body is dismembered into small pieces and fed to a gathering of vultures. The bones are ground into powder and mixed with flour to make bread, which is also fed to the birds. It is the birds that take the body into the sky.'

'Not exactly a proper Christian burial,' Gates groused, disgusted by the idea.

'No, but the symbolism of the ceremony is quite moving. It reinforces the belief of oneness. I have attended sky burials and find them most poetic.'

'But what about cremation?' Kilkenny asked.

'Burning the remains of the dead is an accepted practice, but rarely done in this region as it requires a fuel, which is scarce.'

'At the moment, we have plenty of fuel.' Kilkenny turned to Han. 'You want to give me a hand?'

Kilkenny and Han approached the body of Bob Shen. With the greatest care they moved it to the burning helicopter and cast it into the center of the flames. Next they added the remains of Gene Chun and Jim Chow. Finally, they cast into the fire the helmets of the fallen men and the dismantled wreckage of BAT-2 to prevent the technology from falling into Chinese hands.

Yin joined the Tibetans in a Buddhist prayer for the

dead. Kilkenny did not understand the words but was moved nonetheless.

'We honor the sacrifice of our fallen comrades,' Kilkenny said in conclusion, 'and offer them to the winds that they, too, may find their way home.'

'Nice hecatomb, Nolan,' Gates offered seriously.

'Just what is a hecatomb?' Han asked.

'Originally, it referred to the practice among ancient Greeks and Romans of sacrificing a hundred cows or oxen to commemorate a significant event and curry favor with the gods,' Kilkenny explained. 'It also refers to the slaughter or sacrifice of many victims.'

'I'd say our guys are worth a lot more than a hundred head of cattle,' Gates added.

'After their victory at Troy,' Kilkenny continued, 'many of the Achaeans, impatient to return to their homeland, failed to offer a proper sacrifice. Their gods were displeased, and the Achaeans never made it home.'

Gates leaned close to Han. 'As I said, he's going Greek on us.'

'Keep talking that way and I might go medieval on you instead,' Kilkenny offered.

'Hey!' Gates said excitedly. 'I know *that* movie.'

'I thought you might. Now, to deal with our other problems.'

Kilkenny joined Yin and the Tibetans who were deep in conversation. 'Bishop Yin, I have several requests for our new friends.'

'Yes?' Yin asked.

'First, after the fire dies down, would they please grind the bones of our people to dust? Second, we need to leave soon. Is there a boat we can use? Sadly, we will be unable to return it.'

Yin nodded.

'I don't want them to be harmed for helping us, so when the Chinese arrive, I would like them to be truthful when questioned, but not too truthful.'

Yin relayed Kilkenny's questions, and the Tibetans took a few moments to discuss the matter before responding.

'Norbu, the elder, says they would be honored to scatter the remains of our friends. He also says there is a boat we can use, something that was left by a tourist this past summer. His sons will show you where it is.'

'That's very kind.'

'Relations between the Chinese and Tibetans are not always good,' Yin explained. 'Norbu says he and his brothers will tell whoever comes as little as possible.'

'Perfect. They can say that the bodies of the dead were burned in the fire by the survivors, and that they saw only two people in the aircraft when it left, you and me.'

'And the others?'

'I was hoping they would just "forget" to mention them.'

Yin relayed Kilkenny's comments, starting another round of conversation that ended with Norbu posing another question to Yin.

'They will do as you ask, but they also have a request.'

'I'll do whatever I can,' Kilkenny promised.

'The request is for me. They ask that when we reach the West, I convey their respects to Kundun.'

Kilkenny thought a moment. 'I think we can arrange that.'

Kilkenny left Yin with the Tibetans and rejoined the rest of his team by the fire.

'What's the plan?' Gates asked.

'You three and Yin are taking a boat to India, and I'm going to play decoy in the BAT.'

'You can't be serious,' Tao said.

'It's a bad move,' Gates agreed. 'Anytime a guy splits off from the group in a horror movie, he ends up dead.'

'The Chinese know we're trying to fly out. And since we downed their helo, they have to assume we're still flying. We can't all fit in BAT-1, and if we leave it here they'll know we're trying to get out some other way. If I give them something to chase, you'll have a better chance of making it across the border.'

'I'm the pilot,' Han countered. 'I should be taking the BAT.'

'You have a wife and kids, right?' Kilkenny asked.

'Yeah.'

'I don't, and this expedition has created enough widows and orphans.'

'If being a family man is your criteria, then let me fly,' Gates said. 'There's still hope for you.'

'I appreciate that, Max, but I'd still rather have you in the boat. Look, this isn't a kamikaze run – I fully intend to get out of China alive. We just need a distraction to cover your escape.'

'But why you?' Han asked.

'Peace of mind. If things go bad, I would rather it be me than any of you. Since I'm the boss, my order stands.

Now, if you'll all excuse me, I have a nuke to stow and a message to send.'

Kilkenny strapped BAT-2's RITEG into the back of BAT-1 and pulled on his helmet.

'Satellite uplink on.'

SATELLITE UPLINK ACTIVATED

'Message encrypt, five words: *One born every minute initially*.'

CONFIRM: ONE BORN EVERY MINUTE INITIALLY

'Message confirmed.'

SEND TO?

'Bombadil.'

MESSAGE TRANSMITTED TO BOMBADIL

Kilkenny pulled off the helmet and scratched his head. He looked over at Yin. The Tibetans were treating the Bishop with as much reverence as if he were a high lama of their faith.

'Gather 'round, everybody,' Kilkenny called out.

Everyone, including the Tibetans, joined Kilkenny beside the BAT.

'I just sent word to Rome, so with luck you won't have too much trouble on the other side of the lake. You should get moving and take advantage of this fog for as long as it lasts. Judging by the flow out of these mountains, you'll be moving with the current, so that should help.' Kilkenny turned to Yin. 'Would you please express my deepest thanks to our Tibetan friends for all their help?'

As Yin spoke, Kilkenny bowed deeply to each of the men, who were pleased by the gesture. He turned to his comrades.

'No mushy goodbyes,' Kilkenny said. 'I'll meet up with you on the other side. Take care and get across that border.'

Yin stepped in front of Kilkenny, hands folded and head bowed. He lifted his head, slipped his thumbs inside the collar of his suit, and carefully drew out the hand-carved cross. He held it up for a moment of veneration before lowering it to his chest.

'Bow your head for a blessing,' Yin said softly.

Kilkenny clasped his hands together and lowered his head.

'O Lord Jesus, please watch over this man as he has watched over me. Protect him from harm and guide his journey home. Amen.'

'Amen,' Kilkenny answered.

Kilkenny lifted his head, and Yin extended a hand toward him. He grasped the small, slender hand and discovered warm steel within the grip. And in Yin's gaze Kilkenny found an intensity and clarity reminiscent of the late Pope Leo.

'Only God knows what lies ahead for you and me,' Yin said, 'and if the future differs from our hopes, I wish now to express my gratitude.'

'You're welcome,' Kilkenny replied. 'And Godspeed.'

58

VATICAN CITY

Grin awoke with a start as the riffs of 'Gimme Shelter' poured from the computer's speakers. He adjusted his glasses and clicked on the center of the logo to retrieve Kilkenny's message.

ONE BORN EVERY MINUTE INITIALLY

'Not a story problem,' Grin howled. 'I hate story problems.'

He dismissed this thought as quickly as it came, writing it off to his body's natural desire for an undisturbed sleep cycle – something he had missed over the past two weeks.

Then he thought about the original quote: *There's a sucker born every minute*. It was a cynical expression, to be sure, but it perfectly expressed the view of the master showman who coined it. Grin wondered what message Kilkenny was trying to send with it.

If there's one born every minute initially, Grin thought, *what happens afterward?*

He wondered how time figured into this, and what was causing the initial minute to change. He quickly filled a clean page on his legal pad with every random thought that flashed into his sleep-deprived brain. His mind finally went blank, the well empty.

'Initial minute, initial time,' he said aloud, hoping the sound of his own voice might reignite his synapses.

'Initial,' Grin said again, the word becoming almost a mantra.

Then he saw the first line he'd written on the page.

There's a sucker born every minute – P.T. Barnum

If it isn't time, Grin mused, *maybe it is initials.*

He circled Barnum's first and middle initials and brought up the map of the region where he believed Kilkenny was located. In the middle of one of the valleys that ran from Tibet in Ladakh, he saw a long thin lake shaped like a flattened letter N. On the Tibetan side, the lake was called Bangong Co, but across the border it became Pangong Tso.

P.T. Ah, Pangong Tso! He had it.

Grin picked up the phone and dialed Donoher. The Camerlengo answered before the second ring.

'You've heard from Nolan?' Donoher asked.

'Yeah, and something's happened. I got a very specific message pointing to a lake that straddles the border between China and India. It's right through one of the valleys I thought he'd use.'

'Then you were right.'

'About the valley, yeah, but Nolan's pointing us to the lake, or specifically the Indian side of the lake. I don't think they're in the air anymore – they're traveling by water.

'Which means they'll be on foot once they reach India. I'll pass the word to our people there,' Donoher said. 'Let me know if you hear anything else.'

59

TIBET

The black plume rising against the vivid blue sky provided an unmistakable visual marker of the Harbin's crash site. Liu squirmed impatiently in the rear seat behind the weapons operator, irritable about how the scale of the terrain made distances deceptive.

'How much longer?' he fussed.

'Just a few minutes, sir,' the pilot replied calmly. He had carried VIPs before.

As they neared the site, the plume grew from a thin reed of smoke into a thick black column. Flames licked furiously at the skeletal frame of the helicopter, liquefying soft metals and devouring anything that would burn.

Three Tibetans sat on the ground upwind of the blaze. They watched the helicopter circle, looking for a level place to land, but made no move to flee or welcome the new arrivals.

The Harbin hovered over a relatively level patch of earth, extended its landing gear, and touched down.

The pilot kept the blades running in case the ground proved unstable, and Liu and Peng exited from the rear doors. Both were dressed in flight suits and helmets, and they crouched as they ran beneath the nearly invisible main rotor.

'You there!' Liu shouted as he approached the Tibetans. 'What are you doing here?'

'Watching the fire,' Norbu replied in halting Chinese.

'Did you see what happened?' Peng asked calmly.

'We saw smoke and came to see what was burning. It is a very large fire.'

'Did you see anything else, any other aircraft?'

'We saw two. One was damaged and one was not. The men in gray put the damaged one in the fire. They did not want you to find it. They also put their dead in the fire.'

'Please describe the men,' Peng asked. 'How many and what did they look like?'

'There were two men. An elder, Chinese like you, and a tall foreigner.'

'No others?' Liu demanded.

'They are dead.'

'What happened after they burned their dead?' Peng asked.

'The two men flew away on a strange machine.'

'Where did they go?'

Norbu and the others pointed west, in the direction of the village of Rutog.

'Why didn't you stop them?' Liu said angrily.

'The old one was a holy man,' Norbu explained.

'You spoke with these men?'

'Yes.'

Liu stepped away in a rage, trying to gather his thoughts. He pointed at the burning wreckage. 'That was a military helicopter. Its job is to defend China against foreign aggression. When you discovered a foreigner here, in China, next to a destroyed Chinese helicopter, did you not think this foreigner might have been the cause?'

'We did not see what happened,' Norbu replied calmly. 'We do not know the cause of the accident.'

'Thick-headed fools!' Liu shouted. 'The foreigner shot it down!'

Liu pulled out his pistol and shot Norbu in the head. Norbu's brothers tried to flee but were shot before they could scramble to their feet.

'Why did you do that?' Peng asked, stunned by Liu's brutality.

'They were criminals,' Liu replied as he replaced the spent rounds in his pistol.

'These men had done nothing.'

'They abetted foreign invaders and a fugitive enemy of the state. Their inaction was both criminal and unpatriotic.'

'But that's a matter for the courts to decide.'

'And I have just saved the Ministry of Justice a considerable amount of time and money in reaching the same conclusion,' Liu replied confidently. 'Come, there's still hope we can catch Yin.'

Liu and Peng climbed back into the helicopter and plugged their helmets back into the communications system.

'Sir,' the pilot said, 'there's been a report of an unusual

aircraft flying low over the outskirts of Rutog about twenty-five minutes ago.'

'How far is Rutog?'

'Under five minutes.'

'Get us there.'

60

'Not much of a beach,' Gates said as they walked along the rocky shore of the lake following Norbu's sons, Rinzen and Tashi.

Han dipped his fingers into the cold water, tasted it, and winced. 'Fishing can't be much either. Too salty.'

A helicopter roared overhead, though with the fog they could neither see it nor be seen by it.

'I hope Nolan has a good head start,' Tao said.

'My prayers are with him as well,' Yin added.

Rinzen and Tashi raced forward excitedly, urging the others to follow. Through the mist, they saw a number of large and small shapes on the shore. As they drew close, the shapes took form as boats.

'This must be the marina here in Lake Woebegone,' Gates opined.

Gates walked up to one of the boats. It had a flat wooden top and several large inflated bladders as pontoons underneath. On closer inspection, he noticed stubs sticking out of the bladders and tightly woven seams.

'What is this?'

'Goat, of course,' Yin replied. 'When sealed properly, it makes a good vessel for air.'

'And I thought I'd seen everything.'

'The hide on those boats is yak stretched over a wooden frame,' Yin pointed out. 'Flexible and watertight.'

'Is this what we're taking all the way to India?' Han said skeptically.

'Naw,' Gates replied. 'To carry the four of us, we'd need something bigger, maybe made out of a yeti.'

Norbu's Tibetan sons passed the traditional Tibetan boats and finally stopped at the one they were looking for. Unlike the other boats, this one was slender with a hard finish; to Gates's eyes, it was recognizable. He ran his hand over the smooth granite-gray hulls and found the name molded into the polyethylene: *Windrider Rave*.

'What is it?' Han asked.

'A trimiran,' Gates answered, amazed to find such a craft in the remotest region of Tibet. 'How did *this* get here?'

Yin asked Norbu's sons, and the two alternated in telling the tale.

'Many tourists come to see the lake in the summer,' Yin translated. 'This past summer, a foreigner, a wealthy Japanese man, came with a group of friends. The man brought a boat to sail on the lake. When the time came to leave, the Chinese told him he must pay for a license to take the boat out. The fee was very expensive. The man refused to pay and left the boat instead.'

'Quite a coincidence finding such a boat out here,' Gates mused.

'There is an old saying among the native people of the western provinces,' Yin offered. 'Allah provides.'

'It has only two seats,' Han noticed.

'Yeah,' Gates replied. 'And two of us will be riding on the trampolines, assuming they're stowed in here somewhere.'

Gates peeled the cover off the cockpit and found a bag containing the boat's accessories. With help from Norbu's sons, he stretched the fabric trampolines between the center hull and the outriggers, set the lines, and unfurled the sails. A steady breeze rolled through the valley, fluttering the teal-trimmed translucent sails and promising a good wind for the voyage west.

'Now for the seating arrangements,' Gates announced. 'Roxanne, can you swim?'

'Yes.'

'Good, take a seat on the starboard trampoline. Terry, you're on the port side. Padre, you sit in front of me, and I'll be the even hand, or in this case feet, on the rudder.'

Tao studied the taut triangular trampoline suspended just inches above the water skeptically. 'What would you have done if I said no?'

'I'd have asked if you could sail. And if I got another no, I'd have told you to hang on real tight out there 'cause there's no way I'm putting Yin out on a trampoline. Nolan would kick my ass all the way back to Coronado if he found out. That said, helmets on. Let's get this boat in the water.'

The six easily lifted the sleek craft and set it in knee-deep water. The Tibetans, on the shallow end of the boat, quickly moved back to shore before the icy lake water found a way into their felt boots. Tao and Han held the boat steady as Gates and Yin boarded. Gates gingerly pulled himself into the cockpit, adjusted the seat, and found the pedals. With a shove, Tao and Han leaped onto the trampolines. The *Windrider* responded quickly, catching the wind perfectly. The jib and mainsail billowed, and the craft began to accelerate. Gates threw a wave at the Tibetans as the boat disappeared into the fog.

'Display GPS,' Gates commanded.

A map view of the area appeared in his heads-up display. In the center was a dot indicating their current position. Readouts in the corners of his display indicated his speed, direction, and altitude.

'Display topography.'

Thin lines traced out the forms of mountains, valleys, and ridges in the surrounding terrain.

'Identify lake perimeter and display.'

The view panned out as a bright blue line highlighted the shoreline of the entire lake.

'Identify centerline of lake through long axis, west to east.'

A line appeared running down the middle of the lake from Tibet to Ladakh.

'Centerline defines course and waypoints. Audible alarm if position deviates point five kilometers from course.'

COURSE DEFINED
AUDIBLE ALARM SET

'Do you know where you're going?' Han sounded concerned.

'Yeah, for at least as long as the batteries in my helmet last.'

61

Kilkenny buzzed the outskirts of Rutog fifty feet off the ground. The whine of the turbine engine frightened livestock unfamiliar with the high-pitched sound and drew the curious from their modest dwellings. He waved to the grinning children who raced after the BAT, excitedly trying to keep pace; for many, this was the first aircraft they had ever seen at close range. Kilkenny noticed some adults running toward the center of the village, doubtless to report the sighting. His visit to Rutog was brief but sufficiently sensational to attract attention.

From Rutog, he flew northwest toward the village of Bar, careful to stay above the slowly dissipating blanket of fog. The view as he cruised through the valley was absolutely breathtaking. On either side stood softly rolling mountains, chocolate brown in color and ground into fantastic shapes by eons of glacial weathering. In the distance stood the giants – the sharp-edged peaks of the Himalayas. The granite blues and pure whites of the world's tallest mountains were dazzling in the morning sun.

Near Bar, Kilkenny turned due west following a line

down the center of a narrow canyon that snaked its way toward the Sino-Indian border. He heard the thump of rotors as he approached the first waypoint on his path west. Glancing over his left shoulder, he saw the Harbin, tail high and bearing down on him at three times the BAT's top speed. He checked the seat beside him to confirm that the large bundle of camouflage tarp was securely strapped in place. Then he began flying with evasive maneuvers, trying to make the BAT a harder target for the helicopter's bristling arsenal of weapons to find.

'Blast it out of the sky!' Liu ordered.

The weapons operator selected the Harbin's fixed cannons, opened fire, and twelve-point-seven-millimeter rounds spat from the nose-mounted muzzles – the line of the shell's flight described by bright orange streaks of the tracer rounds. The pilot slowed to avoid overflying the enemy aircraft and adjusted his line of attack, trying to keep pace with his prey's erratic maneuvers.

Kilkenny imagined the smell of cordite as the tracers flew past, his mind recalling from memory the distinct scent of combat. He pitched the BAT's nose down while simultaneously executing a half roll to the right. The BAT's pilot-friendly flight characteristics compensated for Kilkenny's rudimentary skill at the stick, resulting in a passable split-S maneuver. As the BAT dropped into the fog, the roll changed direction 180 degrees. Kilkenny saw the shadow of the Harbin race past overhead, slowing as it reached the spot where he disappeared into the fog.

He reached over to the seat beside him and unlatched the five-point restraint. With his right hand firmly holding the tarp in place, Kilkenny pulled back on the stick and put the BAT into a loop.

'Hah! And Mom thought all those hours playing Chuck Yeager's *Air Combat* were wasted time.'

'Did you hit it?' Liu shouted.

'I don't think so, sir,' the weapons operator replied.

'He may be trying to double back on us,' the pilot said. 'Everyone keep your eyes open.'

The pilot slowed the Harbin and began a cautious turn to the right. Seated behind the pilot on the right side of the aircraft, Peng searched the fathomless haze for any sign of the enemy lurking beneath. He hadn't noticed, but his helmet cropped off the outer edges of his peripheral vision, serving not quite as blinders but reducing his field of view by ten percent. Whether that missing percentage would have made the difference, Peng didn't know, but when he finally saw the BAT, it was shooting straight up out of the fog like a missile.

'He's behind us!' Peng shouted.

The pilot pulled the stick hard to the right, bringing his guns around, but the BAT was now above them. Inverted over the Harbin, Kilkenny pulled the tarp out of the seat and dumped it out behind his wings. The Harbin's main rotors sucked in and devoured the lightweight bundle of fabric. The tarp flapped furiously against the blades like a flag in a gale, creating a camouflage green halo.

'Something's on the rotor!' Peng shouted.

'I feel it,' the pilot cried out. 'It's affecting the controls.'

The pilot's hard right turn continued past the point where the BAT emerged from the fog and raced toward a full revolution. The weapons operator spied the black form overhead and squeezed the trigger on the forward guns. At close range, the Harbin raked the fragile BAT with a punishing fusillade. Heavy rounds pierced the articulating wings and tore the nacelle from its mounts.

The BAT shuddered under the barrage. Kilkenny felt the hair on the back of his neck rise as shells whizzed past, some just inches behind him as he dived through the line of fire. Once hit, the nacelle above Kilkenny's head consumed itself and disgorged a cloud of ceramic fragments. Like the men of BAT-2, Kilkenny felt a stinging rain of shards piercing his skin. He fought to control the BAT as it plunged back into the mist.

Above the Harbin, the main rotor shredded Kilkenny's only weapon, transforming the large tarp into hundreds of ragged strips.

'It's breaking up,' Peng noted.

'*Wa cao!*' the pilot cursed. 'It's going to destroy the engines.'

The Harbin's twin turboshaft engines inhaled the free-flying debris, and layers of camouflage fabric choked the flow of air into the compressors. Destabilized by an unbalanced airflow, the compressor began to disintegrate. As the pilot raced to secure the engines from damage, the cabin filled with a popping sound like that from a rapid-fire gun. The two compressors were self-destructing.

'Brace for impact!' the pilot shouted. 'I'm going to try a power-off landing.'

The pilot declutched the rotor from the now-failed engines, allowing the blades to autorotate. He fully lowered the collective to maintain rotor RPM and pressed down hard on the right pedal to keep the fuselage from spinning beneath the rotor. The Harbin's nose pitched forward with the loss of power, and it slipped into the fog. The pilot pulled back on the cyclic stick to correct his angle of descent and keep air moving steadily through the main rotor. Above the cabin, the main rotor continued to spin like a maple seed corkscrewing through the air to slow the aircraft's fall to earth. The pilot was performing the helicopter equivalent of gliding.

'I'll keep us up as long as I can, but we need to land fast,' the pilot warned. 'Find someplace flat!'

The BAT fell like a wounded goose, wings fluttering im-potently as it tumbled from the sky. The RITEG had shut down, and the controls were dead. Kilkenny wondered if he soon would be as well. His body tensing, he tried to stay loose – the blow that was coming would be hard.

The BAT struck the lake inverted, its widespread wings slapping the water flat like a brake, jarring Kilkenny in his seat. Almost immediately, the BAT began to sink. With his legs braced against the frame to hold himself in place, Kilkenny popped the quick-release button on his five-point restraint. He grabbed the frame where the tubular segments joined at the top, rolled his legs forward out of the seat, and dropped into the lake.

Although most of his body was warm inside the

form-fitting SEALskin suit, the icy salt water found every tiny slit cut by shards from the nacelle. In each wound, the saline solution increased the number of ions available to race through Kilkenny's nervous system, telegraphing signals of pain to his brain. Almost as quickly, the cold numbed the areas around his exposed injuries, resulting in a neurological détente as his brain sorted through the input, deciding which sensation to recognize.

Kilkenny treaded water as he tried to regain his bearings and assess his situation. The heads-up display in his helmet flickered as lake water saturated its electronics – unlike his SEALskin suit, the helmet was not designed for immersion. But before the display shorted out, Kilkenny determined the direction of the nearest shore. He removed the helmet, which had filled with water up to his mouth, and let it sink to the bottom of the lake. He checked for his pistol and combat knife, then swam for shore at breakneck speed.

The surface of Bangong Co was as smooth as glass and deep blue even under the blanket of fog. The constant movement of his arms and legs kept a fresh supply of warm blood flowing in his extremities. The lake's high level of salinity aided his swim by making him more buoyant, but Kilkenny's suit was the key to his survival in the water. Without it, he would have succumbed to hypothermia long before he reached shore.

I wonder what Gates will say, Kilkenny thought, *if I mention Icarus when I tell this story?*

The Harbin limped along in flight, the pilot struggling to maintain altitude. The four men aboard gazed doggedly through the windscreen as if by force of will they could part the veil of mist and find a safe place to land. The fog thinned as they approached the shoreline, the combination of sun and wind flowing down from the mountains stirring the haze. By midday, it would be gone.

'I see something,' the weapons operator said.

Ahead loomed a mountain, and the pilot turned to parallel the shore. The slope fell almost vertically into the water, where the dropoff was steep and close to shore – a hundred feet deep just a stone's throw from the water's edge.

The pilot followed the contour of the lake, noting how the water bent around the mountain, flowing along the path of least resistance. On the far side of the mountain, the curve in the shoreline tapered into one of the long straight segments of the lake.

'Look for a valley or inlet,' the pilot ordered.

Almost as soon as he spoke, a swale between the mountains came into view. The pilot steered the Harbin in a wide arc that brought the aircraft around perpendicular to the shore and nose into the wind. Then he extended the landing gear and flared the helicopter to reduce both the rate of descent and the forward airspeed. The Harbin seemed to float, but the ground still rose up quickly. The pilot leveled out and brought the Harbin down. It landed with a crunch, and the aircraft pitched forward and about ten degrees to the left.

'Everybody out,' the pilot ordered.

The crew and passengers exited from the right side of the aircraft. Smoke wafted from the engine intakes, tingeing the air with a pungent smell. The pilot dropped onto the ground to check the condition of his aircraft. The Harbin employed a retractable tricycle landing gear, and the rear wheel assembly on the right side had collapsed on impact with a large rock.

'Pilot,' Liu growled, 'report our situation and request immediate assistance.'

'I will,' the pilot markedly paced his voice, '*after* I've assessed the condition of the aircraft.'

Peng set his helmet down and stood by the water's edge. The lake was calm and soundlessly lapping along the shore. He picked up a smooth stone and flung it sideways into the water. It skipped twice before submerging, the sound echoing strangely. He picked up another stone and was about to send it after the first when he heard something splashing. The noise was faint, but steady and slowly growing in intensity.

'Do you hear that?' Peng asked.

'What?' Liu replied.

'Listen.'

Liu removed his helmet and cocked an ear toward the lake. 'Probably birds.'

'I don't think so,' Peng said. 'It's too regular.'

Liu listened more intently and picked up on the steady rhythm of the stroke. 'You think someone survived?'

Peng stuck his hand in the water but yanked it out quickly. 'It's freezing. I can't think why anyone else would be swimming, and Kilkenny was once a SEAL – they train in cold water.'

'*Cao!*' Liu spat, staring into the fog. 'If it's a swimmer, where is he?'

'Hard to tell. The sound is bouncing off the rock all around us. But it's definitely approaching shore.'

'You go that way,' Liu ordered, pointing east. 'If you find this swimmer, kill him.'

Peng nodded and the two men set off.

Liu moved carefully along the rocky shore trying to pinpoint the source of the elusive sound. It changed in intensity, but overall it seemed to be moving closer. After ten minutes, Liu estimated he had covered almost fifty meters of difficult terrain. And the sound was definitely nearby.

Through the haze, he spied a lone swimmer cutting a long smooth stroke through the placid water. Liu studied the shore and found a large boulder to conceal himself behind until the swimmer emerged. The man would be cold and tired – an easy kill.

The swimmer slowed, then stopped as he reached the shallows. All but the upper half of the man's head and the barrel of a pistol remained submerged – he exposed only what was essential in order to survey the shore. Seeing no threats, the man dragged himself out of the water and peeled off his balaclava as he crossed the final distance to shore. Liu squeezed off a warning shot that struck the water near the swimmer's feet. It was Kilkenny.

'Throw your weapon into the water behind you!' Liu shouted as he stepped out from behind the boulder.

Kilkenny stopped and shook his head in wonder. 'Just not my day.'

'Your weapon!' Liu shouted again.

Kilkenny tossed his pistol over his shoulder and heard it splash into the lake.

'Now the knife,' Liu commanded.

With his hands in clear view, Kilkenny stripped the knife sheath from his leg and threw it back into the lake.

'Legs apart! Hands on head, now!'

Kilkenny complied, placing his legs shoulder-width apart, slightly bent at the knees.

Liu moved closer. 'Where is Yin Daoming?'

Kilkenny considered the question and decided he was too sore and tired to stonewall. 'Gone.'

'Gone?' Liu spat back angrily. 'Gone where?'

Kilkenny tilted his head toward the water. 'He's in the lake.'

'Is he dead?'

'I don't think he made it to shore,' Kilkenny replied.

Liu smiled at the thought of Yin's body sinking into the frigid depths of the lake. He stepped closer to Kilkenny. 'I should have killed you in Rome.'

'I was just thinking the same thing about you.'

'Why did you do this? What is so important about this priest?'

'Have you ever spoken to him?' Kilkenny asked.

'I have. He is an old fool.'

'Then you weren't listening.'

'I listened enough. You and those who sent you are all fools, deluded by your religion.'

Liu stepped directly in front of Kilkenny and pressed the end of the pistol into his captive's abdomen. The two men stared at each other eye to eye. What Kilkenny saw sickened him.

'You look to the heavens and see something that does not exist,' Liu continued. 'Your religion is nothing more than mass insanity. There is no God, and I am going to prove it to you.'

In a sharp fluid motion, Kilkenny twisted to the right and swept his left hand down and around like the blade of a windmill. The flat of his palm struck the top of Liu's pistol hand. The force of the blow pushed the pistol away from Kilkenny's torso and snapped the metacarpal bones of Liu's three longest fingers. Still, Liu squeezed off a single shot before the weapon flew from his hand out into the lake, the bullet tearing into Kilkenny's right side.

Kilkenny spun back for the return stroke, but the shock of his injury robbed the blow of strength and speed. Liu leaned back and used his right arm to easily deflect Kilkenny's elbow and forearm. Like a gear, Liu turned with his opponent and took control of the exchange. He blocked Kilkenny's right fist with the palm of his left hand, and as it slipped past, he grabbed the wrist and drove his knee into Kilkenny's side.

The pain blinded Kilkenny, leaving him barely aware of his arm being rotated behind his back as he doubled over. Liu spun him around, pinning the trapped forearm up between his shoulder blades and turning Kilkenny toward the lake.

'Move!' Liu shouted, jabbing the thumb of his damaged hand into the wound in Kilkenny's right side.

Kilkenny felt his knees weaken as pain shot through his body, overwhelming his senses. He staggered forward, then planted his right leg, folded his left up to his chest, and pivoted around with what strength he could muster. As he turned, Kilkenny twisted his trapped arm free and grabbed Liu's wrist. With his own center of gravity well off of his right foot, Kilkenny used Liu as a counter-balance. He felt the Asian trying to pull away to avoid the hammer blow from his incoming fist. When he was almost completely around, Kilkenny let go. Released, Liu shot back, avoiding the fist but not the foot.

The blade of Kilkenny's foot landed squarely in the center of Liu's chest and fractured his sternum. Liu toppled back onto the rocky beach, and Kilkenny landed in a foot of water. Liu could barely catch his breath but knew he couldn't wait for the next attack. He pulled the balisong knife from his boot and opened it with a practiced flick of the wrist. As a knife fighter, Liu was ambidextrous.

Both men were slow in gaining their feet. Liu had trouble breathing, and Kilkenny experienced a new level of pain as salty lake water flushed the wound in his side. Liu charged, and Kilkenny backpedaled into the lake. The SEALskin kept Kilkenny's feet warm, but Liu found his freezing to the bone as the icy water seeped into his black leather boots. Kilkenny stood with his left side toward Liu, his left arm raised to block while his right protected his wounded side. Liu mirrored Kilkenny's stance, his damaged hand protecting his chest with the knife hand forward.

Like the shore, the ground they stood on was rocky and uneven, and with each passing second, Liu lost feeling in his feet. He jabbed with the knife and Kilkenny expertly parried the strike. Injured and without a solid footing, neither man could deliver a forceful blow.

Liu telegraphed a second jab, and when Kilkenny moved to block, he turned his hand and drove the knife down. The blade plunged into Kilkenny's thigh. Kilkenny snapped an uppercut that connected with Liu's chin. Liu retracted the knife as he reeled back with the blow, but he regained his footing and charged again. He drove with his whole body, but Kilkenny twisted and the blade found only air. Liu collided with Kilkenny, and both men fell into the icy lake.

Liu's fist plunged into the shallow water and struck a jagged rock. The balisong slipped from his grasp and disappeared. Kilkenny landed prone with Liu on top of him. Recognizing his advantage, Liu sat up and drove his knee down on Kilkenny's wounded side. The air exploded from Kilkenny's mouth and he struggled to stay conscious, to keep his head above water. Liu grabbed a clump of hair and plunged Kilkenny's face into the lake.

Saltwater burned inside Kilkenny's nostrils and leaked into his mouth as his face went numb. Liu pulled Kilkenny's head up, allowing him to catch another breath, prolonging the end.

'*Wo xi wang ni man man si, dan kuai dian xia di yu!*' Liu growled, his guttural cadences primal and menacing.

Liu plunged Kilkenny's head in the water again, pressing his face into the rocks. What little air Kilkenny captured burst from his lungs, and as he choked, Liu pulled him up once again.

'In your barbarian tongue,' Liu hissed, 'I wish you a slow death but a quick ride to hell.'

The icy lake enveloped Kilkenny's head once more, and he knew Liu would not bring him up again. He reached back, trying to grab anything he could use to dislodge his attacker, but Liu shifted his weight and drove his knee down harder into Kilkenny's side.

The air burst from Kilkenny's mouth, and his choked spasms drew in ounce upon ounce of brackish water. He pushed his hands down to the lake bottom and tried to lift himself up, but the uneven rocks beneath him gave way, unable to hold his weight. The palms of his hands lost purchase, and his chest dropped back onto the rocks. More bubbles escaped from his lips as lake water slipped down his throat.

As Kilkenny's consciousness ebbed around him, his thoughts lingered on Kelsey, the child they lost, and the family they would never have. Everything went black.

62

The darkness that enveloped Kilkenny fell away as if he were rising from a watery abyss toward a sunlit surface. Through lidded eyes, he sensed the light's increasing warmth and intensity. Awareness returned slowly, burning through the fog clouding his mind.

A warm breeze stroked his face, and he felt a ripple lap softly against his cheek. Reflexively, he licked an errant droplet from his lips.

Water.

The dual sensations of touch and taste triggered recognition and a trickle of conscious thoughts.

I'm in the water, he reasoned, *but where?*

His memory was elusive. Everything before this moment seemed a blur, images too fleeting to grasp. Nolan remembered water, but not the warm liquid that now cradled his buoyant form. That distant recollection was of a briny sea as cold as death.

A shadow crossed his face, eclipsing the sun. He felt a hand settle gently against the back of his head, and then a pair of lips met his. The kiss was slow and lingering and bespoke the simmering passion of a woman for the love of her life.

'Are you going to float here all day?' she asked, her lips still close to his, her voice melodic and familiar.

'Maybe.'

She laughed and kissed him again before pulling away, wading toward shore. Nolan allowed his legs to sink and his feet landed on a firm bed of smooth sand. He stood and found himself chest-deep in a placid lake, the sun at its midsummer zenith high overhead, and before him the soft curves of rolling dunes along the Lake Michigan shore.

Like Venus, Kelsey slowly emerged from the lake. Nolan stood speechless, watching his wife rise from the water leaving no ripple in her wake. Her long blonde mane dangled between her shoulder blades in a taut French braid. A sheen of water glistened on her tan, slender form, and Nolan smiled when he recognized the brightly colored bikini she had bought for their honeymoon.

Nolan didn't see anyone else but sensed they were not alone. He watched as Kelsey moved up the beach toward a large umbrella that shaded an old beach quilt she had loved since childhood. Something stirred in the shadow, and Kelsey bent down and gently lifted what he knew was their infant son. When she turned toward him, a naked Toby nuzzled contentedly against her breast.

His heart ached at the scene – the future he dreamed of and lost was so tantalizingly close – yet all his desire could not will himself toward shore.

'You know you have to go back,' Kelsey said in that

tone she used to lovingly cajole him out of bed in the morning.

'I can't lose you both again.'

'Nolan, you never lost us. Toby and I are home. And we will be here for you when the time comes. Don't stop swimming, my love. Keep swimming.'

Keep swimming? Nolan tried to move his arms and legs but they were leaden. An icy current pulled him away from shore, and the light faded to total blackness.

63

When he heard the gunshot, Peng raced back across the rocky shore in Liu's direction. He arrived as Liu cursed a final epithet in Kilkenny's ear before plunging his captive's head beneath the water's surface. Peng planted his feet, took aim with a steady, two-handed grip, and fired.

Blood and bone exploded from Liu's left elbow, the entire joint disintegrating as two nine-millimeter rounds hammered home. Instinctively, Liu pulled his damaged arm against his chest, releasing his hold on Kilkenny's head. He glared in the direction of the shots and saw Peng.

'You fool! What are you doing?' Liu howled.

'Ending this insanity,' Peng replied calmly.

With images of the tortured family in Chifeng seared into his memory, Peng fired until the pistol was empty. Wounds blossomed on Liu's forehead and chest as Peng tightly clustered his shots for lethality. Liu toppled into the water, dead.

Peng holstered his pistol as he raced toward the two lifeless forms floating in the shallow water. He lifted Liu's body off Kilkenny's back and pushed it out into deeper water. Kilkenny remained beneath the surface. Straddling Kilkenny's legs, Peng reached down into the water, wrapped his arms around Kilkenny's abdomen, and quickly pulled him from the lake.

Kilkenny's body folded across Peng's forearms, head and shoulders dangling down at the knees but clear of the water. Leaning back with legs bent, braced to support the sodden dead weight, Peng struggled back to shore. With each careful step, he sharply tightened his grip around Kilkenny's abdomen. Briny water drained from Kilkenny's mouth and nose, gouts at first, then only dribbles when Peng finally wrestled Kilkenny to shore.

Peng carefully laid Kilkenny on the relatively smooth patch of the gravely shore and, recalling his training, tilted Kilkenny's head back and began mouth-to-mouth resuscitation. Cleared of water, Kilkenny's chest rose. Peng pulled his mouth away to let Kilkenny's lungs deflate and to see if natural breathing would resume.

Nothing.

Peng checked Kilkenny's neck and found a thready pulse. He repeated the cycle of artificial breathing, and on the third round Kilkenny sputtered and coughed.

'Easy, my friend,' Peng said reassuringly.

He gently rolled Kilkenny onto his side, the stricken man's breathing now coming in stolen gasps as he fought the spasms of a violent coughing jag. When his breathing finally settled into a normal rhythm, Kilkenny rolled onto his back, exhausted.

'Open your eyes,' Peng said.

Kilkenny tried to focus. Peng's voice seemed distant and disconnected.

'Can you hear me?' Peng asked. 'Open your eyes.'

Kilkenny's eyelids fluttered, struggling to open. They felt gritty and raw. The light burned, too bright. He kept blinking, trying to focus.

'That's it. You must try to stay awake. How do you feel?'

His mouth was parched and his throat sore, and his various injuries were now reasserting themselves into his consciousness.

'Shot?' he croaked, his voice raspy.

Peng quickly surveyed Kilkenny and saw numerous wounds of varying severity. Kilkenny winced when Peng extracted a small ceramic shard protruding from a section of Kilkenny's body armor.

'Yes, you were shot. And stabbed, and apparently punctured by many tiny blades.' Peng laughed. 'You are like Wile E. Coyote.'

Kilkenny laughed too. It hurt. 'If Murphy's Laws are religion, I must be a saint.'

'What?'

'A line from an old Tom Smith song – it's about Wile E.'

'Oh, a joke. Good. I think you'll live.'

Kilkenny's eyes began to clear. He lifted his head a little, felt dizzy, and laid back down facing the lake. A dark form floated in the placid water, the body of a man.

'What happened?' Kilkenny asked.

'There was a fight.'

'And I lost,' Kilkenny offered, the details hazy but growing clearer. 'I drowned.'

'Liu was killing you when I arrived.'

Kilkenny turned toward the man, the voice sounding familiar, and dug into his memories. 'Peng?'

Peng nodded.

'You saved me?'

'My weapon simply went off,' Peng explained with a faint smile. 'It happened once before, on Kiritimati. You called it an accidental discharge. I guess I should have it repaired.'

'I think it works just fine. Why did you kill him?'

'Honor.'

'Yours?'

Peng nodded. 'And my country's. Last year, you unmasked a murderer and returned to us our lost heroes. You restored honor to China. To allow you to die at the hands of that *monster* – that is not the China I believe in.'

'But now I've broken more of your country's laws than I care to count.'

'Why?'

Kilkenny closed his eyes and thought about all that had happened, everything that had brought him to this moment. 'Faith.'

'Yours?' Peng asked.

'And Yin's,' Kilkenny said. 'He deserved to be free.'

'I know. My parents and grandparents also shared your faith.'

'Not you?'

'I was very young when my parents were taken away. Their faith did not save them. Or at least that was what I believed until now.'

'Do you remember anything?' Kilkenny asked
'Bits of stories whispered at night. And baijiu.'
'Baijiu?'

'A potent drink that I've never really liked. Most rural villages brew their own. I remember a man coming to my family's home. There would be prayers, and the man would tell some of the same stories my parents whispered to me. Then he would serve bits of bread and baijiu. I haven't thought about this in years,' Peng said, 'not since my parents were arrested. Not until I became involved in this matter.'

The dull thump of helicopter blades beating the air echoed off the rocky terrain around them, and slowly the sound grew louder.

'Don't suppose you could drop me off somewhere on the other side of the border?'

'If it were up to me,' Peng replied, but didn't finish the thought. 'For the moment, you are my prisoner. You will receive medical attention, but what happens afterward I cannot say.'

'Well, at least I'll be healthy enough to be executed.'

64

LADAKH, INDIA

Four hours had passed since the *Windrider* glided away from the eastern shore of Bangong Co, and in that time the sleek craft quietly sailed over a hundred kilometers, across one international border, and through a sliver of disputed territory. The winds had remained steady throughout the voyage, and once the travelers were well inside the Indian-controlled portion of the lake, the fog finally lifted to reveal the glacier-clad Pangong Mountains to the south and the Changchenmo range to the north.

The sun hung high overhead as Gates steered a north-westerly course toward the far end of the lake. The *Windrider* raced over the water, its twin sails capturing enough wind to pull the hulls out of the water atop a trio of T-shaped aluminum hydrofoils. The ride was smooth and fast.

'My God, this is beautiful,' Gates said, awestruck by their surroundings.

'He does very fine work,' Yin agreed.

'So what do you think of your first real taste of freedom?' Tao asked.

'I am savoring it,' Yin replied, 'and I hope my flock in China may one day soon enjoy it in our own land.'

Gates adjusted the sails as he guided the craft into a gentle turn toward shore. Lined up for the approach and still cruising at thirty miles per hour, he released the pins locking the hydrofoils into place and the trimaran slipped down the four-foot struts to the water's surface. Gates locked the hydrofoils in the retracted position, readying the boat to make land. The change in speed and the sound of water rushing past the hulls roused Han from a two-hour nap on the trampoline.

'We there yet?' Han asked sleepily.

'The bustling port of Spangmik is just up ahead,' Gates replied.

Spangmik consisted of a handful of small, rough structures built from local stone and concrete, most painted white. The tiny hamlet was among a handful of villages dotting the southern shore of the lake that were summer homes for a small group of Chang-pa, the nomadic herders of Tibet and southeast Ladakh. This late in the season, the Chang-pa had moved on to their winter pastures, leaving only a small detachment of the Indian army in Spangmik to protect the border.

Gates let out the sail, and the *Windrider* slowed. Compared with the dash down the long alpine lake, they covered the final yards in a crawl. As the boat neared shore, several people emerged from one of the buildings and rushed to the edge of the lake.

'We got company,' Han said.

'Welcoming committee,' Gates said confidently, his attention on reefing the sails. 'Bet Nolan has already charmed these nice people, and there's a hot pot of chicken vindaloo just waiting for us.'

'Max,' Tao said, 'they don't look all that happy to see us.'

Gates looked toward shore and saw the reception party was armed and training their weapons on the trimiran.

'I don't suppose you speak any of the local dialects, Padre,' Gates asked Yin.

'I learned a few phrases from an Indian friend when I was a young man. Sadly, it has been many years since I had need of them.'

'Well, I'd really appreciate it if you'd tickle a few of those old memory cells, just in case,' Gates said. 'Everybody else, just keep your hands where these nice folks can see 'em and hope nobody's got an itchy trigger finger.'

The soldiers closed in as the *Windrider*'s bow touched shore and surrounded the craft. The leader of the group, an army captain with a thick black beard and mustache and a Sikh turban, yelled an incomprehensible order at them, but his hand motions clearly expressed his intent. They were to get out of the boat. Tao and Han were the first ashore, followed by Yin and then Gates. Several soldiers lifted the *Windrider* out of the water and carried it away from the water's edge.

The captain issued another order, this time without gesticulating.

'Padre, any idea what he wants?' Gates asked.

'I believe he wishes us to remove our hats,' Yin replied.

Gates pointed at his helmet, then motioned as if he

was to lift it off. The captain nodded. He scowled at Han, Tao, and Yin when he saw their faces, but seemed genuinely surprised after Gates doffed his helmet.

'English?' the captain asked in a tone as much London as Punjab.

'American, actually,' Gates replied. 'Same with two of my associates. The third's situation is a bit more complicated.'

'That's a relief. Dressed as you are, we thought you might be scouts for the Chinese army.'

'You haven't seen another American dressed like this?'

'No, ought I have?'

'We kinda thought he'd be here by now.'

'Sorry, no sign of him here. Papers?'

'We have none,' Gates admitted. 'We sort of left the People's Republic in a bit of a hurry. You're welcome to search us and our boat – we're not carrying any contraband. In fact, we're carrying only what we have on. I'm sure a few phone calls will clear this whole thing up.'

Just then a young enlisted man rushed down from the outpost. He ran up to the captain and snapped to attention with a crisp textbook salute.

'At ease,' the captain said as he returned the salute.

'Communiqué from Delhi, sir.'

The captain held out his hand, and the young soldier placed in it a folded slip of paper. The captain pursed his lips as he read the page, then he handed it back and dismissed the man.

'It seems we may be able to clear this matter up even sooner,' the captain said.

With his hands clasped behind his back and standing ramrod straight, the captain strode over to Yin Daoming.

'Sir, what is your name?'

'I am Yin Daoming.'

'Are you the Roman Catholic Bishop of Shanghai?'

'I am.'

'Then on behalf of my government, and with the warmest personal greetings from your friend Cardinal Velu of Bombay, I welcome you to the Republic of India.'

'Thank you. I have been looking forward to a visit with my old friend for many years.'

'Then, sir, I will notify Delhi of your arrival and arrange for your transport to Leh. I believe Cardinal Velu's representative is waiting for you there.'

Less than an hour later, a Sikorsky S-92 civilian transport touched down at the helipad at Spangmik. The clean white craft bore a single emblem, a coat of arms consisting of a papal tiara above the crossed keys of Saint Peter. A small detachment of plainclothes Swiss Guards arrived and took formal custody of Yin and the others. As they prepared to leave, Yin approached the captain.

'Captain, I wish to thank you for your hospitality during our brief stay.'

'Your Excellency, your arrival broke the normal tedium of our posting here and provided a story that will be passed on by soldiers here for years to come.'

'If I may ask a favor, please keep an eye out for our missing comrade.'

'We will do what we can for him,' the captain promised.

65

VATICAN CITY

'My Most Eminent Brothers in Christ,' Donoher called out from in front of the altar. The Sistine Chapel grew quiet as all attention focused on him. 'I apologize for being unavailable to you yesterday, but I am certain you all made productive use of the pause in our deliberations. May the Holy Spirit continue to guide us in our work.

'I have two items of news to share with you. First, Cardinal Gagliardi passed away yesterday after a long battle with heart disease. I was with him at the end, and his thoughts and prayers remained with us in this difficult time. I would like to offer at this time a moment of quiet reflection in his memory.'

Donoher struggled to offer a prayer for a man he knew had betrayed the Church, but he left Gagliardi's final judgment in the hands of the Almighty. After a respectful pause, he looked up at the assembled cardinals.

'Regarding the matter of Bishop Yin, I am pleased to announce that on this day, the Feast of All Saints, our brother is free. I received word early today that Bishop Yin crossed the border into India. He is, at this moment, en route to Rome.'

Several of the cardinals smiled broadly, nodding happily to each other like fans of a sports team that had just won an important victory. Others bowed their heads in thankful prayer. Near the center of the chapel, Velu rose from his seat and waited for the Camerlengo to recognize him.

'My Esteemed Lord Velu,' Donoher announced.

'My Lord Cardinal Camerlengo, I believe I speak for all my brothers in expressing my joy at the good news regarding Bishop Yin. Sadly, I now feel compelled to report to you that a cloud has fallen over our conclave, a matter that only you can address.' Velu's words reverberated in the otherwise silent chapel. 'During our informal sessions yesterday, a rumor began to circulate among us. It started at first with a question, one cardinal to another, asking if anything in their rooms seemed out of place. Most noticed no disturbance to their belongings, but the question forced others to reexamine what they initially considered a lapse of memory. Among those asking the question, it became clear that an entire section of Domus Marthae Sanctae had been systematically searched.'

Velu slowly paced as he spoke, his deep brown eyes meeting those of the other cardinals, his voice peaceful and certain. At the chancel screen, he turned and began walking back toward the altar.

'My Lord Brothers, within the sealed confines of this room, I must now break my silence. Mine was one of the rooms searched, and in it something was found. Lord Donoher questioned me about a device that I brought with me into the conclave. I did so for personal reasons and with full knowledge that the Apostolic Constitution explicitly forbade my action, and for breaking my oath I am answerable to our next pontiff. But my transgression, though grave, was not what Lord Donoher sought. Now, with Bishop Yin at long last free, it is time for truth.' Velu now stood directly in front of the Camerlengo. 'I ask you, my Eminent Lord, to share with us the reason for your search.'

Donoher stepped close to Velu, their faces mere inches apart.

'Why?' Donoher asked in a whisper that barely concealed his anger.

'I am sorry to force your hand,' Velu replied softly, 'but to protect Yin, you must name his betrayer.'

Velu bowed and walked slowly back to his seat, providing a brief time for Donoher to collect his thoughts.

'My Most Eminent Lords,' Donoher began, 'the searches that disturbed a number of your rooms were conducted under my authority as Camerlengo and with the approval of the particular congregation. The first rooms searched belonged to the four of us who currently serve on that congregation as we are entrusted with the secrecy of the conclave. The justification for this action comes from evidence that the secrecy of our conclave had been violated with regard to Bishop Yin, and that this violation threatened not only his life but the lives of those who were sent to rescue him.'

Donoher's words hung in the air like a pall of smoke – the sanctity of the conclave had been betrayed, and the Camerlengo believed a prince of the Church was responsible.

'The search was part of a broad effort to unmask the person or persons responsible for this despicable act against the Church,' Donoher continued, 'an effort that I am pleased to report has succeeded. The unfortunate breach is now closed, and we may continue with our work.'

'Who?' Magni shouted, not waiting to be recognized, his face flushed with anger. 'Who is the traitor?'

'The answer to that question,' Donoher thundered back, 'I will give only to the next Pope.'

Magni's gaze remained locked on the Camerlengo for a moment before he resigned with a curt nod and returned to his seat. Donoher wondered if Magni backed down so quickly because he believed the answer would be his in time.

As Pope, Donoher mused, *how will you react when I answer that question with the name of your closest ally?*

Donoher surveyed the room and again found Velu standing, waiting to be recognized.

'My Most Eminent Lord Velu.'

Velu stepped into the center of the chapel and with hands clasped bowed in a brief prayer toward the altar. Drawing on whatever strength he could summon, he stood tall and began to speak.

'My most beloved and esteemed colleagues, when we first entered this magnificent chapel, we called out as one to the Holy Spirit for guidance, and for the wisdom to

411

discern who among us would be the next shepherd of the universal Church. I truly believe that the Holy Spirit answered our prayers immediately. In his final message to us, His Holiness Pope Leo made known what was in his heart. And he, who made all but a handful of us cardinals, reminded us with his suffering why we wear scarlet. This color symbolizes our willingness to die for the Church. His Holiness understood this commitment fully, having shed his own blood to a would-be assassin's bullets in Saint Peter's Square and having suffered for the faith in ways few of us can comprehend.

'We live in a very different world from the one that greeted the dawn of Pope Leo's long and holy reign. The Evil One besets us on all sides, in ways both monstrous and cunningly subtle. The immense challenges facing the Church today compel us to select a man of great faith to illuminate the way of Christ, for it is only on that most difficult path that we can lead the faithful to salvation. To select a politician, a bureaucrat, *a caretaker Pope*,' Velu locked his gaze on the other papabili as he emphasized the last appellation, 'would doom the Church in a time of its most desperate need. Great leaders inspire by their example – that was the key to Leo's success.

'I am humbled that some of you believe I could be Pope, but when I look in my heart,' Velu crossed his arms over his chest, 'I know that it is not my path. At best, I would be a good Pope, but the Church needs more. And when the need is great, God provides. He has done so now, but it is up to us to recognize His divine hand, to feel the presence of Jesus Christ in this room with us, and to act in a way of faith.'

412

With a polite bow to the Camerlengo, Velu returned to his seat. Donoher waited until all eyes turned to him.

'My Lords, does anyone else wish to address the conclave?'

No one stood.

'Then it is time,' Donoher declared.

In silence, each of the cardinals placed a ballot paper on the tables before them and carefully wrote out the name of the man they believed should be the next Pope. Donoher folded his ballot and, looking up, discovered that most of the other electors were also done. Apparently, the pause for prayer and reflection did little to sway minds already made up. His spirits sank at the thought of another deadlocked vote, and the possibility that the election could drift inconclusively for a week until they reached a point where the rules could change. Then, instead of eighty votes, a candidate need only garner an absolute majority, just half the votes plus one. Failing that, they would have to have a runoff between the top two candidates. With an odd number of electors now present, the result of that ballot would be a new Pope.

Following the now-familiar ritual, Cardinal Mizzi approached the altar and, in full view of all present, deposited his ballot in the urn. One by one, the infirmarii cast their ballots next, followed by the rest of the conclave in order of seniority.

Donoher exchanged a subtle nod with Velu as the Indian prelate passed by after casting his ballot. He had to admire the man's selflessness in admitting his failings in service of a greater good. Would any of the remaining papabili have scuttled their ambitions so thoroughly?

The infirmarii returned just as the most junior cardinals approached the altar. They presented the locked box containing the ballots of the ailing cardinals to the three scrutineers, who opened the box and counted the ballots to verify their number. The ballots of the sick were placed one by one into the urn.

Donoher laid a clean sheet of paper on his desk and across the top wrote the date. Down the left side, he wrote: Magni, Escalante, Oromo, and Yin. He suspected Oromo would benefit most from Velu's withdrawal, perhaps allowing the Sudanese cardinal to jump ahead of his two main rivals. The election was now just a game of numbers.

Seated at the long table in front of the altar, the scrutineers chosen for today's vote began opening the ballots. The first passed from Porter to Gensa and finally to Drolet.

'Yin,' Drolet announced in a gravelly voice that rumbled with the seriousness of the proceeding.

Donoher drew a short vertical line beside Yin's name and wondered if any more would join it.

66

BEIJING, CHINA

Tian Yi found himself once again within the red brick walls of the Zhongnanhai compound, seated inside the Qing dynasty pavilion before three of the most powerful men in China. It was a chilly fall evening, the air moist after a day of drizzle. As before, Premier Wen sat in the middle, flanked by President Chong and Minister Fu.

'Is the matter of Yin Daoming resolved?' Wen asked.

'Not in the way we desired,' Tian replied. 'I received confirmation that Yin and three others arrived in India this morning. They are presently aboard an Alitalia flight en route to Rome. Of the team that engineered Yin's escape, most are dead. One, the leader, has been captured.'

'But Yin has escaped to the West,' Fu spat angrily. 'How do you explain this failure?'

'Had the security at Chifeng Prison been adequate, Yin would now be dead,' Tian replied, deflecting the accusation back at Fu, whose ministry directed the nation's prison system. 'Once they were at large, the difficulty in tracking the fugitives grew exponentially. We were very fortunate to intercept them in Tibet, but our luck did not extend to preventing Yin's escape.'

'History tends to repeat itself for those who are foolish enough not to learn its lessons the first time,' Chong offered. 'Yin is going to Rome. If the last Pope felt he was worthy of being a cardinal, we can assume the next will follow suit. Yin's escape will make him as famous in the West as the Dalai Lama. And if Yin is named Pope, he will become as vocal a critic of our government as Pope Leo was of the Soviets.'

'Can the plane be intercepted?' Fu asked.

'Are you suggesting we shoot down a civilian airliner over international waters, thousands of miles from our territory?' Tian asked.

'Something must be done!' Fu raged.

'Yes,' Tian said, 'but what you suggest would brand China a rogue nation.'

'It would bring down this government,' Chong agreed. 'Of course, having Yin free in the West might achieve the same result. The first suggestion notwithstanding, I quite agree with Minister Fu that something must be done, and done quickly. Otherwise, Premier Wen, you may become the Chinese Gorbachev.'

One of you will rule, Wen recalled, *the other will lead.*

'What about our Italian partners?' the Premier asked. 'Were not their interests in line with ours regarding Yin?'

'They were,' Tian replied.

'Then explain the situation to them in terms they will understand. What is at stake here is far more valuable to them than a safe place to launder their money. The billions they earn each year from trade in Chinese opium and weapons are at risk. When Yin reaches Rome, he must die.'

67

ROME

Cusumano climbed aboard the caboose with five workmen. He was dressed in boots and worn gray coveralls with a laminated photo ID clipped to his breast pocket. He carried a dark green sports bag slung over one shoulder with a tall metal thermos protruding from the top of the bag.

The caboose was at the end of a three-car train attached to a small steam locomotive. The engine was something of an anachronism compared with modern high-speed diesel electric engines and magnetic-levitation trains, but the tiny engine was well suited to this particular journey and seemed an appropriate nod to a more elegant era. The train sat on a siding at the Stazione San Pietro under a gray sky, and Cusumano watched tiny droplets of rain streak down the grimy windows of the caboose.

With a lurch, the ancient locomotive began to move. It was, as usual, behind schedule. The tracks it followed ran northwest from the station, parallel to Via Innocenzo

III and just outside the protective walls that surrounded the medieval city of Rome.

Cusumano sat quietly, doing little to draw the attention of his fellow passengers. There was no regular crew for this run; the station manager simply selected however many men were needed to unload the freight once they reached their destination. Fortunately for Cusumano, this train was scheduled to run today.

The sky outside matched the Sicilian's mood. Earlier that afternoon, he received an unexpected visit at his bookshop from Mr Chin. Their meeting was brief and to the point. Yin had escaped from China and was en route to Rome. In a reverse of their first meeting, Chin told Cusumano that it was now the mafia's responsibility to deal with Yin. Failure to do so, Chin implied, would have more than a deleterious effect on their business relationship. The mafia dons conspiring with Gagliardi had decided the matter quickly, and Cusumano – due in equal parts to reputation, current involvement, and immediate availability – found himself pressed again into service as an assassin on an almost impossible assignment. In the parlance of Mario Puzo's *The Godfather*, the dons made Cusumano an offer he couldn't refuse.

A kilometer out of the station, the train veered to the right on a spur built by Mussolini as part of the Lateran pacts of 1929 between the Holy See and the kingdom of Italy. The locomotive moved slowly along the track, as there was little point in building speed for a journey of a few kilometers.

A loud whistle blast announced the train as it neared the twelve-meter-high Leonine Walls surrounding the

Vatican. The iron gates that secured an arched opening in the wall slowly pivoted open. As it passed through the wall, the train crossed the border from Italy into the sovereign state of Vatican City. The section of track ahead was only 862 meters long – the shortest national railroad in the world. Once the train was inside, the gates closed behind it.

At the end of the line stood papal architect Giuseppe Momo's candy-colored Vatican railroad station, a building clad in green, pink, and yellow marble and adorned with sculptures by Eduardo Rubino. Though conceived as a place where the Pope could greet arriving dignitaries, the station was rarely used to serve passengers, and its high-ceilinged gallery had become an ornate storage room. During his many visits with his uncle, Cusumano could not recall ever setting foot inside the station. Gagliardi had snidely dismissed the building as an overdone warehouse and bypassed it in favor of the Vatican's more interesting sites.

The train pulled up to the station, and Cusumano followed his fellow workmen out onto the platform. The rain had slowed to a drizzle, and the workmen, armed with hand trucks from the station, began unloading the freight cars. Much of what they brought into the Vatican was destined for the souvenir stands and duty-free shops. A clerk kept track of the boxes as they were brought into the station, logging each against the manifest, and all the activity occurred under the watchful eyes of a pair of Swiss Guards dressed in blue uniforms.

During a break, Cusumano sat inside the station quietly drinking espresso from his thermos. He listened as his fellow laborers speculated with the engine crew and the Vatican clerk about what might be happening inside the Sistine Chapel. News reports indicated that the conclave had remained locked in session since that morning. Three times today, black smoke spiraled from the chimney flue.

The workers took their time after the break, extending the job to the end of their shift with the hope of being inside the Vatican when, God willing, the new Pope was elected. The boxes slowly disappeared until, at last, Cusumano trucked in the final load.

As the clerk locked the station, Cusumano and the other men boarded the caboose. He sat alone in the front corner of the car where he had left his bag.

'*Stu cazzo!*' Cusumano cursed. 'My thermos leaked all over my bag.'

Two of the workmen laughed at his misfortune; the others sat back with their eyes closed. Cusumano pulled a handkerchief from his breast pocket and slipped his hands inside the bag as if to wipe up the spill. The tall metal thermos contained three chambers, of which only the uppermost contained coffee. Cusumano had used the other two to smuggle weapons through security at the railway station. He deftly unscrewed the bottom of his thermos and carefully removed the contents of the bottom chamber. Piece by piece, the Beretta Px4 pistol took shape as he swiftly reassembled it – a procedure he could accomplish blindfolded in seconds.

The whistle blasted a long tone, then the train shuddered and began to roll. Cusumano kept an eye on the two Swiss Guards through the side window as he attached the laser sight and, last, fitted the silencer into place. The rumble of the train obscured the sound of the twenty-round magazine clicking into place. As soon as the Vatican personnel on the station platform were out of view, he stood and opened fire on the laborers.

Cusumano murdered the men with five quick, expertly placed shots. He slipped the pistol back into his bag, opened the rear door of the caboose, and leaped from the slow-moving train. His feet slipped in the moist gravel, but he kept his balance and stepped away from the rails. The freight cars screened Cusumano as he pulled himself over a short retaining wall and into a secluded corner of the Vatican Gardens. By the time the iron gates in the wall closed, he had concealed himself in the dense foliage where he would wait for Yin's arrival.

68

The chartered Alitalia flight was outfitted like the presidential suite of a luxury hotel, and the four weary travelers were fed well and had all their needs attended to. The aircraft made its final descent into Rome's Leonardo da Vinci – Ciampino airport just before ten o'clock in the evening. It had been overcast and rainy in the Eternal City most of the day, but the skies cleared at sunset and the heavens were full of stars. Yin slept through much of the long flight, but when the pilot announced their impending arrival, he woke and stared down at the city, catching his first glimpse of the illuminated dome of Saint Peter's.

As a Bishop, Yin was required to visit the Vatican every five years to report on the state of his diocese. Due to his incarceration, it was a trip he never made. Now, Yin anticipated at long last fulfilling his episcopal duty. Since he would be unable to return to his See in China, he wondered what new assignment might be offered.

Heavenly Father, Yin prayed, *I ask only for a small parish in need of a priest.*

After landing, the aircraft taxied past the international

terminal and pulled directly into a large hangar used by the airline to service its fleet. After the hangar doors were closed, the passengers and their Swiss Guard escort deplaned in privacy.

Tao, Gates, and Han stepped down the gangway, each wearing a new suit of clothes – a tailor on board customized the fit during the long flight from India. The tailor had also brought enough suits to outfit another eight men. Yin wore a new black cassock piped in amaranth red, with Ke Li's cross displayed openly on his chest.

As they waited for a car, Tao stepped over to the tailor's rack and looked at the collection of unused suits. She found a garment bag tagged with Kilkenny's name and zipped it open. Inside, she found a classic wool pinstripe suit with a double-breasted jacket.

'What's that?' Gates asked.

'Nolan's suit. He would have looked good in it,' Tao suddenly choked back a sob. 'I can't believe I'm already talking about him like he's gone.'

'That's the bitch about not knowing,' Gates offered. 'But I'm not giving up on him, not with all he and I have been through. And if I have to go back into China to get him out, I'll do it.'

Tao embraced Gates and kissed his cheek. 'If that's what it takes, I'm going with you.'

An airport shuttle pulled into the hangar. The travelers boarded it and were transported to a section of the airfield reserved for private planes and helicopters. There they boarded a gleaming white Sikorsky S-92 bearing the Vatican coat of arms.

* * *

Luciano Papiri nursed a drink in the satellite terminal serving international flights. From his seat by the window, he had watched the Alitalia flight land and taxi out to the service buildings without stopping at the terminal. Now, as the Vatican helicopter lifted off, he pulled out his cell phone and selected a preprogrammed number.

'Yes,' Cusumano answered.

'You guessed right. They just took off.'

'Good.'

Papiri ended the call, paid his tab, and left the bar.

The Sikorsky raced over the Eternal City and, after a ten-minute flight, hovered above the far west bastion of the Vatican's medieval walls. The arrowhead-shaped projection of the Leonine Walls surrounded a flat expanse of ground that held two paved areas. Bypassing a smaller circular helipad set close to the tip of the arrowhead, the Sikorsky floated above the larger rectangular pad nearer the access road. This corner of the Vatican lay between the inner and outer walls and was dominated by the massive cylindrical form of Saint John's Tower.

The trees and bushes that lined the old walls rustled with the downwash from the helicopter, shedding tiny droplets of water collected during the day. Cardinals Donoher and Velu sat inside the first of two sedans parked on the access road, both vehicles guarded by a pair of armed Swiss Guards.

Concealed behind a thick grouping of trees and leafy shrubs that thrived alongside the medieval walls, Cusumano watched Yin's helicopter arrive. He was still dressed in sodden coveralls, but had added gloves and a balaclava to his disguise, the latter also soaked with perspiration and itchy. He had concealed himself in the remote copse hours earlier in expectation that Yin would be flown to the Vatican rather than driven – the roads leading to the city-state were packed with the faithful on vigil. When word came that Yin would indeed arrive by air, Cusumano was relieved. The Swiss Guards were on heightened alert in response to the discovery of the dead men in the caboose, and Cusumano knew they would be out in force near the conclave.

As the helicopter touched down, Cusumano gripped a pair of Chinese Type-86P grenades. He had hidden the weapons in the middle chamber of his thermos; they were black-market weapons the mafia profited from and now stood to lose if he didn't kill Yin. It infuriated him that the Chinese had failed to kill a man who had been their prisoner for decades. Now the ludicrous and dangerously suicidal task of killing the Bishop inside the Vatican had fallen to him.

If I get out of this alive, Cusumano thought, *the Chinese will have to pay me enough to buy a library of Gutenberg Bibles.*

The main rotor slowed, and the helicopter door began to open. Cusumano glimpsed the passengers through the row of small windows that dotted the side of the helicopter, then saw the Swiss Guard stepping down the stair. Yin was the next figure in the doorway and the guard turned to help the Bishop deplane. Cusumano rushed out into the clearing. As he ran, he popped the grenade pins with his thumbs, then pivoted his body and swung his right arm around for a side-arm throw to keep the weapon below the rotor blades.

Something bit sharply into Cusumano's left leg just as the grenade slipped from his fingertips. The fifty-caliber round drilled a one-inch hole midthigh, ripping through flesh and muscle and shattering the bone. The damaged leg buckled immediately.

The grenade sailed through the air, its trajectory a low, flat arc toward the helicopter. Too low. It hit the ground short of the tarmac, the soft moist earth absorbing most of its kinetic energy. It rebounded with a weak hop and dribbled onto the tarmac, where the ovoid weapon rolled erratically like a fumbled football.

The guard at the foot of the stair spotted the masked figure running out of the shadows and turned back toward Yin. Looking over the Bishop's shoulder, Tao saw the man too, wrapped her arms around Yin, and pulled him back from the opening.

Cusumano's first grenade detonated at the edge of the tarmac. The weapon's plastic shell all but vaporized with the blast, and sixteen hundred tiny steel balls blossomed out in all directions. The Sikorsky shuddered from the blast, but was distant enough to suffer no damage from the concussive force. Lethal shrapnel peppered the side of the helicopter, puncturing the thin metal skin. Dozens of fragments struck the Swiss Guardsman blocking the doorway, and he toppled forward into the aircraft.

Shifting his weight to his good leg, Cusumano reached back to hurl his remaining grenade. The sniper positioned atop Saint John's Tower fired a second fifty-caliber round from his AS50 rifle. The 660-grain ball projectile drilled through the center of Cusumano's chest. The Sicilian's heart exploded as fragments of lead and bone pureed everything within six inches of the entry point. The impact threw Cusumano onto his back, and he dropped the grenade as he fell. Seconds later, the weapon detonated in a spray of smoke and dirt, shredding the assassin's body.

'Tango is down!' Gates shouted. 'Roxanne, you're with Yin. Terry, grab the med kit. Once we're outside, put your eyes on this bird and see how bad we've been hit.' He turned to the other guards aboard the helicopter. 'You, speak English?'

'*Ja*,' the young soldier replied.

'Great. Help me move your man.'

Gates leaped over the fallen guard down onto the tarmac, then quickly scanned the area for any other threats, finding none. The two guardsmen by the access road raced over to assist, with Velu and Donoher following at a slower pace. The injured guard cursed as Gates and his comrade gingerly carried him through the doorway.

'All clear?' Gates asked as the guardsmen moved to assist.

'Yes, only one man,' one of the guards confirmed.

Han surveyed the side of the helicopter with the pilot as the remaining passengers stepped off. The fuselage was dented and punctured in several places.

'How's it look?' Gates asked.

'I don't think we are in any immediate danger,' the pilot replied, his accent thickly Italian, 'but still, everyone should be a safe distance away.'

'My thinking exactly,' Han concurred.

The wail of an approaching emergency vehicle filled the air. Gates walked with Tao and Yin toward the two approaching churchmen. As Donoher and Velu neared, their expressions of concern melted into joy.

'My Esteemed Brother,' Velu said, 'It is so good to see you again.'

'It has been far too long,' Yin agreed, and he embraced Velu.

'Over all the years,' Velu added, 'you were never forgotten.'

'The Church was always my constant companion.'

Velu pulled away, beaming with delight. 'Bishop, this is Cardinal Donoher, the architect of your liberation.'

Yin moved in front of the Camerlengo and bowed to kiss his ring. Donoher flushed with embarrassment at the gesture, feeling inadequate to be in the presence of the revered Bishop of Shanghai.

'Your Eminence,' Yin said, 'Nolan Kilkenny told me of your passion to win my freedom. For that, I thank you.'

'Bishop Yin, I am humbled to meet a man of your faith,' Donoher replied.

'Has there been word of Nolan Kilkenny?' Yin asked.

'Nothing, I'm afraid.'

'Then I will continue to pray for him.'

'My prayers join yours. Nolan is family to me, and I look with hope to his safe return. Now, if you will excuse me for just a moment, I must have a word with Nolan's collaborators.'

Donoher took Tao, Han, and Gates aside. As more guards and emergency personnel arrived, the men assigned to Donoher took positions around Yin.

Donoher spoke quietly. 'This is where you part company with Bishop Yin. There are matters we must attend to with him that are internal to the Church. On behalf of the Holy See, I thank you for your efforts and your sacrifice in this endeavor. Simple words cannot express our gratitude.' Donoher motioned to the pair of approaching Swiss Guards. 'These men will escort you to a private suite here in Vatican City. I apologize that I cannot be with you right now, and promise to join you as soon as I am able.'

'We understand,' Tao said. 'This is a difficult time for your church.'

'For all of us,' Donoher agreed, 'but even difficult times eventually pass.'

69

Donoher's driver parked the sedan in a small square north of Saint Peter's Basilica, and the Camerlengo led Yin and Velu through a side entry into the Apostolic Palace. The corridors along the way had been cleared of all but the Swiss Guards, and the anteroom of the Sistine Chapel stood empty upon their arrival.

'Why have you brought me here?' Yin asked, realizing where he was. 'I am only a Bishop.'

'In the heart of Pope Leo, you have been a cardinal for many years,' Donoher replied. 'It is true you cannot vote, but you still have a role to play.'

Donoher rapped on the door. Inside, the dean of the College of Cardinals ordered them opened.

Yin looked into the chapel and saw one hundred and seventeen men in scarlet choir dress gazing back. Even the cardinals who had been too ill to attend the voting sessions in person were now present.

Thy will be done, Yin prayed. He crossed the marble threshold.

Velu took his seat, and Donoher escorted Yin to the altar. The junior cardinal dean left the chapel to summon the secretary of the College of Cardinals and the master of papal liturgical celebrations. Donoher and Yin stood with their backs to the assembled cardinals, gazing up at Michelangelo's *Last Judgment*.

'Do you know why you are here?' Donoher asked softly.

'On the flight to Rome, we were told black smoke was seen three times today.'

'There was only one ballot today, but we had to wait for your arrival. You've been through an unimaginable ordeal, only to face this. I want you to know that you do not have to accept election.'

'Just as Christ did not have to accept his fate at Gethsemane,' Yin replied. 'But he did, and I too submit my will to God's.'

'The vote was unanimous,' Donoher said warmly. 'As sure a sign of His will as I've ever seen.'

The junior cardinal dean returned with the pair of Archbishops and led them to the side of the altar. Both men were curious about the presence of another Bishop in the chapel and assumed he was there in a spiritual capacity for the Camerlengo.

'It is time,' Donoher announced.

The two men turned to face the assembled cardinals, then Donoher stepped down from the altar, leaving Yin alone.

Cardinal Scheuermann, the dean, approached Yin.

'Do you accept your canonical election as supreme pontiff?' Scheuermann's voice thundered inside the chapel.

Yin took a deep breath and looked out at the expectant

cardinals. So many different faces, from so many different cultures and peoples. Yin remembered that moment in his cell when he first spoke with Nolan Kilkenny, and from his rescuer learned that the heir of Peter had sent him.

'I do,' Yin answered, his voice clear and strong.

'By what name do you wish to be called?'

'Gousheng, after Saint Peter Wu Gousheng, a martyr for the faith.'

'This way, Your Holiness,' Donoher said, shepherding Yin to a room off to the side of the altar. He stopped at the threshold. 'This is the Room of Tears, for your predecessors have wept in both joy and sorrow at this moment. You enter alone. Inside you will find the white robes of your holy office.'

Donoher bowed and backed away. Yin opened the door and stepped inside. The room was small and red in color. On a table he found three sets of papal robes. Each was a different size, as the papal tailors could not fit the new Pope until after he was elected.

Yin disrobed and carefully laid the black cassock on the table. During most of his years as a Bishop, he wore prison pajamas, and now he was setting aside the uniform of that office forever. He tried on the smallest of the three sets of robes and found the fit acceptable. Next he tested the white zucchettos. Beside the robes lay a brilliant assortment of pectoral crosses – beautiful works of art crafted in gold and precious stones. The crosses set out for him were superior in every way to the one he wore when he entered the Room of Tears, except one.

He picked up the hand-carved wooden cross, kissed

it, and looped the cord around his neck. Tears streamed down his face as he recalled Ke Li's joy when she shared with him this most precious symbol of her faith, and tears of sorrow followed when he felt in his heart that she had died for that faith. Yin knew he would wear the martyred girl's cross to his own grave.

Yin reentered the Sistine Chapel as Pope Gousheng. Donoher guided him to a stool placed before the altar, waited while he seated himself, and placed the fisherman's ring on his finger. One by one, the princes of the Church paid homage to the new Pope. Outside, the crowd spilling out of Saint Peter's Square exploded with cheers as a plume of white smoke rose from the chimney and the bells of Saint Peter's tolled the news.

An hour later, Donoher stepped out onto the main balcony in the basilica's facade overlooking Saint Peter's Square. The crowd quieted, craning to hear the name of the new Pope.

'I announce to you a great joy. We have a Pope,' Donoher said in Latin. 'The Most Reverend Yin Daoming, Bishop of Shanghai, who takes the name Gousheng.'

The crowd roared their approval at the announcement with shouts of *Viva Il Papa*. Reporters covering the event suddenly found themselves at a loss for words as well as pictures, because a man few outside of China had ever heard of or seen was now the supreme pontiff of the universal Church.

Donoher stepped aside, and Pope Gousheng emerged from the shadows and into the light to impart the apostolic blessing *Urbi et Orbi*. For the City and the World.

70

November 2

The flight from Tibet, inside the windowless fuselage of a military transport, was one of the longest Kilkenny had ever endured. After being retrieved from the shore of Bangong Co along with Peng and the crew of the damaged helicopter, Kilkenny had been taken to a military base where his injuries were treated. He was placed in solitary confinement in the base stockade. Aside from routine questions by the attending physician, he was not questioned. It was as if no one there knew quite what to do with him. The brief respite of indecision ended when a squad of military police led by Peng entered his cell and escorted him to the waiting aircraft. Peng spoke to him only once, and that to inform him to remain silent during the flight. The tone in Peng's voice, though curt and official, conveyed that silence was in Kilkenny's best interest.

It was dark when Kilkenny, Peng, and the contingent

of MPs landed at a military airfield. Kilkenny's guards quickly ushered him from the plane into a nearby hangar. There, both he and Peng were provided with a change of clothes – the professional attire of businessmen. Kilkenny dressed slowly, careful of his wounds and the dressings that protected them. As he cinched the Windsor knot on his tie, Peng approached with a pair of hand-cuffs and the final accessory to Kilkenny's wardrobe.

'When we are inside the vehicle, I will place this over your head,' Peng explained as he showed Kilkenny the black hood. 'This is to conceal your presence for where we are going.'

Kilkenny nodded. 'At least it's not a going-away present.'

Peng considered the remark for a moment, then shook his head. 'My orders are only to deliver you.'

Kilkenny sat with Peng in the rear seat of a black SUV. The windows surrounding him were thick and darkly smoked, and the doors closed with the weighty *thunk* of armor plating. When the motorcade was ready to depart the hangar, Peng slipped the hood over Kilkenny's head.

As the journey proceeded, Kilkenny's thoughts retreated from the muffled sounds around him and the uncertainty of what lay ahead. Instead, he found solace in the memories of Kelsey. The bitter anger of his loss was gone, replaced by an acceptance of the tragedy for what it was, and a deep gratitude for the love he shared with her. Of all his life's accomplishments, he was most proud of being her husband.

Thank God, Kilkenny thought, then realized that was exactly what he was doing. His prayer wasn't the rote formula of an ancient catechism, but a sincere expression of his thanks for a relationship through which he defined himself. For the first time since losing his wife and child, he found himself able to pray again.

The motorcade came to a stop. Still hooded, Kilkenny was led from the vehicle. He heard the rustling of dry leaves in the cool night air and their crunch beneath his feet as he trod across a paved walk. Peng wordlessly guided him toward their destination. When Kilkenny heard the sound of two wooden doors close behind him, he knew he was inside a building.

Peng brought him to a stop, and ahead Kilkenny heard a man's voice give an order. Peng responded respectfully and removed Kilkenny's hood. Kilkenny found himself inside a small, ornate pavilion. Seated before him was a stocky man with gray hair and a round face lined with experience. Like Kilkenny and Peng, the man was dressed in business attire as if the three were there to discuss real estate or the stock market.

'Mister Kilkenny, do you know who I am?' the man asked, his accent barely detectable.

'No,' Kilkenny replied honestly.

The man nodded to Peng, who then leaned close to Kilkenny's ear.

'The man you are addressing is Wen Lequan, the Premier of China. Be very careful.'

'Premier Wen, it is an honor to meet you,' Kilkenny offered with a polite bow of his head.

'Mister Kilkenny, Mister Peng describes you as a man of honor. Can I accept your word that I have nothing to fear should your restraints be removed?'

'You have my word.'

Wen gestured with his hand, and Peng removed the handcuffs. With an equally subtle gesture, a circular table and two chairs were placed in front of the Premier.

'Please sit,' Wen said, more an order than a request.

Wen studied Kilkenny as he seated himself and noted he was favoring one side.

'I understand you were injured as a result of your illegal activities inside my country,' Wen began. 'Have you been well treated since your capture?'

'Your doctors have treated me very well, thank you.'

'Mister Kilkenny, as is the custom of your countrymen, I will be direct. You have placed me in a very difficult position.'

'I take complete responsibility for my actions and freely accept the consequences.'

'You are an American with ties to the CIA, yes?'

'I am,' Kilkenny admitted.

'But I presume that you deny any involvement by your government in this—' Wen paused in search of the right word, 'intrusion into China and deliberate interference in our internal affairs?'

'That is the truth.'

'The truth is your actions are considered by some to be a hostile act against the government of China. My military advisers have labeled your assault on our sovereign territory an act of war. The question is, Against whom are we at war?'

'Do you think the United States would risk war with your nation to liberate a political prisoner?' Kilkenny asked.

'Your President, like his predecessors, has an annoying habit of inquiring about certain criminals in the custody of our justice system, but I am certain that the United States is at worst an abettor in this circumstance. In fact, I know you are here on the personal authority of Pope Leo the XIV.'

Kilkenny carefully studied Wen but offered no response to the Premier's statement.

'Peng,' Wen continued, 'in your report following the recovery of the crew of *Shenzhou-7*, you praised Mister Kilkenny as a hero. Why?'

'He risked his life to bring the persons responsible for that tragedy to justice. If I may, though his recent actions have violated our laws and territory, I believe his motivation was the same.'

'Explain,' Wen commanded.

'There are many who view the incarceration of Yin Daoming as unjust. Kilkenny acted with the sole purpose of liberating Yin and correcting this injustice. As with *Shenzhou-7*, he remains consistent.'

Wen considered Peng's logic for a moment, then conceded the point with a nod of his head. From the table beside his chair, the Premier picked up a plain brown envelope and slid it across the table to Kilkenny.

'Open it,' Wen said.

Kilkenny unfastened the clasp and extracted a pair of eight-by-ten black-and-white photographs. The first, an old original print, depicted a class of dour-faced children with their instructor. The children were all dressed in identical uniforms, the future of the Chinese Communist state. The second photo was a computer-enhanced enlargement of the first highlighting the faces of two boys no more than twelve years of age. The boy on the right possessed finer features and a slighter build than his classmate, but Kilkenny's attention was riveted on the clarity in his eyes.

'That photograph is over fifty years old,' Wen said. 'I am the boy on the left.'

'And to your right is Yin Daoming.'

'Yes. Yin and I shared a common childhood, but as adults our paths diverged. His path led to a prison cell in Chifeng. Mine brought me here.'

'Yin had no regrets,' Kilkenny offered.

'Of that I am quite certain,' Wen said, nodding his head knowingly. 'This mission to liberate Yin was a costly one to you and your comrades, but in the end you succeeded. And now, those two boys lead over a third of the world's population.'

'Excuse me?' Kilkenny said.

'Upon his arrival in Rome,' Peng explained, 'Yin Daoming was proclaimed Pope.'

Kilkenny sat rigid in his chair, dumbstruck.

'Which explains the difficult position I find myself in,' Wen added, 'and why you are here. Within the hour of the announcement naming the new Pope, I received a personal communiqué from my former schoolmate. He inquired about your whereabouts, Mister Kilkenny, and made clear his interest in your continued good health.'

'So he doesn't know you have me?' Kilkenny asked.

'Your capture is a state secret. In the minds of those who collaborated in your incursion, you are missing and likely presumed dead. Making you disappear would be a very simple matter. Others counsel me to put you on trial and expose the Western conspiracy that violated our sovereign territory.'

'If you're looking for options, you could just let me go,' Kilkenny offered wryly.

'That is what your Pope suggested. There have been talks in recent years of normalizing relations between China and the Vatican, but only talks. The history between these two states is long and often troubled. There is much distrust on both sides, and this incident only promises to widen that rift.'

'Pope Leo felt much the same after learning the truth about the tragic theater fire,' Kilkenny said. 'And Yin's escape is an affront to your national pride.'

Wen nodded. 'But unlike his predecessor, Mister Kilkenny, the new Pope understands the importance of saving face. Instead of demanding your release in a public way that would surely demean China in the eyes of the world, Pope Gousheng has offered himself as a symbol of Chinese generosity.'

'Yin's arrival in Rome is as big a story as his election, and the media must be going crazy trying to figure it out,' Kilkenny said. 'He's offered to let China take credit for his release?'

'A unilateral gesture of goodwill by the People's Republic of China,' Wen replied, as if quoting a script, 'honoring the long-held wish of the late pontiff and with sincere hope of improved relations with the Vatican in the future. Yin is a very clever man.'

'He's much more than that. Despite his long captivity, Yin bears no ill will toward the government of China.

He's forgiven you, and he prays for you. So all you have to do to get a humanitarian endorsement by the Holy Father of the Roman Catholic Church is quietly let me go and act like none of this ever happened?'

'There are other details – the repatriation of the remains of your fallen comrades and the promise to preserve the site of the theater fire for a Roman Catholic church in Beijing.'

'I might be somewhat biased, Premier Wen, but those terms sound very reasonable.'

'My conclusion as well. Of course, this arrangement relies on all parties involved maintaining the Pope's version of events.'

'To the best of my recollection,' Kilkenny replied, 'I've spent the past month in Rome working on a small project for the Vatican Library.'

'Excellent. Peng, the arrangements have been made. You are to escort Mister Kilkenny to Rome.'

'Yes, Premier,' Peng replied.

'One final thought before you leave China, Mister Kilkenny. My acceptance of the Pope's offer in no way lessens my outrage at what you have done. Once you leave China, you are *never* to return. Now go.'

Kilkenny and Peng stood, and both offered a respectful bow to Wen, who dismissed them with a wave of his hand. Outside the pavilion, one of the Premier's aides handed Peng a folio containing travel documents and the itinerary for transporting Kilkenny to Rome.

'Do I still have to wear the hood?' Kilkenny asked as he stepped into the black SUV.

'No, you are a free man.'

Even in nighttime silhouette, Kilkenny marveled at the beauty of Zhongnanhai. The SUV followed the winding road around the southern lake and out through the New China Gate. As the SUV cleared the gate, Kilkenny looked through the window to his left and saw barricades blocking the street, and beyond was an enormous crowd of people bathed in the white glow of portable light towers. Banners fluttered in the light wind, and people held up placards bearing slogans and images.

'What's that?' Kilkenny asked.

'Tiananmen Square. Many people have gathered to celebrate the Chinese Pope.'

'And the government isn't trying to stop it?'

'No,' Peng replied. 'The crowd is well-behaved and quite large.'

'Since this will likely be my one and only visit to China, could I take a look?'

Peng nodded. 'I am also curious.'

Peng instructed the driver to park along the street – the uniformed police on crowd-control duty would not question a vehicle with government plates. As they passed through the barricades, the immense proportions of the square nearly overwhelmed Kilkenny, as did the sea of people who filled it to capacity.

'There must be hundreds of thousands of people here!'

'Estimates place the number at just over one million,' Peng said. 'Similar crowds are reported in the streets of Hong Kong and Shanghai, and smaller ones elsewhere.'

Chants and songs rippled through the crowd, some familiar to Kilkenny, others totally foreign. The throng immediately around them picked up on one of the chants, and excited youths pumped their fists in the air as if stoking the fires of enthusiasm.

'What are they saying?' Kilkenny asked in a shout barely audible against the rhythmic chant.

'Long live Jesus Christ!' Peng shouted back. 'Long live Pope Gousheng!'

Kilkenny listened for the cadence, then waded into the crowd with his fist held high, parroting the syllables. Like a cloud, the chant slowly drifted away as voices tired. Kilkenny and Peng were grinning with the people around them, taking part in the vast celebration.

'I've never seen anything like this,' Peng offered.

Kilkenny beamed proudly. 'Who would have ever imagined Tiananmen Square would become an extension of Saint Peter's?'

'Until now, a gathering like this wasn't just unimaginable, it was *unthinkable*.'

'Cause enough to be hopeful.'

Author's Note

This novel is a product of the author's imagination; however, the uneasy relations between the Holy See and the People's Republic of China upon which the story is based are real and remain unresolved as of this writing.

Fact: As a political entity, China has existed in some form for millennia. The People's Republic of China (PRC) came to power under Mao Zedong in 1949. China is the fourth-largest nation in the world and home to the world's largest population of 1.3 billion people.

Fact: The significance of the various Popes' secular power has waxed and waned over the past seventeen centuries, but the line of succession for those who served as Bishop of Rome has remained unbroken since the arrival of the Apostle Peter in 42 A.D. Ruling as an absolute monarch, the Pope is the Sovereign of the State of Vatican City – a landlocked city-state with less than one-eighth the area of New York's Central Park and a population of slightly more than nine hundred persons. Of far greater importance is the Pope's role as the spiritual, doctrinal, juridical, and legislative leader of the world's 1.3 billion Roman Catholics.

Fact: The PRC is officially an atheist nation, and religious belief is considered antisocialist. In the years immediately following the Communist takeover and later, during the Cultural Revolution, the government tried to eradicate religion in China. It failed in both instances. Despite periods of intense persecution, religious faith in China has persevered and, in some instances, flourished.

Fact: Unable to eradicate religion, the PRC government has chosen instead to control the content of the message heard by Chinese faithful. Chinese Christians may only use Bibles printed by the government; foreign versions are illegal. The government also places onerous restrictions on contact between Chinese religious organizations and their foreign counterparts to guard against foreign infiltration under the guise of religion. Ironically, covert agents of China's Ministry of State Security have been caught in the West posing as priests to cover their espionage activities.

Fact: The political reliability of religious figures in China is more important to the government than their spiritual training. During a visit to Beijing in 2005, U.S. Secretary of State Condoleezza Rice attended a Palm Sunday service in an officially sanctioned church. The pastor's sermon emphasized how Christ came to Earth not to overthrow a government but the evil in men's hearts.

Fact: The current constitution of the People's Republic of China guarantees its citizens the right to religious belief. This right extends only to those faiths recognized by the government: Buddhism, Taoism, Islam, Protestantism, and Catholicism. The practice of all other religious faiths in China is illegal. Religious instruction is also not permitted to persons under the age of eighteen.

Fact: Although citizens of China have the right to be Catholics, they cannot be Roman Catholics unless they reside in Hong Kong, which has special rules. Taking a cue from England's Henry VIII, the PRC government took control of the Catholic Church in China and usurped the authority of the Pope with the Chinese Catholic Patriotic Association (CCPA). Through the CCPA, the government controls the training of priests and the naming of Bishops in China. The Chinese Patriotic Association controls all other recognized religions.

Fact: The freedom to have religious belief in China is not complemented by the right of free association. All churches sanctioned in China must be registered with the government, and membership in these churches is strictly controlled. As a result, religious activities of many faiths are performed illegally in houses or underground churches.

Fact: The government of China deems the practice of religion an internal matter, and foreign interference, either by missionaries or Popes, is not permitted.

Fact: Ties between China and the Holy See dissolved in 1951 following the expulsion of the last Roman Catholic nuncio from Beijing. Presently, the Holy See is one of only a handful of nations to share full diplomatic relations with Taiwan, which the PRC views as interference in the internal affairs of China.

Fact: A majority of the Bishops of the CCPA have reportedly sought and received recognition from the Vatican with no negative consequence from the Chinese government. Until recently, the CCPA elevated new Bishops only after receiving an indication from the Vatican that the candidate was acceptable. This compromise over the naming of Bishops broke down in 2006, and its status remains in doubt.

Fact: Of the estimated forty Bishops of the underground Roman Catholics in China, most are in prison or under house arrest with the remainder in hiding. Most of these Bishops are very old, and they are dying at a rapid rate. The Holy See has not made any new episcopal appointments to the underground Roman Catholic Church in the past decade and many dioceses, including Shanghai, are vacant.

Fact: Roman Catholic Bishops are required to travel to Rome every five years to report on the condition of their diocese. The Chinese government prohibits this activity, and Roman Catholic Bishops and priests are often charged with espionage.

Fact: The Vatican does not possess an intelligence service comparable to the CIA or the Israeli Mossad, or even to one as modest as the one described in this novel. The Holy See receives information primarily through reports filed by its diplomatic corps and from published sources. During the late 1970s and early 1980s, the Vatican did receive intelligence briefings from the CIA relating to the Solidarity movement in Poland. Anecdotally, the Vatican is considered by many to be the nation most spied upon, yet least capable of spying.

Fact: Diplomatic discussions between China and the Vatican remain stalled over three major issues: recognition of Taiwan, the naming of Bishops, and, most importantly, recognition of the authority of the Pope over the Roman Catholic Church. China demands that the Vatican sever ties with Taiwan as a precondition to further discussions. The Vatican is unlikely to surrender such a valuable bargaining chip for nothing. China further demands that the Vatican refrain from interfering with internal matters, such as the naming of Bishops. Church dogma states that the Pope has final authority in the naming of Bishops.

Fact: Unlike the title of priest or Bishop, the rank of cardinal is not sacramental. Cardinals are primarily assistants and advisers to the Pope, and lay cardinals were permitted until 1918. Since then, with rare exception, only Bishops have been named cardinal. The Pope creates new cardinals by first naming them publicly, then elevating them at a consistory.

Fact: In cases where a Bishop's life would be endangered, the Pope can name him a cardinal *in pectore,* keeping the name a secret in his heart. Pope John Paul II did so with long-imprisoned Bishop Kung Pin-Mei of Shanghai in 1979. The Pope revealed his secret cardinal in 1991, but only after Kung was finally released from prison and exiled to the United States.

Fact: When China regained control of Hong Kong from Britain in 1997, Cardinal Wu Cheng-Chung became the first Chinese cardinal in the Communist nation. Hong Kong enjoys religious freedoms not permitted in the rest of China, and the aging Wu was allowed to remain. Upon Wu's death, Beijing made known it would be displeased if the Vatican created another cardinal in Hong Kong. In 2003, Pope John Paul II named his fourth and final secret cardinal.

Fact: In April 2005, Pope John Paul II died and took to his grave the name of his last secret cardinal, though many believe it was Hong Kong's Bishop Zen Ze-Kiun. One year later, Pope Benedict XVI made Bishop Zen a cardinal, triggering outrage from China. Like Pope John Paul II, Zen is a staunch anti-Communist, and he has taken a strong stand against Beijing's efforts to rein in the rights and liberties enjoyed by the citizens of Hong Kong. The Chinese Catholic Patriotic Association decried Zen's elevation as 'a hostile act' against the government of China.

Fact: Following Zen's elevation, the CCPA named several new Bishops who were not acceptable to the Vatican

– candidates chosen more for their political reliability than their episcopal qualifications. Allegations of kidnapping and forced participation/attendance marred Beijing's claims that the ordinations were proper. The ordinations garnered worldwide condemnation.

Fact: On June 30, 2007, the Vatican posted an open letter on the Vatican web site from the Pope to Catholics in China. The letter expressed the Pope's desire for greater unity among the official and underground Catholics, for strong ties between the faithful of China and the rest of the Roman Catholic Church, for improved relations between China and the Vatican, and for a dialog on the naming of Bishops in China. In response, China reiterated its stance regarding the Vatican's diplomatic relations with Taiwan and on interference in China's internal matters. China also blocked access to the Vatican web site and to domestic web sites that posted the Pope's letter.

Fact: On September 1, 2007, China's State Administration for Religious Affairs implemented Order No. 5, granting the state sole authority over the reincarnation of Living Buddhas. This formalizes a process started in 1995, when China arrested a boy who had recently been recognized as the reincarnated Panchen Lama, and then installed their own Panchen Lama. Through enforcement of this law, China intends to secure control over the most revered figures in Tibetan Buddhism, including the next Dalai Lama. This effort mirrors China's control over the naming of Bishops by the CCPA.

Fact: September 9, 2007, Bishop Han Ding Xiang, the Roman Catholic Bishop of Yang Nian in Heibei Province, died in prison. The Bishop spent nearly 35 years of his life in prisons and labor camps or under house arrest, and his whereabouts during his last six years of incarceration were unknown. The cause of the Bishop's death remains unknown but the circumstances of his death appear suspicious as he died late in the night and was cremated and interred before dawn the next day.

Fact: Chinese Communist Party (CCP) leaders view the pro-democracy movement and Christianity as the greatest threats to their single-party rule, and they are keenly aware of the Vatican's role in toppling Soviet communism. They are particularly fearful of someone with the moral authority to challenge the CCP rising up from within China. Cardinal Zen embodies this perceived danger because the charismatic and popular Bishop of Hong Kong is now in a position to become the next Pope.

ACKNOWLEDGMENTS

I first became aware of the bitter struggle between church and state in China in March 2000 when I read a transcript of Connecticut Senator Joseph Lieberman's eloquent tribute on the floor of the U.S. Senate marking the death of Cardinal Ignatius Kung Pin-Mei. Through Lieberman's recitation of the facts and circumstances of Kung's life, I learned of the ongoing religious repression in China and found the seed of this story in the concept of a secret cardinal. The late Cardinal Kung was a man of great faith and was both an inspiration and a symbol to the oppressed Roman Catholics of China. Although some aspects of my fictional title character may mirror those of Cardinal Kung, this story is a work of fiction and not a biography.

For those interested in the fascinating story of a real secret cardinal, I refer you to www.cardinalkungfoundation.org. I also found Malachi Martin's novel *The Final Conclave* a most insightful exploration of Vatican politics.

My deepest gratitude to Capt. B.J. Keepers (USN/Ret), Fr. Brendan Walsh, Dr David Gorski, Rita Thiron of the

Diocese of Lansing, Billy Downs, Jonathan Swift, Loretta Barrett, and those who cannot be named. Their help was invaluable. As always, any mistakes are mine alone.

My thanks also to Roger Cooper at Vanguard Press, my agent Esther Margolis, and my editors Peter Guzzardi and Ed Stackler for their thoughtful advice and kind support; to my family and friends for their love and encouragement; and to my dog for keeping my feet warm as I write into the night. And last, I recognize my five children and wife Kathy, who make all things possible.

Read on for an exclusive extract from Tom Grace's new novel *Spyder Web* coming in November 2009.

Prologue

'Thank you,' Lin Mei said absently as the owner of the restaurant brought her tea and a bowl of noodles with fish.

She had arrived early at the tiny dockside restaurant, the anticipation of word from her brother in Beijing being almost more than she could contain. Since the handover last summer, each new day brought with it the reality of Hong Kong's transformation from British Crown Colony into a Red Chinese city. Despite Beijing's assurances that little would change, residents of capitalism's strongest beachhead on the Chinese mainland still carried a nagging sense of uncertainty about the future.

Like Hong Kong, Lin was as much a part of China as she was of the West, and the delicate balance between those conflicting forces was difficult for both. An attract-ive young woman in her mid-twenties, she had been fortunate to study in the United States and was soon to marry a young man from San Francisco. On a personal level, Lin Mei's future was full of promise.

She picked at her food, but the anxiety she felt made eating difficult. Instead, she resigned herself to quietly sipping tea while she waited for her brother's emissary.

She spoke with Zhenyi as often as she could, but getting a phone connection to Beijing was still no simple task. Most of her communication with him was through letters carried by private couriers across the slowly dissolving border.

Lin Zhenyi had surprised her when he joined the Party and took a position with the PRC government rather than going West, as she had. He believed that China could change but that the change would have to come from within the government.

Despite his Party membership, Zhenyi maintained discreet contact with democratic reformers. His belief that change was coming deepened with the expansion of China's economy and the return of Hong Kong and, soon, Macao. He felt that strong international ties would draw China out of her self-imposed isolation. When Lin Mei received his call three nights before, she sensed that her brother's optimism had been crushed.

'Mei, I can't talk now,' Zhenyi had apologized at the end of that brief conversation, 'but my next letter will explain everything. You can pick it up at the usual place on Tuesday, at eight o'clock. Read it carefully and you'll understand. I've also enclosed some important research for a friend of mine. He will make arrangements to meet with you. It is crucial that you give him what I found.'

Tonight, she waited, just as he had asked.

*   *   *

Kang Fa circled the restaurant for twenty minutes, looking for watchers before entering. Hong Kong was still Hong Kong, and he knew that there were many eyes in the city that still worked for foreign intelligence services. Through the window, he saw twelve cramped seats, half-filled with evening diners. Near the window sat Lin Mei.

She is beautiful, Kang thought as he approached, more so than any photograph could render.

Her long black hair was drawn back in a French braid that descended to the small of her back like a silken cord against the red satin of her dress. Life in Hong Kong had been very kind to this exquisite young woman.

As Kang entered the restaurant, he saw her look cautiously in his direction.

She's expecting me, he thought, and he smiled back to acknowledge her attention.

'Lin Mei?' he asked politely as he approached her table.

'Yes,' she replied. The man was older than she, well over forty, with graying black hair and a kind face.

'My name is Kang Fa. I am an acquaintance of your brother. I apologize if I have kept you waiting.'

Lin only nodded, almost afraid to speak. Kang sat in the lacquer chair beside hers and ordered tea from the owner of the tiny restaurant.

'Zhenyi asked me to bring you this letter. I know he wished that he could have delivered it himself.'

Lin Mei accepted a sealed envelope that bore the characters of her name; the handwriting was Zhenyi's. She opened it and began to read, devouring each of her brother's quickly drawn characters. He spoke of his disillusion with China, of his lost hope for the future.

As she read, she realized that the rambling letter was her brother's final confession; he wrote as a man facing certain death. She began to weep as the depth of her brother's despair unfolded before her. Zhenyi ended the letter by imploring her to deliver the attached pages to a friend, who, he said, would know what to do with them.

She turned to the next page of the letter. It was a grainy photocopy of an official document that authorized the relocation of the listed individuals into Mainland China for an undetermined period of time. All those named were members of Hong Kong's most prominent Chinese families. The pages were excerpts from Beijing's ten-year plan for the pacification of Hong Kong.

China is going to take hostages to keep Hong Kong in line, Lin Mei realized. The Communists are no different from the warlord emperors who held key families at court to prevent rebellion.

She placed the letter and the list in her purse while struggling to maintain her composure. 'Thank you for delivering this letter.'

Kang saw that she was visibly shaken by what she'd read. 'You must share an uncommonly strong bond with Zhenyi. He has expressed his deepest fears to you, and his news is quite disturbing.'

She looked at Kang's bowed head and sensed that he, too, was concerned for her brother. 'Do you know him well?'

'I've only known Lin for a short time, but it has been long enough to know that he cares a great deal for you.'

'Mr Kang, I really don't feel much like eating right

now, and I have another appointment not far from here. If you have the time, I'd like you to walk with me there. I haven't seen Zhenyi in months, and I want to hear more about him from a friend.'

'I would be honored.'

Kang accompanied her on a meandering walk through the narrow streets of Hong Kong. They talked about Lin Zhenyi, and she was grateful for his presence; Kang was a sympathetic audience. The list had given her a glimpse of something terrible, and she felt as if she held the lives of those people in her hands. Lin hoped that the man she was to meet would know what to do with the list.

An hour slipped by quickly, and Lin ended their walk at the dock where she was to wait. Vessels of all kinds were tied up along the pier, aging junks, fishing boats, and small barges. As evening slipped into darkness, odd circles and squares of light from the boats illuminated the dock in an irregular rhythm of light and shadow.

Lin turned to Kang as they approached the site of her expected rendezvous. 'I would like to thank you for the kindness you have shown me tonight.'

'The pleasure was all mine. Your brother was a decent man.'

Lin nodded and prepared to part company, when a sudden icy fear swept over her. She looked carefully at Kang. He smiled back pleasantly, but his eyes spoke of something deeper and darker beyond the innocent facade. He read her fear and his smile widened.

'Why do you say my brother *was* a decent man? What has happened to him?'

'Your brother was arrested for espionage.'

Lin swallowed back her fears. 'Is he dead?'

'Yes,' Kang replied.

She looked into his eyes and saw the truth, and beyond the truth, she saw something else; Kang Fa seemed to be taking pleasure in her anguish, as only a truly evil person could.

A single tear fell from her eye as she stood there, paralyzed with fear of this man. Kang gently brushed her cheek with his hand to collect the droplet, his touch nearly causing her to faint.

'A tear for the fallen, how poetic. Zhenyi shed many tears before he died, especially when I told him that I would be visiting you.'

The certainty with which he confirmed her brother's death caused Lin's worst fears to explode in her mind. She was in the presence of a sadistic monster.

'I broke your brother's pitiful group of subversives. I infiltrated it with my own agents and destroyed each cell of resistance. With your brother's help, I intercepted the courier who was to meet you tonight. Everyone involved has been captured or killed, and you, my beautiful flower, are all that remains of Lin Zhenyi's ring of spies.'

This man is a killer! her mind screamed out. *Run!*

Lin bolted to one side, trying to escape, but Kang just laughed and grabbed her as she tried to pass, locking his left arm tightly around her torso. His forearm clamped over her breasts, holding her back firmly against his chest. Her warmth aroused him as she trembled in his crushing embrace.

'You are a very beautiful woman, more beautiful than your brother described. When I told him that I would visit you, he pleaded with me not to harm you. He said that you were not involved in his crimes.' Kang pulled at her dress and ran his hand slowly, intimately across her thigh. 'This was the image that I placed in your brother's mind, the single thought that forced him to tell me *everything*.'

'You bastard!' She choked, sobbing.

Kang's free hand moved away from beneath her dress, and with it went the fear of a brutal rape. He'd brought her on a journey from trust to fear, enjoying each subtle turn and its effect upon her, but time grew short and Lin's contact would soon arrive. His grip tightened and her sobbing abruptly halted with the violent snap of her neck.

Neville Axton walked confidently down the darkened pier. Every place in this city held its own special dangers for the inattentive, and a man had to know how to carry himself if he expected to walk about unaccosted. His thirty years as an agent in Her Majesty's Secret Service, most of which had been spent in Hong Kong, allowed him to project an outward demeanor that, while not overtly hostile, left the impression that he was not someone to be trifled with.

He had been worried about tonight's exchange from the moment he learned that Lin Mei would be involved. Axton had warned his Chinese agent about the dangers of using his sister as a mule, but Zhenyi's situation had become desperate and there was simply no alternative.

He strolled along the pier, ignoring the private lives going on inside the floating homes to either side of him. Near the end of the long dock, he saw the silhouette of a woman in the reflected lights of Hong Kong. The woman made no move, no glance toward him as he approached.

At ten feet, he knew that it was Lin Mei seated on the crates near the end of the jetty. Axton sensed something amiss and approached cautiously.

Crouching down in front of her, he stared into the quiet of her eyes. In place of the animation that usually shone out of someone her age, there was emptiness. Her lips were slightly parted, as if to speak, but no words or warning came.

In Lin Mei's hands, Axton found Zhenyi's letter held out like an offering. The list was gone. Axton placed his hand upon her shoulder. His gentle touch caused her to topple forward, crumpling in his arms like a rag doll.

'Lin Mei,' Axton vowed, his mind filling with rage and sorrow, 'I swear to you that I will find your murderer.'

LANGLEY, VIRGINIA

Jackson Barnett wiped the offending smudge from the right lens of his wire-framed bifocals and, satisfied that his vision would be hampered by nothing more than his aging eyes, perched them back on his face. His face was long and thin, favoring his mother's side of the family, and framed with a full head of neatly trimmed silver hair. Barnett possessed the look and demeanor of a lifelong scholar: physically unimposing yet possessing the confidence of a well-trained mind.

Barnett read the intelligence report a second time to clarify his grasp of the details. The report identified the means used to divert the shipment of an American-made supercomputer to a North Korean military testing facility. The machine's sale was restricted to only the closest allies of the United States, and its theft was considered a serious breech of national security. Unfortunately, this was just one of the many problems facing the Director of Central Intelligence this afternoon, problems well beyond those he had faced as a prosecutor in South Carolina a quarter of a century ago.

As Barnett studied the mechanics of the computer theft, his speaker phone buzzed.

'Yes, Sally?' he answered.

'Phillip Moy is here to see you.'

Barnett glanced at his wristwatch and quickly noticed two things. First, the hours between 1:00 and 4:30 P.M. had passed very quickly today, and, second, Phillip Moy was as punctual as ever. 'Show him right in.'

Sally Kirsch escorted an Asian man of average height and build into Barnett's office. The man wore the corporate uniform of highly paid executives around the world – a well-tailored conservative gray suit with a starched white shirt, a floral-print silk tie, and a pair of black Italian loafers whose sheen cast no doubt about the suppleness of the leather. Phillip Moy's face was nearly round and had, as its most dominating feature, a pair of dark brown eyes that burned with a fiery intelligence.

Moy was the founder and CEO of the computer corporation that bore his name. He looked remarkably sharp and unperturbed following a day of briefings and testimony on Capitol Hill. Today's session had, no doubt, added a few more gray hairs to his otherwise blue-black mane.

Kirsch placed several pink message slips on Barnett's desk and collected a small stack of classified files from his out-basket for a return trip to the file room.

Barnett rose to greet his guest. Both men, who had started from humble beginnings, were in their early fifties and nearing the pinnacle of their careers.

'Can I get you a drink, Phillip?' Barnett asked as he poured himself a scotch and soda.

'Sure, just splash a little scotch over some ice. Keep the water.'

Barnett brought the drinks over and sat in a brown leather chair opposite Moy. He sipped on his drink, then loosened his tie, signaling an end to any formality for this meeting. 'How are things going with the Gatekeeper Project?'

'We're still on schedule, so far. Our initial tests show the device is capable of monitoring all the signal traffic moving over a major computer network without degrading that network's performance. The defensive aspects of the Gatekeeper appear to be equally impressive.'

'I'm glad to hear that. Lord knows that we need to get those units in place ASAP. Just last week, some kid broke through an Internet server into one of the Pentagon's low-level computers.' Barnett took a hard swallow of scotch and smacked his lips, sighing.

'She spoofed the router, a real nice hack. It was dumb luck she got caught.' Moy noticed Barnett's eyebrow arch slightly. 'Professional admiration, Jackson – the young lady has talent.'

'Maybe you should hire her.'

'She'd fit right in. Some of my best and brightest programmers have a similar wild, inventive streak. I just give them a constructive way to express their creativity. It's a good thing she wasn't working for someone else, like Ames.'

Barnett nodded in agreement, recalling as if it were yesterday the arrest of the CIA counterintelligence officer on charges of spying for the Soviets. By exploiting the weak internal security on Langley's computer network, Ames used his office PC to steal dozens of files classified beyond his clearance. It was in the aftermath of the Aldrich Ames affair that Moy's security projects with the government began.

'We've come a long way since the early nineties, but the memory of Ames won't soon be forgotten.'

'I understand and share your concerns, Jackson. The Gatekeepers will provide our government's computers with the security they need.'

Moy was a firm believer in the Gatekeeper vision, a strategy for protecting the government's vast computer networks by providing those machines with the tools necessary to thwart a computer-based attack and pursue the attacker. The Gatekeeper vision was born from a fortunate accident in the Moy Electronics research labs. Almost a year earlier, a group of engineers working on a method to increase the flow of information inside a new type of parallel-processing computer hit an impasse. Unlike traditional computer designs, which relied upon a single chip to perform each instruction one after another, the new design linked hundreds of individual chips together like the oarsmen of a Roman galley. Each chip in the new design would tackle just a piece of a larger problem, allowing the team of small processors to outperform the massive single processor of a supercomputer.

The problem the engineers encountered was a simple matter of communication. The faster they tried to run the team of parallel processors, the more tangled the flow of information among individual chips became. They were ready to start over, when the project leader of the parallel-processing team had a discussion about their problems with the young woman who led Moy Electronics' most esoteric group of researchers – the neural and cognitive sciences team.

Over a two-hour lunch, the two project leaders brainstormed an idea that later evolved into the Gatekeeper, an artificially intelligent device capable of learning and adapting itself to its host computer's environment.

It was a giant step in programming, giving the Gatekeeper the ability to determine from where a user was calling and if the user was legitimate. In its current form, the device could discover a hacker trying to break into its host computer and trace the connection back to its source. Like taking a picture of a burglar in your house, Moy's Gatekeeper could follow the electronic trail to the hacker's computer and even strip evidence from the intruder's machine. The hacker wouldn't know he had been traced until the police showed up at the front door.

'Phillip, I've been thinking about something since you first explained these neural-network systems to me. Given that a Gatekeeper is capable of learning everything about the computer environment that it's attached to – and I believe you said that includes every machine that it comes into contact with – can it be taught to look for *other things* while it's out there?'

Moy arched an eyebrow at his friend as he thought about the question. 'You want to turn my Gatekeeper into a hacker?'

Barnett nodded and took another sip of his drink as Moy settled back a little farther into the soft leather chair to consider the idea. He didn't disturb his colleague, knowing that Moy's outward calm belied the furious pace of thought within. True geniuses, he mused, seemed to possess a remarkable ability to block out distractions and focus their minds completely. While different thoughts floated in and out of his consciousness, Barnett knew that Moy's mind was racing through the possibilities posed by his question. After a few quiet moments, Moy looked up from his swirling glass with a mischievous smile.

Barnett broke the silence. 'Judging from that look on your face, I assume you've found an answer. Can you program your Gatekeeper to break into another computer?'

'Of course, the tools are already there.' To Moy, the technical issues seemed trivial. 'The Gatekeeper is driven to learn about its computer environment in order to protect that environment. This includes the host computer and every system within its network. Each time another computer comes into contact with the Gatekeeper, it becomes a learned part of the Gatekeeper's experience. This mutant Gatekeeper would share a similar thirst to learn, but the intentions behind its actions would be markedly different.'

'Give me an example, Phillip.'

'Okay,' Moy replied, relishing his role as computer villain. 'Say I wanted to break into the network here at Langley. Your high-security computers aren't on the Net, so I can't hack my way in. And breaking into this building is obviously a little more difficult than getting into the English Department at Podunk State University.'

'Obviously,' Barnett agreed, playing along.

'If I wanted to get into your information, and I had one of these devices, I would find out where the CIA buys their personal computers and laptops. Then I would get a job at that company, say testing the computers before they get delivered. As soon as an order for the CIA came through, I'd plant my device in one of your computers and ship it. With any luck, that computer would be connected to the information that I'm interested in. The odds are also very high that the CIA's well-protected intranet has at least one dedicated phone line to the outside world. My device would find that line and stealthily contact me for further instructions.'

Barnett was intrigued by the hacker-Gatekeeper scenario Moy proposed. 'Could such a device be easily detected?'

Moy shook his head. 'I envision this device as something very similar physically to our Gatekeeper, just one of a hundred anonymous black chips on a circuit board. Operationally, it would be completely invisible, and it would have total control over its host. In all likelihood, no one would ever know the device was there. Even if its activities could be detected, they would be dismissed as the work of a person. After all, who in their right mind would suspect a computer of espionage?'

Barnett sipped his drink, then smiled. 'I think you've reached the conclusion that I was hoping for. Recent international events are forcing the White House to reevaluate our diplomatic and trade relations with several countries, including Iraq, Iran, North Korea, and the People's Republic of China.'

'The Red Chinese will rot in hell before I sell them any of my computers, regardless of what the White House thinks of them.'

Barnett showed no surprise at Moy's reaction. The defection of Moy's father, a Chinese Oppenheimer, had resulted in the imprisonment of several relatives. Little word ever came out of China about the people they left behind.

'I would never ask you to deal with the PRC. I know your family history well enough not to make such a request.' With that assurance made, Barnett returned to his original point. 'What I wanted you to consider is what might happen if a computer equipped with one of these devices was to *disappear* in shipment and find itself someplace that we don't officially want it. Further suppose that once our electronic spy had learned its way

471

around this hostile nation's computer network, it found a way to call home.'

'Interesting.' Moy's eyes narrowed as he studied the DCI's face. 'Is China to be a target for this type of operation?'

Barnett just shrugged his shoulders. 'This is purely speculation on my part, nothing more than an exercise in wishful thinking. I will admit that our current shortage of intelligence assets in the PRC, coupled with their desire for high-end computers, make them an ideal target.'

Moy took the hint. 'The modifications you propose would require significant funding and man-hours – at least a year of software development and testing. I expect that you'll want the accounting for this little venture kept separate from the Gatekeeper Project.'

'That's correct. We'll assign some of our technical people to work with yours on developing the . . .' Barnett paused as he found himself at a momentary loss for words. 'What shall we call this new device?'

'I'm not sure. What's the word you used to describe someone like Aldrich Ames, a hidden spy working for your enemies?'

'Ames was a mole. Like its namesake, intelligence moles burrow deep and are difficult to root out.'

'Mole,' Moy mused. 'I'm sure my marketing people could dream up something from that, but it just doesn't sound right. It's too cute. The device we're talking about is coldly logical, calculating and precise. It's a finely tuned machine.'

'Sounds like one of your sports cars.'

'Exactly.' A glint then appeared in Moy's eyes, a flash of

inspiration that could only have been more obvious had a cartoonist drawn a lightbulb over his head. He flipped to a blank page on his legal pad and sketched something very quickly. 'I recently acquired an old Porsche, one identical to the car that James Dean drove into oblivion. This particular model had a very unique name. If the goal of this project is to create an electronic spy, one that operates exclusively in a World Wide Web of networked computers, then the resulting device would be a . . .'

Moy paused dramatically as he handed the legal pad to Barnett. Barnett saw on it a menacing arachnid leering at him, and one word in large block letters.

'*Spyder*,' Barnett said, finishing the sentence. He thought about the name for a minute as Moy sat back, pleased with his quick wit. 'I give up, Phillip; Spyder it is. I'll get everything arranged on this end to get you started. I'll fund the project through my discretionary budget. That should keep it hidden long enough for us to complete development.'

What's next?

Tell us the name of an author you love

and we'll find your next great book.